BEAR ISLAND

ALISTAIR MACLEAN, the son of a Scots Minister, was
brought up in the Scottish Highlands. In 1941 at the
age of eighteen, he joined the Royal Navy; two and a
half years spent aboard a cruiser was later to give him
the background for *HMS Ulysses*, his first novel, the
outstanding documentary novel on the war at sea. He
is now the author of twenty-three best-selling novels,
of which *Athabasca* is the most recent; most of them
have now sold more than a million copies throughout
the world.

Many of his novels have also been filmed – *Force 10
from Navarone*, *The Guns of Navarone*, *Where Eagles
Dare*, and *Bear Island* are among the most famous –
and there are plans to film many more books.

ALISTAIR MACLEAN

Bear Island

FONTANA / Collins

First published in 1971 by William Collins Sons & Co. Ltd
First issued in Fontana Paperbacks 1973
Twenty-second impression January 1982

© Alistair MacLean 1971

Made and printed in Great Britain by
William Collins Sons & Co. Ltd, Glasgow

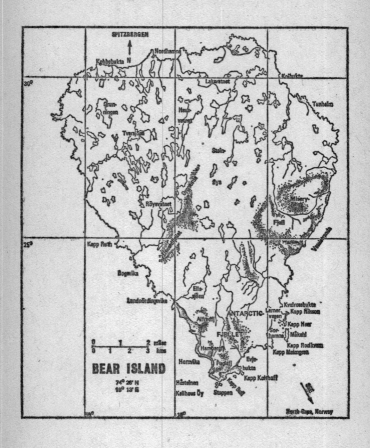

SPITZBERGEN

Kobbebukta   N   Nordhamna

30°   Lakavatnet   Kolbukta

                Grun-   Tunheim
                ningen   Haus-
                                    vatnet
            Tverelva
                                    Stein-

                                    fiya
            Røyevatnet   Miseryv

                                                    Fjell

25°   Kapp Ruth

        Bogevika

        Lundnordingsvika
                        Ella-
                        sjøen
                            Alfredf   ANTARCTIC   Lerner- Kvalrossbukta
                                                      vagen   Kapp Nilsson
                            Alfredf   Kapp Hær
                            FJELLE   Sør-
                                                      hamna   Måkehl
                            Hambergf   Kapp Roolkvam
                        Hornvika   Fuglef Evje-   Kapp Malmgren
                                                bukta   Kapp Kolthoff
                Håstelnen   Kapp Rull
                Kellhøus Øy   Støppen

BEAR ISLAND

74° 26′ N
10° 13′ E

0   1   2   miles
0   1   2   3   kms

                                        North Cape, Norway

CHAPTER ONE

To even the least sensitive and perceptive beholder the *Morning Rose,* at this stage of her long and highly chequered career, must have seemed ill-named, for if ever a vessel could fairly have been said to be approaching, if not actually arrived at, the sunset of her days it was this one. Officially designated an Arctic Steam Trawler, the *Morning Rose,* 560 gross tons, 173 feet in length, 30 in beam and with a draught, unladen but fully provisioned with fuel and water, of 14.3 feet, had, in fact, been launched from the Jarrow slipways as far back as 1926, the year of the General Strike.

The *Morning Rose,* then, was far gone beyond the superannuation watershed, she was slow, creaking, unstable and coming apart at the seams. So were Captain Imrie and Mr Stokes. The *Morning Rose* consumed a great deal of fuel in relation to the foot-pounds of energy produced. So did Captain Imrie and Mr Stokes, malt whisky for Captain Imrie, Jamaican rum for Mr Stokes. And that was what they were doing now, stoking up on their respective fuels with the steadfast dedication of those who haven't attained septuagenarian status through sheer happenstance.

As far as I could see, none of the sparse number of diners at the two long fore-and-aft tables was stoking up very much on anything. There was a reason for this, of course, the same reason that accounted for the poor attendance at dinner that night. It was not because of the food which, while it wouldn't cause any sleepless nights in the kitchens of the Savoy, was adequate enough, nor was it because of any aesthetic objections our cargo of creative artists might have entertained towards the dining saloon's decor, which was, by any standards, quite superb: it was a symphony in teak furniture and wine-coloured carpets and curtains, not, admittedly, what one would look to find on the average trawler, but then, the average trawler, when its fishing days are over—as the *Morning Rose*'s were deemed to be in 1956—doesn't have the good fortune to be re-engined and converted to a luxury yacht by, of all people, a shipping millionaire whose enthusiasm for the sea was matched only by his massive ignorance of all things nautical.

The trouble tonight lay elsewhere, not within the ship but without. Three hundred miles north of the Arctic Circle, where we at the present moment had the debatable fortune to be, the weather conditions can be as beautifully peaceful as any on earth, with mirror-smooth, milky-white seas stretching from horizon to horizon under a canopy of either washed-out blue or stars that are less stars than little chips of frozen fire in a black, black sky. But those days are rare and, usually, to be found only in that brief period that passes for summer in those high latitudes. And whatever summer there had been was long gone. We were deep into late October now, the period of the classical equinoctial gales, and there was a real classical equinoctial beauty blowing up right then. Moxen and Scott, the two stewards, had prudently drawn the dining saloon curtains so that we couldn't see quite how classical it was.

We didn't have to see it. We could hear it and we could feel it. We could hear the wild threnody of the gale in the rigging, a high-pitched, ululating, atonic sound, as lonely, lost and eerie as a witch's lament. We could hear, at monotonously regular intervals, the flat explosive clap of sound as the bluff bows of the trawler crashed into the troughs of the steep-sided waves marching steadily eastwards under the goad of that bitter wind born on the immensity of the Greenland ice-cap, all of seven hundred miles away. We could hear the constantly altering variation in the depth of the engine note as the propeller surged upwards, almost clearing water level, then plunged deep down into the sea again.

And we could feel the storm, a fact that most of those present clearly found a great deal more distressing than just listening to it. One moment, depending upon which side of the fore-and-aft tables we were sitting, we would be leaning sharply to our left or right as the bows lurched and staggered up the side of a wave: the next, we would be leaning as sharply in the other direction as the stern, in turn, rode high on the crest of the same wave. To compound the steadily increasing level of misery and discomfort the serried ranks of waves beyond the damask drapes were slowly but ominously beginning to break down into confused seas which violently accentuated the *Morning Rose*'s typical fishing-boat propensity for rolling continuously in anything short of mill-pond conditions. The two different motions, lateral and transverse, were now combining to produce an extremely unpleasant corkscrewing effect indeed.

Because I'd spent most of the past eight years at sea, I wasn't experiencing any distressing symptoms myself, but I didn't have to be a doctor—which my paper qualifications declared me to be—to diagnose the symptoms of *mal de mer*. The wan smile, the gaze studiously averted from anything that resembled food, the air of rapt communication with the inner self, all the signs were there in plenty. A very mirth-provoking subject, sea-sickness, until one suffers from it oneself: then it ceases to be funny any more. I'd dispensed enough sea-sickness pills to turn them all buttercup-yellow, but these are about as effective against an Arctic gale as aspirin is against cholera.

I looked round and wondered who would be the first to go. Antonio, I thought, that tall, willowy, exquisite, rather precious but oddly likeable Roman with the shock of ludicrously blond and curling hair. It is a fact that when a person reaches that nadir of nausea which is the inevitable prelude to violent sickness the complexion does assume a hue which can only be described as greenish: in Antonio's case it was more a tinge of apple-green chartreuse, an odd coloration that I'd never seen before, but I put it down to his naturally sallow complexion. Anyway, no question but that it was the genuine symptom of the genuine illness: another particularly wild lurch and Antonio was on his feet and out of the saloon at a dead run—or as near a dead run as his land-lubber legs could achieve on that swaying deck—without either farewell or apology.

Such is the power of suggestion that within a very few seconds and on the very next lurch three other passengers, two men and a girl, hurriedly rose and left. And such is the power of suggestion compounded that within two minutes more there were, apart from Captain Imrie, Mr Stokes and myself, only two others left: Mr Gerran and Mr Heissman.

Captain Imrie and Mr Stokes, seated at the heads of their respective and now virtually deserted tables, observed the hurried departure of the last of the sufferers, looked at each other in mild astonishment, shook their heads and got on with

9

the business of replenishing their fuel reserves. Captain Imrie, a large and splendidly patriarchal figure with piercing blue eyes that weren't much good for seeing with, had a mane of thick white hair that was brushed straight back to his shoulders, and, totally obscuring the dinner tie he affected for dinner wear, an even more impressively flowing beard that would have been the envy of many a biblical prophet: as always, he wore a gold-buttoned, double-breasted jacket with the thick white ring of a commodore of the Royal Navy, to which he wasn't entitled, and, partly concealed by the grandeur of his beard, four rows of medal ribbons, to which he was. Now, still shaking his head, he lifted his bottle of malt scotch from its container—not until that evening had I understood the purpose of that two-foot-high wrought-iron contraption bolted to the saloon deck by the side of his chair —filled his glass almost to the top and added the negligible amount of water required to make it brimming full. It was at this precise moment that the *Morning Rose* reared unusually high on the crest of a wave, hovered for what appeared to be an unconscionably long time, then fell both forwards and sideways to plunge with a resounding, shuddering crash into the shoulder of the next sea. Captain Imrie didn't spill a drop: for any indication he gave to the contrary he might have been in the tap-room of the Mainbrace in Hull, which was where I'd first met him. He quaffed half the contents of his glass in one gulp and reached for his pipe. Captain Imrie had long mastered the art of dining gracefully at sea.

Mr Gerran, clearly, hadn't. He gazed down at his lamb chops, brussels sprouts, potatoes, and glass of hock which weren't where they ought to have been—they were on his napkin and his napkin was on his lap—with a vexed frown on his face. This was, in its small way, a crisis, and Otto Gerran could hardly be said to be at his ineffectual best when faced with crisis of any kind. But for young Moxon, the steward, this was routine: his own napkin at the ready and bearing a small plastic bucket he'd apparently conjured from nowhere, he set about effecting running repairs while Gerran gazed downwards with an expression of perplexed distaste.

Seated, Otto Gerran, apart from his curiously narrow, pointed cranium that widened out to broad, fleshy jowls, looked as if he might have been cast in one of the standard moulds which produce the vast majority of human shapes and forms: it was not until he stood up, a feat he performed with great difficulty and as infrequently as possible, that one appreciated how preposterous this misconception was. Gerran stood five feet two inches in his elevator shoes, weighed two hundred and forty-five pounds and, were it not for his extremely ill-fitting clothes—one would assume that the tailor just gave up—was the nearest thing to a perfect human sphere I'd ever clapped eyes on. He had no neck, long slender sensitive hands and the smallest feet I've ever seen for a man of his size. The salvage operation over, Gerran looked up and at Imrie. His complexion was puce in colour, with the purple much more in evidence than the brown. This did not mean that he was angry, for Gerran never showed anger and was widely believed to be incapable of it: puce was as standard for him as the peaches and cream of the mythical English rose. His coronary was at least fifteen years overdue.

'Really, Captain Imrie, this is preposterous.' For a man of his vast bulk, Gerran had a surprisingly high-pitched voice: surprisingly, that is, if you weren't a medical practitioner. 'Must we keep heading into this dreadful storm?'

'Storm?' Captain Imrie lowered his glass and looked at Gerran in genuine disbelief. 'Did you say "storm"? A little blow like this?' He looked across to the table where I was sitting with Mr Stokes. 'Force Seven, you would say, Mr Stokes? A touch of Eight, perhaps?'

Mr Stokes helped himself to some more rum, leaned back and deliberated. He was as bereft of cranial and facial hair as Captain Imrie was over-endowed with it. With his gleaming pate, tightly-drawn brown face seamed and wrinkled into a thousand fissures, and a long, thin, scrawny neck, he looked as aged and as ageless as a Galapagos turtle. He also moved at about the same speed. Both he and Captain Imrie had gone to sea together—in mine-sweepers, as incredibly far back as World War I—and had remained together until they had officially retired ten years previously. Nobody, the legend went, had ever heard them refer to each other except as Captain Imrie and Mr Stokes. Some said that, in private, they used the terms Skipper and Chief (Mr Stokes was the Chief Engineer) but this was discounted as an unsubstantiated and unworthy rumour which did justice to neither man.

Moments passed, then Mr Stokes, having arrived at a

measured opinion, delivered himself of it. 'Seven,' he said.

'Seven.' Captain Imrie accepted the judgement as unhesitatingly as if an oracle had spoken and poured himself another drink: I thanked whatever gods there be for the infinitely reassuring presence of Smithy, the mate, on the bridge. 'You see, Mr Gerran? Nothing.' As Gerran was at that moment clinging frantically to a table that was inclined at an angle of 30 degrees, he made no reply. 'A storm? Dearie me, dearie me. Why, I remember the very first time that Mr Stokes and I took the *Morning Rose* up to the Bear Island fishing grounds, the very first trawler ever to fish those waters and come back with full holds, 1928, I think it was—'

'1929,' Mr Stokes said.

'1929.' Captain Imrie fixed his bright blue eyes on Gerran and Johann Heissman, a small, lean, pale man with a permanently apprehensive expression: Heissman's hands were never still. 'Now, that was a storm! We were with a trawler out of Aberdeen, I forget its name—'

'The *Silver Harvest*,' Mr Stokes said.

'The *Silver Harvest*. Engine failure in a Force Ten. Two hours she was broadside to the seas, two hours before we could get a line aboard. Her skipper—her skipper—'

'MacAndrew. John MacAndrew.'

'Thank you, Mr Stokes. Broke his neck. Towed his boat— and him with his broken neck in splints—for thirty hours in a Force Ten, four of them in a Force Eleven. Man, you should have seen yon seas. I tell you, they were mountains, just mountains. The bows thirty feet up and down, up and down, rolling over on our beam ends, hour after hour, every man except Mr Stokes and myself coughing his insides up—' He broke off as Heissman rose hurriedly to his feet and ran from the saloon. 'Is your friend upset, Mr Gerran?'

'Couldn't we heave to or whatever it is you do?' Gerran pleaded. 'Or run for shelter?'

'Shelter? Shelter from what? Why, I remember—'

'Mr Gerran and his company haven't spent their lives at sea, Captain,' I said.

'True, true. Heave to? Heaving to won't stop the waves. And the nearest shelter is Jan Mayen—and that's three hundred miles to the west—into the weather.'

'We could run before the weather. Surely that would help?'

'Aye, we could do that. She'd steady up then, no doubt

about it. If that's what you want, Mr Gerran. You know what the contract says—captain to obey all orders other than those that will endanger the vessel.'

'Good, good. Right away, then.'

'You appreciate, of course, Mr Gerran, that this blow might last another day or so?'

With amelioration of the present sufferings practically at hand Gerran permitted himself a slight smile. 'We cannot control the caprices of Mother Nature, Captain.'

'And that we'll have to turn almost ninety east?'

'In your safe hands, Captain.'

'I don't think you are quite understanding. It will cost us two, perhaps three days. And if we run east, the weather north of North Cape is usually worse than it is here. Might have to put into Hammerfest for shelter. Might lose a week, maybe more. I don't know how many hundred pounds a day it costs you to hire the ship and crew and pay your own camera crew and all those actors and actresses—I hear tell that some of those people you call stars can earn a fortune in just no time at all—' Captain Imrie broke off and pushed back his chair. 'What am I talking about? Money will mean nothing to a man like you. You will excuse me while I call the bridge.'

'Wait.' Gerran looked stricken. His parsimony was legendary throughout the film world and Captain Imrie had touched, not inadvertently, I thought, upon his tenderest nerve. 'A week! Lose a whole week?'

'If we're lucky.' Captain Imrie pulled his chair back up to the table and reached for the malt.

'But I've already lost three days. The Orkney cliffs, the sea, the *Morning Rose*—not a foot of background yet.' Gerran's hands were out of sight but I wouldn't have been surprised if he'd been wringing them.

'And your director and camera crew on their backs for the past four days,' Captain Imrie said sympathetically. It was impossible to say whether a smile lay behind the obfuscatory luxuriance of moustache and beard. 'The caprices of nature, Mr Gerran.'

'Three days,' Gerran said again. 'Maybe another week. A thirty-three day location budget, Kirkwall to Kirkwall.' Otto Gerran looked ill, clearly both the state of his stomach and his film finances were making very heavy demands upon him. 'How far to Bear Island, Captain Imrie?'

'Three hundred miles, give or take the usual. Twenty-eight hours, if we can keep up our best speed.'

'You *can* keep it up?'

'I wasn't thinking about the *Morning Rose*. It can stand anything. It's your people, Mr Gerran. Nothing against them, of course, but I'm thinking they'd be more at home with those pedal boats in the paddling ponds.'

'Yes, of course, of course.' You could see that this aspect of the business had just occurred to him. 'Dr Marlowe, you must have treated a great deal of sea-sickness during your years in the Navy.' He paused, but as I didn't deny it, he went on: 'How long do people take to recover from sickness of this kind?'

'Depends how sick they are.' I'd never given the matter any thought, but it seemed a logical enough answer. 'How long they've been ill and how badly. Ninety rough minutes on a cross-Channel trip and you're as right as rain in ten minutes. Four days in an Atlantic gale and you'll be as long again before you're back on even keel.'

'But people don't actually *die* of sea-sickness, do they?'

'I've never known of a case.' For all his usual indecisiveness and more than occasional bumbling ineptitude which tended to make people laugh at him—discreetly and behind his back, of course—Otto, I realized for the first time and with some vague feeling of surprise, was capable of determination that might verge on the ruthless. Something to do with money, I suppose. 'Not by itself, that is. But with a person already suffering from a heart condition, severe asthma, bronchitis, ulcerated stomach—well, yes, it could see him off.'

He was silent for a few moments, probably carrying out a rapid mental survey of the physical condition of cast and crew, then he said: 'I must admit that I'm a bit worried about our people. I wonder if you'd mind having a look over them, just a quick check? Health's a damn sight more important than any profit—hah! profit, in these days!—that we might make from the wretched film. As a doctor I'm sure you whole-heartedly agree.'

'Of course,' I said. 'Right away.' Otto had to have something that had made him the household name that he had become in the past twenty years and one had to admire this massive and wholly inadmirable hypocrisy that was clearly part of it. He had me all ways. I had said that sea-sickness alone did not kill so that if I were to state categorically that some member or members of his cast or crew were in no condition to withstand any further punishment from the sea he would insist on proof of the existence of some disease which, in conjunction with sea-sickness, might be potentially lethal, a proof that, in the first place, would have been very difficult for me to adduce in light of the limited examination facilities available to me aboard ship and, in the second place, would have been impossible anyhow, for every single member of cast and crew had been subjected to a rigorous insurance medical before leaving Britain: if I gave a clean bill of health to all, then Otto would press on with all speed for Bear Island, regardless of the sufferings of 'our people' about whom he professed to be so worried, thereby effecting a considerable saving in time and money: and, in the remote event of any of them inconsiderately dying upon our hands, why, then, as the man who had given the green light, I was the one in the dock.

I drained my glass of inferior brandy that Otto had laid on in such meagre quantities and rose. 'You'll be here?'

'Yes. Most co-operative of you, Doctor, most.'

'We never close,' I said.

I was beginning to like Smithy though I hardly knew him or anything about him: I was never to get to know him, not well. That I should ever get to know him in my professional capacity was unthinkable: six feet two in his carpet slippers and certainly nothing short of two hundred pounds, Smithy was as unlikely a candidate for a doctor's surgery as had ever come my way.

'In the first-aid cabinet there.' Smithy nodded towards a cupboard in a corner of the dimly-lit wheel-house. 'Captain Imrie's own private elixir. For emergency use only.'

I extracted one of half a dozen bottles held in place by felt-lined spring clamps and examined it under the chart-table lamp. My regard for Smithy went up another notch. In latitude 70° something north and aboard a superannuated trawler, however converted, one does not look to find Otard-Dupuy VSOP.

'What constitutes an emergency?' I asked.

'Thirst.'

I poured some of the Otard-Dupuy into a small glass and offered it to Smithy, who shook his head and watched me as I sampled the brandy, then lowered the glass with suitable reverence.

'To waste this on a thirst,' I said, 'is a crime against nature. Captain Imrie isn't going to be too happy when he comes up here and finds me knocking back his special reserve.'

'Captain Imrie is a man who lives by fixed rules. The most fixed of the lot is that he never appears on the bridge between 8 p.m. and 8 a.m. Oakley—he's the bo'sun—and I take turns during the night. Believe me, that way it's safer for everyone all round. What brings you to the bridge, Doctor —apart from this sure instinct for locating VSOP?'

'Duty. I'm checking on the weather prior to checking on the health of Mr Gerran's paid slaves. He fears they may start dying off like flies if we continue on this course in these conditions.' The conditions, I'd noted, appeared to be deteriorating, for the behaviour of the *Morning Rose,* especially its degree of roll, was now distinctly more uncomfortable than it had been: perhaps it was just a function of the height of the bridge but I didn't think so.

'Mr Gerran should have left you at home and brought along his palm-reader or fortune-teller.' A very contained man, educated and clearly intelligent, Smithy always seemed to be slightly amused. 'As for the weather, the 6 p.m. forecast was as it usually is for these parts, vague and not very encouraging. They haven't,' he added superfluously, 'a great number of weather stations in those parts.'

'What do you think?'

'It's not going to improve.' He dismissed the weather and smiled. 'I'm not a great man for the small-talk, but with the Otard-Dupuy who needs it? Take the weight off your feet for an hour, then go tell Mr Gerran that all his paid slaves, as you call them, are holding a square dance on the poop.'

'I suspect Mr Gerran of having a suspicious checking mind. However, if I may—?'

'My guest.'

I helped myself again and replaced the bottle in the cabinet. Smithy, as he'd warned, wasn't very talkative, but the silence was companionable enough. Presently he said: 'Navy, aren't you, Doc?'

'Past tense.'

'And now this?'

'A shameful come-down. Don't you find it so?'

'Touché.' I could dimly see the white teeth as he smiled in the half-dark. 'Medical malpractice, flogging penicillin to the wogs or just drunk in charge of a surgery?'

'Nothing so glamorous. "Insubordination" is the word they used.'

'Snap. Me too.' A pause. 'This Mr Gerran of yours. Is he all right?'

'So the insurance doctors say.'

'I didn't mean that.'

'You can't expect me to speak ill of my employer.' Again there was that dimly-seen glimpse of white teeth.

'Well, that's one way of answering my question. But, well, look, the bloke must be loony—or is that an offensive term?'

'Only to psychiatrists. I don't speak to them. Loony's fine by me. But I'd remind you that Mr Gerran has a very distinguished record.'

'As a loony?'

'That, too. But also as a film-maker, a producer.'

'What kind of producer would take a film unit up to Bear Island with winter coming on?'

'Mr Gerran wants realism.'

'Mr Gerran wants his head examined. Has he any idea what it's like up there at this time of year?'

'He's also a man with a dream.'

'No place for dreamers in the Barents Sea. How the Americans ever managed to put a man on the moon—'

'Our friend Otto isn't an American. He's a central European. If you want the makers of dreams or the peddlers of dreams, there's the place to find them—among the headwaters of the Danube.'

'And the biggest rogues and confidence men in Europe?'

'You can't have everything.'

'He's a long way from the Danube.'

'Otto had to leave in a great hurry at a time when a large number of people had to leave in a great hurry. Year before the war, that was. Found his way to America—where else?—then to Hollywood—again, where else? Say what you like about Otto—and I'm afraid a lot of people do just that—you have to admire his recuperative powers. He'd left a thriving film business behind him in Vienna and arrived in California with what he stood up in.'

'That's not so little.'

'It was then. I've seen pictures. No greyhound, but still about a hundred pounds short of what he is today. Anyway, inside just a few years—chiefly, I'm told, by switching at the psychologically correct moment from anti-Nazism to anti-Communism—Otto prospered mightily in the American film industry on the strength of a handful of nauseatingly super-patriotic pictures, which had the critics in despair and the audiences in raptures. In the mid-fifties, sensing that the cinematic sun was setting over Hollywood—you can't see it but he carries his own built-in radar system with him—Otto's devotion to his adopted country evaporated along with his bank balance and he transferred himself to London, where he made a number of avant-garde films that had the critics in rapture, the audiences in despair and Otto in the red.'

'You seem to know your Otto,' Smithy said.

'Anybody who has read the first five pages of the prospectus for his last film would know his Otto. I'll let you have a copy. Never mentions the film, just Otto. Misses out words like "nauseating" and "despair" of course and you have to read between the lines a bit. But it's all there.'

'I'd like a copy.' Smithy thought some, then said: 'If he's in the red where's the money coming from? To make this film, I mean.'

'Your sheltered life. A producer is always at his most affluent when the bailiffs are camped outside the studio gates —rented studio, of course. Who, when the banks are foreclosing on him and the insurance companies drafting their ultimatums, is throwing the party of the year at the Savoy? Our friend the big-time producer. It's kind of like the law of nature. You'd better stick to ships, Mr Smith,' I added kindly.

'Smithy,' he said absently. 'So who's bank-rolling your friend?'

'My employer. I've no idea. Very secretive about money matters is Otto.'

'But someone is. Backing him, I mean.'

'Must be.' I put down my glass and stood up. 'Thanks for the hospitality.'

'Even after he's produced a string of losers? Seems barmy to me. Fishy, at least,'

18

'The film world, Smithy, is full of barmy and fishy people.'
I didn't, in fact, know whether it was or not but if this ship-
load was in any way representative of the cinema industry it
seemed a pretty fair extrapolation.

'Or perhaps he's just got hold of the story to end all
stories.'

'The screenplay. There, now, you may have a point—but
it's one you would have to raise with Mr Gerran personally.
Apart from Heissman, who wrote it, Gerran is the only one
who's seen it.'

It hadn't been a factor of the height of the bridge. As I
stepped out on to the starboard ladder on the lee side—there
were no internal communications between bridge and deck
level on those elderly steam trawlers—I was left in no doubt
that the weather had indeed deteriorated and deteriorated
sharply, a fact that should have probably been readily
apparent to anyone whose concern for the prevailing meteorological conditions hadn't been confronted with the unfair
challenge of Otard-Dupuy. Even on this, what should have
been the sheltered side of the ship, the power of the wind,
bitter cold, was such that I had to cling with both hands to
the handrails: and with the *Morning Rose* now rolling,
erratically and violently, through almost fifty degrees of arc
—which was wicked enough but I'd once been on a cruiser
that had gone through a hundred degrees of arc and still
survived—I could have used another pair of arms.

Even on the blackest night, and this was incontestably one
of the blackest, it is never wholly dark at sea: it may never
be possible precisely to delineate the horizon line where sea
and sky meet, but one can usually look several vertical degrees
above or below the horizon line and say with certainty that
here is sky or here is sea: for the sea is always darker than
the sky. Tonight, it was impossible to say any such thing
and this was not because the violently rolling *Morning Rose*
made for a very unstable observation platform nor because
the big uneven seas bearing down from the east made for a
tumbling amorphous horizon: because tonight, for the first
time, not yet dense but enough to obscure vision beyond two
miles, smoke frost lay on the surface of the sea, that peculiar
phenomenon which one finds in Norway where the glacial
land winds pass over the warm fjord waters or, as here, where

the warm Atlantic air passed over the Arctic waters. All I could see, and it was enough to see, was that the tops were now being torn off the waves, white-veined on their leeward sides, and that the seas were breaking ciear across the foredeck of the *Morning Rose,* the white and icy spume hissing into the sea on the starboard. A night for carpet slippers and the fireside.

I turned for'ard towards the accommodation door and bumped into someone who was standing behind the ladder and holding on to it for support. I couldn't see the person's face for it was totally obscured by wind-blown hair but I didn't have to, there was only one person aboard with those long straw-coloured tresses and that was Mary dear: given my choice of people to bump into on the *Morning Rose* I'd have picked Mary dear any time. 'Mary dear', not 'Mary Dear': I'd given her that name to distinguish her from Gerran's continuity girl whose given name was Mary Darling. Mary dear was really Mary Stuart but that wasn't her true name either: Ilona Wisniowecki she'd been christened but had prudently decided that it wasn't the biggest possible asset she had for making her way in the film world. Why she'd chosen a Scots name I didn't know: maybe she just liked the sound of it.

'Mary dear,' I said. 'Aboard at this late hour and on such a night.' I reached up and touched her cheek, we doctors can get away with murder. The skin was icily cold. 'You can carry this fresh air fanatic bit too far. Come on, inside.' I took her arm—I was hardly surprised to find she was shivering quite violently—and she came along docilely enough.

The accommodation door led straight into the passenger lounge which, though fairly narrow, ran the full width of the ship. At the far end was a built-in bar with the liquor kept behind two glassed-in iron-grilled doors: the doors were kept permanently locked and the key was in Otto Gerran's pocket.

'No need to frog-march me, Doctor.' She habitually spoke in a low-pitched quiet voice. 'Enough is enough and I was coming in anyway.'

'Why were you out there in the first place?'

'Can't doctors always tell?' She touched the middle button of her black leather coat and from this I understood that her internal economy wasn't taking too kindly to the roller-coaster antics of the *Morning Rose.* But I also understood that even had the sea been mirror-smooth she'd still have been out on that freezing upper deck: she didn't talk much to the others nor the others to her.

She pushed the tangled hair back from her face and I could see she was very pale and the skin beneath the brown eyes tinged with the beginnings of exhaustion. In her high-cheek-boned Slavonic way—she was a Latvian but, I supposed, no less a Slav for that—she was very lovely, a fact that was freely admitted and slightingly commented upon as being her only asset: her last two pictures—her only two pictures—were said to have been disasters of the first magnitude. She was a silent girl, cool and aloofly remote and I liked her, which made me a lonely minority of one.

'Doctors aren't infallible,' I said. 'At least, not this one.' I peered at her in my best clinical fashion. 'What's a girl like you doing in these parts on this floating museum?'

She hesitated. 'That's a personal question.'

'The medical profession are a very personal lot. How's your headache? Your ulcer? Your bursitis? We don't know where to stop.'

'I need the money.'

'You and me both.' I smiled at her and she didn't smile back so I left her and went down the companionway to the main deck.

Here was located the *Morning Rose's* main passenger accommodation, two rows of cabins lining the fore-and-aft central passage-way. This had been the area of the former fish-holds and although the place had been steam-washed, fumigated and disinfected at the time of conversion it still stank most powerfully and evilly of cod liver oil that has lain too long in the sun. In ordinary circumstances, the atmosphere was nauseating enough: in those extraordinary ones it was hardly calculated to assist sufferers in a rapid recovery from the effects of sea-sickness. I knocked on the first door on the starboard side and went in.

Johann Heissman, horizontally immobile on his bunk, looked like a cross between a warrior taking his rest and a medieval bishop modelling for the stone effigy which in the fullness of time would adorn the top of his sarcophagus. Indeed, with his thin waxy fingers steepled on his narrow chest, his thin waxy nose pointing to the ceiling and his curiously transparent eyelids closed, the image of the tomb seemed particularly opposite in this case: but it was a deceptive image for a man does not survive twenty years in a Soviet hard-labour camp in Eastern Siberia just to turn in his cards from *mal de mer*.

'How do you feel, Mr Heissman?'

'Oh, God!' He opened his eyes without looking at me, moaned and closed them again. 'How do I feel?'

'I'm sorry. But Mr Gerran is concerned—'

'Otto Gerran is a raving madman.' I didn't take it as any indication of some sudden upsurge in his physical condition but, no question, this time his voice was a great deal stronger. 'A crackpot! A lunatic!'

While privately conceding that Heissman's diagnosis lay somewhere along the right lines, I refrained from comment and not out of some suitably due deference to my employer. Otto Gerran and Johann Heissman had been friends much too long for me to risk treading upon the delicate ground that well might lie between them. They had known each other, as far as I had been able to discover, since they had been students together at some obscure Danubian gymnasium close on forty years ago and had, at the time of the Anschluss in 1938, been the joint owners of a relatively prosperous film studio in Vienna. It was at this point in space and time that they had parted company suddenly, drastically and, it seemed at the time, permanently, for while Gerran's sure instinct had guided his fleeing footsteps to Hollywood, Heissman had unfortunately taken off in the wrong direction altogether and, only three years previously, to the total dis-belief of all who had known him and believed him dead for a quarter of a century, had incredibly surfaced from the bitter depths of his long Siberian winter. He had sought out Gerran and now it appeared that their friendship was as close as ever it had been. It was assumed that Gerran knew about the hows and whys of Heissman's lost years and if this were indeed the case then he was the only man who did so for Heissman, understandably enough, never discussed his past. Only two things about the men were known for certain —that it was Heissman, who had a dozen pre-war screen-plays to his credit, who was the moving spirit behind this venture to the Arctic, and that Gerran had taken him into full partnership in his company, Olympus Productions. In light of this, it behooved me to step warily and keep my comments on Heissman's comments strictly to myself.

'If there's anything you require, Mr Heissman—'

'I require nothing.' He opened his transparent eyelids again and this time looked—or glared—at me, eyes of washed-out grey streaked with blood. 'Save your treatment for that cretin Gerran.'

'Treatment?'

'Brain surgery.' He lowered his eyelids wearily and went back to being a medieval bishop again, so I left him and went next door.

There were two men in this cabin, one clearly suffering quite badly, the other equally clearly not suffering in the slightest. Neal Divine, the unit director, had adopted a death's door resignation attitude that was strikingly similar to that favoured by Heissman and although he wasn't even within hailing distance of death's door he was plainly very sea-sick indeed. He looked at me, forced a pale smile that was half apology, half recognition, then looked away again. I felt sorry for him as he lay there, but then I'd felt sorry for him ever since he'd stepped aboard the *Morning Rose*. A man dedicated to his craft, lean, hollow-cheeked, nervous and perpetually balanced on what seemed to be the knife-edge of agonizing decisions, he walked softly and talked softly as if he were perpetually afraid that the gods might hear him. It could have been a meaningless mannerism but I didn't think so: no question, he walked in perpetual fear of Gerran, who was at no pains to conceal the fact that he despised him as a man just as much as he admired him as an artist. Why Gerran, a man of indisputably high intelligence, should behave in this way, I didn't know. Perhaps he was one of that far from small group of people who harbour such an inexhaustible fund of ill-will towards mankind in general that they lose no opportunity to vent some of it on the weak, the pliant or those who are in no position to retaliate. Perhaps it was a personal matter. I didn't know either man or their respective backgrounds well enough to form a valid judgement.

'Ah, 'tis the good healer,' a gravelly voice said behind me. I turned round without haste and looked at the pyjama-clad figure sitting up in his bunk, holding fast with his left hand to a bulkhead strap while with the other he clung equally firmly to the neck of a scotch bottle, three parts empty. 'Up the ship comes and down the ship goes but naught will come between the kindly shepherd and his mission of mercy to his queasy flock. You will join me in a post-prandial snifter, my good man?'

'Later, Lonnie, later.' Lonnie Gilbert knew and I knew and we both knew that the other knew that later would be too late, three inches of scotch in Lonnie's hands had as much hope as the last meringue at the vicar's tea-party; but the conventions had been observed, honour satisfied. 'You weren't at dinner, so I thought—'

'Dinner!' He paused, examined the word he'd just said for inflexion and intonation, decided his delivery had been lacking in a proper contempt and repeated himself. 'Dinner! Not the høgswash itself, which I suppose is palatable enough for those who lack my esoteric tastes. It's the hour at which it's served. Barbaric. Even Attila the Hun—'

'You mean you no sooner pour your apéritif than the bell goes?'

'Exactly. What does a man do?'

Coming from our elderly production manager, the question was purely rhetorical. Despite the baby-clear blue eyes and faultless enunciation, Lonnie hadn't been sober since he'd stepped aboard the *Morning Rose*: it was widely questioned whether he'd been sober for years. Nobody—least of all Lonnie—seemed to care about this, but this was not because nobody cared about Lonnie. Nearly all people did, in greater or lesser degrees, dependent on their own natures. Lonnie, growing old now, with all his life in films, was possessed of a rare talent that had never bloomed and never would now, for he was cursed—or blessed—with insufficient drive and ruthlessness to take him to the top, and mankind, for a not always laudable diversity of reasons, tends to cherish its failures: and Lonnie, it was said, never spoke ill of others and this, too, deepened the affection in which he was held except by the minority who habitually spoke ill of everyone.

'It's not a problem I'd care to be faced with myself,' I said. 'How are you feeling?'

'Me?' He inclined his bald pate 45 degrees backwards, tilted the bottle, lowered it and wiped a few drops of the elixir from his grey beard. 'Never been ill in my life. Who ever heard of a pickled onion going sour?' He cocked his head sideways. 'Ah!'

'Ah, what?' He was listening, that I could see, but I couldn't hear a damned thing except the crash of bows against

24

seas and the metallic drumming vibration of the ancient steel hull which accompanied each downwards plunge.

' "The horns of Elfland faintly blowing," ' Lonnie said. ' "Hark! The Herald Angels." '

I harked and this time I heard. I'd heard it many times, and with steadily increasing horror, since boarding the *Morning Rose,* a screechingly cacophonous racket that was fit for heralding nothing short of Armageddon. The three perpetrators of this boiler-house bedlam of sound, Josh Hendriks's young sound crew assistants, might not have been tone stone deaf but their classical musical education could hardly be regarded as complete, as not one of them could read a note of music. John, Luke and Mark were all cast in the same contemporary mould, with flowing shoulder-length hair and wearing clothes that gave rise to the suspicion that they must have broken into a gurus' laundry. All their spare time was spent with recording equipment, guitar, drums and xylophone in the for'ard recreation room where they rehearsed, apparently night and day, against the moment of their big break-through into the pop-record world where they intended, appropriately enough, to bill themselves as 'The Three Apostles'.

'They might have spared the passengers on a night like this,' I said.

'You underestimate our immortal trio, my dear boy. The fact that you may be one of the most excruciating musicians in existence does not prevent you from having a heart of gold. They have *invited* the passengers along to hear them perform in the hope that this might alleviate their sufferings.' He closed his eyes as a raucous bellow overlaid with a high-pitched scream as of some animal in pain echoed down the passageway outside. 'The concert seems to have begun.'

'You can't fault their psychology,' I said. 'After that, an Arctic gale is going to seem like a summer afternoon on the Thames.'

'You do them an injustice.' Lonnie lowered the level in the bottle by another inch then slid down into his bunk to show that the audience was over. 'Go and see for yourself.'

So I went and saw for myself and I had been doing them an injustice. The Three Apostles, surrounded by that plethora of microphones, amplifiers, speakers and arcane electronic equipment without which the latter-day troubadours will not —and, more importantly, cannot—operate, were performing on a low platform in one corner of the recreation room and maintaining their balance with remarkable ease largely, it seemed, because their bodily gyrations and contortions, as inseparable a part of their art as the electronic aids, seemed to synchronize rather well with the pitching and rolling of the *Morning Rose*. Rather conservatively, if oddly, clad in blue jeans and psychedelic caftans, and bent over their microphones in an attitude of almost acolytic fervour, the three young sound assistants were giving of their uninhibited best and from what little could be seen of the ecstatic expressions on faces eighty per cent concealed at any given moment by wildly swinging manes of hair, it was plain that they thought that their best approximated very closely to the sublime. I wondered, briefly, how angels would look with ear-plugs, then turned my attention to the audience.

There were fifteen in all, ten members of the production crew and five of the cast. A round dozen of them were very clearly the worse for the wear, but their sufferings were being temporarily held in abeyance by the fascination, which stopped a long way short of rapture, induced by the Three Apostles who had now reached a musical crescendo accompanied by what seemed to be some advanced form of St Vitus' Dance. A hand touched me on the shoulder and I looked sideways at Charles Conrad.

Conrad was thirty years old and was to be the male lead in the film, not yet a big-name star but building up an impressive international reputation. He was cheerful, ruggedly handsome, with a thatch of thick brown hair that kept falling over his eyes: he had eyes of the bluest blue and most gleamingly white perfect teeth—like his name, his own— that would have transported a dentist into ecstasies or the depths of despair, depending upon whether he was primarily interested in the aesthetic or economic aspects of his profession. He was invariably friendly, courteous and considerate, whether by instinct or calculated design it was impossible to say. He cupped his hand to my ear, nodded towards the performers.

'Your contract specifies hairshirts?'

'No. Why? Does yours?'

'Solidarity of the working classes.' He smiled, looking at me with an oddly speculative glint in his eyes. 'Letting the opera buffs down, aren't you?'

'They'll recover. Anyway, I always tell my patients that a change is as good as a rest.' The music ceased abruptly and I lowered my voice about fifty decibels. 'Mind you, this is carrying it too far. Fact is, I'm on duty. Mr Gerran is a bit concerned about you all.'

'He wants his herd delivered to the cattle market in prime condition?'

'Well, I suppose you all represent a pretty considerable investment to him.'

'Investment? Ha! Do you know that that twisted old skinflint of a beer-barrel has not only got us at fire-sale prices but also won't pay us a penny until shooting's over?'

'No, I didn't.' I paused. 'We live in a democracy, Mr Conrad, the land of the free. You don't have to sell yourselves in the slave market.'

'Don't we just! What do you know about the film industry?'

'Nothing.'

'Obviously. It's in the most depressed state in its history. Eighty per cent of the technicians and actors unemployed. I'd rather work for pennies than starve.' He scowled, then his natural good humour reasserted itself. 'Tell him that his prop and stay, that indomitable leading man Charles Conrad, is fit and well. Not happy, mind you, just fit and well. To be happy I'd have to see him fall over the side.'

'I'll tell him all of that.' I looked around the room. The Three Apostles, mercifully, were refreshing themselves, though clearly in need of something stronger than ginger ale. I said to Conrad: 'This little lot will get to market.'

'Instant mass diagnosis?'

'It takes practice. It also saves time. Who's missing?'

'Well.' He glanced around. 'There's Heissman—'

'I've seen him. And Neal Divine. And Lonnie. And Mary Stuart—not that I'd expect her to be here anyway.'

'Our beautiful but snooty young Slav, eh?'

'I'll go half-way with that. You don't have to be snooty to avoid people.'

'I like her too.' I looked at him. I'd only spoken to him twice, briefly. I could see he meant what he said. He sighed. 'I wish she were my leading lady instead of our resident Mata Hari.'

'You can't be referring to the delectable Miss Haynes?'

'I can and I am,' he said moodily. 'Femmes fatales wear

me out. You'll observe she's not among those present. I'll bet she's in bed with those two damned floppy-eared hounds of hers, all of them having the vapours and high on smelling salts.'

'Who else is missing?'

'Antonio.' He was smiling again. 'According to the Count —he's his cabin-mate—Antonio is *in extremis* and unlikely to see the night out.'

'He did leave the dining-room in rather a hurry.' I left Conrad and joined the Count at his table. The Count, with a lean · aquiline face, black pencil moustache, bar-straight black eyebrows and greying hair brushed straight back from his forehead, appeared to be in more than tolerable health. He held a very large measure of brandy in his hand and I did not have to ask to know that it would be the very best cognac obtainable, for the Count was a renowned connoisseur of everything from blondes to caviare, as precisely demanding a perfectionist in the pursuit of the luxuries of life as he was in the performance of his duties, which may have helped to make him what he was, the best lighting cameraman in the country and probably in Europe. Nor did I have to wonder where he had obtained the cognac from: rumour had it that he had known Otto Gerran a very long time indeed, or at least long enough to bring his own private supplies along with him whenever Otto went on safari. Count Tadeusz Leszczynski—which nobody ever called him because they couldn't pronounce it—had learned a great deal about life since he had parted with his huge Polish estates, precipitately and for ever, in mid-September, 1939.

'Evening, Count,' I said. 'At least, you look fit enough.'

'Tadeusz to my peers. In robust health, I'm glad to say. I take the properly prophylactic precautions.' He touched the barely perceptible bulge in his jacket. 'You will join me in some prophylaxis? Your penicillins and aureomycins are but witches' brews for the credulous.'

I shook my head. 'Duty rounds, I'm afraid. Mr Gerran wants to know just how ill this weather is making people.'

'Ah! Our Otto himself is fit?'

'Reasonably.'

'One can't have everything.'

'Conrad tells me that your room-mate Antonio may require a visit.'

'What Antonio requires is a gag, a straight-jacket and a nursemaid, in that order. Rolling around, sick all over the floor, groaning like some miscreant stretched out on the rack.' The Count wrinkled a fastidious nose. 'Most upsetting, most.'

'I can well imagine it.'

'For a man of delicate sensibilities, you understand.'

'Of course.'

'I simply *had* to leave.'

'Yes. I'll have a look at him.' I'd just pushed my chair back to the limit of its securing chain when Michael Stryker sat down in a chair beside me. Stryker, a full partner in Olympus Productions, combined the two jobs, normally separate, of production designer and construction manager—Gerran never lost the opportunity to economize. He was a tall, dark and undeniably handsome man with a clipped moustache and could readily have been mistaken for a matinee idol of the mid-thirties were it not for the fashionably long and untidy hair that obscured about ninety per cent of the polo-necked silk sweater which he habitually affected. He looked tough, was unquestionably cynical and, from what little I had heard of him, totally amoral. He was also possessed of the dubious distinction of being Gerran's son-in-law.

'Seldom we see you abroad at this late hour, Doctor,' he said. He screwed a long black Russian cigarette into an onyx holder with all the care of a precision engineer fitting the tappets on a Rolls-Royce engine, then held it up to the light to inspect the results. 'Kind of you to join the masses, *esprit de corps* and what have you.' He lit his cigarette, blew a cloud of noxious smoke across the table and looked at me consideringly. 'On second thoughts, no. You're not the *esprit de corps* type. We more or less have to be. You don't. I don't think you could. Too cool, too detached, too clinical. too observant—and a loner. Right?'

'It's a pretty fair description of a doctor.'

'Here in an official capacity, eh?'

'I suppose so.'

'I'll wager that old goat sent you.'

'Mr Gerran sent me.' It was becoming increasingly apparent to me that Otto Gerran's senior associates were unlikely ever to clamour for the privilege of voting him into the Hall of Fame.

'That's the old goat I mean.' Stryker looked thoughtfully

at the Count. 'A strange and unwonted solicitude on the part of our Otto, wouldn't they say, Tadeusz? I wonder what lies behind it?'

The Count produced a chased silver flask, poured himself another generous measure of cognac, smiled and said nothing. I said nothing either because I'd already decided that I knew the answer to that one: even later on, in retrospect, I could not and did not blame myself, for I had arrived at a conclusion on the basis of the only facts then available to me. I said to Stryker: 'Miss Haynes is not here. Is she all right?'

'No, I'm afraid she's no sailor. She's pretty much under the weather but what's a man to do? She's pleading for sedatives or sleeping drugs and asking that I send for you, but of course I had to say no.'

'Why?'

'My dear chap, she's been living on drugs ever since we came aboard this damned hell-ship.' It was as well for his health, I thought, that Captain Imrie and Mr Stokes weren't sitting at the same table. 'Her own sea-sick tablets one moment, the ones you doled out the next, pep pills in between and barbiturates for dessert. Well, you know what would happen if she took sedatives or more drugs on top of that lot.'

'No, I don't. Tell me.'

'Eh?'

'Does she drink? Heavily, I mean?'

'Drink? No. I mean, she never touches the stuff.'

I sighed. 'Why don't cobblers stick to their own lasts? I'll leave films to you, you leave medicine to me. Any first-year medical student could tell you—well, never mind. Does she know what kind of tablets she's taken today and how many —not that it could have been all that many or she'd have been unconscious by now?'

'I should imagine so.'

I pushed back my chair. 'She'll be asleep in fifteen minutes.'

'Are you sure? I mean—'

'Which is her room?'

'First on the right in the passageway.'

'And yours?' I asked the Count.

'First left.'

I nodded, rose, left, knocked on the first door on the right and went inside in response to a barely-heard murmur. Judith Haynes was sitting propped up in her bed with, as Conrad

30

had predicted, a dog on either side of her—two rather beautiful and beautifully groomed cocker spaniels: I could not, however, catch any trace of smelling salts. She blinked at me with her rather splendid eyes and gave me a wan smile, at once tremulous and brave. My heart stayed where it was.

'It was kind of you to come, Doctor.' She had one of those dark molasses voices, as effective at close personal quarters as it was in a darkened cinema. She was wearing a pink quilted bed-jacket which clashed violently with the colour of her hair and, high round her neck, a green chiffon scarf, which didn't. Her face was alabaster white. 'Michael said you couldn't help.'

'Mr Stryker was being over-cautious.' I sat down on the edge of the mattress and took her wrist. The cocker spaniel next me growled deep in its throat and bared its teeth. 'If that dog bites me, I'll clobber it.'

'Rufus wouldn't harm a fly, would you, Rufus darling?'

It wasn't flies I was worried about but I kept silence and she went on with a sad smile: 'Are you allergic to dogs, Doctor Marlowe?'

'I'm allergic to dog bites.'

The smile faded until her face was just sad. I knew nothing about Judith Haynes except what I'd heard at second hand, and as all I'd heard had been from her colleagues in the industry I heavily discounted about ninety per cent of what had been told me: the only thing I had so far learned with any certainty about the film world was that back-biting, hypocrisy, double-dealing, innuendo and character assassination formed so integral a part of its conversational fabric that it was quite impossible to know where the truth ended and falsehood began. The only safe guide, I'd discovered, was to assume that the truth ended almost immediately.

Miss Haynes, it was said, claimed to be twenty-four and had been, on the best authority, for the past fourteen years. This, it was said darkly, explained her predilection for chiffon scarves, for it was there that the missing years showed: equally, she may just have liked chiffon scarves. With equal authority it was stated that she was a complete bitch, her only redeeming quality being her total devotion to her two cocker spaniels and even this back-handed compliment was qualified by the observation that as a human being she had to have something or somebody to love, something or somebody to return her affection. She had tried cats, it was said, but that hadn't worked: the cats, apparently, didn't love her back. But one thing was indisputable. Tall, slender, with wonderful titian hair and classically beautiful in the sculptured Greek fashion, Miss Haynes, it was universally conceded, couldn't act for toffee. Nonetheless, she was a very hot box office attraction indeed: the combination of the wistfully regal expression, which was her trade-mark, and the startling contrast of her lurid private life saw to that. Nor was her career in any way noticeably hindered by the facts that she was the daughter of Otto Gerran, whom she was said to despise, the wife of Michael Stryker, whom she was said to hate, and a full partner in the Olympus Productions company.

There was nothing much wrong with her physical condition that I could see. I asked her how many tablets of various kinds she had consumed in the course of the day and after dithering about helplessly for a bit and totting up the score with the shapely and tapering forefinger of her right hand on the shapely and tapering fingers of her left—she was alleged to be able to add up pounds and dollars with the speed and accuracy of an IBM computer—she gave me some approximate figures and in return I gave her some tablets with instructions as to how many and when to take them, then left. I didn't prescribe any sedatives for the dogs—they looked OK to me.

The cabin occupied by the Count and Antonio was directly opposite across the passageway. I knocked twice, without reply, went inside and saw why there had been no reply: Antonio was there all right, but I could have knocked until doomsday and Antonio would not have heard me, for Antonio would never hear anything again. From the Via Veneto via Mayfair to die so squalidly in the Barents Sea: for the gay and laughing Antonio there could never have been a right or proper or suitable place to die, for if ever I'd met a man in love with life it had been Antonio: and for this cosseted creature of the sybaritic salons of the capitals of Europe to die in those bleak and indescribably bitter surroundings was so incongruous as to be shocking, so unreal as to momentarily suspend both belief and comprehension. But there he was, just there, lying there at my feet, very real, very dead.

The cabin was full of the sour-sweet smell of sickness and

there was physical evidence of that sickness everywhere. Antonio lay not on his bunk but on the carpeted deck beside it, his head arched impossibly far back until it was at right angles to his body. There was blood, a great deal of blood, not yet congealed, on his mouth and on the floor by his mouth. The body was contorted into an almost impossible position, arms and legs outflung at grotesque angles, the knuckles showing ivory. Rolling around, the Count had said, sick, a man on the rack, and he hadn't been so far out at that, for Antonio had died as a man on the rack dies, in agony. Surely to God he must have cried out, even although his throat would have been blocked most of the time, he must have screamed, he *must* have, he would have been unable to prevent himself: but with the Three Apostles in full cry, his cries would have gone unheeded. And then I remembered the scream I had heard when I'd been talking to Lonnie Gilbert in his cabin and I could feel the hairs prickling on the back of my neck: I should have known the difference between the high-pitched yowling of a rock singer and the scream of a man dying in torment.

I knelt, made a cursory examination, finding out no more in the process than any layman would have done, closed the staring eyes and then, with the advent of *rigor mortis* in mind, straightened out the contorted limbs with an ease that I found vaguely surprising. Then I left the cabin, locked the door and hesitated for only a moment before dropping the key in my pocket: if the Count were possessed of the delicate sensibilities he claimed, he'd be glad I'd taken the key with me.

CHAPTER TWO

'Dead?'. Otto Gerran's puce complexion had deepened to
a shade where I could have sworn it was overlaid with indigo.
'Dead, did you say?'

'That's what I said.' Otto and I were alone in the dining
saloon: it was ten o'clock now and at nine-thirty sharp
Captain Imrie and Mr Stokes invariably left for their cabins,
where they would remain incommunicado for the next ten
hours. I lifted from Otto's table a bottle of raw fire-water
on which someone had unblushingly stuck a label claiming
that the contents were brandy, took it to the stewards' pantry,
returned with a bottle of Hine and sat down. It said much for
Otto's unquestioned state of shock that not only had he
not appeared to note my brief absence, he even stared
directly at me, unblinkingly and I'm sure unseeingly, as I
poured out two fingers for myself: he registered no reaction
whatsoever. Only something pretty close to a state of total
shock could have held Otto's parsimonious nature in check
and I wondered what the source of this shock might be.
True, the news of the death of anyone you knew can come
as a shock, but it comes as a numbing shock only when the
nearest and dearest are involved, and if Otto had even a
measurable amount of affection for anyone, far less for the
unfortunate Antonio, he concealed it with great skill. Perhaps he was, as many are, superstitious about death at sea,
perhaps he was concerned with the adverse effect it might
have on cast and crew, maybe he was bleakly wondering where,
in the immensity of the Barents Sea, he could lay hands on a
make-up artist, hairdresser and wardrobe man, for Otto, in
the sacred name of economy, had combined all three normally separate jobs in the person of one man, the late
Antonio. With a visibly conscious effort of will-power he
looked away from the Hine bottle and focused his eyes on
me.

'How can he be dead?'

'His heart's stopped. His breathing's stopped. That's how
he can be dead. That's how anyone can be dead.'

Otto reached out for the bottle of Hine and splashed some brandy into a glass. He didn't pour it, he literally splashed it, the spreading stain on the white tablecloth as big as my hand: his own hand was shaking as badly as that. He poured out three fingers as compared to my two, which may not sound so very much more but then Otto was using a balloon glass whereas mine was a tulip. Tremblingly, he lifted the glass to his mouth and half of its contents disappeared in one gulp, most of it down his throat but a fair proportion on his shirt-front. It occurred to me, not for the first time, that if ever I found myself in a situation where all seemed lost, and the only faint hope of life depended on having one good man and true standing by my right shoulder, the name of Otto Gerran was not one that would leap automatically to my mind.

'How did he die?' The brandy had done some good, Otto's voice was low, just above a whisper, but it was steady.

'In agony, I would say. If you mean why did he die, I don't know.'

'You don't know? You—you're supposed to be a doctor.' Otto was having the greatest difficulty in remaining in his seat: with one hand clutching the brandy glass, the other was barely sufficient to anchor his massive weight against the wild plunging of the *Morning Rose*. I said nothing so he went on: 'Was it sea-sickness? Could that have done it?'

'He was sea-sick, all right.'

'But you said a man doesn't die just from that.'

'He didn't die just from that.'

'An ulcerated stomach, you said. Or heart. Or asthma—'

'He was poisoned.'

Otto stared at me for a moment, his face registering no comprehension, then he set his glass on the table and pushed himself abruptly to his feet, no mean accomplishment for a man of his bulk. The trawler rolled wickedly. I leaned quickly forward, snatched up Otto's glass just as it began to topple and at the same moment Otto lurched to one side and staggered across to the starboard—the lee—door of the saloon leading to the upper deck. He flung this open and even above the shrieking of the wind and the crash of the seas I could hear him being violently sick. Presently he re-entered, closed the door, staggered across the deck and collapsed into his chair. His face was ashen. I handed him his glass and he drained the contents, reached out for the bottle and re-filled his glass. He drank some more and stared at me.

'Poison?'

'Looked like strychnine. Had all—'

'Strychnine? Strychnine! Great God! Strychnine! You—you'll have to carry out a post-mortem, an—an autopsy.'

'Don't talk rubbish. I'll carry out no such thing, and for a number of excellent reasons. For one thing, have you any idea what an autopsy is like? It's a very messy business indeed, I can assure you. I haven't the facilities. I'm not a specialist in pathology—and you require one for an autopsy. You require the consent of the next of kin—and how are you going to get that in the middle of the Barents Sea? You require a coroner's order—no coroner. Besides, a coroner only issues an order where there's a suspicion of foul play. No such suspicion exists here.'

'No—no foul play? But you said—'

'I said it looked like strychnine. I didn't say it was strychnine. I'm sure it's not. He seemed to show the classical symptoms of having had tetanic spasms and opisthotonos—that's when the back arches so violently that the body rests on the head and the heels only—and his face showed pure terror: there's nearly always this conviction of impending death at the onset of strychnine poisoning. But when I straightened him out there were no signs of tetanic contractions. Besides, the timing is all wrong. Strychnine usually shows its first effects within ten minutes and half an hour after taking the stuff you're gone. Antonio was at least twenty minutes here with us at dinner and there was nothing wrong with him then—well, sea-sickness, that's all. And he died only minutes ago—far too long. Besides, who on earth would want to do away with a harmless boy like Antonio? Do you have in your employ a raving psycho who kills just for the kicks of it? Does it make any kind of sense to you?'

'No. No, it doesn't. But—but poison. You said—'

'Food poisoning.'

'Food poisoning! But people don't die of food poisoning. You mean ptomaine poisoning?'

'I mean no such thing for there is no such thing. You can eat ptomaines to your heart's content and you'll come to no harm. But you can get all sorts of food poisoning—chemically contaminated—mercury in fish, for instance—edible mushrooms that aren't edible mushrooms, edible mussels that aren't edible mussels—but the nasty one is *salmonella*. And that can kill, believe me. Just at the end of the war one variety of it, *salmonella enteritidis*, laid low about thirty people in Stoke-on-Trent. Six of them died. And there's an even nastier one called *clostridium botulinum*—a kind of half-cousin of botulinus, a charming substance that is guaranteed to wipe out a city in a night—the Ministry of Health makes it. This *clostidium* secretes an exotoxin—a poison—which is probably the most powerful occurring in nature. Between the wars a party of tourists at Loch Maree in Scotland had a picnic lunch—sandwiches filled with potted duck paste. Eight of them had this. All eight died. There was no cure then, there is no cure now. Must have been this or something like this that Antonio ate.'

'I see, I see.' He had some more brandy, then looked up at me, his eyes round. 'Good God! Don't you see what this means, man! We're all at risk, all of us. This *clostridium* or whatever you call it could spread like wildfire—'

'Rest easy. It's neither infectious nor contagious.'

'But the galley—'

'You think that hadn't occurred to me? The source of infection can't be there. If it were, we'd all be gone—I assume that Antonio—before his appetite deserted him, that was—had the same as all of us. I didn't pay any particular attention but I can find out probably from the people on either side of him—I'm sure they were the Count and Cecil.'

'Cecil?'

'Cecil Golightly—your camera focus assistant or something like that.'

'Ah! The Duke.' For some odd reason Cecil, a diminutive, shrewd and chirpy little Cockney sparrow was invariably known as the Duke, probably because it was so wildly unsuitable. 'That little pig see anything! He never lifts his eyes from the table. But Tadeusz—well, now, he doesn't miss much.'

'I'll ask. I'll also check the galley, the food store and the cold room. Not a chance in ten thousand—I think we'll find that Antonio had his own little supply of tinned delicacies —but I'll check anyway. Do you want me to see Captain Imrie for you?'

'Captain Imrie?'

I was patient. 'The master must be notified. The death must be logged. A death certificate must be issued—normally, he'd do it himself but not with a doctor aboard—but I'll have to be authorized. And he'll have to make preparations for the funeral. Burial at sea. Tomorrow morning, I should imagine.'

He shuddered. 'Yes, please. Please do that. Of course, of course, burial at sea. I must go and see John at once and tell him about this awful thing.' By 'John' I assumed he meant John Cummings Goin, production accountant, company accountant, senior partner in Olympus Production and widely recognized as being the financial controller—and so in many ways the virtual controller—of the company. 'And then I'm going to bed. Yes, yes, to bed. Sounds terrible, I know, poor Antonio lying down there, but I'm dreadfully upset, really dreadfully upset.' I couldn't fault him on that one, I'd rarely seen a man look so unhappy.

'I can bring a sedative to your cabin.'

'No, no, I'll be all right.' Unthinkingly, almost, he picked up the bottle of Hine, thrust it into one of the capacious pockets of his tent-like jacket and staggered from the saloon. As far as insomnia was concerned, Otto clearly preferred home-made remedies to even the most modern pharmaceutical products.

I went to the starboard door, opened it and looked out. When Smithy had said that the weather wasn't going to improve, he'd clearly been hedging his bets: conditions were deteriorating and, if I were any judge, deteriorating quite rapidly. The air temperature was now well below freezing and the first thin flakes of snow were driving by overhead, almost parallel to the surface of the sea. The waves were now no longer waves, just moving masses of water, capriciously tending, it seemed, in any and all directions, but in the main still bearing mainly easterly. The *Morning Rose* was no longer just cork-screwing, she was beginning to stagger, falling into a bridge-high trough with an explosive impact more than vaguely reminiscent of the flat, whip-like crack of a not so distant naval gun, then struggling and straining to right herself only to be struck by a following wall of water that smashed her over on her beam ends again. I leaned farther outwards, looking upwards and was vaguely puzzled by the dimly seen outline of the madly flapping flag on the foremast: puzzled, because it wasn't streaming out over the starboard side, as it should have been, but towards the starboard quarter. This meant that the wind was moving round to the north-east and what this could portend I could not even guess: I vaguely suspected that it wasn't anything good. I went inside, yanked the door closed with some effort, made a silent prayer for the infinitely reassuring and competent presence of Smithy on the bridge, made my way to the stewards' pantry again and helped myself to a bottle of Black Label, Otto having made off with the last of the brandy —the drinkable brandy, that is. I took it across to the captain's table, sat in the captain's chair, poured myself a small measure and stuck the bottle in Captain Imrie's convenient wrought-iron stand.

I wondered why I hadn't told Otto the truth. I was a convincing liar, I thought, but not a compulsive one: probably because Otto struck me as being far from a stable character and with several more pegs of brandy inside him, in addition to what he had already consumed, he seemed less than the ideal confidant.

Antonio hadn't died because he'd taken or been given strychnine. Of that I was quite certain. I was equally certain that he hadn't died from *clostridium botulinum* either. The exotoxin from this particular anaerobe was quite as deadly as I had said but, fortunately, Otto had been unaware that the incubation period was seldom less than four hours and, in extreme cases, had been known to be as long as forty-eight—not that the period of incubation delay made the final results any less fatal. It was faintly possible that Antonio might have scoffed, say, a tin of infected truffles or suchlike from his homeland in the course of the afternoon, but in that case the symptoms would have been showing at the dinner table, and apart from the odd chartreuse hue I'd observed nothing untoward. It had to be some form of systematic poison, but there were so many of them and I was a long way from being an expert on the subject. Nor was there any necessary question of foul play: more people die from accidental poisoning than from the machinations of the ill-disposed.

The lee door opened and two people came staggering into the room, both young, both bespectacled, both with faces all but obscured by wind-blown hair. They saw me, hesitated, looked at each other and made to leave, but I waved them in and they came, closing the door behind them. They staggered across to my table, sat down, pushed the hair from their faces and I identified them as Mary Darling, our continuity girl, and Allen—nobody knew whether he had another name or whether that was his first or second one—the clapper/loader. He was a very earnest youth who had recently been asked to leave his university. He was an intelligent lad but easily bored. Intelligent but a bit short on wisdom—he regarded film-making as the most glamorous job on earth.

'Sorry to break in on you like this, Dr Marlowe.' Allen was very apologetic, very respectful. 'We had no idea—to tell you the truth we were both looking for a place to sit down.'

'And now you've found a place. I'm just leaving. Try some of Mr Gerran's excellent scotch—you both look as if you could do with a little.' They did, indeed, look very pale indeed.

'No, thank you, Dr Marlow. We don't drink.' Mary Darling—everyone called her Mary darling—was cast in an even more earnest mould than Allen and had a very prim voice to go with it. She had very long, straight, almost platinum hair that fell any old how down her back and that clearly hadn't been submitted to the attentions of a hairdresser for years: she must have broken Antonio's heart. She wore a habitually severe expression, enormous horn-rimmed glasses, no make-up —not even lipstick—and had about her a businesslike, competent, no-nonsense, I can-take-care-of-myself-thank-you attitude that was so transparently false that no one had the heart to call her bluff.

'No room at the inn?' I asked.

'Well,' Mary darling said, 'it's not very private down in the recreation room, is it? As for those three young—young—'

'The Three Apostles do their best,' I said mildly. 'Surely the lounge was empty?'

'It was not.' Allen tried to look disapproving but I thought his eyes crinkled. 'There was a man there. In his pyjamas. Mr Gilbert.'

'He had a big bunch of keys in his hands.' Mary darling paused, pressed her lips together, and went on: 'He was trying to open the doors where Mr Gerran keeps all his bottles.'

'That sounds like Lonnie,' I agreed. It was none of my business. If Lonnie found the world so sad and so wanting there was nothing much I or anybody could do about it: I just hoped that Otto didn't catch him at it. I said to Mary: 'You could always try your cabin.'

'Oh, no! We couldn't do *that*.'

'No, I suppose not.' I tried to think why not, but I was too old. I took my leave and passed through the stewards' pantry into the galley. It was small, compact, immaculately clean, a minor culinary symphony in stainless steel and white tile. At this late hour I had expected it to be deserted, but it wasn't: Haggerty, the chief cook, with his regulation chef's hat four-square on his greying clipped hair, was bent over some pots on a stove. He turned round, looked at me in mild surprise.

'Evening, Dr Marlowe.' He smiled. 'Carrying out a medical inspection of my kitchen?'

'With your permission, yes.'

He stopped smiling. 'I'm afraid I do not understand, sir.' He could be very stiff, could Haggerty, twenty-odd years in the Royal Navy had left their mark.

'I'm sorry. Just a formality. We seem to have a case of food poisoning aboard. I'm just looking around.'

'Food poisoning! Not from this galley, I can assure you. Never had a case in my life.' Haggerty's injured professional pride quite overcame any humanitarian concern he might have had about the identity of the victim or how severe his case was. 'Twenty-seven years as a cook in the *Andrew*, Dr Marlowe, last six as Chief on a carrier, and if I'm to be told I don't run a hygienic galley—'

'Nobody's telling you anything of the sort.' I used to him the tone he used to me. 'Anyone can see the place is spotless. If the contamination came from this galley, it won't be your fault.'

'It didn't come from this galley.' Haggerty had a square ruddy face and periwinkle blue eyes: the complexion, suffused with anger, was now two shades deeper and the eyes hostile. 'Excuse me, I'm busy.' He turned his back and started rattling his pots about. I do not like people turning their backs on me when I am talking to them and my instinctive reaction was to make him face me again, but I reflected that his pride had been wounded, justifiably so from his point of view, so I contented myself with the use of words.

'Working very late, Mr Haggerty?'

'Dinner for the bridge,' he said stiffly. 'Mr Smith and the bo'sun. They change watches at eleven and eat together then.'

'Let's hope they're both fit and well by twelve.'

He turned very slowly. 'What's that supposed to mean?'

'I mean that what's happened once can happen again. You know you haven't expressed the slightest interest in the identity of the person who's been poisoned or how ill that person is?'

'I don't know what you mean, sir.'

'I find it very peculiar. Especially as the person became violently ill just after eating food prepared in this galley.'

'I take orders from Captain Imrie,' he said obliquely. 'Not from passengers.'

'You know where the captain is at this time of night. In bed and very, very sound. It's no secret. Wouldn't you like to come with me and see what you've done? To look at this poisoned person.' It wasn't very nice of me but I didn't see what else I could do.

'To see what *I've* done!' He turned away again, deliberately placed his pots to one side and removed his chef's hat. 'This had better be good, Doctor.'

I led the way below to Antonio's cabin and unlocked the door. The smell was revolting. Antonio lay as I had left him, except that he looked a great deal more dead now than he had done before: the blood had drained from face and hands leaving them a transparent white. I turned to Haggerty.

'Good enough?'

Haggerty's face didn't turn white because ruddy faces with a mass of broken red veins don't turn that way, but it did become a peculiar muddy brick colour. He stared down at the dead man for perhaps ten seconds, then turned away and walked quickly up the passage. I locked the door and followed, staggering from side to side of the passage as the *Morning Rose* rolled wickedly in the great troughs. I made my erratic way through the dining saloon, picked up the Black Label from Captain Imrie's wrought-iron stand, smiled pleasantly at Mary darling and Allen—God knows what thoughts were in their minds as I passed through—and returned to the galley. Haggerty joined me after thirty seconds. He was looking ill and I knew he had been ill. I had no doubt that he had seen a great deal during his lifetime at sea but there is something peculiarly horrifying about the sight of a man who has died violently from poisoning. I poured him three fingers of scotch and he downed it at a gulp. He coughed, and either the coughing or the scotch brought some colour back to his face.

'What was it?' His voice was husky. 'What—what kind of poison could kill a man like that? God, I've never seen anything so awful.'

'I don't know. That's what I want to find out. May I look round now?'

'Christ, yes. Don't rub it in, Doctor—well, I didn't know, did I? What do you want to see first?'

'It's ten past eleven,' I said.

'Ten past—my God, I'd forgotten all about the bridge.' He prepared the bridge dinner with remarkable speed and efficiency—two cans of orange juice, a tin opener, a flask of soup, and then the main course in snap-lidded metal canteens. Those he dumped in a wicker basket along with cutlery and two bottles of beer and the whole preparation took just over a minute.

While he was away—which wasn't for more than two minutes—I examined what little open food supplies Haggerty carried in his galley, both on shelves and in a large refrigerator. Even had I been capable of it, which I wasn't, I'd no facilities aboard for analysing food, so I had to reply on sight, taste and smell. There was nothing amiss that I could see. As Haggerty had said, he ran a hygienic galley, immaculate food in immaculate containers.

Haggerty returned. I said, 'Tonight's menu, again.'

'Orange juice or pineapple juice, oxtail—'

'All tinned?' He nodded. 'Let's see some.' I opened two tins of each, six in all, and sampled them under Haggerty's now very apprehensive eye. They tasted the way those tinned products usually taste, which is to say that they didn't taste of anything very much at all, but all perfectly innocuous in their pallid fashion.

'Main course?' I said. 'Lamb chops, brussels, horseradish, boiled potatoes?'

'Right. But these things aren't kept here.' He took me to the adjacent cool room, where the fruits and vegetables were stored, thence below to the cold room, where sides of beef and pork and mutton swung eerily from steel hooks in the harsh light of naked bulbs. I found precisely what I had

43

expected to find, nothing, told Haggerty that whatever had happened was clearly no fault of his, then made my way to the upper deck and along an interior passage till I came to Captain Imrie's cabin. I tried the handle, but it was locked. I knocked several times, without result. I hammered it until my knuckles rebelled, then kicked it, all with the same result: Captain Imrie had still about nine hours' sleep coming up and the relatively feeble noises I was producing had no hope of penetrating to the profound depths of unconsciousness he had now reached. I desisted. Smithy would know what to do.

I went to the galley, now deserted by Haggerty, and passed through the pantry into the dining saloon. Mary darling and Allen were sitting on a bulkhead settee, all four hands clasped together, pale—very pale—faces about three inches apart, gazing into each other's eyes in a kind of mystically miserable enchantment. It was axiomatic, I knew, that shipboard romances flourished more swiftly than those on land, but I had thought those phenomena were confined to the Bahamas and suchlike balmy climes: aboard a trawler in a full gale in the Arctic I should have thought that some of the romantically essential prerequisites were wholly absent or at least present in only minimal quantities. I took Captain Imrie's chair, poured myself a small drink and said 'Cheers!'

They straightened and jumped apart as if they'd been connected to electrodes and I'd just made the switch. Mary darling said reproachfully: 'You did give us a fright, Dr Marlowe.'

'I'm sorry.'

'Anyway, we were just leaving.'

'Now I'm really sorry.' I looked at Allen. 'Quite a change from university, isn't it?'

He smiled wanly. 'There is a difference.'

'What were you studying there?'

'Chemistry.'

'Long?'

'Three years. Well, almost three years.' Again the wan smile. 'It took me all that time to find out I wasn't much good at it.'

'And you're now?'

'Twenty-one.'

'All the time in the world to find out what you are good

at. I was thirty-three before I qualified as a doctor.'

'Thirty-three.' He didn't say it but his face said it for him: if he was that old when he qualified what unimaginable burden of years is he carrying now? 'What did you do before then?'

'Nothing I'd care to talk about. Tell me, you two were at the captain's table for dinner tonight, weren't you?' They nodded. 'Seated more or less opposite Antonio, weren't you?'

'I think so,' Allen said. That was a good start. He just thought so.

'He's not well. I'm trying to find out if he ate something that disagreed with him, something he may have been allergic to. Either of you see what he had to eat?'

They looked at each other uncertainly.

'Chicken?' I said encouragingly. 'Perhaps some French fries?'

'I'm sorry, Dr Marlowe,' Mary darling said. 'I'm afraid —well, we're not very observant.' No help from this quarter, obviously they were so lost in each other that they couldn't even remember what they had eaten. Or perhaps they just hadn't eaten anything. I hadn't noticed. I hadn't been very observant myself. But then, I hadn't been expecting a murder to happen along.

They were on their feet now, clinging to each other for support as the deck tried to vanish from beneath their feet. I said: 'If you're going below I wonder if you'd ask Tadeusz if he'd be kind enough to come up and see me here. He'll be in the recreation room.'

'He might be in bed,' Allen said. 'Asleep.'

'Wherever he is,' I said with certainty, 'he's not in bed.'

Tadeusz appeared within a minute, reeking powerfully of brandy, a vexed expression on his aristocratic features. He said without preamble: 'Damned annoying. Most damned annoying. Do you know where I can find a master key? That idiot Antonio has gone and locked our cabin door from the inside and he must be hopped to the eyebrows with sedatives. Simply can't waken him. Cretin!'

I produced his cabin key. 'He didn't lock the door from the inside. I did from the outside.' The Count looked at me for an uncomprehending moment, then mechanically reached for his flask as shocked understanding showed in his face. Not too much shock, just a little, but I was sure that what little there was was genuine. He tilted the flask and two or three drops trickled into his glass. He reached for the Black Label, helped himself with a steady but generous hand and drank deeply.

'He couldn't hear me? He—he is beyond hearing?'

'I'm sorry. Something he ate, I can't think what else, some killer toxin, some powerful, quick-acting and deadly poison.'

'Quite dead?' I nodded. 'Quite dead,' he repeated. 'And I told him to stop making such a grand opera Latin fuss and walked away and left a dying man.' He drank some more scotch and grimaced, an expression that was no reflection on Johnnie Walker. 'There are advantages in being a lapsed Catholic, Dr Marlowe.'

'Rubbish. Sackcloth and ashes not only don't help, they're simply just not called for here. All right, so you didn't suspect there was anything wrong with him. I saw him at table and I wasn't any cleverer and I'm supposed to be a doctor. And when you left him in the cabin it was too late anyway: he was dying then.' I helped him to some more scotch but left my own glass untouched: even one relatively sober mind around might prove to be of some help, although just how I couldn't quite see at that moment. 'You sat beside him at dinner. Can you remember what you ate?'

'The usual.' The Count, it was clear, was more shaken than his aristocratic nature would allow him to admit. 'Rather, he didn't eat the usual.'

'I'm not in the right frame of mind for riddles, Tadeusz.'

'Grapefruit and sunflower seeds. That was about what he lived on. One of those vegetarian nuts.'

'Walk softly, Tadeusz. Those nuts may yet be your pall-bearers.'

The Count grimaced again. 'A singularly ill-chosen remark. Antonio never ate meat. And he'd a thing against potatoes. So all he had were the sprouts and horseradish. I remember particularly well because Cecil and I gave him our horseradish, to which, it seems, he was particularly partial.' The Count shuddered. 'A barbarian food, fit only for ignorant Anglo-Saxon palates. Even young Cecil has the grace to detest that offal.' It was noteworthy that the Count was the only person in the film unit who did not refer to Cecil Golightly as the Duke: perhaps he thought he was being upstaged in the title stakes but, more probably, as a dyed-in-the-wool aristocrat himself, he objected to people taking frivolous liberties with titles.

'He had fruit juice?'

'Antonio had his own homemade barley water.' The Count smiled faintly. 'It was his contention that everything that came out of a can had been adulterated before it went into that can. Very strict on those matters, was Antonio.'

'Soup? Any of that?'

'*Ox*-tail?'

'Of course. Anything else? That he ate, I mean?'

'He didn't even finish his main course—well, his sprouts and radish. You may recall that he left very hurriedly.'

'I recall. Was he liable to sea-sickness?'

'I don't know. Don't forget, I've known him no longer than yourself. He's been a bit off-colour for the past two days. But then, who hasn't?'

I was trying to think up another penetrating question when John Cummings Goin entered. His unusual surname he'd inherited from a French grandfather in the High Savoy, where, apparently, this was not an altogether uncommon name. The film crew, inevitably, referred to him as Comin' and Goin', but Goin was probably wholly unaware of this: he was not the sort of man with whom one took liberties.

Any other person entering the dining saloon from the main deck on a night like that would have presented an appearance that would have varied from the wind-blown to the dishevelled. Not one hair of Goin's black, smooth, centre-parted, brushed-back hair was out of place: had I been told that he eschewed the standard proprietary hairdressing creams in favour of cow-hide glue, I would have seen no reason to doubt it. And the hairstyle was typical of the man—everything smooth, calm, unruffled and totally under control. In one area only did the comparison fall down. The hairstyle was slick, but Goin wasn't: he was just plain clever. He was of medium height, plump without being fat, with a smooth, unlined face. He was the only man I'd ever seen wearing *pince-nez*, and that only for the finest of fine print which, in Goin's line of business, came his way quite often: the *pince-nez* looked so inevitable that it was unthinkable that he should ever wear any other type of reading aid. He was, above all, a civilized man and urbane in the best sense of the word.

He picked up a glass from a rack, timed the wild staggering of the *Morning Rose* to walk quickly and surely to the seat on my right, picked up the Black Label and said: 'May I?'

'Easy come, easy go,' I said. 'I've just stolen it from Mr Gerran's private supply.'

'Confession noted.' He helped himself. 'This makes me an accessory. Cheers.'

'I assume you've just come from Mr Gerran,' I said.

'Yes. He's most upset. Sad, sad, about that poor young boy. An unfortunate business.' That was something else about Goin, he always got his priorities right: the average company accountant, confronted with the news of the death of a member of a team, would immediately have wondered how the death would affect the project as a whole: Goin saw the human side of it first. Or, I thought, he spoke of it first: I knew I was being unfair to him. He went on: 'I understand you've so far been unable to establish the cause of death.' Diplomacy, inevitably, was second nature to Goin: he could so easily and truthfully have said that I just hadn't a clue.

So I said it for him. 'I haven't a clue.'

'You'll never get to Harley Street talking that way.'

'Poison, that's certain. But that's all that's certain. I carry the usual sea-going medical library around with me, but that isn't much help. To identify a poison you must be able either to carry out a chemical analysis or observe the poison at work on the victim—most of the major poisons have symptoms peculiar to themselves and follow their own highly idiosyncratic courses. But Antonio was dead before I got to him and I lack the facilities to do any pathological work, assuming I could do it in the first place.'

'You're destroying all my faith in the medical profession. Cyanide?'

'Impossible. Antonio took time to die. A couple of drops of hydrocyanic—prussic acid—or even a tiny quantity of pharmacopoeial acid, and that's only two per cent of anhydrous prussic acid—and you're dead before your glass hits the floor. And cyanide makes it murder, it always makes it murder. There's no way I know of it can be administered by accident. Antonio's death, I'm certain, was an accident.'

Goin helped himself to some more scotch. 'What makes you so certain it was an accident?'

'What makes me so certain?' That was a difficult one to answer off the cuff owing to the fact that I was convinced it was no accident at all. 'First, there was no opportunity for the administering of poison. We know that Antonio was alone in his cabin all afternoon right until dinner-time.' I looked at the Count. 'Did Antonio have any private food supplies with him in his cabin?'

'How did you guess?' the Count looked surprised.

'I'm not guessing. I'm eliminating. He had?'

'Two hampers. Full of glass jars—I think I mentioned that Antonio would never eat anything out of a tin—with all sorts of weird vegetable products inside, including dozens of baby food jars with all sorts of purées in them. A very finicky eater, was poor Antonio.'

'So I'm beginning to gather. I think our answer will lie there. I'll have Captain Imrie impound his supplies and have them analysed on our return. To get back to the opportunity factor. Antonio came up to the dining saloon here, had the same as the rest of us—'

'No fruit juices, no soup, no lamb chops, no potatoes,' the Count said.

'None of those. But what he did have we all had. Then straight back to his cabin. In the second place, who would want to kill a harmless person like that—especially as Antonio was a total stranger to all of us and only joined us at Wick for the first time? And who but a madman would administer a deadly poison in a closed community like this, knowing that he couldn't escape and that Scotland Yard would be leaning over the quay walls in Wick, just waiting for our return?'

'Maybe that's the way a madman would figure a sane person would figure,' Goin said.

'What English king was it who died of a surfeit of lampreys?' the Count said. 'If you ask me, our unfortunate Antonio may well have perished from a surfeit of horseradish.'

'Like enough.' I pushed back my chair and made to rise. But I didn't get up immediately. Way back in the dim and lost recesses of my mind the Count had triggered off a tiny bell, an infinitesimal tinkle so distant and remote that if I hadn't been listening with all my ears I'd have missed it completely: but I had been listening, the way people always listen when they know, without knowing why, that the old man with the scythe is standing there in the wings, winding up for the back stroke. I knew both men were watching me. I sighed. 'Decisions, decisions. Antonio has to be attended to—'

'With canvas?' Goin said.

'With canvas. Count's cabin cleaned up. Death has to be logged. Death certificate. And Mr Smith will have to make the funeral arrangements.'

'Mr Smith?' The Count was vaguely surprised. 'Not our worthy commanding officer.'

'Captain Imrie is in the arms of Morpheus,' I said. 'I've tried.'

'You have your deities mixed up,' Goin said. 'Bacchus is the one you're after.'

'I suppose it is. Excuse me, gentlemen.'

I went directly to my cabin but not to write out any death certificate. As I'd told Goin, I did carry a medical library of sorts around with me and it was of a fair size. I selected several books, including Glaister's *Medical Jurisprudence and Toxicology,* 9th edition (Edinburgh 1950), Dewar's *Textbook of Forensic Pharmacy* (London 1946) and Gonzales, Vance and Helpern's *Legal Medicine and Toxicology,* which seemed to be a pre-war book. I started consulting indices and within five minutes I had it.

The entry was listed under 'Systematic Poisons' and was headed '*Aconite*. Bot. A poisonous plant of the order *Ranunculaceae.* Particular reference *Monkshood* and *Wolfsbane.* Phar. *Aconitum napellus*. This, and *aconitine,* an alkaloid extract of the former, is commonly regarded as the most lethal of all poisons yet identified: a dose of not more than 0.004 gm is deadly to man. Aconite and its alkaloid produce a burning and peculiar tingling and numbing effect where applied. Later, especially with larger doses, violent vomiting results, followed by paralysis of motion, paralysis of sensation and great depression of the heart, followed by death from syncope.

'Treatment. To be successful must be immediate as possible. Gastric lavage, 12 gm of tannic acid in two gallons of warm water, followed by 1.2 gm tannic acid in 180 ml tepid water: this should be followed by animal charcoal suspended in water. Cardiac and respiratory stimulants, artificial respiration and oxygen will be necessary as indicated.

'N.B. The root of aconite has frequently been eaten in mistake for that of horseradish.'

CHAPTER THREE

I was still looking at, but no longer reading the article on *Aconite* when it was gradually borne in upon my preoccupation that there was something very far amiss with the *Morning Rose*. She was still under way, her elderly oil-fired steam engines throbbing along as dependably as ever, but her motion had changed. Her rolling factor had increased till she was swinging wickedly and dismayingly through an angle of close on 70 degrees: the pitching factor had correspondingly decreased and the thudding jarring vibration of the bluff bows smashing into the quartering seas had fallen away to a fraction of what it had previously been.

I marked the article, closed the book, then lurched and stumbled—I could not be said to have run for it was physically impossible—along the passageway, up the companionway, through the lounge and out on to the upper deck. It was dark but not so dark as to prevent me from gauging direction by the feel of the gale wind, by the spume blowing off the top of the confused seas. I shrank back and tightened my grip on a convenient handrail as a great wall of water, black and veined and evil, reared up on the port side, just for'ard of the beam: it was at least ten feet higher than my head. I was certain that the wave, with the hundreds of tons of water it contained, was going to crash down square on the fore-deck of the trawler, I couldn't see how it could fail to, but but fail it did: as the wave bore down on us, the trough to starboard deepened and the *Morning Rose,* rolling over to almost forty degrees, simple fell into it, pressed down by the great weight of water on its exposed port side. There came the familiar flat explosive thunderclap of sound, the *Morning Rose* vibrated and groaned as over-stressed plates and rivets adjusted to cope with the sudden shearing strain, white, icily-cold water foamed over the starboard side and swirled around my ankles, and then it was gone, gurgling through the scuppers as the *Morning Rose* righted itself and rolled far over on its other side. There was no worry about any of this, no threat to safety and life, this was what Arctic trawlers had been built for and the *Morning Rose* could continue to absorb this punishment indefinitely. But there *was* cause for worry, if such a word can be used to express a desperately acute anxiety: that massive wave which had caught the trawler on her port bow, had knocked her almost 20 degrees off course. She was still 20 degrees off course, and 20 degrees off course she remained: nobody was making any attempt to bring her round. Another, and a smaller sea, and then she was lying five more degrees over to the east and here, too, she remained. I ran for the bridge ladder.

I bumped into and almost knocked down a person at the precise spot where I'd bumped into Mary dear an hour ago. Contact this time was much more solid and the person said 'Oof!' or something of that sort. The kind of gasp a winded lady makes is quite different from a man's and instinct and a kind of instantaneous reasoning told me that I had bumped into the same person again: Judith Haynes would be in bed with her spaniels and Mary darling was either with Allen or in bed dreaming about him: neither, anyway, was the outdoor type.

I said something that might have been misconstrued as a brusque apology, side-stepped and had my foot on the first rung when she caught my arm with both hands.

'Something's wrong. I know it is. What?' Her voice was calm, just loud enough to make itself heard over the high-pitched obbligato of the wind in the rigging. Sure she knew something was wrong, the sight of Dr Marlowe moving at anything above his customary saunter was as good as a police or air raid siren any day. I was about to say something to this effect when she added: 'That's why I came on deck,' which effectively rendered stillborn any cutting remarks I'd been about to make, because she'd been aware of trouble before I'd been: but, then, she hadn't had her thoughts taken up with *Aconitum napellus*.

'The ship's not under command. There's nobody in charge on the bridge, nobody trying to keep a course.'

'Can I do anything?'

She was wonderful. 'Yes. There's a hot-water electric geyser on the galley bulkhead by the stove. Bring up a jug of hot water, not too hot to drink, a mug and salt. Lots of salt.'

I sensed as much as saw her nod and then she was gone. Four seconds later I was inside the wheel-house. I could dimly see one figure crumpled against the chart-table, another apparently sitting straight by the wheel, but that was all I could see. The two overhead lights were dull yellow glows. It took me almost fifteen frantic seconds to locate the instrument panel just for'ard of the wheel, but only a couple of seconds thereafter to locate the rheostat and twist it to its clockwise maximum. I blinked in the hurtfully sudden wash of white light.

Smithy was by the chart-table, Oakley by the wheel, the former on his side, the latter upright, but that, I could see, didn't mean that Oakley was in any better state of health than the first mate, it was just that neither appeared capable of moving from the positions they had adopted. Both had their heads arched towards their knees, both had their hands clasped tightly to their midriffs. Neither of them was making any sound. Possibly neither was suffering pain and the contracted positions they had assumed resulted from some wholly involuntary motor mechanism: it was equally possible that their vocal cords were paralysed.

I looked at Smithy first. One life is as important as the next, or so any one of a group of sufferers will think, but in this case I was concerned with the greatest good of all concerned and the fact that the 'all' here just coincidentally included me had no bearing on my choice: if the *Morning Rose* was running into trouble, and I had a strange fey conviction that it was, Smithy was the man I wanted around.

Smithy's eyes were open and the look in them intelligent. Among other things the aconite article had stated that full intelligence is maintained to the very end. Could this be the end? Paralysis of motion, the article had said and paralysis of motion we undoubtedly had here. Then paralysis of sensation—maybe that's why they weren't crying out in agony, it could have been that they had been screaming their heads off up on the bridge here with no one around to hear them, but now they weren't feeling anything any more. I saw and vaguely recorded the fact that there were two metal canteens lying close together on the floor, both of them very nearly emptied of food. Both of them, I would have thought, were *in extremis* but for one very odd factor: there was no sign of the violent vomiting of which the article had spoken. I wished to God that somewhere, sometime, I had taken the trouble to learn something about poisons, their causes, their effects, their symptoms and aberrant symptoms—which we seemed to have here—if any.

Mary Stuart came in. Her clothes were soaking and her hair was in a terrible mess, but she'd been very quick and she'd got what I'd asked her to—including a spoon, which I'd forgotten. I said: 'A mug of hot water, six spoons of salt. Quick. Stir it well.' Gastric lavage, the book had said, but as far as the availability of tannic acid and animal charcoal was concerned I might as well have been on the moon. The best and indeed the only hope lay in a powerful and quick-acting emetic. Alum and zinc sulphate was what the old boy in my medical school had preferred but I'd never come across anything better than sodium chloride—common salt. I hoped desperately that aconitine absorption into the bloodstream hadn't progressed too far—and that it was aconitine I didn't for a moment doubt. Coincidence is coincidence but to introduce some such fancy concoction as curare at this stage would be stretching things a bit. I levered Smithy into a sitting position and was just getting my hands under his armpits when a dark-haired young seaman, clad—in that bitter weather—in only jersey and jeans came hurrying into the wheel-house. It was Allison, the senior of the two quarter-masters. He looked—not stared—at the two men on the deck: he was very much a seaman cast in Smithy's mould.

'What's wrong, Doctor?'

'Food poisoning.'

'Had to be something like that. I was asleep. Something woke me. I knew something was wrong, that we weren't under command.' I believed him, all experienced seamen have this in-built capacity to sense trouble. Even in their sleep. I'd come across it before. He moved quickly to the chart-table then glanced at the compass. 'Fifty degrees off course, to the east.'

'We've got all the Barents Sea to rattle about in,' I said. 'Give me a hand with Mr Smith, will you?'

We took an arm each and dragged him towards the port door. Mary dear stopped stirring the contents of the metal mug she held in her hand and looked at us in some perplexity.

'Where are you going with Mr Smith?'

'Taking him out on the wing.' What did she think we were going to do with him, throw him over the side? 'All that fresh air. It's very therapeutic.'

'But it's snowing out there! And bitterly cold.'

'He's also—I hope—going to be very, very sick. Better outside than in. How does that concoction taste?'

She sipped a little salt and water from her spoon and screwed up her face. 'It's awful!'

'Can you swallow it?'

She tried and shuddered. 'Just.'

'Another three spoons.' We dragged Smithy outside and propped him in a sitting position. The canvas wind-dodger gave him some protection but not much. His eyes were open and following our actions and he seemed aware of what was going on. I put the emetic to his lips and tilted the mug but the fluid just trickled down his chin. I forced his head back and poured some of the emetic into his mouth. Clearly, all sensation wasn't lost, for his face contorted into an involuntary grimace of distaste: more importantly, his Adam's apple bobbed up and down and I knew he'd swallowed some of it. Encouraged, I poured in twice as much, and this time he swallowed it all. Not ten seconds later he was as violently ill as ever I've seen a man be. Over Mary's protests and in spite of Allison's very evident apprehension I forced some more of the salt and water on him: when he started coughing blood I turned my attention to Oakley.

Within fifteen minutes we had two still very ill men on our hands, clearly suffering violent abdominal pains and weak to the point of exhaustion, but, more importantly, we had two men who weren't going to go the same way as the unfortunate Antonio had gone. Allison was at the wheel, with the *Morning Rose* back on course: Mary dear, her straw-coloured hair now matted with snow, crouched beside a very groggy Oakley: Smithy was now sufficiently recovered to sit on the storm-sill of the wheel-house, though he still required my arm to brace him against the staggering of the *Morning Rose*. He was beginning to recover the use of his voice although only to a minimal extent.

'Brandy,' he croaked.

I shook my head. 'Contra-indicated. That's what the textbooks say.'

'Otard-Dupuy,' he insisted. At least his mind was clear enough. I rose and got him a bottle from Captain Imrie's private reserve. After what his stomach had just been through, nothing short of carbolic acid was going to damage it any more. He put the bottle to his head, swallowed and was immediately sick again.

'Maybe I should have given you cognac in the first place,' I said. 'Salt water comes cheaper, though.'

He tried to smile, a brief and painful effort, and tilted the bottle again. This time the cognac stayed down, he must have had a stomach lined with steel or asbestos. I took the bottle from him and offered it to Oakley, who winced and shook his head.

'Who's got the wheel?' Smithy's voice was a hoarse and strained whisper as if it hurt him to speak, which it almost certainly did.

'Allison.'

He nodded, satisfied. 'Damn boat,' he said. 'Damn sea. I'm sea-sick. Me. Sea-sick.'

'You're sick, all right. Nothing to do with the sea. This damn boat wallowing about in this damn sea was all that saved you: a flat calm and Smithy was among the immortals.' I tried to think why anyone who was not completely unhinged should want Smithy and Oakley among the immortals but the idea was so preposterous that I abandoned it almost the moment it occurred to me. 'Food poisoning and I was lucky. I got here in time.'

He nodded but kept quiet. It probably hurt him too much to talk. Mary dear said: 'Mr Oakley's hands and face are freezing and he's shaking with the cold. So am I, for that matter.'

And so, I realized, was I. I helped Smithy to a bolted chair beyond the wheel, then went to assist Mary dear who was trying to get a jelly-kneed Oakley to his feet. We'd just got Oakley approximately upright, no easy task, for he was practically a dead weight and we required one hand for him and one for ourselves, when Goin and the Count appeared at the top of the ladder.

'Thank God, at last!' Goin was slightly out of breath but not one hair was out of place. 'We've been looking for you every—what on earth! Is that man drunk?'

'He's sick. The same sickness as Antonio had, only he's been lucky. What's the panic?'

'The same sickness—you must come at once, Marlowe. My God, this is turning into a regular epidemic.'

'A moment.' I helped Oakley inside and lowered him into as comfortable a position as possible atop some kapok life-jackets. 'Another casualty, I take it?'

'Yes, Otto Gerran.' Maybe I lifted an eyebrow, I forget, I do know I felt no particular surprise, it seemed to me that anyone who had been within sniffing distance of that damned aconite was liable to keel over at any moment. 'I called at his cabin ten minutes ago, there was no reply and I went in and there he was, rolling about the carpet—'

The irreverent thought came to me that, with his almost perfectly spherical shape, no one had ever been better equip-ped for rolling about a carpet than Otto was: it seemed un-likely that Otto was seeing the humorous side of it at that moment. I said to Allison: 'Can you get anyone up here to help you?'

'No trouble.' The quartermaster nodded at the small ex-change in the corner. 'I've only to phone the mess-deck.'

'No need.' It was the Count. 'I'll stay.'

'That's very kind.' I nodded at Smithy and Oakley in turn. 'They're not fit to go below yet. If they try to, they'll like as not end up over the side. Could you get them some blankets?'

'Of course.' He hesitated. 'My cabin—'

'Is locked. Mine's not. There are blankets on the bed and extra ones at the foot of the hanging locker.' The Count left and I turned to Allison. 'Short of dynamiting his door open, how do I attract the captain's attention? He seems to be a sound sleeper.'

Allison smiled and again indicated the corner exchange. 'The bridge phone hangs just above his head. There's a resistance in the circuit. I can make the call-up sound like the QE 2's fog-horn.'

'Tell him to come along to Mr Gerran's room and tell him it's urgent.'

'Well.' Allison was uncertain. 'Captain Imrie doesn't much like being woken up in the middle of the night. Not without an awfully good reason, that is, and now that the mate and bo'sun are all right again, like—'

'Tell him Antonio is dead.'

CHAPTER FOUR

At least Otto wasn't dead. Even above the sound of the wind and the sound of the sea, the creakings and groanings as the elderly trawler slammed her way into the Arctic gale, Otto's voice could be distinctly heard at least a dozen feet from his cabin door. What he was saying, however, was far from distinct, the tearing gasps and agonized moans boded ill for what we would see when we opened the door.

Otto Gerran looked as he sounded, not quite *in extremis* but rapidly heading that way. As Goin had said, he was indeed rolling about the floor, both hands clutching his throat as if he was trying to throttle himself: his normally puce complexion had deepened to a dark and dangerous-looking purple, his eyes were bloodshot and a purplish foam at his mouth had stained his lips to almost the same colour as his face: or maybe his lips were purplish anyway, like a man with cyanosis. As far as I could see he hadn't a single symptom in common with Smithy and Oakley: so much for the toxicological experts and their learned textbooks.

I said to Goin: 'Let's get him on his feet and along to the bathroom.' As a statement of intent it was clear and simple enough, but its execution was far from simple: it was impossible. The task of hoisting 245 lbs of unco-operative jellyfish to the vertical proved to be quite beyond us. I was just about to abandon the attempt and administer what would certainly be a very messy first aid on the spot when Captain Imrie and Mr Stokes entered the cabin. My surprise at the remarkable promptness with which they had put in an appearance was as nothing compared to my initial astonishment at observing that both men were fully dressed: it was not until I noticed the horizontal creases in their trousers that I realized that they had gone to sleep with all their clothes on. I made a brief prayer for Smithy's swift and complete recovery.

'What in the name of God goes on?' Whatever condition Captain Imrie had been in an hour or so ago, he was completely sober now. 'Allison says that Italian fellow's dead and—' He stopped abruptly as Goin and I moved sufficiently apart to let him have his first glimpse of the prostrate, moaning Gerran. 'Jesus wept!' He moved forward and stared down. 'What the devil—an epileptic fit?'

'Poison. The same poison that killed Antonio and nearly killed the mate and Oakley. Come on, give us a hand to get him along to the bathroom.'

'Poison!' He looked at Mr Stokes as if to hear from him confirmation that it couldn't possibly be poison, but Mr Stokes wasn't in the mood for confirming anything, he just stared with a kind of numbed fascination at the writhing man on the floor. 'Poison! On *my* ship. What poison? Where did they get it? Who gave it to them. Why should—'

'I'm a doctor, not a detective. I don't know anything about who, where, when, why, what. All I know is that a man's dying while we're talking.'

It took the four of us less than thirty seconds to get Otto Gerran along to the bathroom. It was a pretty rough piece of manhandling but it was a fair assumption that he would rather be Otto Gerran, bruised but alive, than Otto Gerran, unmarked but dead. The emetic worked just as swiftly and effectively as it had with Smithy and Oakley and within three minutes we had him back in his bunk under a mound of blankets. He was still moaning incoherently and shivering so violently that his teeth chattered uncontrollably, but the deep purple had begun to recede from his cheeks and the foam had dried on his lips.

'I think he's OK now but please keep an eye on him, will you?' I said to Goin. 'I'll be back in five minutes.'

Captain Imrie stopped me at the door. 'If you please, Dr Marlowe, a word with you.'

'Later.'

'Now. As master of this vessel—' I put a hand on his shoulder and he became silent. I felt like saying that as master of this vessel he'd been awash in scotch and snoring in his bunk when people were all around dropping like flies but it would have been less than fair: I was irritable because unpleasant things were happening that should not have been happening and I didn't know why, or who was responsible.

'Otto Gerran will live,' I said. 'He'll live because he was lucky enough to have Mr Goin here stop by his cabin. How many other people are lying on their cabin floors who haven't been lucky enough to have someone stop by, people so far gone that they can't even reach their doors? Four casualties so far: who's to say there isn't a dozen?'

'A dozen? Aye. Aye, of course.' If I was out of my depth, Captain Imrie was submerged. 'We'll come with you.'

'I can manage.'

'Like you managed with Mr Gerran here?'

We made our way directly to the recreation room. There were ten people there, all men, mostly silent, mostly unhappy: it is not easy to be talkative and cheerful when you're hanging on to your seat with one hand and your drink with the other. The Three Apostles, whether because of exhaustion or popular demand, had laid the tools of their trade aside and were having a drink with their boss Josh Hendriks, a small, thin, stern and middle-aged Anglo-Dutchman with a perpetual worried frown. Even when off-duty, he was festooned with a mass of strap-hung electronic and recording equipment: word had it that he slept so accoutred. Stryker, who appeared far from overcome by concern for his ailing wife, sat at a table in a corner, talking to Conrad and two other actors, Gunther Jungbeck and Jon Heyter. At a third table John Halliday, the stills photographer and Sandy, the props man, made up the company. No one, as far as I could judge, was suffering from anything that couldn't be accounted for by the big dipper antics of the *Morning Rose*. One or two glances of mildly speculative curiosity came our way, but I volunteered no explanation for our unaccustomed visit there: explanations take time but the effects of *aconitine*, as was being relentlessly borne in upon me, waited for no man.

Allen and Mary darling we found in the otherwise deserted lounge, more green-faced than ever but clasping hands and gazing at each other with the rapt intensity of those who know there will be no tomorrow: their noses were so close together that they must have been cross-eyed from their attempts to focus. For the first time since I'd met her Mary darling had removed her enormous spectacles—misted lenses due to Allen's heavy breathing, I had no doubt—and without them she really was a very pretty young girl with none of that rather naked and defenceless look that so often characterizes the habitual wearer of glasses when those are removed. One thing was for sure, there was nothing wrong with Allen's eyesight.

I glanced at the liquor cupboard in the corner. The glass-fronted doors were intact from which I assumed that Lonnie Gilbert's bunch of keys were capable of opening most things: had they failed here I would have looked for signs of the use of some other instrument, not, perhaps, the berserk wielding of a fire-axe but at least the discreet employment of a wood chisel: but there were no such signs.

Heissman was asleep in his cabin, uneasily, restlessly asleep, but clearly not ill. Next door Neal Divine, his bed-board raised so high that he was barely visible, looked more like a medieval bishop than ever, but a happily unconscious one this time. Lonnie was sitting upright in his bunk, his arms folded across his ample midriff, and from the fact that his right hand was out of sight under the coverlet, almost certainly and lovingly wrapped round the neck of a bottle of purloined scotch, and the further fact that he wore a beatific smile, it was clear that his plethora of keys could be put to a very catholic variety of uses.

I passed up Judith Haynes's cabin—she'd had no dinner—and went into what I knew to be, at that moment, the last occupied cabin. The unit's chief electrician, a large, fat, red-faced and chubby-cheeked individual rejoicing in the name of Frederick Crispin Harbottle, was propped on an elbow and moodily eating an apple: appearances to the contrary, he was an invincibly morose and wholly pessimistic man. For reasons I had been unable to discover, he was known to all as Eddie: rumour had it that he had been heard to speak, in the same breath, of himself and that other rather better-known electrician, Thomas Edison.

'Sorry,' I said. 'We've got some cases of food poisoning. You're not one of them, obviously.' I nodded towards the recumbent occupant of the other bed, who was lying curled up with his back to us. 'How's the Duke?'

'Alive.' Eddie spoke in a tone of philosophical resignation. 'Moaning and groaning about his bellyache before he dropped off. Moans and groans nearly every night, come to that. You know what the Duke's like, he just can't help himself.'

We all knew what he was like. If it is possible for a person to become a legend within the space of four days then Cecil

Golightly had become just that. His unbridled gluttony lay just within the bounds of credibility and when Otto, less than an hour previously, had referred to him as a little pig who never lifted his eyes from the table he had spoken no more than the truth. The Duke's voracious capacity for food was as abnormal as his obviously practically defunct metabolic system, for he resembled nothing so much as a man newly emerged from a long stay in a concentration camp.

More out of habit than anything I bent over to give him a cursory glance and I was glad I did, for what I saw were wide-open, pain-dulled eyes moving wildly and purposelessly from side to side, ashen lips working soundlessly in an ashen face and the hooked fingers of both hands digging deep into his stomach as if he were trying to tear it open.

I'd told Goin that I'd be back in Otto's cabin in five minutes: I was back in forty-five. The Duke, because he had been so very much longer without treatment than Smithy, Oakley or Gerran, had gone very, very close to the edge indeed, to the extent that I had on one occasion almost given up his case as being intractably hopeless, but the Duke was a great deal more stubborn than I was and that skeletal frame harboured an iron constitution: even so, without almost continuous artificial respiration, a heart stimulant injection and the copious use of oxygen, he would surely have died: now he would as surely live.

'Is this the end of it, then? Is this the end?' Otto Gerran spoke in a weakly querulous voice and, on the face of it, I had to admit that he had every right to sound both weak and querulous. He hadn't as yet regained his normal colour, he looked as haggard as a heavily-jowled man ever can and it was clear that his recent experience had left him pretty exhausted: and with this outbreak of poisoning coming on top of the continuously hostile weather that had prevented him from shooting even a foot of background film, Otto had reason to believe that the fates were not on his side.

'I should think so,' I said. In view of the fact that he had aboard some ill-disposed person who was clearly a dab hand with some of the more esoteric poisons this was as unwarrantedly optimistic a statement as I could remember making, but I had to say something. 'Any other victims would have shown the symptoms before now: and I've checked every-one.'

'Have you now?' Captain Imrie asked. 'How about my crew? They eat the same food as you do.'

'I hadn't thought of that.' And I hadn't. Because of some mental block or simply because of lack of thought, I'd assumed, wholly without reason, that the effects would be confined to the film unit people: Captain Imrie was probably thinking that I regarded his men as second-rate citizens who, when measured against Otto's valuable and expensive cast and crew, hardly merited serious consideration. I went on: 'What I mean is, I didn't know that. That they ate the same food. Should have been obvious. If you'll just show me—'

With Mr Stokes in lugubrious attendance, Captain Imrie led me round the crew quarters. Those consisted of five separate cabins—two for the deck staff, one for the engine-room staff, one for the two cooks and the last for the two stewards. It was the last one that we visited first.

We opened the door and just stood there for what then seemed like an unconscionably long time but was probably only a few seconds, mindless creatures bereft of will and speech and power of motion. I was the first to recover and stepped inside.

The stench was so nauseating that I came close to being sick for the first time that night and the cabin itself was in a state of indescribable confusion, chairs knocked over, clothes strewn everywhere and both bunks completely denuded of sheets and blankets which were scattered in a torn and tangled mess over the deck. The first and overwhelming im-pression was that there had been a fight to the death, but both Moxen and Scott, the latter almost covered in a shredded sheet, looked curiously peaceful as they lay there, and neither bore any marks of violence.

'I say we go back. I say we return now.' Captain Imrie wedged himself more deeply into his chair as if establishing both a physically and argumentatively commanding position. 'You gentlemen will bear in mind that I am the master of this vessel, that I have responsibilities towards both passengers and crew.' He lifted his bottle from the wrought-iron stand and helped himself lavishly and I observed, automatically and with little surprise, that his hand was not quite steady. 'If I'd typhoid or cholera aboard I'd sail at once for quarantine in the nearest port where medical assistance is available. Three dead and four seriously ill, I don't see that cholera or typhoid could be any worse than we have here on the *Morning Rose*. Who's going to be the next to die?' He looked at me almost accusingly. Imrie seemed to be adopting the understandable attitude that, as a doctor, it was my duty to preserve life and that as I wasn't making a very good job of it what was happening was largely my fault. 'Dr Marlowe here admits that he is at a loss to understand the reasons for this—this lethal outbreak. Surely to God that itself is reason enough to call this off?'

'It's a long, long way back to Wick,' Smithy said. Like Goin, seated beside him, Smithy was swathed in a couple of blankets and, like Otto, he still looked very much under the weather. 'A lot can happen in that time.'

'Wick, Mr Smith? I wasn't thinking of Wick. I can be in Hammerfest in twenty-four hours.'

'Less,' said Mr Stokes. He sipped his rum, deliberated and made his pronouncement. 'With the wind and the sea on the port quarter and a little assistance from me in the engine-room? Twenty hours.' He went over his homework and found it faultless. 'Yes, twenty hours.'

'You see?' Imrie transferred his piercing blue gaze from myself to Otto. 'Twenty hours.'

When we'd established that there had been no more casualties among the crew Captain Imrie, in what was for him a very peremptory fashion, had summoned Otto to the saloon and Otto in turn had sent for his three fellow directors, Goin, Heissman and Stryker. The other director, Miss Haynes, was, Stryker had reported, very deeply asleep, which was less than surprising in view of the sedatives I'd prescribed for her. The Count had joined the meeting without invitation but everyone appeared to accept his presence there as natural.

To say that there was an air of panic in the saloon would have been exaggeration, albeit a forgivable one, but to say that there was a marked degree of apprehension, concern and uncertainty would have erred on the side of understatement. Otto Gerran, perhaps, was more upset than any other person present, and understandably so, for Otto had a great deal more to lose than any other person present.

'I appreciate the reasons for your anxiety,' Otto said, 'and your concern for us all does you the greatest credit. But I think this concern is making you over-cautious. Dr Marlowe says that this—ah—epidemic is definitely over. We are going to look very foolish indeed if we turn and run now and then nothing more happens.'

Captain Imrie said: 'I'm too old, Mr Gerran, to care what I look like. If it's a choice between looking a fool and having another dead man on my hands, then I'd rather look a fool any time.'

'I agree with Mr Gerran,' Heissman said. He still looked sick and he sounded sick. 'To throw it all away when we're so near—just over a day to Bear Island. Drop us off there and then go to Hammerfest—just as in the original plan. That means—well, you'd be in Hammerfest in say sixty hours instead of twenty-four. What's going to happen in that extra thirty-six hours that's not going to happen in the next twenty-four? Lose everything for thirty-six hours just because you're running scared?'

'I am not running scared, as you say.' There was something impressive about Imrie's quiet dignity. 'My first—'

'I wasn't referring to you personally,' Heissman said.

'My first concern is for the people under my charge. And they are under *my* charge. *I* am the person responsible. *I* must make the decision.'

'Granted, Captain, granted.' Goin was his usual imperturbable self, a calm and reasonable man. 'But one has to strike a balance in these matters, don't you think. Against what Dr Marlow now regards as being a very remote possibility of another outbreak of food poisoning occurring, there's the near certainty—no, I would go further and say that there's the inevitability—that if we go directly to Hammerfest we'll be put in quarantine for God knows how long. A week, maybe two weeks, before the port medical authorities give us clearance. And then it'll be too late, we'd just have to abandon all ideas about making the film at all and go home.' Less than a couple of hours previously, I recalled, Heissman had been making most disparaging remarks about Otto's mental capacities, but he'd backed him up against Captain Imrie and now here was Goin doing the same thing: both men knew which side of their bread required butter. 'The losses to Olympus Productions will be enormous.'

'Don't be telling me that, Mr Goin,' Imrie said. 'What you

mean is that the losses to the insurance company—or companies—will be enormous.'

'Wrong,' Stryker said and from his tone and attitude it was clear that directorial solidarity on the board of Olympus Productions was complete. 'Severally and personally, all members of the cast and crew are insured. The film project—a guarantee as to its successful conclusion—was uninsurable, at least in terms of the premiums demanded. We, and we alone, bear the loss—and I would add that for Mr Gerran, who is by far and away the biggest shareholder, the effects would be ruinous.'

'I am very sorry about that.' Captain Imrie seemed genuinely sympathetic but he didn't for a moment sound like a man who was preparing to abandon his position. 'But that's your concern, I'm afraid. And I would remind you, Mr Gerran, of what you yourself said earlier on this evening. "Health," you said, "is a damned sight more important than any profit we might make from this film." Wouldn't you say this is a case in point?'

'That's nonsense to say that,' Goin said equably. He had the rare gift of being able to make potentially offensive statements in a quietly rational voice that somehow robbed them of all offence. ' "Profit", you say was the word Mr Gerran used. Certainly, Mr Gerran would willingly pass up any potential profit if the need arose, and that need wouldn't have to be very pressing or demanding. He's done it before.' This was at variance with the impression I'd formed of Otto, but then Goin had known him many more years than I had days. 'Even without profit we could still make our way by breaking even, which is as much as most film companies can hope for these days. But you're not talking—we're not talking —about lack of profit, we're talking about a total and non-recoverable loss, a loss that would run into six figures and break us entirely. We've put our collective shirt on this one, Captain Imrie, yet you're talking airily of liquidating our company, putting dozens of technicians—and their families —on the breadline and damaging, very likely beyond repair, the careers of some very promising actors and actresses. And all of this for what? The remote chance—according to Dr Marlowe, the very remote chance—that someone may fall ill again. Haven't you got things just a little bit out of proportion, Captain Imrie?'

If he had, Captain Imrie wasn't saying so. He wasn't saying anything. He didn't exactly have the look of a man who was thinking and thinking hard.

'Mr Goin puts it very succinctly,' Otto said. 'Very succinctly indeed. And there's a major point that seems to have escaped you, Captain Imrie. You have reminded me of something I said earlier. May I remind you of something *you* said earlier. May I remind you—'

'And may I interrupt, Mr Gerran,' I said. I knew damn well what he was going to say and the last thing I wanted was to hear him say it. 'Please. A peace formula, if you wish. You want to continue. So does Mr Goin, so does Mr Heissman. So do I—if only because my reputation as a doctor seems to depend on it. Tadeusz?'

'No question,' said the Count. 'Bear Island.'

'And, of course, it would be unfair to ask either Mr Smith or Mr Stokes. So I propose—'

'This isn't Parliament, Dr Marlowe,' Imrie said. 'Not even a local town council. Decisions aboard a vessel at sea are not arrived at by popular vote.'

'I've no intention that they should be. I suggest we draw up a document. I suggest we note Captain Imrie's proposals and considered opinions. I suggest if more illness occurs we run immediately for Hammerfest, even although we are at the time only one hour distant from Bear Island. I suggest it be recorded that Captain Imrie be protected and absolved from any accusation of hazarding the health of his crew and passengers in light of the medical officer's affidavit—which I will write out and sign—that no such hazard exists: the only charge the captain has to worry about at any time is the physical hazarding of his vessel and that doesn't exist here. Then we will state that the captain is absolved from all blame and responsibility for any consequences arising from our decision: the navigation and handling of the vessel remain, of course, his sole responsibility. Then all five of us sign it. Captain Imrie?'

'Agreed.' There is a time to be prompt and Captain Imrie clearly regarded this as such a time. At best, the proposal was a lame compromise, but one he was glad to accept. 'Now, if you gentlemen will excuse me. I have to be up betimes —4 a.m. to be precise.' I wondered when he had last risen at that unearthly hour—not, probably, since his fishing days had ended: but the illness of mate and bo'sun made for exceptional circumstances. He looked at me. 'I will have that document at breakfast?'

'At breakfast. I wonder, Captain, if on your way to bed you could ask Haggerty to come to see me. I'd ask him personally, but he's a bit touchy about civilians like myself.'

'A lifetime in the Royal Navy is not forgotten overnight. Now?'

'Say ten minutes? In the galley.'

'Still pursuing your inquiries, is that it? It's not your fault, Dr Marlowe.'

If it wasn't my fault, I thought, I wished they'd all stop making me feel it was. Instead I thanked him and said good night and he said good night to us and left accompanied by Smithy and Mr Stokes. Otto steepled his fingers and regarded me in his best chairman of the board fashion.

'We owe you our thanks, Dr Marlowe. That was well done, an excellent face-saving proposal.' He smiled. 'I am not accustomed to suffering interruption lightly but in this case it was justified.'

'If I hadn't interrupted we'd all be on our way to Hammerfest now. You were about to remind him of that part of your contract with him which states that he will obey all your orders other than those that actually endanger the vessel. You were about to point out that, as no such physical danger exists, he was technically in breach of contract and so would be legally liable to the forfeiture of the entire contract fee, which would certainly have ruined him. But for a man like that money ranks a long, long way behind pride and Captain Imrie is a very proud man. He'd have told you to go to hell and turned his ship for Hammerfest.'

'I'd say that our worthy physician's assessment is a hundred per cent accurate.' The Count had found some brandy and now helped himself freely. 'You came close there, Otto, my boy.'

If the company chairman felt annoyance at being thus familiarly addressed by his cameraman, he showed no evidence of it. He said: 'I agree. We are in your debt, Dr Marlowe.'

'A free seat at the première,' I said, 'and all debts discharged.' I left the board to its deliberations and weaved my unsteady way down to the passenger accommodation. Allen and Mary darling were still in the same place in the lounge, only now she had her head on his shoulder and seemed to be asleep. I gave him a casually acknowledging wave of my hand and he answered in kind: he seemed to be becoming accustomed to my peripatetic presence.

I entered the Duke's cabin without knocking, lest there was someone there asleep. There was. Eddie, the electrician, was very sound indeed and snoring heavily, the sight of his cabin mate's close brush with the reaper hadn't unnerved him any that I could see. Cecil Golightly was awake and looking understandably very pale and drawn but not noticeably suffering, largely, it seemed very likely, because Mary Stuart, who was just as pale as he was, was sitting by his bedside and holding his far from reluctant hand. I was beginning to think that perhaps she had more friends than either she or I thought she had.

'Good lord!' I said. 'You still here?'

'Didn't you expect me to be? You asked me to stay and keep an eye on him. Or had you forgotten?'

'Certainly not,' I lied. 'Didn't expect you to remain so long, that's all. You've been very kind.' I looked down upon the recumbent Duke. 'Feeling a bit better?'

'Lots, Doctor. Lots better.' With his voice not much more than a strained whisper he didn't sound it, but then, after what he'd been through in the past hour I didn't expect him to.

'I'd like to have a little talk with you,' I said. 'Just a couple of minutes. Feel up to it?'

He nodded. Mary dear said: 'I'll leave you then,' and made to rise but I put a restraining hand on her shoulder.

'No need. The Duke and I share no secrets.' I gave him what I hoped would be translated as a thoughtful look. 'It's just possible, though, that the Duke might be concealing a secret from me.'

'Me? A—a secret?' Cecil was genuinely puzzled.

'Tell me. When did the pains start?'

'The pains? Half-past nine. Ten. Something like that, I can't be sure.' Temporarily bereft of his quick wit and chirpy humour, the Duke was a very woebegone Cockney sparrow indeed. 'When this thing hit me I wasn't feeling much like looking at watches.'

'I'm sure you weren't,' I said sympathetically. 'And dinner was the last bite you had tonight?'

'The last bite.' His voice even sounded firm.

'Not even another teeny-weeny snack? You see, Cecil, I'm puzzled. Miss Stuart has told you that others have been ill, too?' He nodded. 'Well, the odd thing is that the others began to be ill almost at once after eating. But it took well over an hour in your case. I find it very strange. You're absolutely sure? You'd nothing?'

'Doctor!' He wheezed a bit. 'You know me.'

'Yes. That's why I'm asking.' Mary dear was looking at me with coolly appraising and rather reproachful brown eyes, any moment now she was going to say didn't I know Cecil was a sick man. 'You see, I know that the others who were sick were suffering from some kind of food poisoning that they picked up at dinner and I know how to treat them. But your illness must have had another cause, I've no idea what it was or how to treat it and until I can make some sort of diagnosis I can't afford to take chances. You're going to be very hungry tomorrow morning and for some time after that but I have to give your system time to settle down: I don't want you to eat *anything* that might provoke a reaction so violent that I mightn't be able to cope with it this time. Time will give the all clear.'

'I don't understand, Doctor.'

'Tea and toast for the next three days.'

The Duke didn't turn any paler than he was because that was impossible: he just looked stricken.

'Tea and toast?' His voice was a weak croak. 'For three days!'

'For your own good, Cecil.' I patted him sympathetically on the shoulder and straightened, preparing to leave. 'We just want to see you on your feet again.'

'I was feeling peckish, like,' the Duke explained with some pathos.

'When?'

'Just before nine.'

'Just before—half an hour after dinner?'

'That's when I feel the most peckish. I nipped up into the galley, see, and there was this casserole on a hot plate but I'd only time for one spoonful when I heard two people coming so I jumped into the cool room.'

'And waited?'

'I had to wait.' The Duke sounded almost virtuous. 'If I'd opened the door even a crack they'd have seen me.'

71

'So they didn't see you. Which means they left. Then?'

'They'd scoffed the bleedin' lot,' the Duke said bitterly.

'Lucky you.'

'Lucky?'

'Moxen and Scott, wasn't it? The stewards?'

'How—how did you know?'

'They saved your life, Duke.'

'They what?'

'They ate what you were going to eat. So you're alive. They're both dead.'

Allen and Mary darling had obviously given up their midnight vigil for the lounge was deserted. I'd five minutes before I met Haggerty in the galley, five minutes in which to collect my thoughts: the trouble was that I had to find them first before I could collect them. And then I realized I was not even going to have the time to find them for there were footsteps on the companionway. Trying with very little success to cope with the wild staggering of the *Morning Rose,* Mary Stuart made her unsteady way towards an armchair opposite me and collapsed into rather than sat in it. Insofar as it was possible for such an extraordinarily good-looking young woman to look haggard, then she looked haggard: her face was grey. I should have felt annoyed with her for interrupting my train of thought, assuming, that was, that I ever managed to get the train under way, but I could feel no such emotion: I was beginning to realize, though only vaguely, that I was incapable of entertaining towards this Latvian girl any feeling that remotely bordered on the hostile. Besides, she had clearly come to talk to me, and if she did she wanted some help, or reassuring or understanding and it would come very hardly indeed for so proud, so remote, so aloof a girl to ask for any of those. In all conscience, I couldn't make things difficult for her.

'Been sick?' I asked. As a conversational gambit it lacked something but doctors aren't supposed to have manners. She nodded. She was clasping her hands so tightly that I could see the faint ivory gleam of knuckles.

'I thought you were a good sailor?' The light touch.

'It is not the sea that makes me ill.'

I abandoned the light touch. 'Mary dear, why don't you lie down and try to sleep?'

'I see. You tell me that two more men have been poisoned and died and then I am supposed to drop off to sleep and have happy dreams. Is that it?' I said nothing and she went on wryly: 'You're not very good at breaking bad news, are you?'

'Professional callousness. You didn't come here just to reproach me with my tactlessness. What is it, Mary dear?'

'Why do you call me "Mary dear"?'

'It offends you?'

'Oh, no. Not when you say it.' From any other woman the words would have carried coquettish overtones, but there were none such here. It was meant as a statement of fact, no more.

'Very well, then.' I don't know what I meant by 'Very well, then,' it just made me feel obscurely clever. 'Tell me.'

'I'm afraid,' she said simply.

So she was afraid. She was tired, overwrought, she'd tended four very, very sick men who'd been poisoned, she'd learnt that three others whom she knew had died of poison and the violence of the Arctic gale raging outside was sufficient to give pause to even the most intrepid. But I said none of those things to her.

'We're all afraid at times, Mary.'

'You too?'

'Me too.'

'Are you afraid now?'

'No. What's there to be afraid of?'

'Death. Sickness and death.'

'I have to live with death, Mary. I detest it, of course I do, but I don't fear it. If I did, I'd be no good as a doctor. Would I now?'

'I do not express myself well. Death I can accept. But not when it strikes out blindly and you know that it is not blind. As it is here. It strikes out carelessly, recklessly, without cause or reason, but you know there is cause and reason. Do you —do you know what I mean?'

I knew perfectly well what she meant. I said: 'Even at my brightest and best, metaphysics are hardly my forte. Maybe the old man with the scythe does show discrimination in his indiscrimination, but I'm too tired—'

'I'm not talking about metaphysics.' She made an almost angry little gesture with her clasped hands. 'There's something terribly far wrong aboard this ship, Dr Marlowe.'

'Terribly far wrong?' Heaven only knew that I couldn't have agreed with her more. 'What should be wrong, Mary dear?'

She said gravely: 'You would not patronize me, Dr Marlowe? You would not humour a silly female?'

I had to answer at once so I said obliquely but deliberately: 'I would not insult you, Mary dear. I like you too much for that.'

'Do you really?' She smiled faintly, whether amused by me or pleased at what I'd said I couldn't guess. 'Do you like all the others, too?'

'Do I—I'm sorry.'

'Don't you find something odd, something very strange about the people, about the atmosphere they create?'

I was on safer ground here. I said frankly: 'I'd have to have been born deaf and blind not to notice it. One is warding off barely-expressed hostilities, elbowing aside tensions, wading through undercurrents the whole of the livelong day, and at the same time, if you'll forgive the mixing of the metaphors, trying to shield one's eyes from the constant shower of sparks given off by everyone trying to grind their own axes at the same time. Everyone is so frighteningly friendly to everyone else until the moment comes, of course, when everyone else is so misguided as to turn his or her back. Our esteemed employer, Otto Gerran, cannot speak too highly of his fellow directors, Heissman, Stryker, Goin and his dear daughter, all of whom he vilifies most fearfully the moment they are out of earshot, all of which would be wholly unforgivable were it not for the fact that Heissman, Stryker and his dear daughter each behave in the same fashion to Otto and *their* co-directors. You get the same petty jealousies, the same patently false sincerities, the same smilers with the knives beneath the cloaks on the lower film unit crew level —not that they, and probably rightly, would regard themselves as being any lower than Otto and his chums—I use the word 'chums', you understand, without regard to the strict meaning of the word. And, just to complicate matters, we have this charming interplay between the first and second divisions. The Duke, Eddie Harbottle, Halliday, the stills man, Hendriks and Sandy all cordially detest what we might call the management, a sentiment that is strongly reciprocated by the management themselves. And everybody seems to have a down on the unfortunate director, Neal Divine. Sure, I've noticed all of this, I'd have to be a zombie not to have, but I disregard ninety-odd per cent and just put it down to the normally healthy backbiting bitchery inseparable from the cinema world. You get fakes, cheats, liars, mountebanks, sycophants, hypocrites the world over, it's just that the movie-making milieu appears to act as a grossly distorting magnifying-glass that selects and highlights all the more undesirable qualities while ignoring or at best diminishing the more desirable ones—one has to assume that there are some.'

'You don't think a great deal of us, do you?'

'Whatever gave you that impression?'

She ignored that. 'And we're all bad?'

'Not all. Not you. Not the other Mary or young Allen—but maybe that's because they're too young yet or too new in this business to have come to terms with the standard norms of behaviour. And I'm pretty sure that Charlie Conrad is on the side of the angels.'

Again the little smile. 'You mean he thinks along the same lines as you?'

'Yes. Do you know him at all?'

'We say good morning.'

'You should get to know him better. He'd like to know you better. He likes you—he said so. And, no, we weren't discussing you—your name cropped up among a dozen others.'

'Flatterer.' Her tone was neutral, I didn't know whether she was referring with pleasure to Conrad or with irony to myself. 'So you agree with me? There is something very strange in the atmosphere here?'

'By normal standards, yes.'

'By any standards.' There was a curious certainty about her. 'Distrust, suspicion, jealousy, one looks to find those things in our unpleasant little world, but one does not look to find them on the scale that we have here. Do not forget that I know about those things. I was born in a Communist country, I was brought up in a Communist country. You understand?'

'Yes. When did you get away?'

'Two years ago. Just two years.'

'How?'

'Please. Others may wish to use the same way.'

'And I'm in the pay of the Kremlin. As you wish.'

'You are offended?' I shook my head. 'Distrust, suspicion, jealousy, Dr Marlowe. But there is more here, much more. There is hate and there is fear. I—I can smell it. Can't you?'

'You have a point to make, Mary dear, and you're leading up to it in a very tortuous fashion. I wish you would come to it.' I looked at my watch. 'I do not wish to be rude to you but neither do I wish to rude to the person who is waiting to see me.'

'If people hate and fear each other enough, terrible things can happen.' This didn't seem to require even an affirmative, so I kept silent and she went on: 'You say that those illnesses, those deaths, are the result of accidental food poisoning. Are they, Dr Marlowe? *Are* they?'

'So this is what has taken you all this long time to lead up to? You think—you think it may have been deliberate, have been engineered by someone. *That's* what you think?' I hoped it was clear to her that the idea had just occurred to me for the first time.

'I don't know what to think. But yes—yes, that's what I think.'

'Who?'

'Who?' She looked at me in what appeared to be genuine astonishment. 'How should I know who? Anybody, I suppose.'

'You'd be a sensation as a prosecuting counsel. Then if not who, why?'

She hesitated, looked away, glanced briefly back at me, then looked at the deck. 'I don't know why, either.'

'So you've no basis for this incredible suggestion other than your Communist-trained instincts.'

'I've put it very badly, haven't I?'

'You'd nothing to put, Mary. Just examine the facts and see how ridiculous your suggestion is. Seven disparate people affected and all struck down completely at random—or can you give me a reason why so wildly diverse a group as a film producer, a hairdresser, a camera focus assistant, a mate, a bo'sun and two stewards should be the victims? Can you tell me why some lived, why some died? Can you tell me why two of the victims assimilated this poison from food served at the saloon table, two from food consumed in the galley and one, the Duke, who may have been poisoned in either the galley or the saloon? Can you, Mary?'

She shook her head, the straw-coloured hair fell over her eyes and she let it stay there. Maybe she didn't want to look at me, maybe she didn't want me to look at her.

'After today,' I said, 'I've been left standing, I've been widely given to understand, among the ruins of my professional reputation but I'll wager what's left of it, together with anything else you care to name, that this whole-sale poisoning is completely accidental and that no person aboard the *Morning Rose* wished to, hoped to or intended to poison those seven men.' Which was a different thing entirely from claiming that there was no one aboard the *Morning Rose* who was responsible for the tragedy. 'Not unless we have a madman aboard, and you can say what you like—you've already said it—about our highly—ah—individualistic shipboard companions, none of them is unhinged. Not, that is, criminally unhinged.'

She hadn't looked at me once when I was speaking, and even when I'd finished, continued to present me with a view of the crown of her head. I rose, lurched across to the armchair where she was sitting, braced myself with one hand on the back of her chair and placed a finger of the other under her chin. She straightened and brushed back the hair from her eyes, brown eyes, large and still and full of fear. I smiled at her and she smiled back and the smile didn't touch her eyes. I turned and left the lounge.

I was quite ten minutes late for my appointment in the galley and as Haggerty had already made abundantly clear to me that he was a stickler for the proprieties, I expected to find him in a mood anywhere between stiff outrage and cool disapproval. Haggerty's attention, however, was occupied with more immediate and pressing matters, for as I approached the galley through the stewards' pantry I could hear the sound of a loud and very angry altercation. At least, Haggerty was being loud and angry.

It wasn't so much an altercation as a monologue and it was Haggerty, his red face crimson now with anger and his periwinkle blue eyes popping, who was conducting it: Sandy, our props man, was the unfortunate party on the other side of this very one-sided argument and his silent acceptance of the abuse that was being heaped upon him stemmed less from the want of something to say than from the want of air. I thought at first that Haggerty had his very large red hand clamped round Sandy's scrawny neck but then realized that he had the two lapels of Sandy's jacket crushed together in one hand: the effect, however, was about the same, and as Sandy was only about half the cook's size there was very little he could do about it. I tapped Haggerty on the shoulder.

'You're choking this man,' I said mildly. Haggerty glanced at me briefly and got back to his choking. I went on, just as mildly: 'This isn't a naval vessel and I'm not a Master-At-Arms so I can't order you about. But I am what the courts would accept as an expert witness and I don't think they'd question my testimony when you're being sued for assault and battery. Could cost you your life's savings, you know.'

Haggerty looked at me again and this time he didn't look away. Reluctantly, he removed his hand from the little man's collar and just stood there, glaring and breathing heavily, momentarily, it seemed, at a loss for words.

Sandy wasn't. After he'd massaged his throat a bit to see if it were still intact, he addressed a considerable amount of unprintable invective to Haggerty, then continued, shouting: 'You see? You heard, you great big ugly baboon. It's the courts for you. Assault and battery, mate, and it'll cost you—'

'Shut up,' I said wearily. 'I didn't see a thing and he didn't lay a finger on you. Be happy you're still breathing.' I looked at Sandy consideringly. I didn't really know him, I knew next to nothing about him, I wasn't even sure whether I liked him or not. Like Allen and the late Antonio, if Sandy had another name no one seemed to know what it was. He claimed to be a Scot but had a powerful Liverpool accent. He was a strange, undersized, wizened leprechaun of a man, with a wrinkled walnut-brown face and head—his pate was gleamingly bald—and stringy white hair that started about earlobe level and cascaded in uncombed disarray over his thin shoulders. He had quick-moving and almost weasel-like eyes but maybe that was unfair to him, it may have been the effect of the steel-legged rimless glasses that he affected. He was given to claiming, when under the influence of gin, which was as often as not, that he not only didn't know his birthday, he didn't even know the year in which he had been born, but put it around 1919 or 1920. The consensus of informed shipboard opinion put the date, not cruelly, at 1900 or slightly earlier.

I noticed for the first time that there were some tins of sardines and pilchards on the deck, and a larger one of corned beef. 'Aha!' I said. 'The midnight skulker strikes again.'

'What was that?' Haggerty said suspiciously.

'You couldn't have given our friend here a big enough helping for dinner,' I said.

'It wasn't for myself.' Sandy, under stress, had a high-pitched squeak of a voice. 'I swear it wasn't. You see—'

'I ought to throw the little runt over the side. Little sneaking robbing bastard that he is. Down here, up to his thieves' tricks, the minute any back's turned. And who's blamed for the theft, eh, tell me that, who's blamed for the theft? Who's got to account to the captain for the missing supplies? Who's got to make the loss good from his own pocket? And who's going to get his pay docked for not locking the galley door?' Haggerty's blood pressure, as he contemplated the injustices of life, was clearly rising again. 'To think,' he said bitterly, 'that I've always trusted my fellow men. I ought to break his bloody neck.'

'Well, you can't do that now,' I said reasonably. 'You can't expect me, as a professional man, to perjure myself in the witness box. Besides, there's no harm done, nothing stolen. You've no losses to pay for, so why get in bad with Captain Imrie?' I looked at Sandy, then at the tins on the floor; 'Was that all you stole?'

'I swear to God—'

'Oh, do be quiet.' I said to Haggerty: 'Where was he, what was he doing when you came in?'

'He'd his bloody great long nose stuck in the big fridge there, that was what he was doing. Caught him red-handed, I did.'

I opened the refrigerator door. Inside it was packed with a large number of items of very restricted variety—butter, cheeses, long-life milk, bacon and tinned meats. That was all. I said to Sandy: 'Come here. I want to look through your clothes.'

'*You* want to look through my clothes?' Sandy had taken heart from his providential deliverance from the threat of physical violence and the knowledge that he would not now be reported to those in authority. 'And who do you think *you* are then? A bleedin' cop? The CID, eh?'

'Just a doctor. A doctor who's trying to find out why three people died tonight.' Sandy stared at me, his eyes widening behind his rimless glasses, and his lower jaw fell down. 'Didn't you know that Moxen and Scott were dead? The two stewards?'

'Aye, I'd heard.' He ran his tongue over his lips. 'What's that got to do with me?'

'I'm not sure. Not yet.'

'You can't pin that on me. What are you talking about?' Sandy's brief moment of truculence was vanished as if it had never been. 'I've nothing to do—'

'Three men died and four almost did. They died or nearly died from food poisoning. Food comes from the galley. I'm interested in people who make unauthorized visits to the galley.' I looked at Haggerty. 'I think we'd better have Captain Imrie along here.'

'No! Christ, no!' Sandy was close to panic. 'Mr Gerran would kill me—'

'Come here.' He came to me, the last resistance gone. I went through his pockets but there was no trace of the only instrument he could have used to infect foodstuffs in the refrigerator, a hypodermic syringe. I said: 'What were you going to do with those tins?'

'They weren't for me. I told you. What would I want with them? I don't eat enough to keep a mouse alive. Ask anyone. They'll tell you.'

I didn't have to ask anyone. What he said was perfectly true: Sandy, like Lonnie Gilbert, depended almost exclusively upon the Distillers Co., Ltd to maintain his calorific quota. But he could still have been using those tins of meat as an insurance, as a red herring, if he'd been caught out as he had been.

'Who were the tins for, then?'

'The Duke. Cecil. I've just been to his cabin. He said he was hungry. No, he didn't. He said he was *going* to be hungry 'cos you'd put him on tea and toast for three days.' I thought back to my interview with the Duke. I'd only used the tea and toast threat to extract information from him and it wasn't until now that I recalled that I had forgotten to withdraw the threat. This much of Sandy's story had to be true.

'The Duke asked you to get some supplies for him?'

'No.'

'You told him you were going to get them?'

'No. I wanted to surprise him. I wanted to see his face when I turned up with the tins.'

Impasse. He could be telling the truth. He could equally well be using the story as a cloak for other and more sinister activities. I couldn't tell and probably would never know. I said: 'You better go and tell your friend the Duke that he'll be back on a normal diet as from breakfast.'

'You mean—I can go?'

'If Mr Haggerty doesn't wish to press a charge.'

'I wouldn't lower myself.' Haggerty clamped his big hand round the back of Sandy's neck with a grip tight enough to make the little man squeal in pain. 'If I ever catch you within sniffing distance of my galley again I won't just squeeze your neck, I'll break the bloody thing.' Haggerty marched him to the door, literally threw him out and returned. 'Got off far too easy if you ask me, sir.'

'He's not worth your ire, Mr Haggerty. He's probably telling the truth—not that makes him any less a sneak-thief. Moxen and Scott ate here tonight after the passengers had dinner?'

'Every night. Waiting staff usually eat before the guests —they preferred it the other way round.' With the departure of Sandy, Haggerty was looking a very troubled and upset man, the loss of the two stewards had clearly shaken him badly and was almost certainly responsible for the violence of his reaction towards Sandy.

'I think I've traced the source of the poison. I believe the horseradish was contaminated with a very unpleasant organism called *clostridium botulinum*, a sporing anaerobe found most commonly in garden soil.' I'd never heard of such a case of contamination but that didn't make it impossible. 'No possible reflection on you—it's totally undetectable before, during and after cooking. Were there any leftovers tonight?'

'Some. I made a casserole for Moxen and Scott and put the rest away.'

'Away?'

'For throwing. There wasn't enough to re-use for anything.'

'So it's gone.' Another door locked.

'On a night like this? No fear. The gash is sealed in poly-thene bags, then they're punctured and go over the side—in the morning.'

The door had opened again. 'You mean it's still here?'

'Of course.' He nodded towards a rectangular plastic box secured to the bulkhead by butterfly nuts. 'There.'

I crossed to the box and lifted the lid. Haggerty said: 'You'll be going to analyse it, is that it?'

'That's what I intended. Rather, to keep it for analysis.' I dropped the lid. 'That won't be possible now. The bin's empty.'

'Empty? Over the side—in this weather?' Haggerty came and unnecessarily checked the bin for himself. 'Bloody funny. And against regulations.'

'Perhaps your assistant—'

'Charlie? That bone-idle layabout. Not him. Besides, he's off-duty tonight.' Haggerty scratched the grey bristle of his hair. 'Lord knows why they did it but it must have been Moxen or Scott.'

'Yes,' I said. 'It must have been.'

I was so tired that I could think of nothing other than my cabin and my bunk. I was so tired that it wasn't until I had arrived at my cabin and looked on the bare bunk that I recalled that all my blankets had been taken away for Smithy and Oakley. I glanced idly at the small table where I'd left the toxicological books that I had been consulting and my tiredness very suddenly left me.

The volume on Medical Jurisprudence that had provided me with the information on *aconitine* was lying with its base pressed hard against the far fiddle of the table, thrown there, of course, by one of the violent lurches of the *Morning Rose*. The silken bookmark ribbon attached to the head of the book stretched out most of its length on the table, which was an unremarkable thing in itself were it not for my dear and dis-tinct recollection that I'd carefully used the bookmark to mark the passage I'd been reading.

I wondered who it was who knew I'd been reading the article on *aconitine*.

CHAPTER FIVE

I suddenly didn't fancy my cabin very much any more. Not, that was, as a place to sleep in. The eccentric shipping millionaire who'd had the *Morning Rose* completely stripped and fitted for passenger accommodation had had a powerful aversion to locks on cabin doors and, having had the means and the opportunity to do so, had translated his theories into practice. It may have been just a phobia or it may have stemmed from his assertion that many people had unnecessarily lost their lives at sea through being trapped in locked cabins as their ships went down—which, in fact, I knew to be true. However it was, it was impossible to lock a cabin door in the *Morning Rose* from the inside: it didn't even have a sliding bolt.

The saloon, I decided, was the place for me. It had, as I recalled, a very comfortable corner bulkhead settee where I could wedge myself and, more importantly, protect my back. The lockers below the settee seats had a splendid assortment of fleecy steamer rugs, another legacy, like the lockless doors, from the previous owner. Best of all, it was a brightly lit and public place, a place where people were liable to come and go even at that late hour, a place where no one could sneak up on you unawares. Not that any of this would offer any bar to anyone so ill-disposed as to take a potshot at me through the saloon's plate glass windows. It was, I supposed, some little consolation that the person or persons bent on mayhem had not so far chosen to resort to overt violence, but that hardly constituted a guarantee that they wouldn't: why the hell couldn't the publishers of reference books emulate the prestigious *Encyclopædia Britannica* and do away with book-marks altogether?

It was then that I recalled that I'd left the board of Olympus Productions in full plenary session up in the saloon. How long ago was that? Twenty minutes, not more. Another twenty minutes, perhaps, and the coast would be clear. It wasn't that I harboured any particular suspicion towards any of the four: they might just consider it very odd if I were to elect to sleep up there for the night when I'd a perfectly comfortable cabin down below.

Partly on impulse, partly to kill some of the intervening time, I decided to have a look at the Duke, to check on his condition, to ensure him a restful night by promising he'd be back on full rations come breakfast time and to find out if Sandy had been telling the truth. His was the third door to the left: the second to the right was wide open, the door stayed back at 90 degrees. It was Mary Stuart's cabin and she was inside but not asleep: she sat in a chair wedged between table and bunk, her eyes wide open, her hands in her lap.

'What's this, then?' I said. 'You look like someone taking part in a wake.'

'I'm not sleepy.'

'And the door open. Expecting company?'

'I hope not. I can't lock the door.'

'You haven't been able to lock the door since you came aboard. It doesn't have a lock.'

'I know. It didn't matter. Not till tonight.'

'You—you're not thinking that someone might sneak up and do you in while you're sleeping?' I said in a tone of a person who could never conceive of such a thing happening to himself.

'I don't know what to think. I'm all right. Please.'

'Afraid? Still?' I shook my head. 'Fie on you. Think of your namesake, young Mary Darling. She's not scared to sleep alone.'

'She's not sleeping alone.'

'She isn't? Ah, well, we live in a permissive age.'

'She's with Allen. In the recreation room.'

'Ah! Then why don't you join them? If it's safety you wrongly imagine you need, why then, there's safety in numbers.'

'I do not like to play—what you say—gooseberry.'

'Oh, fiddlesticks!' I said and went to see the Duke. He had colour, not much but enough, in his cheeks and was plainly on the mend. I asked him how he was.

'Rotten,' said the Duke. He rubbed his stomach.

'Still pretty sore?'

'Hunger pains,' he said.

'Nothing tonight. Tomorrow, you're back on the strength—

forget the tea and toast. By the way, that wasn't very clever of you to send Sandy up to raid the galley. Haggerty nabbed him in the act.'

'Sandy? In the galley?' The surprise was genuine. '*I* didn't send him up.'

'Surely he told you he was going there?'

'Not a word. Look, Doc, you can't pin—'

'Nobody's pinning anything on anybody. I must have taken him up wrong. Maybe he just wanted to surprise you—he said something about you feeling peckish.'

'I said that all right. But honest to God—'

'It's all right. No harm done. Good night.'

I retraced my steps, passing Mary Stuart's open door again. She looked at me but said nothing so I did the same. Back in my cabin I looked at my watch. Five minutes only had elapsed, fifteen to go. I was damned if I was going to wait so long, I was feeling tired again, tired enough to drop off to sleep at any moment, but I had to have a reason to go up there. For the first time I devoted some of my rapidly waning powers of thought to the problem and I had the answer in seconds. I opened my medical bag and extracted three of the most essential items it contained—death certificates. For some odd reason I checked the number that was left—ten. All told, thirteen. I was glad I wasn't superstitious. I stuffed the certificates and a few sheets of rather splendidly headed ship's notepaper—the previous owner hadn't been a man to do things by half—into my briefcase.

I opened the cabin door wide so as to have some light to see by, checked that the passage was empty and swiftly un-screwed the deck-head lamp. This I dropped on the deck from gradually increasing heights starting with about a foot or so until a shake of the lamp close my ear let me hear the unmistakable tinkle of a broken filament. I screwed the now useless lamp back into its holder, took up my briefcase, closed the door and made for the bridge.

The weather, I observed during my very hurried passage across the upper deck and up the bridge ladder, hadn't im-proved in the slightest. I had the vague impression that the seas were moderating slightly but that may have been because of the fact that I was feeling so tired that I was no longer capable of registering impressions accurately. But one aspect of the weather was beyond question: the almost horizontally driving snow had increased to the extent that the masthead light was no more than an intermittent glow in the gloom above.

Allison was at the wheel, spending more time looking at the radarscope than at the compass, and visibility being what it was, I could see his point. I said: 'Do you know where the captain keeps his crew lists? In his cabin?'

'No.' He glanced over his shoulder. 'In the chart-house there.' He hesitated. 'Why would you want those, Dr Marlowe?'

I pulled a death certificate from the briefcase and held it close to the binnacle light. Allison compressed his lips.

'Top drawer, port locker.'

I found the lists, entered up the name, address, age, place of birth, religion and next of kin of each of the two dead men, replaced the book and made my way down to the saloon. Half an hour had elapsed since I'd left Gerran, his three co-directors and the Count sitting there, and there all five still were, seated round a table and studying cardboard-covered folders spread on the table before them. A pile of those lay on the table, some more were scattered on the floor where the rolling of the ship had obviously precipitated them. The Count looked at me over the rim of his glass: his capacity for brandy was phenomenal.

'Still abroad, my dear fellow? You do labour on our behalf. Much more of this and I suggest that you be co-opted as one of our directors.'

'Here's one cobbler that sticks to his last.' I looked at Gerran. 'Sorry to interrupt, but I've some forms to fill up. If I'm interrupting some private session—'

'Nothing private going on here, I assure you.' It was Goin who answered. 'Mainly studying our shooting script for the next fortnight. All the cast and crew will have one tomorrow. Like a copy?'

'Thank you. After I've finished this. Afraid my cabin light has gone on the blink and I'm not much good at writing by the light of matches.'

'We're just leaving.' Otto was still looking grey and very tired but he was mentally tough enough to keep going long after his body had told him to stop. 'I think we could all do with a good night's sleep.'

'It's what I would prescribe. You could postpone your

departure for five minutes?'

'If necessary, of course.'

'We've promised Captain Imrie a guarantee or affidavit or what will you exonerating him from all blame if we have any further outbreaks of mysterious illness. He wants it on his breakfast table, and he wants it signed. And as Captain Imrie will be up at 4 a.m. and I suspect his breakfast will be correspondingly early, I suggest it would be more convenient if you all signed it now.'

They nodded agreement. I sat at a nearby table and in my best handwriting, which was pretty bad, and best legal jargon, which was awful, I drafted a statement of responsibility which I thought would meet the case. The others apparently thought so too or were too tired to care, for they signed with only a cursory glance at what I had written. The Count signed too and I didn't as much as raise an eyebrow. It had never even crossed my mind that the Count belonged to those elevated directorial ranks, I had thought that the more highly regarded cameramen, of which the Count was undoubtedly one, were invariably freelance and therefore ineligible for election to any film company board. But at least it helped to explain his lack of proper respect for Otto.

'And now, to bed.' Goin eased back his chair. 'You, too, Doctor?'

'After I've filled out the death certificates.'

'An unpleasant duty.' Goin handed me a folder. 'This might help amuse you afterwards.'

I took it from him and Gerran heaved himself upright with the usual massive effort. 'Those funerals, Dr Marlowe. The burials at sea. What time do they take place?'

'First light is customary.' Otto closed his eyes in suffering. 'After what you've been through, Mr Gerran, I'd advise you to give it a miss. Rest as long as possible tomorrow.'

'You really think so?' I nodded and Otto removed his mask of suffering. 'You will stand in for me, John?'

'Of course,' Goin said. 'Good night, Doctor. Thank you for your co-operation.'

'Yes, yes, thank you, thank you,' Otto said.

They trooped off unsteadily and I fished out my death certificate forms and filled them out. I put those in one sealed envelope, the signed affidavit—I just in time remembered to add my own signature—in another, addressed them to Captain

Imrie and took them up to the bridge to ask Allison to hand them over to the captain when he came on watch at four in the morning. Allison wasn't there. Instead, Smithy, heavily clad and muffled almost to the eyebrows, was sitting on a high stool before the wheel. He wasn't touching the wheel, which periodically spun clockwise and counter-clockwise as of its own accord, and he'd turned up the rheostat. He looked pale and had dark circles under his eyes but he didn't have a sick look about him any more. His recuperative powers were quite remarkable.

'Automatic pilot,' he explained, almost cheerfully, 'and all the lights of home. Who needs night-sight in zero visibility?'

'You ought to be in bed,' I said shortly.

'I've just come from there and I'm just going there. First Officer Smith is not yet his old self and he knows it. Just come up to check position and give Allison a break for coffee. Also, I thought I might find you here. You weren't in your cabin.'

'I'm here now. What did you want to see me about?'

'Otard-Dupuy,' he said. 'How does that sound?'

'It sounds fine.' Smithy slid off his stool and headed for the cupboard where Captain Imrie kept his private store of restoratives. 'But you weren't hunting the ship to offer me a brandy.'

'No. Tell you the truth, I've been trying to figure out some things. No dice with the figuring, if I was bright enough for that I'd be too bright to be where I am now. Thought you could help me.' He handed me a glass.

'We should make a great team,' I said.

He smiled briefly. 'Three dead and four half dead. Food poisoning. What poisoning?'

I told him the story about the sporing anaerobes, the one I'd given Haggerty. But Smithy wasn't Haggerty.

'Mighty selective poison, isn't it? Clobbers A and kills him, passes up B, clobbers C and doesn't kill him, passes up D and so on. And we all had the same food to eat.'

'Poisons are notoriously unpredictable. Six people at a picnic can eat the same infected food: three can land in hospital while the others don't feel a twinge.'

'So, some people get tummy-aches and some don't. But that's a bit different from saying that a poison that is deadly enough to kill, and to kill violently and quickly, is going to leave others entirely unaffected. I'm no doctor but I flat out don't believe it.'

'I find it a bit odd myself. You have something in mind?'

'Yes. The poisoning was deliberate.'

'Deliberate?' I sipped some more of the Otard-Dupuy while I wondered how far to go with Smithy. Not too far, I thought, not yet. I said: 'Of course it was deliberate. And so easily done. Take our poisoner. He has this little bag of poison. Also, he has this little magic wand. He waves it and turns himself invisible and then flits around the dining tables. A pinch for Otto, none for me, a pinch for you, a pinch for Oakley, no pinches for, say, Heissman and Stryker, a double pinch for Antonio, none for the girls, a pinch for the Duke, two each for Moxen and Scott, and so on. A wayward and capricious lad, our invisible friend: or would you call it being selective?'

'I don't know what I'd call it,' Smithy said soberly. 'But I know what I'd call you—devious, off-putting, side-tracking and altogether protesting too much. Without offence, of course.'

'Of course.'

'I wouldn't rate you as anybody's fool. You can't tell me that you haven't had some thoughts along those lines.'

'I had. But because I've been thinking about it a lot longer than you, I've dismissed them. Motive, opportunity, means— impossible to find any. Don't you know that the first thing a doctor does when he's called in to a case of accidental poisoning is to suspect that it's not accidental?'

'So you're satisfied?'

'As can be.'

'I see.' He paused. 'Do you know we have a transmitter in the radio office that can reach just about any place in the northern hemisphere? I've got a feeling we're going to have to use it soon.'

'What on earth for?'

'Help.'

'Help?'

'Yes. You know. The thing you require when you're in trouble. I think we need help now. Any more funny little accidents and I'll be damn certain we need help.'

'I'm sorry,' I said. 'You're way beyond me. Besides, Britain's a long long way away from us now.'

'The NATO Atlantic forces aren't. They're carrying out fleet exercise somewhere off the North Cape.'

'You're well informed,' I said.

'It pays to be well informed when I'm talking to someone who claims to be as satisfied as can be over three very mysterious deaths when I'm certain that someone would never rest and could never be satisfied until he knew exactly how those three people had died. I've admitted I'm not very bright but don't completely under-estimate what little intelligence I have.'

'I don't. And don't overestimate mine. Thanks for the Otard-Dupuy.'

I went to the starboard screen door. The *Morning Rose* was still rolling and pitching and shaking and shuddering as she battered her way northwards through the wild seas but it was no longer possible to see the wind-torn waters below: we were in a world now that was almost completely opaque, a blind and bitter world of driving white, a world of snowy darkness that began and ended at scarcely an arm length's distance. I looked down at the wing bridge deck and in the pale light of wash from the wheel-house I could see footprints in the snow. There was only one set of them, sharp and clearly limned as if they had been made only seconds previously. Somebody had been there, for a moment I was certain that someone had been there, listening to Smith and myself talking. Then I realized there was *only* one set, the set I had made myself, and they hadn't been filled in or even blurred because the blizzard driving horizontally across the wind-dodger was clearing the deck at my feet. Sleep, I thought, and sleep now: for with that lack of sleep, the tiring events of the past few hours, the sheer physical exhaustion induced by the violent weather and Smithy's dark forebodings, I was beginning to imagine things. I realized that Smithy was at my shoulder.

'You levelling with me, Dr Marlowe?'

'Of course. Or do you think *I'm* the invisible Borgia who's flitting around, a little pinch here, a little pinch there?'

'No, I don't. I don't think you're levelling with me, either.' His voice was sombre. 'Maybe some day you are going to wish you were.'

Some day I was going to wish I had, for then I wouldn't have had to leave Smithy behind in Bear Island.

Back in the saloon, I picked up the booklet Goin had given me, went to the corner settee, found myself a steamer blanket, decided I didn't require it yet and wedged myself into the corner, my feet comfortably on a swivel chair belonging to the nearest table. I picked up, without much interest, the cardboard file and was debating whether to open it when the lee door opened and Mary Stuart came in. There was snow on the tangled corn-coloured hair and she was wearing a heavy tweed coat.

'So this is where you are.' She banged the door shut and looked at me almost accusingly.

'This,' I acknowledged, 'is where I am.'

'You weren't in your cabin. And your light's gone. Do you know that?'

'I know that. I'd some writing to do. That's why I came here. Is there something wrong?'

She lurched across the saloon and sat heavily on the settee opposite me. 'Nothing more than has been wrong.' She and Smithy should meet up, they'd get on famously. 'Do you mind if I stay here?'

I could have said that it didn't matter whether I minded or not, that the saloon was as much hers as mine, but as she seemed to be a touchy sort of creature I just smiled and said: 'I would take it as an insult if you left.' She smiled back at me, just an acknowledging flicker, and settled as best she could in her seat, drawing the tweed coat around her and bracing herself against the violent movements of the *Morning Rose*. She closed her eyes and with the long dark lashes lying along pale wet cheeks her high cheek-bones were more pronounced than ever, her Slavonic ancestry unmistakable.

It was no great hardship to look upon Mary Stuart but I still felt an increasing irritation as I watched her. It wasn't so much her fey imaginings and need for company that made me uneasy, it was the obvious discomfort she was experiencing in trying to keep her seated balance while I was wedged so very comfortably in my own place: there is nothing more uncomfortable than being comfortable oneself and watching another in acute discomfort, not unless, of course, one has a feeling of very powerful antagonism towards the other party, in which case a very comfortable feeling can be induced: but I had no such antagonism towards the girl opposite. To compound my feeling of guilt she began to shiver involuntarily.

'Here,' I said. 'You'd be more comfortable in my seat. And there's a rug here you can have.'

She opened her eyes. 'No, thank you.'

'There are plenty more rugs,' I said in something like exasperation. Nothing brings out the worst in me more quickly than sweetly-smiling suffering. I picked up the rug, did my customary two-step across the heaving deck and draped the rug over her. She looked at me gravely and said nothing.

Back in my corner I picked up the booklet again but instead of reading it got to wondering about my cabin and those who might visit it during my absence. Mary Stuart had visited it, but then she'd told me she had and the fact that she was here now confirmed the reason for her visit. At least, it seemed to confirm it. She was scared, she said, she was lonely and so she naturally wanted company. Why my company? Why not that of, say, Charles Conrad who was a whole lot younger, nicer, and better-looking than I was? Or even his other two fellow actors, Gunther Jungbeck and Jon Heyter, both very personable characters indeed? Maybe she wanted to be with me for all the wrong reasons. Maybe she was watching me, maybe she was virtually guarding me, maybe she was giving someone the opportunity to visit my cabin while—I was suddenly very acutely aware that there were things in my cabin that I'd rather not be seen by others.

I put the book down and headed for the lee door. She opened her eyes and lifted her head.

'Where are you going?'

'Out.'

'I'm sorry. I just—are you coming back?'

'I'm sorry, too. I'm not rude,' I lied, 'just tired. Below. Back in a minute.'

She nodded, her eyes following me until I closed the door behind me. Once outside I remained still for twenty seconds or so, ignoring the vagrant flurries of snow that even here, on the lee side, seemed bent on getting down my collar and up the trouser cuffs, then walked quickly for'ard. I peered through the plate glass window and she was sitting as I'd left her, only now she had her elbows on her knees and her face in her hands, shaking her head slowly from side to side. Ten years ago I'd have been back in that saloon pretty rapidly, arms round her and telling her that all her troubles were over. That was ten years ago. Now I just looked at her, wondered if she had been expecting me to take a peek at her, then made my way for'ard and down to the passenger accommodation.

It was after midnight but not yet closing hours in the lounge bar, for Lonnie Gilbert, with a heroically foolhardy disregard for what would surely be both Otto's fearful wrath when the crime was discovered, had both glass doors swung open and latched in position, while he himself was ensconced in some state behind the bar itself, a bottle of malt whisky in one hand, a soda-siphon in the other. He beamed paternally at me as I passed through and as it seemed late in the day to point out to Lonnie that the better-class malts stood in no need of the anaemic assistance of soda I just nodded and went below.

If anybody had been in my cabin and gone through my belongings, he'd done it in a very circumspect way. As far as I could recall everything was as I had left it and nothing had been disturbed, but then, a practised searcher rarely left any trace of his passing. Both my cases had elasticized linen pockets in the lids and in each pocket in each lid, holding the lids as nearly horizontal as possible, I placed a small coin just at the entrance to the pocket. Then I locked the cases. In spite of the trawler's wildly erratic behaviour those coins would remain where they were, held in place by the pressure of the clothes inside but as soon as the lid was opened, the pressure released, and the lid then lifted even part way towards the vertical, the coins would slide down to the feet of the pockets. I then locked my medical bag—it was considerably large and heavier than the average medical bag but then it held a considerably greater amount of equipment— and put it out in the passage. I closed the door behind me, carefully wedging a spent book match between the front of the door and the sill: that door would have to open only a crack and the match would drop clear.

Lonnie, unsurprisingly, was still at his station in the lounge when I reached there.

'Aha!' He regarded his empty glass with an air of surprise, then reached out with an unerring hand. 'The kindly healer with his bag of tricks. Hotfoot to the succour of suffering mankind? A new and dreadful epidemic, is it? Your old Uncle Lonnie is proud of you, boy, proud of you. This Hippocratic spirit—' He broke off, only to resume almost at once. 'Now that we have touched, inadvertently chanced upon, as one might say, this topic—spirit, the blushful Hippocrene—I wonder if by any chance you would care to join me in a thimbleful of the elixir I have here—'

'Thank you, Lonnie, no. Why don't you get to bed? If you keep it up like this, you won't be able to get up tomorrow.'

'And that, my dear boy, is the whole point of the exercise. I don't want to get up tomorrow. The day after tomorrow? Well, yes, if I must, I'll face the day after tomorrow. I don't want to, mind you, for tomorrows, I've found, are always distressingly similar to todays. The only good thing you can say about a today is that at any given moment such and such a portion of it is already irrevocably past—' he paused to admire his speech control—'irrevocably past, as I say, and, with the passing of every moment, so much less of it to come. But *all* of tomorrow is still to come. Think of it. *All* of it—the livelong day.' He lifted his recharged glass. 'Others drink to forget the past. But some of us—very, very few and it would not be right of me to say that we're gifted with a prescience and understanding and intelligence far beyond the normal ken, so I'll just say we're different—some of us, I say, drink to forget the future. How, you will ask, can one forget the future? Well, for one thing, it takes practice. And, of course, a little assistance.' He drank half his malt in one gulp and intoned: ' "Tomorrow and tomorrow and tomorrow creeps in this petty pace from day to day to the last syllable—" '

'Lonnie,' I said, 'I don't think you're the least little bit like Macbeth.'

'And there you have it in a nutshell. I'm not. A tragic figure, a sad man, fated and laden with doom. Now, me, I'm not like that at all. We Gilberts have the indomitable spirit, the unconquerable soul. Your Shakespeares are all very well, but Walter de la Mare is my boy.' He lifted his glass and squinted myopically at it against the light. ' "Look your last on all things lovely every hour." '

'I don't think he quite meant it in that way, Lonnie. Anyway, doctor's orders and do me a favour—get to hell out of here. Otto will have you drawn and quartered if he finds you here.'

'Otto? Do you know something?' Lonnie leaned forward confidentially. 'Otto's really a very kindly man. I like Otto. He's always been good to me, Otto has. Most people are good, my dear chap, don't you know that? Most people are kind.

Lots of them very kind. But none so kind as Otto. Why, I remember—'

He broke off as I went round the back of the bar, replaced the bottles, locked the doors, placed the keys in his dressing-gown pocket and took his arm.

'I'm not trying to deprive you of the necessities of life,' I explained. 'Neither am I being heavy-handed and moralistic. But I have a sensitive nature and I don't want to be around when you find out that your assessment of Otto is a hundred per cent wrong.' Lonnie came without a single murmur of protest. Clearly, he had his emergency supplies cached in his cabin. On our stumbling descent of the companionway he said: 'You think I'm headed for the next world with my gas pedal flat on the floor, don't you?'

'As long as you don't hit anybody it's none of my business how you drive, Lonnie.'

He stumbled into his cabin, sat heavily on his bed, then moved with remarkable swiftness to one side: I could only conclude that he'd inadvertently sat on a bottle of scotch. He looked at me, pondering, then said: 'Tell me, my boy, do you think they have bars in heaven?'

'I'm afraid I have no information on that one, Lonnie.'

'Quite, quite. It makes a gratifying change to find a doctor who is not the source of all wisdom. You may leave me now, my good fellow.'

I looked at Neal Divine, now quietly asleep, and at Lonnie, impatiently and for obvious reasons awaiting my departure, and left them both.

Mary Stuart was sitting where I'd left her, arms straight out on either side and fingers splayed to counteract the now noticeably heavier pitching of the *Morning Rose*: the rolling effect, on the other hand, was considerably less, so I assumed that the wind was still veering in a northerly direction. She looked at me with the normally big brown eyes now preternaturally huge in a dreadfully tired face, then looked away again.

'I'm sorry,' I found myself apologizing. 'I've been discussing classics and theology with our production manager.' I made for my corner seat and sat down gratefully. 'Do you know him at all?'

'Everybody knows Lonnie.' She tried to smile. 'We worked

together in the last picture I made.' Again she essayed a smile. 'Did you see it?'

'No.' I'd heard about it though, enough to make me walk five miles out of my way to avoid it.

'It was awful. I was awful. I can't imagine why they gave me another chance.'

'You're a very beautiful girl,' I said. 'You don't have to be able to act. Performance detracts from appearance. Anyway, you may be an excellent actress. I wouldn't know. About Lonnie?'

'Yes. He was there. So were Mr Gerran and Mr Heissman.' I said nothing so she went on: 'This is the third picture we've all made together. The third since Mr Heissman—well, since he—'

'I know. Mr Heissman was away for quite a bit.'

'Lonnie's such a nice man. He's so helpful and kind and I think he's a very wise man. But he's a funny man. You know that Lonnie likes to take a drink. One day, after twelve hours on the set and all of us dead tired, when we got back to the hotel I asked for a double gin and he became very angry with me. Why should he be like that?'

'Because he's a funny man. So you like him?'

'How could I not like him? He likes everybody so everybody just likes him back. Even Mr Gerran likes him—they're very close. But then, they've known each other for years and years.'

'I didn't know that. Has Lonnie a family? Is he married?'

'I don't know. I think he was. Maybe he's divorced. Why do you ask so many questions about him?'

'Because I'm a typically knowing, prying sawbones and I like to know as much as possible about people who are or may be my patients. For instance, I know enough about Lonnie now never to give him a brandy if he were in need of a restorative for it wouldn't have the slightest effect.'

She smiled and closed her eyes. Conversation over. I took another steamer rug from under my seat, wrapped it around me—the temperature in the saloon was noticeably dropping —and picked up the folder that Goin had given me. I turned to Page 1, which, apart from being titled 'Bear Island', started off without any preamble.

'It is widely maintained,' it read, 'that Olympus Productions is approaching the making of this, its latest production, in

96

conditions so restrictive as to amount to an aura of almost total secrecy. Allegations to this effect have subsequently made their appearance in popular and trade presses and in light of the absence of production office denials in the contrary those uncorroborated assertions have achieved a considerable degree of substance and credence which one might regard, in the circumstances, as being a psychological inevitability.' I read through this rubbish again, a travesty of the Queen's English fit only for the columns of the more learned Sunday papers, and then I got it: they were making a hush-hush picture and didn't care who knew. And very good publicity it was for the film, too, I thought, but, no, I was doing the boys an injustice. Or so the boys said. The article continued:

'Other cinematic productions'—I assumed he meant films —'have been approached and, on occasion, even executed under conditions of similar secrecy but those other and, one is afraid spurious *sub rosa* ventures have had for their calculated aim nothing less, regrettably, than the extraction of the maximum free publicity. This, we insist, and with some pride, is not the objective of Olympus Productions.' Good old Olympus, this I had to see, a cinema company who didn't want free publicity: next thing we'd have the Bank of England turning its nose up at the sound of the word 'money'. 'Our frankly cabbalistic approach to this production, which has given rise to so much intrigued and largely ill-informed speculation, has, in fact, been imposed upon us by considerations of the highest importance: the handling of this, a story which in the wrong hands might well generate potentially and dangerously explosive international repercussions, calls for the utmost in delicacy and finesse, essential qualities for the creation of what we confidently expect will be hailed as a cinematic masterpiece, but qualities which even we feel —nay, are certain—would not be able to overcome the immense damage done by—and we are certain of this—the world-wide furore that would immediately and automatically follow the premature leaking of the story we intend to film.

'We are confident, however, that when—there is no "if"— this production is made in our own way, in our own time, and under the very strictest security conditions—this is why we have gone to the quite extraordinary lengths of obtaining notarized oaths of secrecy from every member of the cast and crew of the film project under discussion, including the managing director and his co-directors—we will have upon our hands, when this production is presented to a public, which will have been geared by that time to the highest degree of expectancy, a *tour de force* of so unparalleled an order that the justification for—'

Mary Stuart sneezed and I blessed her, twice, once for her health and once for the heaven-sent interruption of the reading of this modestly phrased manifesto. I glanced at her again just as she sneezed again. She was sitting in a curiously huddled fashion, hands clasped tightly together, her face white and pinched. I laid down the Olympus manifesto, unwrapped my rug, crossed the saloon in a zigzag totter which resulted from the now very pronounced pitching of the *Morning Rose,* sat beside her and took her hands in mine. They were icily cold.

'You're freezing,' I said somewhat unnecessarily.

'I'm all right. I'm just a bit tired.'

'Why don't you go below to your cabin? It's at least twenty degrees warmer down there and you'll never sleep up here if you have to keep bracing yourself all the time from falling off your seat.'

'No. I don't sleep down there either. I've hardly slept since—' She broke off. 'And I don't feel nearly so—so queasy up here. Please.'

I don't give up easily. I said: 'Then at least take my corner seat, you'll be much more comfortable there.'

She took her hands away. 'Please. Just leave me.'

I gave up. I left her. I took three wavering steps in the direction of my seat, halted in irritation, turned back to her and hauled her none too gently to her feet. She looked at me, not speaking, in tired surprise, and continued to say nothing, and to offer no resistance, as I led her across to my corner, brought out another two steamer rugs, cocooned her in those, lifted her feet on to the settee and sat beside her. She looked up at me for a few seconds, her gaze transferring itself from my right eye to my left and back again, then she turned her face to me, closed her eyes and slid one of her icy hands under my jacket. During all this performance she didn't speak once or permit any expression to appear on her face and I would have been deeply moved by this touching trust in me were it not for the reflection that if it were her purpose or instructions to keep as close an eye as possible on me she could hardly, even in her most optimistic moments, have hoped to arrive at a situation where she could keep an eye within half an inch of my shirt-front. I couldn't even take a deep breath without her knowing all about it. On the other hand, if she were as innocent as the driven snow that had now completely obscured the plate glass not six inches from my head, then it was less than likely that any ill-disposed citizen or citizens would contemplate taking action of a violent and permanent nature against me as long as I had Mary Stuart practically sitting on my lap. It was, I thought, a pretty even trade. I looked down at the half-hidden lovely face and reflected that I was possibly having a shade the better of the deal.

I reached for my own rug, draped it round my shoulders in Navaho style, picked up the Olympus manifesto again and continued to read. The next two pages were largely a hyperbolic expansion of what had gone before, with the writer—I assumed it was Heissman—harping on at nauseating length on the twin themes of the supreme artistic merit of the production and the necessity for absolute secrecy. After this self-adulatory exercise, the writer got down to facts.

'After long consideration, and the close examination and subsequent rejection of a very considerable number of possible alternatives, we finally decided upon Bear Island as the location for this project. We are aware that all of you, and this includes the entire crew of the *Morning Rose* from Captain Imrie downwards, believed that we were heading for a destination in the neighbourhood of the Lofoten Islands off Northern Norway and it was not exactly, shall we say, through fortuitous circumstances, that this rumour was gaining some currency in certain quarters in London immediately prior to our departure. We make no apologies for what may superficially appear to be an unwarranted deception, for it was essential to our purposes and the maintenance of secrecy that this subterfuge be adopted.

'For the following brief description of Bear Island we are indebted to the Royal Geographical Society of Oslo, who have also furnished us with a translation.' That was a relief, just as long as the translator wasn't Heissman I might be able to get it on the first reading. 'This information, it is perhaps superfluous to add, was obtained for us through the good offices of a third party entirely unconnected with Olympus Productions, a noted ornithologist who must remain entirely incognito. It may be mentioned in the passing that the Norwegian government has given us permission to film on the island. We understand that it is their understanding that we propose to make a wild life documentary: such an understanding, far less a commitment, was not obtained from us.'

I wondered about that last bit—not the cleverer-than-thou smugness of it, that was clearly inseparable from everything Heissman wrote—but the fact that he should say it at all. Heissman, clearly, was not a man much given to hiding his own brilliance—the phrase 'low cunning' would not have occurred to him—under a bushel but equally he wasn't a man who would permit this particular type of self-gratification to lead him into danger. Almost certainly if the Norwegians did find out they had been deluded there would be nothing in international law they could do about it—Olympus wouldn't have overlooked anything so obvious—other than ban the completed film from their country, and as Norway could hardly be regarded as a major market this would cause few sleepless nights. On the other hand, it would be effective in stilling any qualms of conscience—true, this was the world of the cinema but Heissman would be unlikely to overlook even the most remote possibility—that might have arisen had the project been denied even this superficial official blessing, and the very fact that they were being made privy to the secret inner workings of Olympus would tend to bind both cast and crew closer to the company, for it is an almost universal law of nature that mankind, which is still in the painful process of growing up, dearly loves its little closed and/or secret societies, whether those be the most remote Masonic Lodge in Saskatchewan or White's of St James's, and tends to form an intense personal attachment and loyalty to other members of that group while presenting a united front to the world of the unfortunates beyond their doors. I did not overlook the possibility that there might be another, and conceivably sinister, interpretation of Heissman's confidential frankness but as it was now into the early hours of the morning I didn't particularly feel like seeking it out.

'Bear Island,' the résumé began. 'One of the Svalbard group, of which Spitzbergen is much the largest. This group remained neutral and unclaimed until the beginning of the twentieth century when, because of its very considerable investments in the exploitation of mineral resources and the establishment of whaling operations, Norway requested sovereignty of the area, placing her petition before the Conference'—they didn't specify what conference—'at Christiania (Oslo) in 1910, 1912 and again in 1914. On each occasion Russian objections prevented ratification of the proposals. However, in 1919 the Allied Supreme Council granted Norway sovereignty, formal possession being taken on August 14th, 1925.'

Having established the ownership beyond all doubt the report proceeded: 'The (Bear) island, 74° 28′N., 19° 13′E., lies some 260 miles N.N.W. of North Cape, Norway, and some 140 miles south of Spitzbergen and may be regarded as the meeting point of the Norwegian, Greenland and Barents Seas. In terms of distance from its nearest neighbours, this is the most isolated island in the Arctic.'

There followed a long and for me highly uninteresting account of the island's history which seemed to consist mainly of interminable squabbles between Norwegians, Germans and Russians over whaling and mining rights—although I was mildly intrigued to learn that as recently as the twenties there had been as many as a hundred and eighty Norwegians working the coal mines at Tunheim in the north-east of the island—I would have imagined that even the polar bears, after whom the island was named, would have given this desolation as wide a berth as possible. The mines, it seemed, had been closed down following a geological survey which showed that the purity and thickness of the seams were not sufficient to make it a profitable proposition. The island, however, was not entirely uninhabited even today: it appeared that the Norwegian Government maintained a meteorological and radio station at Tunheim.

Then came articles on the natural resources, vegetation and animal life, all of which I took as read. The references to the climate, however, which might be expected to concern us all, I found much more intriguing and highly discouraging. 'The meeting of the Gulf Stream and the Polar Drift,' it read, 'makes for extremely poor weather conditions, with large rainfall and dense fogs. The average summer temperature rises to not more than five degrees above freezing. Not until mid-July do the lakes become ice-free and the snow melts. The midnight sun lasts for 106 days from April 30th to

August 13th: the sun remains below the horizon from November 7th to February 4th.' This last item made our presence there, this late in the year, very odd indeed as Otto couldn't expect more than a few hours of daylight at the most: perhaps the script called for the whole story to be shot in darkness.

'Physically and geologically,' it went on, 'Bear Island is triangular in shape with its apex to the south, being approximately twelve miles long on its north-south axis in width varying from ten miles in the north to two miles in the south at the point where the southernmost peninsula begins. Generally speaking the north and west consist of a fairly flat plateau at an elevation of about a hundred feet, while the south and east are mountainous, the two main complexes being the Misery Fell group in the east and the Antarcticfjell and its associated mountains, the Alfredfjell, Harbergfjell and Fuglefjell in the extreme south-east.

'There are no glaciers. The entire area is covered with a network of shallow lakes, none more than a few yards in depth: those account for about one-tenth of the total area of the island: the remainder of the interior of the island consists largely of icy swamps and loose scree which makes it extremely difficult to traverse.

'The coastline of Bear Island is regarded as perhaps the most inhospitably bleak in the world. This is especially true in the south where the island ends in vertical cliffs, the streams entering the sea by waterfalls. A characteristic feature of this area is the detached pillars of rock that stand in the sea close to the foot of the cliffs, remnants from that distant period when the island was considerably larger than it is now. The melting of the snows and ice in June/July, the powerful tidal streams and the massive erosion undermine those coastal hills so that large masses of rock are constantly falling into the sea. The great polomite cliffs of Hambergfjell drop sheer for over 1400 feet: at their base, projecting from the seas are sharp needles of rock as much as 250 feet high, while the Fuglefjell (Bird Fell) cliffs are almost as high and have at their most southerly point a remarkable series of high stacks, pinnacles and arches. To the east of this point, between Kapp Bull and Kapp Kolthoff, is a bay surrounded on three sides by vertical cliffs which are nowhere less than 1000 feet high.

'Those cliffs are the finest bird breeding grounds in the Northern Hemisphere.'

It was all very fine for the birds, I supposed. That was the end of the Geographical Society's report—or as much of it as the writer had chosen to include—and I was bracing myself for a return to Heissman's limpid prose when the lee door opened and John Halliday staggered in. Halliday, the unit's highly competent stills photographer, was a dark, swarthy, taciturn and unsmiling American. Even by his normal cheerless standards Halliday looked uncommonly glum. He caught sight of us and stood there uncertainly, holding the door open.

'I'm sorry.' He made as if to go. 'I didn't know—'

'Enter, enter,' I said. 'Things are not as they seem. What you see before you is a strictly doctor-patient relationship.' He closed the door and sat down morosely on the settee that Mary Stuart had so lately occupied. 'Insomnia?' I asked. 'A touch of the *mal de mer*?'

'Insomnia.' He chewed dispiritedly on the wad of black tobacco that never seemed to leave his mouth. 'The *mal de mer*'s all Sandy's.' Sandy, I knew, was his cabin-mate. True, Sandy hadn't been looking very bright when last I'd seen him in the galley but I'd attributed this to Haggerty's yearning to eviscerate him: at least it explained why he hadn't called in to see the Duke after he'd left us.

'Bit under the weather, is he?'

'Very much under the weather. Kind of a funny green colour and sick all over the damned carpet.' Halliday wrinkled his nose. 'The smell—'

'Mary.' I shook her gently and she opened sleep-dulled eyes. 'Sorry, I've got to go for a moment.' She said nothing as I half helped her to a sitting position, just glanced incuriously at Halliday and closed her eyes again.

'I don't think he's all that bad,' Halliday said. 'Not poisoning or anything like that, I mean. I'm sure of it.'

'No harm to take a look,' I said. Halliday was probably right: on the other hand Sandy had had the freedom of the galley before Haggerty had caught him and with Sandy's prehensile and sticky fingers anything was conceivable, including the possibility that his appetite was not quite as birdlike as he claimed. I picked up my medical bag and left.

As Halliday had said, Sandy was of a rather peculiar green-

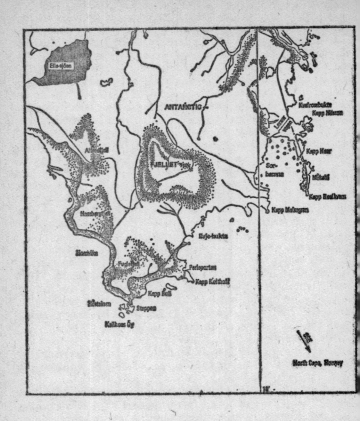

ish shade and he'd obviously been very sick indeed. He was sitting propped up in his bunk, with both forearms wrapped round his middle: he glared at me balefully as I entered.

'Christ, I'm dying,' he wheezed. He swore briefly, pungently and indiscriminately at life in general and Otto in particular. 'Why that crazy bastard wants to drag us aboard this bloody old stinking hell-ship—'

I gave him some sleeping-sedatives and left. I was beginning to find Sandy a rather less than sympathetic character:

more importantly, sufferers from *aconitine* poisoning couldn't speak, far less indulge in the fluent Billingsgate in which Sandy was clearly so proficient.

Swaying from side to side and again with her arms stretched out to support herself, Mary Stuart still had her eyes shut: Halliday, dejectedly chewing his wad of tobacco, looked up at me in lackadaisical half-inquiry as if he didn't much care whether Sandy was alive or dead.

'You're right,' I said. 'Just the weather.' I sat down a little way from Mary Stuart and not as much as by a flicker of a closed eyelid did she acknowledge my presence. I shivered involuntarily and drew the steamer rug around me. I said: 'It's getting a bit nippy in this saloon. Why don't you take one of these and kip down here?'

'No thanks. I'd no idea it would be so damn cold here. My blankets and pillow and it's me for the lounge.' He smiled faintly. 'Just as long as Lonnie doesn't trample all over me with his hob-nailed boots in the middle watch.' It was apparently common knowledge that the liquor in the lounge drew Lonnie like a lodestone. Halliday chewed some more, then nodded at the bottle in Captain Imrie's wrought-iron stand. 'You're a whisky man, Doc. That's the stuff to warm you up.'

'Agreed. But I'm a very choosy whisky man. What is it?' Halliday peered. 'Black Label.'

'None better. But I'm a malt man myself. You're cold, you try some. It's on the house. Stole it from Otto.'

'I'm not much of a one for scotch. Now bourbon—'

'Corrodes the digestive tract. I speak as a medical man. Now, one sip of that stuff there and you'll swear off those lethal Kentucky brews for ever. Go on. Try it.'

Halliday looked at the bottle, as if uncertainly. I said to Mary Stuart: 'How about you? Just a little? You've no idea how it warms the cockles.'

She opened her eyes and gave me that oddly expressionless look. 'No thank you. I hardly ever drink.' She closed her eyes again.

'The flaw that makes for perfection,' I said absently, because my mind was on other things. Halliday wouldn't drink from that bottle, Mary Stuart wouldn't drink from that bottle, but Halliday seemed to think it was a good idea that I should. Had they both remained in their seats during my absence or had they been busy little bees, one keeping guard against my premature return while the other altered the character of the Black Label with ingredients not necessarily made in Scotland? Why else had Halliday come up to the saloon if not to lure me away? Why hadn't he gone direct to the lounge with blankets and pillow instead of wandering aimlessly up here to the saloon where he must have known from mealtimes that the temperature was considerably colder than it was down below? Because, of course, before Mary Stuart had made her presence known to me here, she'd seen me through the outer windows and had reported to Halliday that a certain problem had arisen that could only be solved by bringing about my temporary absence from the saloon. Sandy's sickness had been a convenient coincidence—if it had been a coincidence, I suddenly thought: if Halliday was the person, or was in cahoots with the person who was so handy with poisons, then the introduction of some mildly emetic potion into Sandy's drink would have involved no more problem than that of opportunity. It all added up.

I became aware that Halliday was on his feet and was lurching unsteadily in my direction, bottle in one hand and glass in the other: the bottle, I noticed almost mechanically, was about one-third full. He halted, swaying, in front of me and poured a generous measure into the glass, bowed lightly, offered me the glass and smiled. 'Maybe we're both on the hide-bound and conservative side, Doc. In the words of the song, I will if you will so will I.'

I smiled back. 'Your willingness to experiment does you credit. But no thanks. I told you, I just don't like the stuff. I've tried it. Have you?'

'No, but I—'

'Well, how can you tell, then?'

'I don't think—'.

'You were going to try it anyway. Go on. Drink it.'

Mary Stuart opened her eyes. 'Do you always make people drink against their will? Is this what doctors do—force alcohol on those who don't want it?'

I felt like scowling and saying, 'Why don't you shut up?' but instead I smiled and said: 'Teetotal objections overruled.'

'So what's the harm?' Halliday said. He had the glass to his lips. I stared at him until I remembered I shouldn't be staring, which was all of a fraction of a second, smiled indulgently, glanced at Mary Stuart whose ever so slightly compressed lips registered no more than a trace of prudish disapproval, then looked back in time to see Halliday lowering his half empty glass.

'Not bad,' he pronounced. 'Not bad at all. Kind of a funny taste, though.'

'You could be arrested in Scotland for saying that,' I said mechanically. The villain had nonchalantly quaffed the hemlock while his accomplice had looked on with indifference. I felt very considerably diminished, a complete and utter idiot: as a detective, my inductive and deductive powers added up to zero. I even felt like apologizing to them except that they wouldn't know what I was talking about.

'You may in fact be right, Doc, one could even get to like this stuff.' Halliday topped up his glass, drunk again, took the bottle across to its wrought-iron rest and resumed his former seat. He sat there silently for perhaps half a minute, finished off the scotch with a couple of swallows and rose abruptly to his feet. 'With that lot inside me I can even ignore Lonnie's hob-nails. Good night.' He hurried from the saloon.

I looked at the doorway through which he had vanished, my mind thoughtful, my face not. I still didn't understand why he had come to the saloon in the first place: and what thought had so suddenly occurred to him to precipitate so abruptly a departure? An unprofitable line of thinking to pursue, I couldn't even find a starting-point to begin theorizing. I looked at Mary Stuart and felt very guilty indeed: murderesses, I knew, came in all shapes, sizes and guises but if they came in this particular guise then I could never trust my judgement again. I wondered what on earth could have led me to entertain so ludicrous a suspicion: I must be even more tired than I thought.

As if conscious of my gaze she opened her eyes and looked at me. She had this extraordinary ability to assume this still and wholly expressionless face, but beneath this remoteness, this distance, this aloofness lay, I thought, a marked degree of vulnerability. Wishful thinking on my part, it was possible: but I was oddly certain it wasn't. Still without speaking, still without altering her expression or lack of it, she half-rose, hobbled awkwardly in her cocoon of steamer rugs and sat close beside me. In my best avuncular fashion I put my arm round her shoulders, but it didn't stay there for long for she took hold of my wrist and deliberately and without haste lifted my arm over the top of her head and pushed it clear of her. Just to show that doctors are suprahuman and incapable of being offended by patients who aren't really responsible for their own behaviour, I smiled at her. She smiled back at me and her eyes, I saw with an astonishment that I knew was not reflected in my face, were filled with unshed tears: almost as if she were aware of those tears and wished to hide them, she suddenly swung her legs up on the settee, turned towards me and got back to the short-range examination of my shirt-front, only this time she put both her arms around me. As far as freedom of mobility was concerned I was as good as handcuffed, which was doubtless what she wanted anyway. That she harboured no lethal intent towards me I was sure: I was equally sure that she was determined not to let me out of her sight and that this was the most effective way she knew of doing just that. How much it cost that proud and lonely person to behave like this I couldn't guess: even less could I imagine what made her do it at all.

I sat there and tried to mull things over in my now thoroughly befogged mind and, predictably, made no progress whatsoever. Besides, my tired eyes were being almost hypnotized by the behaviour of the scotch inside the Black Label bottle, with the almost metronomic regularity with which the liquid ascended and descended the opposite sides of the bottle in response to the regular pitching of the *Morning Rose*. One thing led to another and I said: 'Mary dear?'

'Yes?' She didn't turn her face up to look at me and I didn't have to be told why: the area around the level of my fourth shirt-button was becoming noticably damp.

'I don't want to disturb you but it's time for my nightcap.'

'Whisky?'

'Ah! Two hearts that beat as one.'

'No.' She tightened her arms.

'No?'

'I hate the smell of whisky.'

'I'm glad,' I said *sotto voce*, 'I'm not married to you.'

'What was that?'

'I said "Yes, Mary dear".'

Five more minutes passed and I realized that my mind had closed down for the night. Idly I picked up the Olympus manifesto, read some rubbish about the sole completed copy of the screen-play being deposited in the vaults of a London bank, and put it down again. Mary Stuart was breathing quietly and evenly and seemed to be asleep. I bent and blew lightly on the left eyelid which was about the only part of her face that I could see. It didn't quiver. She was asleep. I shifted my position experimentally, not much, and her arms automatically tightened round me, she'd clearly left a note to her subconscious before turning in for the night. I resigned myself to remaining where I was, it wasn't a form of imprisonment that was likely to scar me permanently: I wondered vaguely whether the idea behind this silken incarceration was to prevent me from doing things or from chancing upon some other devilry that might well be afoot. I was too tired to care. I made up my mind just to sit there and keep a sleepless vigil until the morning came: I was asleep within not more than two minutes.

Mary Stuart was not and didn't look as if she was built along the lines of a coal-heaver but she wasn't stuffed with swansdown either, for when I woke my left arm was asleep, wholly numb and almost useless, a realization that was brought home to me when I had to reach across my right hand to lift up my left wrist to see what time the luminous hands of my watch said it was. They said it was 4.15.

It says much for my mental acuity that at least ten seconds elapsed before it occurred to me why it had been necessary for me to consult the luminous hands. Because it was dark, of course, but why was the saloon dark? Every light had been on when I'd gone to sleep. And what had wakened me? Something had, I knew without knowing why that I hadn't wakened naturally but that there had been some external cause. What and where was the cause? A sound or a physical contact, it couldn't be anything else, and whoever was responsible for whatever it had been was still with me. He had to be, insufficient time had elapsed since I'd worked for him to have left the saloon: more importantly the hairs on the back of my neck told me there was another and inimical presence in the saloon with me.

Gently I took hold of Mary Stuart's wrists to ease her arms away. Again the resistance was automatic, hers was not a subconscious to go to sleep on the job, but I was in no mood to be balked by any subconscious. I prised her arms free, slid along the settee, lowered her carefully to the horizontal, rose and moved out towards the middle of the saloon.

I stood quite still, my hands grasping the edge of a table to brace myself, my breathing almost stopped as I listened intently. I could have spared myself the trouble. I was sure that the weather had moderated, not a great deal but enough to be just noticeable, since I'd gone to sleep, but it hadn't moderated to the extent where any stealthy movements—and I could expect none other—could possibly be heard above the sound of the wind and the seas, the metallic creakings and groanings of the ancient plates and rivets of the *Morning Rose*.

The nearest set of light switches—there was a duplicate set by the stewards' pantry—was by the lee door. I took one step in the remembered direction then stopped. Did the presence in the room know that I was awake and on my feet? Were his eyes more attuned to the darkness than my newly opened ones? Could he dimly discern my figure? Would he guess that my first move would be towards the switches and was he preparing to block my way? If he were, how would he block my way? Would he be carrying a weapon and what kind of weapon—I was acutely aware that all I had were two hands, the left one still a fairly useless lump of tingling pins and needles. I stopped, irresolute.

I heard the metallic click of a door handle and a gust of icy air struck me: the presence was leaving by the lee door. I reached the door in four steps, stepped outside on to the deck, flung up an instinctively protective right forearm as a bright light abruptly struck my eyes and immediately wished I had used my left forearm instead for then it might have offered me some measure of protection against something hard, heavy and very solid that connected forcibly and painfully with the left side of my neck. I clung to the outside edge of the door to support myself but I didn't seem to have much strength left in my hands: and I seemed to have none at all in my legs for although I remained quite conscious I sank to the deck as if my legs had been filleted: by the time the momentary paralysis had passed and I was able to use the support of the door to drag myself shakily to my feet, I was alone on the deck. I had no idea where my assailant had gone and the matter was one of only academic interest, my legs could barely cope with supporting my weight in a static position: even the thought of running or negotiating ladders and companionways at speed was preposterous.

Still clinging to whatever support was to hand I stepped back into the saloon, fumbled the lights on and pulled the lee door closed behind me. Mary Stuart was propped on an elbow, the heel of one palm rubbing an eye while the lid of the other was half open in the fashion of a person just rousing from a very deep or drugged sleep. I looked away, stumbled towards Captain Imrie's table and sat down heavily in his chair. I lifted the bottle of Black Label from its stand. It was half full. For what seemed quite a long time but could have been no more than seconds I stared at this bottle, not seeing it, then looked away to locate the glass that Halliday had been using. It was nowhere to be seen, it could have fallen and rolled out of sight in a dozen different directions. I selected another glass from the table rack, splashed some scotch into it, drank it and made my way back to my seat. My neck felt awful. One good shake of my head and it would fall off.

'Don't breathe through your nose,' I said, 'and you'll hardly smell the demon drink at all.' I propped her up to a sitting position, rearranged her rugs and forestalled her by, for a change, putting my arms around her. I said: 'There now.'

'What was it? What happened?' Her voice was low and had a shake to it.

'Just the door. Wind blew it open. Had to close it, that's all.'

'But the lights were off.'

'I put them off. Just after you'd gone to sleep.'

She wriggled an arm free from the blankets and gently touched the side of my neck.

'It's colouring already,' she whispered. 'It's going to be a huge ugly bruise. And it's bleeding.' I reached up with my handkerchief and she wasn't making any mistake: I stuffed my handkerchief into my collar and left it there. She went on in the same little voice: 'How did it happen?'

'One of those stupid things. I slipped on the snow and struck my neck on the storm-sill of the door. Does ache a bit, I must say.'

She didn't answer. She freed her other arm, caught me by both lapels, stared at me with a face full of misery and put her forehead on my shoulder. Now it was my collar's turn to become damp. It was the most extraordinary behaviour for a wardress—that her function was to keep tabs on and effectively immobilize me I was increasingly sure—but then, she was the most extraordinary wardress I'd ever come across. And the nicest. Dr Marlowe, I said, the lady is in distress and you are but human. I let my suspicions take five and stroked the tangled yellow hair. I'd been led to believe, I forget by what or by whom, that nothing was as conducive to the calming of upset feminine feelings as that soothing gesture: only seconds later I was wondering where I'd picked up this piece of obviously blatant misinformation for she suddenly pushed herself upright and struck me twice on the shoulder with the base of her clenched left fist. I was more than ever convinced that she wasn't made of swansdown.

'Don't do that,' she said. 'Don't *do* that.'

'All right,' I said agreeably. 'I won't do that. I'm sorry.'

'No, no, please! *I'm* sorry. I don't know what made me— I really—' She stopped speaking, although her lips kept on moving, and stared at me with tear-filled eyes, the no longer beautiful face defenceless and defeated and full of despair: it made me feel acutely uncomfortable for I do not like to see proud and self-contained people thus reduced. There was a quick indrawing of breath, then, astonishingly, she had her arms wound round my neck and so tightly that it would appear that she was bent upon my instant asphyxiation. She wept in silence, her shoulders shaking.

Splendidly done, I thought approvingly, quite splendidly done. Irrespective of for whose benefit it might be—and then I despised myself for my cynicism. Quite apart from the fact that her acknowledged limitations as an actress put such a performance out of the question I was convinced, without knowing why I was convinced, that what I was seeing was genuine uninhibited emotion. And what on earth had she to gain by pretending to lower her defences in front of me?

For whom, then, the tears? Not for me, of that I was certain, why in the world for me? I scarcely knew her, she scarcely knew me, I was only a shoulder to cry on, likely enough I was only a doctor's shoulder to cry on, people have the oddest misconceptions about doctors and maybe their shoulders are regarded as being more reliable and comforting than the average. Or more absorbent. Nor were the tears for herself, I was equally certain of that, to survive, intact, the kind of upbringing she'd hinted she'd had, one had to be possessed of an unusual degree of self-reliance and mental toughness that almost automatically excluded considerations of self-pity. So for whom, then, the tears?

I didn't know and, at that moment, I hardly cared. In normal circumstances and with no other matter so significantly important as to engage my attention, so lovely a girl in such obvious distress would have had my complete and undivided concern, but the circumstances were abnormal and my thoughts were elsewhere engaged with an intensity that made Mary Stuart's odd behaviour seem relatively unimportant.

I couldn't keep my eyes from the bottle of scotch by the captain's table. When Halliday had had, at my insistence as I now bitterly recalled, his first drink, the bottle had been about a third full: after his second drink it had been about a quarter full: and now it was half full. The quiet and violent man who had so recently switched off the lights and moved through the saloon had switched bottles and, for good measure, had removed the glass that Halliday had used.

Mary Stuart said something, her voice so muffled and indistinct that I couldn't make it out: what with salt tears and salt blood this night's work was going to cost me a new shirt. I said: 'What?'

She moved her head, enough to enable her to speak more clearly, but not enough to let me see her face.

'I'm sorry. I'm sorry I was such a fool. Will you forgive me?'

I squeezed her shoulder in what was more or less an automatic gesture, my eyes and my thoughts were still on that bottle, but she seemed to take it as sufficient answer. She said hesitantly: 'Are you going to sleep again?' She hadn't stopped being as foolish as she thought: or perhaps she wasn't being foolish at all.

'No, Mary dear, I'm not going to sleep again.' Whatever tone of firm resolution my tone carried, it was superfluous: the throbbing pain in my neck was sufficient guarantee of my wakefulness.

'Well, that's all right then.' I didn't ask what this cryptic remark was intended to convey. Physically, we couldn't have been closer but mentally I was no longer with her. I was with Halliday, the man whom I had thought had come to kill me, the man I'd practically forced to have a drink, the man who'd drunk what had been intended for me.

I knew I would never see him again. Not alive,

CHAPTER SIX

Dawn, in those high latitudes and at that time of year, did not come until half-past ten in the morning, and it was then that we buried the three dead men, Antonio and Moxen and Scott, and surely their shades would have forgiven us for the almost indecent dispatch with which their funerals were carried out, for that driving blizzard was still at its height, the wind was full of razored knives and struck through both clothes and flesh and laid its icy fingers on the marrow. Captain Imrie, a large and brass-bound Bible in his mittened hands, read swiftly through the burial service, or at least I assumed he did, he could have been reading the Sermon on the Mount for all I could tell, the wind just plucked the inaudible words from his mouth and carried them out over the grey-white desolation of waters. Three times a canvas-wrapped bundle slid smoothly out from beneath the *Morning Rose*'s only Union Flag, three times a bundle vanished soundlessly beneath the surface of the sea: we could see the splashes but not hear them for our ears were full of the high and lonely lament of the wind's requiem in the frozen rigging.

On land, mourners customarily find it difficult to tear themselves away from a newly-filled grave, but here there was no grave, there was nothing to look at and the bitter cold was sufficient to drive from every mind any thought other than that of immediate shelter and warmth: besides, Captain Imrie had said that it was an old fisherman's custom to drink a toast to the dead. Whether it was or not I had no idea, it could well have been a custom that Imrie had invented himself, and certainly the deceased had been no fishermen: but whatever its origin I'm sure that it made its contributory effect towards the extremely rapid clearing of the decks.

I remained where I was. I felt inhibited from joining the others not because I found Captain Imrie's proposal distasteful or ethically objectionable—only the most hypocritical could find in the Christian ethic a bar to wishing *bon voyage* to the departed—but because, in crowded surroundings, it

115

could be very difficult to see who was filling my glass and what he was filling it with. Moreover, I'd had no more than three hours' sleep the previous night, my mind was tired and a bit fuzzy round the edges and it was my hope that the admittedly heroic treatment of exposure to an Arctic blizzard might help to blow some of the cobwebs away. I took a firm hold on one of the numerous lifelines that were rigged on deck, edged my way out to the largest of one of the numerous deck cargoes we were carrying, took what illusory shelter was offered in its lee and waited for the cobwebs to fly away.

Halliday was dead. I hadn't found his body, I'd searched, casually and unobtrusively, every likely and most of the unlikely places of concealment on the *Morning Rose*: he had vanished and left no trace. Halliday, I knew, was lying in the black depths of the Barents Sea. How he'd got there I didn't know and it didn't seem to be important: it could be that someone had helped him over the side but it was even more probable that he had required no assistance. He'd left the saloon as abruptly as he had because the poison in his scotch—my scotch—had been as fast acting as it had been deadly. He had felt the urgent need to be sick and the obvious place to be sick was over the side: a slip on the snow or ice, one of the hundreds of trough-seeking lurches that the trawler had experienced during the night and in what must have been by that time his ill, weakened and dazed state, and he would have been quite unable to prevent himself from pitching over the low guard-rails. The only consolation, if consolation it was, was that he had probably succumbed to poison before his lungs had filled with water. I did not subscribe to the popular belief that death from drowning was a relatively easy and painless way to go, if for no other reason than that it was a theory that in the nature of things lacked positive documentation.

I was as certain as could be that Halliday's absence had so far gone unnoticed by everyone except myself and the person responsible for his death, and there was not even certainty about that last point, it was quite possible that he knew nothing of Halliday's brief visit to the saloon. True, Halliday had not appeared for breakfast but as a few others had done the same and those who had come had done so intermittently over the best part of a couple of hours, his

116

absence had gone unremarked. His cabin-mate, Sandy, was still feeling under the weather to the extent that Halliday's presence or absence was a matter of total indifference to him: and as Halliday had been very much a solitary there was no one who would be sufficiently concerned to inquire anxiously as to his whereabouts. I hoped that his absence remained undiscovered as long as possible: although the signed guarantee given to Captain Imrie that morning had contained no specific reference as to the action to be taken in the event of someone going missing, he was quite capable of seizing upon this as a pretext to abandon the trip and make with all speed for Hammerfest.

The match I'd left jammed between the foot of my cabin door and the sill had no longer been in position when I'd returned to my cabin early in the morning. The coins I'd left in the linen pockets of the lids of my suitcases had shifted position from the front to the back of the pockets, sure evidence that my cases had been opened in my absence. It says much for my frame of mind that the discovery occasioned me no particular surprise—which was in itself surprising, for although someone aboard was aware that the good doctor had been boning up on *aconitine* and so had more than a fair idea that the poisoning had not been accidental, that in itself was hardly reason to start examining the doctor's hand luggage. More than ever, it behooved me to watch my back.

I heard a sound behind my back. My instinctive reaction was to take a couple of rapid steps forward, who knew what hard or sharp implement might be coming at my occiput or shoulder-blades, then whirl round, but a simultaneous reasoning told me that it was unlikely that anyone would propose to do me in on the upper deck in daylight under the interested gaze of watchers on the bridge, so I turned round leisurely and saw Charles Conrad moving into what little shelter was offered in the lee of the bulk deck cargo.

'What's this, then?' I said. 'The morning constitutional at all costs? Or don't you fancy Captain Imrie's scotch?'

'Neither.' He smiled. 'Curiosity is all.' He tapped the tarpaulin-covered bulk beside us. It was close on ten feet in height, semi-cylindrical—the base was flat—and was lashed in position by at least a dozen steel cables. 'Do you know what this is?'

'Is this a clever question?'

'Yes.'

'Prefabricated Articized huts. Or so the word went in Wick. Six of them, designed to fit one inside the other for ease of transportation.'

'That's it. Made of bonded ply, kapok insulation, asbestos and aluminium.' He pointed to another bulky item of deck cargo immediately for'ard of the one behind which we were sheltering. This peculiarly shaped object appeared to be roughly oval along its length, perhaps six feet high. 'And this?'

'Another clever question?'

'Of course.'

'And my answer will be wrong? Again?'

'If you still believe what you were told in Wick, yes. Those aren't huts because we don't need huts. We're heading for an area called the Sor-hamna—the South Haven—where there already *are* huts, and perfectly usable ones. Bloke called Lerner came there seventy years ago, prospecting for coal—which he found, by the way: a bit of an odd-ball who painted the rocks on the shore in the German colours to indicate that this was private property. He built huts—he even built a road across the headland to the nearest bay, the Kvalross Bukta or Walrus Bay. After him a German fishing company based themselves here—and *they* built huts. More importantly, a Norwegian scientific expedition spent nine months here during the most recent International Geophysical Year—and *they* built huts. Whatever else is lacking at South Haven it's not accommodation.'

'You're very well informed.'

'I don't forget something that I finished reading only half an hour ago. Comin' and Goin's been making the rounds this morning handing out copies of the prospectus of what's going to be the greatest film ever made. Didn't you get one from him?'

'Yes. He forgot to give me a dictionary, though.'

'A dictionary would have helped.' He tapped the tarpaulin beside us. 'This is a mock-up of the central section of a submarine—just a shell, nothing inside it. When I say it's a mock-up, I don't mean it's made of cardboard—it's made of steel and weighs ten tons, including four tons of cast-iron ballast. That other item in front is a conning-tower which is to be bolted on to this once it's in the water.'

'Ah!' I said because I couldn't think of any other comment. 'And those alleged tractors and drums of fuel on the after deck—they'll be tanks and anti-aircraft guns?'

'Tractors and fuel, as stated.' He paused. 'Do you know there's only one copy of the screen-play for this film and that's locked up in the Bank of England or some such?'

'I went to sleep about that bit.'

'They haven't even got a shooting script for the scenes to be shot on the island. Just a series of unrelated incidents which, taken together, make no sense at all. Sure, there must be connecting links to make sense of it all: but they're all in the vaults in Threadneedle Street or whatever this damned bank is. No part of it makes sense.'

'Maybe it's not meant to make sense.' I was conscious that my feet were slowly turning into blocks of ice. 'Not at this stage. There may be excellent reasons for the secretiveness. Besides, don't some producers encourage directors who play it off the cuff, who improvise as they go along and as the mood takes them?'

'Not Neal Divine. He's never shot an off-the-cuff scene in his life.' Not much of Conrad's forehead was to be seen beneath the thick brown hair that the snow and wind had brought down almost to eyebrow level, but what little was visible was very heavily corrugated indeed. 'If a Divine shooting script calls for you to be wearing a bowler hat and doing the can-can in Scene 289, then you're doing a bowler-hatted can-can in 289. As for Otto, he never moves until everything's calculated out to the last matchstick and the last penny. Especially the last penny.

'He has the reputation for being careful.'

'Careful!' Conrad shivered. 'Doesn't the whole set-up strike you as being crazy.'

'The entire film world,' I said candidly, 'strikes me as being crazy, but as an ordinary human being exposed to it for the first time I wouldn't know whether this current particular brand of craziness differs from the norm or not. What do your fellow actors think of it?'

'What fellow actors?' Conrad said glumly. 'Judith Haynes is still closeted with those two pooches of hers. Mary Stuart is writing letters in her cabin, at least she says it's letters, it's probably her last will and testament. And if Gunther Jungbeck and Jon Heyter have any opinion on everything they're carefully keeping it to themselves. Anyway, *they* are a couple of odd-balls themselves.'

'Even for actors?'

'Touché.' He smiled, but he wasn't trying too hard. 'Sea burials bring out the misanthrope in me. No, it's just that they know so little about the film world, at least the British film world, understandable enough I suppose, Heyter's done all his acting in California, Jungbeck in Germany. They're not odd, really, it's just that we have nothing in common to talk about, no points of reference.'

'But you must know of them?'

'Not even that, but that's not surprising. I like acting but the film world bores me to tears and I don't mix socially. That makes me an odd-ball too. But Otto vouches for them —in fact, he speaks pretty highly of them, and that's good enough for me. They'll both probably act me off the screen when it comes to the bit.' He shivered again. 'Conrad's curiosity remains unsatisfied, but Conrad has had enough. As a doctor, wouldn't you prescribe some of this scotch which old Imrie is supposed to be dispensing so liberally?'

We found Captain Imrie dispensing the scotch with so heavy a hand that plainly it came from his own private supplies and not from Otto's, for Otto, heavily wrapped in a coloured blanket and with his puce complexion still a pale shadow of its former self, was sitting in his accustomed dining chair and raising no objections that I could see. There must have been at least twenty people present, ship's crew and passengers, and they were very far indeed from being a merry throng. I was surprised to see Judith Haynes there, with her husband, Michael Stryker, hovering attentively over her. I was surprised to see Mary darling there, her sense of duty or what was the done thing must have been greater than her aversion to alcohol, and was even more surprised to note that she had so abandoned all sense of the proprieties as to be holding young Allen by the arm in a positively proprietorial fashion: I was not surprised to see that Mary Stuart was absent. So were Heissman and Sandy. The two actors with whom Conrad claimed to have so little in common, Jungbeck and Heyter, were together in one corner and for the first time I looked at them with some degree of real interest. They *looked* like actors, no question of that, or, more accurately, they looked like what I thought actors ought to look like. Heyter was tall, fair, good-looking, young and twenty years ago would have been referred to as clean-cut: he had a mobile, expressive, animated face. Jungbeck was at least fifteen years his senior, a thick-set man with heavy shoulders, a five o'clock shadow and dark, curling hair just beginning to grey: he had a ready, engaging smile. He was cast, I knew, as the villain in the forthcoming production and despite the appropriate build and blue jowls didn't look the least bit like one.

The almost complete silence in the saloon, I soon realized, didn't stem entirely from the solemnity of the occasion, although that element must have been there: Captain Imrie had been holding the floor and had only broken off to acknowledge our entrance and to take the opportunity of dispensing some more liquor, which I refused. And now, it was clear, Captain Imrie was taking up where he had left off.

'Aye,' he said heavily, ''tis fitting, 'tis fitting. They have gone today, sadly, tragically gone, three of Britain's sons—' I was almost glad, for the moment, that Antonio was no longer around—'but it comes to us all, sooner or later the hour strikes, and if they must rest where better to lie than in those honoured waters of Bear Island where ten thousand of their countrymen sleep?' I wondered, uncharitably, what hour struck when Captain Imrie poured himself his first restorative of the morning but then recalled that as he had been up since 4 a.m. he was no doubt now rightly regarding the day as being pretty far advanced, a supposition which he proceeded to prove correct by replenishing his glass without, however, interrupting the smooth flow of his monologue. His audience, I noted with regret, had about them the look of men and women who wished themselves elsewhere.

'I wonder what Bear Island means to you people,' he went on. 'Nothing, I suppose, why should it? It's just a name, Bear Island, just a name. Like the Isle of Wight or what's yon place in America, Coney Island: just a name. But for people like Mr Stokes here and myself and thousands of others it's a wee bit more than that. It was a kind of turning-point, a dividing point in our lives, what those geography or geology fellows would call a watershed: when we came to know the name we knew that no name had ever meant so much to us before—and no name would ever mean so

121

much again. And we knew that nothing would ever be the same again. Bear Island was the place where boys grew up, just over the night, as it were: Bear Island was the place where middle-aged men like myself grew old.' This was a different Captain Imrie speaking now, quietly reminiscent, sad without bitterness, and the captive audience was now voluntarily so, no longer glancing longingly at the saloon exits.

'We called it "the Gate",' he went on. 'The gate to the Barents Sea and the White Sea and those places in Russia where we took those convoys through all the long years of the war, all those long years ago. If you passed the Gate and came back again, you were a lucky man: if you did it half-a-dozen times you'd used up all your luck for a lifetime. How many times did we pass the Gate, Mr Stokes?'

'Twenty-two times.' For once, Mr Stokes had no need for deliberation.

'Twenty-two times. I am not saying it because I was there but people on those convoys to Murmansk suffered more terribly than people have ever suffered in war before or will ever suffer in war again, and it was here, in those waters, at the Gate, that they suffered most of all, for it was here that the enemy waited by night and by day and it was here that the enemy struck us down. The fine ships and the fine boys, our boys and the German boys, more of them lie in those waters than anywhere in the world, but the waters run clean now and the blood is washed away. But not in our minds, not in our minds: thirty years have passed now and I cannot hear the words "Bear Island", not even when I say them myself, but my blood runs cold. The graveyard of the Arctic and we hope they are at peace now, but still my blood runs cold.' He shivered, as if he felt a physical chill, then smiled slightly. 'The old talk too much, a blether talks too much, so you know now how terrible it is to have an old blether stand before you. All I'd really meant to say is that our shipmates are in good company.' He raised his glass. '*Bon voyage.*'

Bon voyage. But not the last goodbye, not the last time we would be saying goodbye, I felt it deep in my bones and I knew that Captain Imrie felt it also. I knew that it was some sort of fore-knowledge or premonition that had made him talk as he had done, that had been responsible for a rambling reminiscence as uncalled for as it was irrelevant—or appeared to be. I wondered if Captain Imrie was even dimly aware of this thought transference process, of the substitution of the fearful things, the dreadful things of long ago for the unrealized awareness that such things were not confined to the actions of overt warfare, that violent death acknowledged no restrictions in time and space, that the bleak and barren waters of the Barents Sea were its habitat and its home.

I wondered how many others of those present felt this atavistic fear, this oddly nameless dread so often encountered in the loneliest and most desolate places on earth, a dread that reaches back over the aeons to primitive man who as yet knew not fire, to those unthinkably distant ancestors who crouched in terror in their lightless caves while the forces of evil and darkness walked abroad in the night: a fear that, here and now, was all too readily reinforced and compounded by the sudden, violent and inexplicable deaths of three of their company the previous night.

It was hard to tell, I thought, just who was feeling affected by such primeval stirrings of foreboding, for mankind does not readily acknowledge even to itself, far less show or discuss, the existence of such irrationally childlike superstitions. Captain Imrie and Mr Stokes, without a doubt: they had gone into a corner by themselves and were staring down, unseeingly, I was sure, and certainly without speaking, at the glasses in their hands, and as the two of them rarely if ever sat together without discussing, at great length, matters of the gravest import, this was highly significant in itself. Neal Divine, more hollow-cheeked than ever but apparently slightly recovered from his very low state of the previous evening, sat by himself, continuously twirling the empty glass in his hand, his usual nervous preoccupied self, but whether he was preoccupied with *mal de mer,* the thought that he was about to begin his directorial duties and so consequently be exposed to the lash of Gerran's tongue or whether he, too, was feeling fingers from the dead past reach deep into him was impossible to say.

Comin' and Goin' was seated by Otto at the head of the table and they, too, were silent. I wondered just what the relationship between the two men was. They seemed to be on cordial enough terms but they only sought each other out, I had observed, when questions of business were to be discussed. It could well have been that, personally, they had little in common, but the fact that Comin' and Goin' had recently been made Vice-President and heir-apparent to Olympus Productions seemed to speak highly enough of Otto's regard for him. And as they were together now and not talking I assumed that they were pondering over matters similar to those that were engaging the attention of Imrie and myself.

The Three Apostles weren't talking, but that meant nothing, when they were deprived of their instruments, their music magazines and their garishly primary-coloured comics, the presence of all of which they had probably deemed as being inappropriate in the present circumstances, they were habitually bereft of speech. Stryker, still in solicitously close attendance upon his wife, was talking quietly to the Count, while the Duke was conspicuously not talking to his cabin-mate Eddie, but as they were rarely on speaking terms anyway, this was hardly significant. I became aware that Lonnie Gilbert was at my elbow and I wondered what degree, if any, of the underlying significance of Captain Imrie's words had penetrated his befuddled mind. Lonnie was clutching a glass of scotch, both container and contents of genuine family size, a marked contrast to the relatively small portions he'd been pouring himself in the lounge bar about midnight: I could only assume that somewhere in the remoter recesses of Lonnie's mind there lurked some vestigial traces of conscience which permitted him only modest amounts of hooch not honestly come by.

'"Envy and calumny and hate and pain, and that unrest which men miscall delight shall touch them not and torture not again,"' Lonnie intoned. He tilted his glass, lowered the liquid level by two fingers and smacked his lips. '"From the contagion—"'

'Lonnie.' I nodded at the glass. 'When did you start this morning?'

'Start? My dear fellow, I never stopped. A sleepless night. "From the contagion of the world's slow stain they are secure, and now can never mourn the heart grown cold, the head grown grey—"'

Aware that he had lost his audience, Lonnie broke off and followed my line of sight. Mary darling and Allen, proprieties observed, were leaving. Mary hesitated, stopped in front of Judith Haynes's chair, smiled and said: 'Good morning, Miss Haynes. I hope you're feeling better today?'

Judith Haynes smiled, a fractionally glimpsed set of perfect teeth, then looked away: a false smile meant to be seen and understood as a false smile, followed by a complete and contemptuous dismissal. I saw colour stain Mary darling's cheeks and she made as if to speak, but Allen, his lips tight, took her arm and urged her gently towards the lee door.

'Well, well,' I said. 'I wonder what all that was about. A clearly offended Miss Haynes but I can't conceive of our little Mary giving offence to anybody.'

'But she has done, my boy, she has done. Our Judith is one of those sad and unfortunate females who can't abide any other female who is younger, better-looking or more intelligent than she is. Our little Mary offends on at least two of those counts.'

'You disappoint me,' I said. 'Here I was, manfully trying to discount—or at least ignore—what appears to be the universally held opinion that Judith Haynes is a complete and utter bitch and now—'

'And you were right.' Lonnie regarded his empty glass with an expression of faint astonishment. 'She isn't a bitch, at least she doesn't make a career out of it, except inadvertently. To those who offer no threat or competition, little children or pets, she is capable of generous impulses, even affection. But that apart, a poor, poor creature, incapable of loving or inspiring love in others, to wit and in short, a loveless soul, perverse but pitiable, a person who having once seen herself and not liking what she has seen, turns away from reality and takes refuge in misanthropic fantasy.' Lonnie executed a swift sideways scuttle in the direction of an unattended scotch bottle, replenished his glass with the speed and expertise born of a lifetime of practice, returned happily and warmed to his theme.

'Sick, sick, sick, and it is the sick, not the whole, who require our help and sympathy.' Lonnie could, on occasion, sound very pontifical indeed. 'She's one of the hapless band of the world's willing walking wounded—how's that, four w's and never a stutter—who takes a positive delight in being hurt, in being affronted, and if the hurt is not really there, why, then, all the better, they can imagine one even closer to the heart's desire. For those unfortunates who love only themselves the loving embrace of self-pity, close hugged like an old and dear friend, is the supreme, the most precious luxury in life. I can assure you, my dear fellow, that no hippo ever wallowed in his African mud-bath with half the relish—'

'I'm sure you're right, Lonnie,' I said, 'and a very apt analogy that is, too.' I wasn't listening to him any more, my attention had been caught and held by the fleeting glimpse I'd had of a figure hurrying by on the deck outside. Heissman, I was almost sure it was Heissman, and if it were I'd three immediate questions that asked for equally immediate answers. Heissman was rarely observed to move at any but the most deliberate and leisurely speed so why the uncharacteristic haste? Why, if he were moving aft, did he choose the weather instead of the lee side of the superstructure unless he hoped to avoid being observed through the large snow-obscured windows on the weather side of the saloon? And what, in view of his well-known and almost pathological aversion to cold—an inevitable legacy, one supposed, of his long years in Siberia—was he doing on the upper deck anyway? I clapped Lonnie on the shoulder. 'Back, as the saying goes, in a trice. I have to visit the sick.'

I left, not hurriedly, through the lee door, then paused to see if anyone was interested enough in my departure to follow me out. And someone did follow me, almost immediately, but if he had any interest in my movements he wasn't letting me see it. Gunther Jungbeck smiled at me briefly, indifferently, and hurried forward to the entrance to the passenger accommodation. I waited a few more seconds, then climbed up the vertical steel ladder to the boat deck, immediately abaft the bridge and radio office.

I circled the funnel and engine intake fans casing and found no one there. I hadn't expected to, even a polar bear wouldn't have hung around that bitter and totally exposed boat deck without a very compelling reason. I moved aft by one of our two motorized lifeboats, took what illusory shelter I could find beside a ventilator and peered out over the after-deck.

For the first few moments I could see nothing, nothing, that was, that was likely to be of any interest to me, not so much because of the driving snow as the fact that all objects crowding the after-deck—and there were well over a score of them, ranging from fuel drums to a sixteen-foot work-boat on a special cradle—were so deeply shrouded in their shapeless cocoons of snow that, in most cases, it was virtually impossible to decide upon not only their identity but whether they were inanimate or not. Not until any of them might move.

One of the cocoons stirred, a slender ghostly form detaching itself from the shelter of a square bulky object which I knew to be the cabin for a Sno-Cat. The figure half-turned in my direction and although the face was almost entirely hidden by a hand that held both sides of the parka hood closed against the snow, enough of straw-coloured hair showed to let me identify the only person aboard with that colour of hair. Almost at once she was joined by a person moving into my line of vision from behind the break of the boat deck and I didn't even have to see the thin ascetic face to know that this was Heissman.

He approached the girl directly, took her arm without, as far as I could see, any kind of opposition being offered, and said something to her. I sank to my knees, partly to reduce the risk of detection if either chanced to look up, partly to try and make out what was being said. The concealment part worked but the eavesdropping failed, partly because the wind was in the wrong direction but chiefly because they had their heads very close together either because they regarded suitably low and conspiratorial conversation as being appropriate to the occasion or because they were affording each other's faces protection from the snow. I inched forward to the very end of the boat deck and squatted back on my heels with my head bent forward but this was of no help either.

Heissman now had an arm around Mary Stuart's shoulders and this time the gesture of intimacy did produce a reaction although scarcely the expected one for she reached up an arm around his neck and put her head on his shoulder. At least another two minutes were spent in this highly confidential tête-à-tête, then they walked slowly away towards the living accommodation, Heissman still with his arm around the girl's shoulders. I made no move to follow them, for such a move would not only have almost certainly resulted in quick detection but it would have been pointless: whatever personal they'd had to say had already been said.

'Yoga in the Barents Sea,' a voice said behind me. 'That's

127

dedication for you.'

'Fanatics always carry everything to excess,' I said. I rose awkwardly but without too much haste before turning round for I knew I had nothing to fear from Smithy. Clad in a hooded duffel-coat and looking a great deal fitter than he had been doing just before midnight, he was looking at me with what might have been an expression of quizzical amusement except that his eyes didn't seem to find anything humorous in what they saw. 'You have to be regular in these things,' I explained.

'Of course.' He walked past me, looked over the boat deck guard-rail and examined the deep tracks left in the snow by Mary and Heissman. 'Bird-watching?'

'The haunts of coot and hern.'

'Yes, indeed. But an oddly assorted pair of love-birds, wouldn't you say?'

'It's this film world, Smithy. It seems to be full of very oddly assorted birds.'

'Odd birds, period.' He nodded for'ard, towards the chart-house. 'Warmth and cheer, Doc, just the place for some more ornithological research.'

There wasn't a great deal of warmth owing to the fact that Smithy had left the side door open after he'd looked out through the window and observed me moving cautiously along the boat deck but there was a certain amount of cheer in the shape of a bottle he produced from a cupboard. He said: 'Shall we send for the king's taster?'

I looked at the unbroken lead seal. 'Not unless you think someone has brought his own bottling plant aboard.'

'I've checked.' Smithy broke the seal. 'We talked last night. At least, I did. You may or may not have listened. I was worried last night. I thought you might not be levelling with me. I'm worried stiff now. Because I know you're not.'

'Because I've taken up ornithology?' I said mildly.

'That among other things. This wholesome poisoning, now. I've had time to think, just a bit. Of course you couldn't have had any idea who the poisoner was—it's hardly conceivable that if you knew the person who had done in that Italian boy that you'd have let him do the same to six others, two of whom were to die. In fact you couldn't even have been sure that the whole thing wasn't accidental, the poisoning was on so apparently haphazard a basis.'

'Thank you kindly,' I said. My opinion of Smithy had fallen sharply. 'Except that it wasn't on an apparently haphazard basis. It *was* haphazard.'

'That was last night.' It was as if he hadn't heard me. 'Then you couldn't have had any idea. Now you can. Things have happened, haven't they?'

'What things?' My opinion of Smithy had risen sharply. He was sure that there was mayhem afoot, but why? Was he making a mental short list, guessing as to who might be the handy lad with the aconite—not that he could possibly know the poison used was aconite—wondering where he had got it, where he kept it now, where he had learned to prepare it so skilfully that it could indetectably be introduced into food? And not only who was the poisoner but *why* was the poisoner acting as he did? And why the random nature of the poisoning? Was he basing his guesses just on my stealthy behaviour?

'Lots of things, not all of which have necessarily lately happened, just things that have come to light or seem odd in view of what we might call recent developments. For instance, why have Captain Imrie and Mr Stokes been chosen for the job instead of any two young and efficient yacht and charter skippers and engineers who usually find themselves unemployed at this time of year? Because they're so old and so soaked in scotch and rum that they can't tell the time of day twenty hours out of the twenty-four. They just don't see what goes on and even if they were to they'd probably attach no significance to it anyway.'

I didn't put down my glass, look keenly at Smithy or in any other way indicate that I was listening with undivided attention. But I was. This thought had never occurred to me.

Smithy continued. 'I said last night that I thought the presence of Mr Gerran and his company up here at this time in the year was a bit odd. I don't think so any more. I think it's damned peculiar and calls for some sort of rational explanation from your friend Otto, which we're not likely to get.'

'He's not my friend,' I said.

'And this.' He pulled out a copy of the Olympus Productions manifesto. 'A load of meaningless rubbish that old smoothie Goin has been inflicting on everybody in sight. Have you—'

'Goin? A smoothie?'

'An untrustworthy, time-serving, money-grubbing smoothie

with his two hands never on speaking terms, and I'd say that even if he weren't a professional accountant.'

'Maybe he'd better not be my friend either,' I said.

'All this ridiculous secrecy they harp on in this clap-trap. To protect the importance of their damned screen-play. A hundred gets one it's a screen to protect something an awful lot more important than their screen-play. Another hundred gets one that there's no screen-play in the bank vaults they speak of for the reason that there is no screen-play. And their shooting schedule for Bear Island. Have you read that? It's not even comic. Just a lot of unrelated incidents about caves, and mysterious motor-boats and shooting dummy submarines and climbing cliffs and falling into the sea and dying in Arctic snows that any five-year-old could have dreamed up.'

'You've got a very suspicious mind, Smithy,' I said.

'Have I not? And this young Polish actress, the blonde one—'

'Latvian. Mary Stuart. What of her?'

'A strange one. Aloof and alone. Never mixes. But when there's illness on the bridge, or in Otto's cabin or in the cabin of that young lad they call the Duke, who's there? Who but our friend Mary Stuart.'

'She's a kind of Samaritan. Would you be so conspicuous if you wanted to avoid attention?'

'Might be the very best way to achieve it. But if that's not the case, why make a point of being so damned inconspicuous just now when meeting Heissman in a blizzard on the after-deck?'

I would very much rather, I thought, have Smith for me than against me. I said: 'A romantic assignation, perhaps?'

'With *Heissman*?'

'You're not a girl, Smithy.'

'No.' He grinned briefly. 'But I've met 'em. Why are all the big nobs on the management side so pally with Otto in public and so critical in private? Why is a cameraman a director? Why—'

'How did you know that?'

'Uh-huh. So you knew too. Because Captain Imrie showed me this guarantee thing that you and the directors of Olympus had signed: the Count had signed as one of them. Why is the director, this Divine fellow who is supposed to be so good at his job, so scared of Otto, while Lonnie, who is not only a permanent alcoholic layabout but latches on to Otto's private hooch supplies with impunity, doesn't give a damn about him?'

'Tell me, Smithy,' I said, 'just how much time have you been devoting lately to steering and navigating this boat?'

'Hard to say. Just about as much time, I would say, as you have been to the practice of medicine.'

I didn't say 'Touché' or anything like that, I just let Smithy pour some more of the aconite-free drink into my glass and looked out of the window at the grey swirling icy world beyond. So many whys, Smithy, so many whys. Why had Mary been foregathering clandestinely with Heissman when the Heissman I'd observed last night had been so clearly unwell as to be unable to indulge in any skullduggery—not that this ruled out the chilling possibility that Heissman might be one of two or more who held life so lightly and might easily be either a principal or a go-between. Why had Otto, though himself a poisoning victim, reacted so violently—including having been violently ill—when he'd heard that Antonio had been a poisoning victim? Had Cecil's larder raid been as innocuous as he had claimed? Had Sandy's? Who had checked on the *aconitine* article, disposed of the left-overs in the galley, been in my cabin during the night and searched my baggage? Why had he searched my baggage—this extremely active poisoner, the same man, perhaps, who had doctored the scotch bottle, clobbered me and been responsible for Halliday's death? Again, was there more than one of them? And if Halliday had died accidentally, as I was sure he had, then why had he come to the saloon, where his visit, I was equally sure, had not been accidental?

It was all so full of 'ifs' and 'buts' that I was beginning to clutch at ridiculous straws rather than fight my way through the impenetrable fog. What accounted for Lonnie's diatribe—for it had amounted to no less—against Judith Haynes to the effect that she detested all mankind, especially when they were womankind? No doubt Miss Haynes was as capable of being catty and jealous as many other otherwise likeable females are, but one would have thought that she had too much going for her in the way of wealth, success, fame, position and looks to have to bother too much about despising every woman she met. But if that were so, why had she cold-shouldered Mary darling?

But what could that have to do with murder? I didn't know, but nothing the slightest bit odd, I thought gloomily, could be dismissed out of hand as having nothing to do with the very odd goings-on aboard the *Morning Rose*. Were Jungbeck and Heyter, for instance, to be considered as being possibly under suspicion because one had recently followed me from the saloon—especially as Conrad had earlier thrown a degree of suspicion on them by disclaiming all knowledge of them as actors? Or did this factor of apparently throwing suspicion bring Conrad himself under just the tiniest cloud? Dammit to hell, I thought wearily, if I keep on thinking like this I'll be casting young Allen as the master poisoner just because he'd told me that he'd once studied chemistry, briefly, at university.

'A penny for your thoughts, Dr Marlowe.' Smithy wasn't very much of a one for letting his face act as a front man for his mind.

'Don't throw your money away. What thoughts?'

'Two thoughts. Two kinds of thoughts. All the thoughts you're having about all the things you're not telling me and all the guilty thoughts you're having about not telling me them.'

'It's like a rule of nature,' I said. 'Some people are always more liable to have injustices done to them than others.'

'So you've told me all your thoughts?'

'No. But the ones I haven't told aren't worth the telling. Now, if I had some facts—'

'So you admit something is pretty far wrong?'

'Of course.'

'And you've told me everything you know, just not everything you think?'

'Of course.'

'I speak in sorrow,' Smithy said, 'for my lost illusions about the medical profession.' He reached up under the hood of my parka, pulled down the scarf around my neck and stared at what was by now the great multi-coloured and blood-encrusted weal on my neck. 'Jesus! That is something. What happened to you?'

'I fell.'

'The Marlowes of this world don't fall. They're pushed. Where did you fall?' I didn't much care for the all but imper-

132

ceptible accent on the word 'fall'.

'Upper deck. Port side. I struck my neck on the storm-sill of the saloon door.'

'Did you now? I would say that this was caused by what the criminologists call a solid object. A very solid object about half-an-inch wide and sharp-edged. The saloon door sill is three inches wide and made of sorbo-rubber. All the storm doors on the *Morning Rose* are—it's to make them totally windproof and waterproof. Or perhaps you hadn't noticed? The way you perhaps haven't noticed that John Halliday, the unit's still photographer, is missing?'

'How do you know?' He'd shaken me this time, not just a little, or my face would have shown it, but so much that I knew my features stayed rigidly fixed in the same expression.

'You don't deny it?'

'I don't know. How do you?'

'I went down to see the props man, this elderly lad they call Sandy. I'd heard he was sick and—'

'Why did you go?'

'If it matters, because he's not the sort of person that people visit very much. He doesn't seem liked. Seems a bit hard to be sick *and* unpopular at the same time.' I nodded, this would be in character with Smithy. 'I asked him where his room-mate Halliday was as I hadn't seen him at breakfast. Sandy said he'd gone for breakfast. I didn't say anything to Sandy but this made me a bit curious so I had a look in the recreation room. He wasn't there either, so I got curiouser until I'd searched the *Morning Rose* twice from end to end. I think I covered every nook and cranny in the vessel where even a stray seagull could be hiding and you can take my word for it. Halliday's not in the *Morning Rose*.'

'Reported this to the captain?'

'Well, well, what an awful lot of reaction. No, I haven't reported it to the captain.'

'Why not?'

'Same reason as you haven't. If I know my Captain Imrie, he'd at once declare that there was no clause in that agreement you signed that was binding on this particular case, that saying that foul play wasn't involved in this case also would be altogether too much of a good thing, and turn the *Morning Rose* straight for Hammerfest.' Smithy looked at me dead-pan over the rim of his glass. 'I'm rather curious to see what does happen when we get to Bear Island.'

'It might be interesting.'

'Very non-committal. It might, says he thoughtfully, be equally interesting to provoke some kind of reaction in Dr Marlowe. Just once. Just for the record—my own private record. I wonder if I could do it. Do you remember I said on the bridge in the very early hours of this morning that we might just possibly have to call for help and that if we had to we had a transmitter here that could reach almost anywhere in the northern hemisphere. Not, perhaps, my exact words, but the gist is accurate?'

'The gist is accurate.' Even to myself the repetition of the words sounded mechanical and I had to make a conscious effort not to shiver as an ice-shod centipede started up a fandango between my shoulder-blades.

'Well, we can call for help till we're blue in the face, this transmitter here can no longer reach as far as the galley.' For once, almost unbelievably, Smithy's face was registering an emotion other than amusement. His face tight with anger, he produced a screwdriver from his pocket and turned to the big steel-blue receiver-transmitter on the inner bulkhead.

'Do you always carry a screwdriver about with you?' The sheer banality of the question made it apposite in the circumstances.

'Only when I call up the radio station at Tunheim in north-east Bear Island and get no reply. And that's no ordinary radio station, it's an official Norwegian Government base.' Smithy set to work on the face-plate screws. 'I've already had this damned thing off about an hour ago. You'll see in a jiffy why I put it back on again.'

While I was waiting for this jiffy to pass I recalled our conversation on the bridge in the very early hours of the morning, the time he'd referred to the radio and the relative closeness—and, by inference, the availability—of the NATO Atlantic forces. It had been immediately afterwards that I'd looked through the starboard screen door and seen the sharp fresh footprints in the snow, footprints I'd been immediately certain, that had been made by an eavesdropper, a preposterous idea I'd almost as quickly put out of my mind when I'd appreciated that there had been only one set of footprints there, those which I made myself. For some now inexplicable reason it had never occurred to me that any person clever enough to have been responsible for the series of undetected crimes that had taken place aboard the *Morning Rose* would have been far too clever to have overlooked the blinding obviousness of the advantage that lay in using footsteps already there. The footsteps had, indeed, been newly made, our ubiquitous friend had been abroad again.

Smithy removed the last of the screws and, not without some effort, removed the face-plate. I looked at the revealed interior for about ten seconds, then said: 'I see now why you put the face-plate back on. The only thing that puzzles me is that that cabinet looks a bit small for a man to get inside it with a fourteen pound sledge-hammer.'

'Looks just like it, doesn't it?' The tangled mess of wreckage inside was, literally, indescribable. The vandal who had been at work had seen to it that, irrespective of how vast a range of spares were carried, the receiver-transmitter could never be made operable again. 'You've seen enough?'

'I think so.' He started to replace the cover and I said: 'You've radios in the lifeboats?'

'Yes. Hand-cranked. They'll reach farther than the galley but a megaphone would be about as good.'

'You'll have to report this to the captain, of course.'

'Of course.'

'Then it's heigh-ho for Hammerfest?'

'Twenty-four hours from now and he can heigh-ho for Tahiti as far as I'm concerned.' Smithy tightened the last screw. 'That's when I'm going to tell him. Twenty-four hours from now. Maybe twenty-six.'

'Your outside limit for dropping anchor in Sor-hamna?'

'Tying up. Yes.'

'You're a very deceitful man, Smithy.'

'It's the company I keep. And the life I lead.'

'You're not to blame yourself, Smithy,' I said kindly. 'We live in vexed and troubled times.'

CHAPTER SEVEN

When the Norwegian compilers of the report on Bear Island had spoken of it as possessing perhaps the most inhospitably bleak coastline in the world, they had been speaking with the measured understatement of true professional geographers. As we approached it in the first light of dawn—which in those latitudes, at that time of year, and under grey and lowering skies which were not only full of snow but getting rid of it as fast as they could, was as near mid forenoon as made no difference—it presented the most awesome, awe-inspiring and, in the true sense of the word, awful spectacle of nature it had ever been my misfortune to behold. A frightening desolation, it was a weird combination of the wickedly repellent and unwillingly fascinating, an evil and dreadful and sinister place, a place full of the terrifying intimation of mortality, the culmination of all the terrors for our long-lost Nordic ancestors, for whom hell was the land of eternal cold and for whom this would be the eternally frozen purgatory to be visited only in their dying nightmares.

Bear Island was black. That was the shocking, the almost frightful thing about it. Bear Island was black, black as a widow's weeds. Here in the regions of year-long snow and ice, where, in winter, even the waters of the Barents Sea ran a milky white, to find this ebony mass towering 1500 vertical feet up into the grey overcast evoked the same feeling of total disbelief, the same numbing impact, although here magnified a hundredfold, as does the first glimpse of the black cliff of the north face of the Eiger rearing up its appalling grandeur among the snows of the Bernese Oberland: this benumbment of the senses stemmed from a dichotomous struggle to accept the evidence before the eyes, for while reason said that it had to be so, that primeval part of the mind that existed long before man knew what reason was just flatly refused to accept it.

We were just south-west of the most southerly tip of Bear Island, steaming due east through the calmest seas that we had encountered since leaving Wick, but even that term was only relative, it was still necessary to hang on to something if one wished to maintain the perpendicular. Overall, the weather hadn't changed any for the better, the comparative moderating of the seas was due entirely to the fact that the wind blew now directly from the north and we were in the lee of whatever little shelter was afforded by those giant cliffs. We were making this particular approach to our destination at Otto's request for he was understandably anxious to build up a library of background shots which, so far, was completely non-existent, and those bleak precipices would have made a cameraman's or director's dream: but Otto's luck was running true to form, those driving gusts of snow, which would in any event have driven straight into the camera lens and completely obscured it, more often than not obscured the cliffs themselves.

Due north lay the highest cliffs of the island, the polomite battlements of the Hambergfjell dropping like a stone into the spume-topped waves that lashed its base, with, standing out to sea, an imposing rock needle thrusting up at least 250 feet: to the north-east, and less than a mile distant, stood the equally magnificent Bird Fell cliffs with, clustered at their foot, an incredible series of high stacks, pinnacles and arches that could only have been the handiwork of some Herculean sculptor, at once both blind and mad.

All this we—about ten others and myself—could see purely by courtesy of the fact that we were on the bridge which had its for'ard screen windows equipped with a high-speed Kent clear-view screen directly in front of the helmsman—which at this particular moment was Smithy—while on either side were two very large windscreen-wipers which coped rather less effectively with the gusting snow.

I was standing with Conrad, Lonnie and Mary Stuart in front of the port wiper. Conrad, who was by no means as dashing in real life as he was on the screen, appeared to have struck up some kind of diffident friendship with Mary, which, I reflected, was as well for her social life as she'd barely spoken to me since the morning of the previous day, which might have been interpreted as being a bit graceless of her considering I'd incurred a large variety of aches and cramps in preventing her from falling to the floor during most of the preceding night. She hadn't exactly avoided me in the past twenty-four hours but neither had she sought me out, maybe she had certain things on her mind, such as her conscience and her unforgiveable treatment of me: nor had I exactly sought her out for I, too, had a couple of things on my mind, the first of which was herself.

I had developed towards her a markedly ambivalent feeling: while I had to be grateful to her for having, however unwittingly, saved my life because her aversion to scotch had prevented me from having the last nightcap I'd ever have had in this world, at the same time she'd prevented me from moving around and, just possibly, stumbling upon the lad who had been wandering about in the middle watches with ill-intent in his heart and a sledge-hammer in his hand. That she, and for whomsoever she worked, knew beyond question that I was a person who might have reason to be abroad at inconvenient hours I no longer doubted. And the second thing in my mind was the 'whomsoever': I no longer doubted that it was Heissman and perhaps he didn't even stand in need of an accomplice: doctors, by the nature of their profession, are even more fallible and liable to error than the average run of mankind and I might well have been in error when I'd seen him on his bed in pain and judged him unfit to move around. Moreover, Goin apart, he was the only man with a cabin to himself and so able to sally out and return undetected by a room-mate. And, of course, there was always this mysterious Siberian background of his. None of which, not even his secret meeting with Mary Stuart, was enough to hang a cat on.

Lonnie touched my arm and I turned. He smelt like a distillery. He said: 'Remember what we were talking about? Two nights ago.'

'We talked about a lot of things.'

'Bars.'

'Don't you ever think of anything else, Lonnie? Bars? What bars?'

'In the great hereafter,' Lonnie said solemnly. 'Do you think there are any there? In heaven, I mean. I mean, you couldn't very well call it heaven if there are no bars there, now could you? I mean, I wouldn't call it an act of kindness to send an old man like me to a prohibition heaven, now would you? It wouldn't be kind.'

'I don't know, Lonnie. On biblical evidence I should expect there would be some wine around. And lots of milk and honey.' Lonnie looked pained. 'What leads you to expect that you're ever going to be faced with the problem?'

'I was but posing a hypothetic question.' The old man spoke with dignity. 'It would be positively *un*Christian to send me there. God, I'm thirsty. Unkind is what I mean. I mean, charity is the greatest of Christian virtues.' He shook his head sadly. 'An act of the greatest uncharity, my dear boy, the very negation of the spirit of kindness.' Lonnie gazed out through a side window at the fantastically shaped islets of Keilhous Oy, Hosteinen and Stappen, now directly off our port beam and less than half a mile distant. His face was set in lines of tranquil sacrifice. He was as drunk as an owl.

'You do believe in this kindness, Lonnie?' I said curiously. After a lifetime in the cinema business I didn't see how he possibly could.

'What else is there, my dear boy?'

'Even to those who don't deserve it?'

'Ah! Now. There is the point. Those are the ones who deserve it most.'

'Even Judith Haynes?'

He looked as if I had struck him and when I saw the expression on his face I felt as if I had struck him, even although I felt his to be a mysteriously exaggerated reaction. I reached out a hand even as I was about to apologize for I knew not what, but he turned away, a curious sadness on his face, and left the bridge.

'Now I've seen the impossible,' Conrad said. He wasn't smiling but he wasn't being censorious either. 'Someone has at last given offence to Lonnie Gilbert.'

'One has to work at it,' I said. 'I've transgressed against Lonnie's creed. He thinks that I'm unkind.'

'Unkind?' Mary Stuart laid a hand on the arm I was using to steady myself. The skin under the brown eyes was perceptibly darker than it had been thirty-six hours ago and was even beginning to look puffy and the whites of the eyes themselves were dulled and slightly tinged with red. She hesitated, as if about to say something, then her gaze shifted to a point over my left shoulder. I turned.

Captain Imrie closed the starboard wheel-house door behind him. Insofar as it was possible to detect the shift and play of expression on that splendidly bewhiskered and bearded face, it seemed that the captain was upset, even agitated. He crossed directly to Smithy and spoke to him in a low and urgent voice. Smithy registered surprise, then shook his head. Captain Imrie spoke again, briefly. Smithy shrugged his shoulders, then said something in return. Both men looked at me and I knew there was more trouble coming, if not actually arrived, if for no reason other than that so far nothing untowards had happened with which I hadn't been directly or indirectly concerned. Captain Imrie fixed me with his piercing blue eyes, jerked his head with most uncharacteristic peremptoriness towards the chart-room door and headed for it himself. I shrugged my own shoulders in apology to Mary and Conrad and followed. Captain Imrie closed the door behind me.

'More trouble, mister.' I didn't much care for the way he called me 'mister'. 'One of the film crew, John Halliday, has disappeared.'

'Disappeared where?' It wasn't a very intelligent question but then it wasn't meant to be.

'That's what I'd like to know.' I didn't much care for the way he looked at me either.

'He can't just have disappeared. I mean, you've searched for him?'

'We've searched for him, all right.' The voice was harsh with strain. 'From anchor locker to stern-post. He's not aboard the *Morning Rose*.'

'My God,' I said. 'This is awful.' I looked at him in what I hoped registered as puzzlement. 'But why tell me all this?'

'Because I thought you might be able to help us.'

'Help you? I'd like to, but how? I assume that you can only be approaching me in my medical capacity and I can assure you that there's absolutely nothing in what I've seen of him or read in his medical history—'

'I wasn't approaching you in your bloody medical capacity!' Captain Imrie had started to breathe very heavily. 'I just thought you might help me in other ways. Bloody strange, isn't it, mister, that you've been in the thick of everything that's been happening?' I'd nothing to say to this, I'd just been thinking the same thing myself. 'How it was you who just "happened" to find Antonio dead. How it was you who just "happened" to go to the bridge when Smith and Oakley were ill. How was it you who went straight to the stewards' cabin in the crew quarters. Next thing, I suppose, you'd have gone straight to Mr Gerran's cabin and found him dead also, if Mr Goin hadn't had the good luck to go there first. And isn't it bloody strange, mister, that a doctor, the one person who could have helped those people and seemingly couldn't is the one person aboard with enough medical knowledge to make them sick in the first place?'

No question—looking at it from his angle—Captain Imrie was developing quite a reasonable point of view. I was more than vaguely surprised to find that he was capable of developing a point of view in the first place. Clearly, I'd been underestimating him: just how much I was immediately to realize.

'And just why were you spending so much time in the galley late the night before last—when I was in my bed, damn you? The place where all the poison came from. Haggerty told me. He told me you were poking around—*and* got him out of the galley for a spell. You didn't find what you wanted. But you came back later, didn't you? Wanted to find out where the food left-overs were, didn't you? Pretended you were surprised when they were gone. That would look good in court.'

'Oh, for heaven's sake, you silly old—'

'And you were very, very late abroad that night, weren't you? Oh, yes, I've been making inquiries. Up in the saloon—Mr Goin told me: up on the bridge—Oakley told me: down in the lounge—Gilbert told me: and—' he paused dramatically —'in Halliday's cabin—his cabin-mate told me. And, most of all, who was the man who stopped me from going to Hammerfest when I wanted to and persuaded the others to sign this worthless guarantee of yours absolving me from all blame? Tell me that, eh, mister?'

His trump card played, Captain Imrie rested his case. I had to stop the old coot, he was working himself up to having me clapped in irons. I sympathized with him, I was sorry for what I would have to say to him, but clearly this wasn't my morning for making friends anyway. I looked at him coldly and without expression for about ten seconds then said: 'My name's "Doctor" not "mister". I'm not your damned mate.'

'What? What was that?'

I opened the door to the wheel-house and invited him to pass through.

'You just mentioned the word "court". Just step out there and repeat those slanderous allegations in the presence of witnesses and you'll find yourself standing in a part of a court you never expected to be in. Can you imagine the extent of the damages?'

From his face and the perceptible shrinking of his burly frame it was apparent that Captain Imrie immediately could. I was a long, long way from being proud of myself, he was a worried old man saying honestly what he thought had to be said, but he'd left me with no option. I closed the door and wondered how best to begin.

I wasn't given the time to begin. The knock on the door and the opening of the door came on the same instant. Oakley had an urgent and rather apprehensive look about him.

'I think you'd better come down to the saloon right away, sir,' he said to Imrie. He looked at me. 'You, too, I'm afraid, Dr Marlowe. There's been a fight down there, a bad one.'

'Great God Almighty!' If Captain Imrie still had had any lingering hopes that he was running a happy ship, the last of them was gone. For a man of his years and bulk he made a remarkably rapid exit: I followed more leisurely.

Oakley's description had been reasonably accurate. There had been a fight and a very unpleasant affair it must have been too during the period it had lasted—obviously, the very brief period it had lasted. There were only half a dozen people in the saloon altogether—one or two were still suffering sufficiently from the rigours of the Barents Sea to prefer the solitude of their cabins to forbidding beauties of Bear Island, while the Three Apostles, as ever, were down in the recreation room, still cacophonously searching for the bottom rung on the ladder to musical immortality. Three of the six were standing, one sitting, one kneeling and the last stretched out on the deck of the saloon. The three on their feet were Lonnie and Eddie and Hendriks, all with the air of concerned but hesitant helplessness that afflicts uncommitted bystanders on such occasions. Michael Stryker was sitting in a chair at the captain's table, using a very bloodstained handkerchief to dab a deep cut on the right cheekbone: it was noticeable that the knuckles of the hand that held the handkerchief were quite badly skinned. The kneeling figure was Mary Darling. All I could see was her back, the long blonde tresses falling to the deck and her big horn-rimmed spectacles lying about two feet away. She was crying, but crying silently, the thin shoulders shaking convulsively in incipient hysteria. I knelt and raised her, still kneeling, to an upright position. She stared at me, ashen-faced, no tears in her eyes, not recognizing me: without her glasses she was as good as blind.

'It's all right, Mary,' I said. 'Only me. Dr Marlowe.' I looked at the figure on the floor and recognized him, not without some difficulty, as young Allen. 'Come on, now, be a good girl. Let me have a look at him.'

'He's terribly hurt, Dr Marlowe, terribly hurt!' She had difficulty in getting her words out during long and almost soundless gasps. 'Oh, look at him, look at him, it's awful!' Then she started crying in earnest, not quietly this time. Her whole body shook. I looked up.

'Mr Hendriks, will you please go to the galley and ask Mr Haggerty for some brandy? Tell him I want it. If he's not there, take it anyway.' Hendriks nodded and hurried away. I said to Captain Imrie: 'Sorry, I should have asked permission.'

'That's all right, Doctor.' We were back on professional terms again, however briefly: perhaps it was because his reply was largely automatic for the bulk of his interest, and all that clearly hostile, was for the moment centred on Michael Stryker. I turned back to Mary.

'Go and sit on the settee, there. And take some of that brandy. You hear?'

'No! No! I—'

'Doctor's orders.' I looked at Eddie and Lonnie and without a word from me they took her across to the nearest settee. I didn't wait to see whether she followed doctor's orders or not: a now stirring Allen had more pressing claims on my attention. Stryker had done a hatchet job on him: he had a cut forehead, a bruised cheek, an eye that was going to be closed by night, blood coming from both nostrils, a split lip, one tooth missing and another so loose that it was going to be missing very soon also. I said to Stryker: 'You do this to him?'

'Obvious, isn't it?'

'You have to savage him like this? Christ, man, he's only a kid. Why don't you pick on someone your own size next time?'

'Like you, for instance?'

'Oh, my God!' I said wearily. Beneath Stryker's tissue-thin veneer of civilization lay something very crude indeed. I ignored him, asked Lonnie to get water from the galley and cleaned up Allen as best I could. As was invariable in such cases the removal of surface blood improved his appearance about eighty per cent. A plaster on his forehead, two cotton-wool plugs for his nose, and two stitches in a frozen lip and I'd done all I could for him. I straightened as an indignant Captain Imrie started questioning Stryker.

'What happened, Mr Stryker?'

'A quarrel.'

'A quarrel, was it now?' Captain Imrie was being heavily ironic. 'And what started the quarrel?'

'An insult. From him.'

'From that—from that child?' The captain's feelings clearly matched my own. 'What kind of insult to do that to a boy?'

'A private insult.' Stryker dabbed the cut on his cheek and, Hippocrates in temporary abeyance, I felt sorry that it wasn't deeper, even although it looked quite unpleasant enough as it was. 'He just got what anyone gets who insults me, that's all.'

'I shall endeavour to keep a still tongue in my head,' Captain Imrie said drily. 'However, as captain of this ship—'

'I'm not a member of your damned crew. If that young fool there doesn't lodge a complaint—and he won't—I'd be obliged if you'd mind your own business.' Stryker rose and left the saloon. Captain Imrie made as if to follow, changed his mind, sat down wearily at the head of his own table and reached for his own private bottle. He said to the three men now clustered round Mary: 'Any of you see what happened?'

'No, sir.' It was Hendriks. 'Mr Stryker was standing alone over by the window there when Stuart went up to speak to him, I don't know what, and next moment they were rolling about the floor. It didn't last more than seconds.'

Captain Imrie nodded wearily and poured a considerable measure into his glass, he was obviously and rightly depending on Smithy to make the approach to anchorage. I got Allen, now quite conscious, to his feet and led him towards the saloon door. Captain Imrie said: 'Taking him below?'

I nodded. 'And when I come back I'll tell you all about how I started it.' He scowled at me and returned to his scotch. Mary, I noticed, was sipping at the brandy and shuddering at every sip. Lonnie held her glasses in his hand and I escaped with Allen before he gave them back to her.

I got Allen into his bunk and covered him up. He had a little colour in his battered cheeks now but still hadn't spoken.

I said: 'What was all that about?'

He hesitated. 'I'm sorry. I'd rather not say.'

'Why ever not?'

'I'm sorry again. It's a bit private.'

'Someone could be hurt?'

'Yes, I—' He stopped.

'It's all right. You must be very fond of her.' He looked at me for a few silent moments, then nodded. I went on: 'Shall I bring her down?'

'No, Doctor, no! I don't want—I mean, with my face like this. No, no, I couldn't!'

'Your face was an awful sight worse just five minutes ago. She was doing a fair job of breaking her heart even then.'

'Was she?' He tried to smile and winced. 'Well, all right.'

I left and went to Stryker's cabin. He answered my knock and his face didn't have welcome written all over it. I looked at the still bleeding cut.

'Want me to have a look at that?' Judith Haynes, clad in a fur parka and trousers and looking rather like a red-haired Eskimo, was sitting on the cabin's only chair, her two cocker spaniels in her lap. Her dazzling smile was in momentary abeyance.

'No.'

'It might scar.' I didn't give a damn whether it scarred or not.

'Oh.' The factor of his appearance, it hadn't been too hard to guess, was of importance to Stryker. I entered, closed the door, examined and dabbed the cut, put on astringent and applied a plaster. I said: 'Look, I'm not Captain Imrie. Did you have to bang that boy like that? You could have flattened him with a tap.'

'You were there when I told Captain Imrie that it was a purely personal matter.' I'd have to revise my psychological thinking, clearly neither my freely offered medical assistance nor my reasonableness of approach nor the implied flattery had had the slightest mollifying effect. 'Having MD hung round your neck doesn't give you the right to ask impertinent prying questions. Remember what else I said to Imrie?'

'You'd be obliged if I minded my own damned business?'
'Exactly.'
'I'll bet young Allen feels that way too.'
'That young Allen deserves all he got,' Judith Haynes said. Her tone wasn't any more friendly than Stryker's. I found what she said interesting for two reasons. She was widely supposed to loathe her husband but there was no evidence of it here: and here might lie a more fruitful source for inquiry for, clearly, she wasn't as good at keeping her emotions and tongue under wraps as her husband was.

'How do you know, Miss Haynes? You weren't there.'
'I didn't have to be. I—'
'Darling!' Stryker's voice was abrupt, warning.
'Can't trust your wife to speak for herself, is that it?' I said. His big fists balled but I ignored him and looked again at Judith Haynes. 'Do you know there's a little girl up in the saloon crying her eyes out over what your big tough husband did to that kid? Does that mean nothing to you?'

'If you're talking about that little bitch of a continuity girl, she deserves all that comes her way too.'

'Darling!' Stryker's voice was urgent. I stared at Judith Haynes in disbelief but I could see she meant what she said. Her red slash of a mouth was contorted into a line as straight and as thin as the edge of a ruler, the once beautiful green eyes were venomous and the face ugly in its contorted attempts to conceal some hatred or viciousness or poison in the mind. It was an almost frightening display of what must have been a very, very rare public exhibition of what powerful rumour in the film world—to which I now partially apologized for my former mental strictures—maintained to be a fairly constant private amalgam of the peasant shrew and the screaming fishwife.

'That—harmless—child?' I spaced the words in slow incredulity. 'A bitch?'

'A tramp, a little tramp! A slut! A little gutter—'
'Stop it!' Stryker's voice was a lash, but it had strained overtones. I had the feeling that only desperation would make him talk to his wife in this fashion.

'Yes, stop it,' I said. 'I don't know what the hell you're talking about, Miss Haynes, and I'm damned sure you don't either. All I know is you're sick.'

I turned to go. Stryker barred my way. He'd lost a little colour from his cheeks.

'Nobody talks to my wife that way.' His lips hardly moved as he spoke.

I was suddenly sick of the Strykers. I said: 'I've insulted your wife?'

'Unforgivably.'

'And so I've insulted you?'

'You're getting the point, Marlowe.'

'And anyone who insults you gets what's coming to them. That's what you said to Captain Imrie.'

'That's what I said.'

'I see.'

'I thought you might.' He still barred my way.

'And if I apologize?'

'An apology?' He smiled coldly. 'Let's try one out for size, shall we?'

I turned to Judith Haynes. I said: 'I don't know what the hell you're talking about, Miss Haynes, and I'm damned sure you don't either. All I know is you're sick.'

Her face looked as if invisible claws had sunk deep into both cheeks all the way from temple to chin and dragged back the skin until it was stretched drumtight over the bones. I turned to face Stryker. His facial skin didn't look tight at all. The strikingly handsome face wasn't handsome any more, the contours seemed to have sagged and jellied and the cheeks were bereft of colour. I brushed by him, opened the door and stopped.

'You poor bastard,' I said. 'Don't worry. Doctors never tell.'

I was glad to make my way up to the clean biting cold of the upper deck. I'd left something sick and unhealthy and more than vaguely unclean down there behind me and I didn't have to be a doctor to know what the sickness was. The snow had eased now and as I looked out over the weather side—the port side—I could see that we were leaving one promontory about a half-mile behind on the port quarter while another was coming up about the same distance ahead on the port bow. Kapp Kolthoff and Kapp Malmgrem, I knew from the chart, so we had to be steaming north-east across the Evjebukta. The cliffs here were less high, but we were even more deeply into their lee than twenty minutes previously and the sea had moderated even more. We had less than three miles to go.

I looked up at the bridge. The weather, obviously, was improving considerably or interest and curiosity had been stimulated by the close proximity of our destination, for there was now a small knot of people on either wing of the bridge but with hoods so closely drawn as to make features indistinguishable. I became aware that there was a figure standing close by me huddled up against the fore superstructure of the bridge. It was Mary Darling with the long tangled blonde tresses blowing in every direction of the compass. I went towards her, put my arm round her with the ease born of recent intensive practice, and tilted her face. Red eyes, tear-splotched cheeks, a little woebegone face half-hidden behind the enormous spectacles: the slut, the bitch, the little tramp.

'Mary Darling,' I said. 'What are you doing here? It's far too cold. You should be inside or below.'

'I wanted to be alone.' There was still the catch of a dying sob in her voice. 'And Mr Gilbert kept wanting to give me brandy—and, well—' she shuddered.

'So you've left Lonnie alone with the restorative. That'll be an eminently satisfactory all-round conclusion as far as Lonnie—'

'Dr Marlowe!' She became aware of the arm round her and made a half-hearted attempt to break away. 'People will see us!'

'I don't care,' I said. 'I want the whole world to know of our love.'

'You want the whole—' She looked at me in consternation, her normally big eyes huge behind her glasses, then came the first tremulous beginnings of a smile. 'Oh, Dr Marlowe!'

'There's a young man below who wants to see you immediately,' I said.

'Oh!' The smile vanished, heaven knows what gravity of import she found in my words. 'Is he—I mean, he'll have to go to hospital, won't he?'

'He'll be up and around this afternoon.'

'Really? Really and truly?'

'If you're calling my professional competence into question—'

'Oh, Dr Marlowe! Then what—why does he—'

'I should imagine he wants you to hold his hand. I'm putting myself in his shoes, of course.'

'Oh, Dr Marlowe! Will it—I mean in his cabin—'

'Do I have to drag you down there?'

'No.' She smiled. 'I don't think that will be necessary.' She hesitated. 'Dr Marlowe?'

'Yes?'

'I think you're wonderful. I really do.'

'Hoppit.'

She smiled, almost happily now, and hopped it. I wished I even fractionally shared her opinion of me, for if I was in a position to do so there would be a good number fewer of dead and sick and injured around. But I was glad of one thing, I hadn't had to hurt Mary Darling as I'd feared I might, there had been no need to ask her any of the questions that had half-formed in my mind even as I had left the Strykers' cabin. If she were even remotely capable of being any of those things that Judith Haynes had, for God knew what misbegotten reasons, accused her of being, then she had no right to be in the film industry as a continuity girl, she was in more than a fair way to making her fame and fortune as one of the great actresses of our time. Besides, I didn't have to ask any questions now, not where she and Allen and the Strykers were concerned: it was hard to say whether my contempt for Michael Stryker was greater than my pity.

I remained where I was for a few minutes watching some crew members who had just come on to the foredeck begin to remove the no longer necessary lashings from the deck cargo, strip off tarpaulins and set slings in places, while another two set about clearing away the big fore derrick and testing the winch. Clearly, Captain Imrie had no intention of wasting any time whatsoever upon our arrival: he wanted, and understandably, to be gone with all dispatch. I went aft to the saloon.

Lonnie was the sole occupant, alone but not lonely, not as long as he had that bottle of Hine happily clutched in his fist. He lowered his glass as I sat down beside him.

'Ah! You have assuaged the sufferings of the walking wounded? There is a preoccupied air about you, my dear fellow.' He tapped the bottle. 'For the instant alleviation of workaday cares—'

'That bottle belongs to the pantry, Lonnie.'

'The fruits of nature belong to all mankind. A soupçon?'

'If only to stop you from drinking it all. I have an apology to make to you, Lonnie. About our delectable leading lady. I don't think there's enough kindness around to waste any in throwing it in her direction.'

'Barren ground, you would say? Stony soil?'

'I would say.'

'Redemption and salvation are not for our fair Judith?'

'I don't know about that. All I know is that I wouldn't like to be the one to try and that, looking at her, I can only conclude that there's an awful lot of unkindness around.'

'Amen to that.' Lonnie swallowed some more brandy. 'But we must not forget the parables of the lost sheep and the prodigal son. Nothing and nobody is ever entirely lost.'

'I dare say. Luck to leading her back to the paths of the righteous—you shouldn't have to fight off too much competition for the job. How is it, do you think, that a person like that should be so different from the other two?'

'Mary dear and Mary darling? Dear, dear girls. Even in my dotage I love them dearly. Such sweet children.'

'They could do no wrong?'

'Never!'

'Ha! That's easy to say. But what if, perhaps, they were deeply under the influence of alcohol?'

'What?' Lonnie appeared genuinely shocked. 'What are you talking about? Inconceivable, my dear boy, inconceivable!'

'Not even, say, if they were to have a double gin?'

'What piffling nonsense is this? We are speaking of the influence of alcohol, not about apéritifs for swaddling babes.'

'You would see no harm in either of them asking for, say, just one drink?'

'Of course not.' Lonnie looked genuinely puzzled. 'You do harp on so, my dear fellow.'

'Yes, I do rather. I just wondered why once, after a long day on the set, when Mary Stuart had asked you for just that one drink you flew completely off the handle.'

In curiously slow-motion fashion Lonnie put bottle and glass on the table and rose unsteadily to his feet. He looked old and tired and terribly vulnerable.

'Ever since you came in—now I can see it.' He spoke in a kind of sad whisper. 'Ever since you came in you've been leading up to this one question.'

He shook his head and his eyes were not seeing me. 'I thought you were my friend,' he said quietly, and walked uncertainly from the saloon.

CHAPTER EIGHT

The north-west corner of the Sor-hamna bight, where the *Morning Rose* had finally come to rest, was just under three miles due north-east, as the crow flies, from the most southerly tip of Bear Island. The Sor-hamna itself, U-shaped and open to the south, was just over a thousand yards in width on its east-west axis and close on a mile in length from north to south. The eastern arm of the harbour was discontinuous, beginning with a small peninsula perhaps three hundred yards in length, followed by a two hundred-yard gap of water interspersed with small islands of various sizes then by the much larger island of Makehl, very narrow from east to west, stretching almost half a mile to its most southerly point of Kapp Roalkvam. The land to the north and east was low-lying, that to the west, or true island side, rising fairly steeply from a shallow escarpment but nowhere higher than a small hill about 400 feet high about halfway down the side of the bight. Here were none of the towering precipices of the Hambergfjell or Bird Fell ranges to the south: but, on the other hand, here the entire land was covered in snow, deep on the north-facing slopes and their valleys where the pale low summer sun and the scouring winds had passed them by.

The Sor-hamna was not only the best, it was virtually the only reasonable anchorage in Bear Island. When the wind blew from the west it offered perfect protection for vessels sheltering there, and for a northerly wind it was only slightly less good. From an easterly wind, dependent upon its strength and precise direction, it afforded a reasonable amount of cover—the gap between Kapp Heer and Makehl was the deciding factor here and, when the wind stood in this quarter and if the worst came to the worst, a vessel could always up anchor and shelter under the lee of Makehl Island: but when the wind blew from the south a vessel was wide open to everything the Barents Sea cared to throw at it.

And this was why the degree of unloading activity aboard the *Morning Rose* was increasing from the merely hectic to the nearly panic-stricken. Even as we had approached the

Sor-hamna the wind, which had been slowly veering the past thirty-six hours, now began rapidly to increase its speed of movement round the compass at disconcerting speed so that by the time we had made fast it was blowing directly from the east. It was now a few degrees south of east, and strengthening, and the *Morning Rose* was beginning to feel its effects: it only had to increase another few knots or veer another few degrees and the trawler's position would become untenable.

At anchor, the *Morning Rose* could comfortably have ridden out the threatened blow, but the trouble was that the *Morning Rose* was not at anchor. She was tied up alongside a crumbling limestone jetty—neither iron nor wooden structures would have lasted for any time in those stormy and bitter waters—that had first been constructed by Lerner and the *Deutsche Seefischerei-Verein* about the turn of the century and then improved upon—if that were the term—by the International Geophysical Year expedition that had summered there. The jetty, which would have been condemned out of hand and forbidden for public use almost anywhere else in the northern hemisphere, had originally been T-shaped, but the left arm of the T was now all but gone while the central section leading to the shore was badly eaten away on its southward side. It was against this dangerously dilapidated structure that the *Morning Rose* was beginning to pound with increasing force as the south-easterly seas caught her under the starboard quarter and the cushioning effect as the trawler struck heavily and repeatedly against the jetty was sufficient to make those working on deck stagger and clutch on to the nearest support. It was difficult to say what effect this was having on the *Morning Rose*, for apart from the scratching and slight indentations of the plates none was visible, but trawlers are legendarily tough and it was unlikely that she was coming to any great harm: but what was coming to harm, and very visibly so, was the jetty itself, for increasingly large chunks of masonry were beginning to fall into the Sor-hamna with dismaying frequency, and as most of our fuel, provisions and equipment still stood there, the seemingly imminent collapse of the pier into the sea was not a moment to be viewed with anything like equanimity.

When we'd first come alongside shortly before noon, the unloading had gone ahead very briskly and smoothly indeed, except for the unloading of Miss Haynes's snarling pooches,

153

Even before we'd tied up, the after derrick had the sixteen-foot work-boat in the water and three minutes later an only slightly smaller fourteen-footer with an outboard had followed it: those boats were to remain with us. Within ten minutes the specially strengthened for'ard derrick had lifted the weirdly-shaped—laterally truncated so as to have a flat bottom—mock-up of the central section of a submarine over the side and lowered it gently into the water, where it floated with what appeared to be perfect stability, no doubt because of its four tons of cast-iron ballast. It was when the mock-up conning-tower was swung into position to be bolted on to the central section of the submarine that the trouble began.

It just wouldn't bolt on. Goin and Heissman and Stryker, the only three who had observed the original tests, said that in practice it had operated perfectly: clearly, it wasn't operating perfectly now. The conning-tower section, elliptical in shape, was designed to settle precisely over a four-inch vertical flange in the centre of the mid-section, but settle it just wouldn't do: it turned out that one of the shallow curves at the foot of the conning-tower was at least a quarter-inch out of true, a fact that was almost certainly due to the pounding that we'd taken on the way up from Wick: just one lashing not sufficiently bar-taut would have permitted that microscopic freedom of vertical movement that would have allowed the tiny distortion to develop.

The solution was simple—just to hammer the offending curve back into shape—and in a dockyard with skilled plate-layers available this would probably have been no more than a matter of minutes. But we'd neither technical facilities nor skilled labour available and the minutes had now stretched into hours. A score of times now the for'ard derrick had offered up the offending conning-tower piece to the flange: a score of times it had had to be lifted again and painstakingly assaulted by hammers. Several times a perfect fit had been achieved where it had been previously lacking only to find the distortion had mysteriously and mischievously transferred itself a few inches farther along the metal. Nor, now, despite the fact that the submarine section was in the considerable lee afforded by both pier and vessel, were matters being made any easier by the little waves that were beginning to creep around the bows of the *Morning Rose* and rock it, gently at first but with increasing force, to the extent that the ultimate good fit was clearly going to depend as much on the luck of timing as the persuasion of the hammers.

Captain Imrie wasn't frantic with worry for the sound reason that it wasn't in his nature to become frantic about anything, but the depth of his concern was evident enough from the fact that he had not only skipped lunch but hadn't as much as fortified himself with anything stronger than coffee since our arrival in the Sor-hamna. His main concern, apart from the well-being of the *Morning Rose*—he clearly didn't give a damn about his passengers—was to get the fore-deck cleared of its remaining deck cargo because, as I'd heard Otto rather unnecessarily and unpleasantly reminding him, it was part of his contractual obligations to land all passengers and cargo before departure for Hammerfest. And, of course, what was exercising Captain Imrie's mind so powerfully was that, with darkness coming on and the weather blowing up, the for'ard deck cargo had not yet been unloaded and would not be until the fore derrick was freed from its present full-time occupation of holding the conning-tower suspended over the mid-section.

The one plus factor about Captain Imrie's concentration was that it gave him little time to worry about Halliday's disappearance. More precisely, it gave him little time to try to do anything constructive about it, for I knew it was still very much on his mind from the fact that he had taken time off to tell me that upon his arrival in Hammerfest his first intention would be to contact the law. There were two things I could have said at this stage, but I didn't. The first was that I failed to see what earthly purpose this could serve—it was just, I suppose, that he felt that he had to do something, anything, however ineffectual that might be: the second was that I felt quite certain that he would never get the length of Hammerfest in the first place, although just then hardly seemed the time to tell him why I thought so. He wasn't then in the properly receptive mood: I had hopes that he would be shortly after he had left Bear Island.

I went down the screeching metal gangway—its rusty iron wheels, apparently permanently locked in position, rubbed to and fro with every lurch of the *Morning Rose*—and made my way along the ancient jetty. A small tractor and a small Sno-Cat—they had been the third and fourth items to be unloaded from the trawler's after-deck—were both equipped with towing sledges and everybody from Heissman downwards was helping to load equipment aboard those sledges for haulage up to the huts that lay on the slight escarpment not more than twenty yards from the end of the jetty. Everybody was not only helping, they were helping with a will: when the temperature is fifteen degrees below freezing the temptation to dawdle is not marked. I followed one consignment up to the huts.

Unlike the jetty, the huts were of comparatively recent construction and in good condition, relics from the latest IGY—there could have been no possible economic justification in dismantling them and taking them back to Norway. They were not built of the modern kapok, asbestos and aluminium construction so favoured by modern expeditions in Arctic regions as base headquarters: they were built—although admittedly pre-sectioned—in the low-slung chalet design fairly universally found in the higher Alpine regions of Europe. They had about them that four-square hunch-shouldered look, the appearance of lowering their heads against the storm, that made it seem quite likely that they would still be there in a hundred years' time. Provided they are not exposed to prevailing high winds and the constant fluctuation of temperature above and below the freezing point, man-made structures can last almost indefinitely in the deep-freeze of the high Arctic.

There were five structures here altogether, all of them set a considerable distance apart—as far as the shoulder of the hill beyond the escarpment would permit. Little as I knew of the Arctic, I knew enough to understand the reason for this spacing: here, where exposure to cold is the permanent and dominating factor of life, it is fire which is the greatest enemy, for unless there are chemical fire-fighting appliances to hand, and there nearly always are not, a fire, once it has taken hold, will not stop until everything combustible has been destroyed: blocks of ice are scarcely at a premium when it comes to extinguishing flames.

Four small huts were set at the corners of a much larger central block. According to the rather splendid diagram Heissman had drawn up in his manifesto, those were to be given over, respectively, to transport, fuels, provisions and equipment: I was not quite sure what he meant by equipment. Those were all square and windowless. The central and very much larger building was of a peculiar starfish shape with a pentagonal centrepiece and five triangular annexes all forming an integral whole: the purpose of this design was difficult to guess, I would have thought it one conducive to maximum heat-loss. The centrepiece was the living, dining and cooking area: each arm held two tiny bare rooms for sleeping quarters. Heating was by electric oil-filled black heaters bolted to the walls, but until we got our own portable generator going we were dependent on simple oil stoves: lighting was by pressurized Coleman kerosene lamps. Cooking, which was apparently to consist of the endless opening and heating of contents of tins, was to be done on a simple oil stove. Otto, needless to say, hadn't brought a cook along: cooks cost money.

With the notable exception of Judith Haynes everyone, even the still groggy Allen, worked willingly and as quickly as the unfamiliar and freezing conditions would permit: they also worked silently and joylessly, for although no one had been on anything approaching terms of close friendship with Halliday, the news of his disappearance had added fresh gloom and apprehension to a company who believed themselves to be evilly jinxed before even the first day of shooting. Stryker and Lonnie, who never spoke to each other except when essential, checked all the stores, fuel, oil, food, clothing, arctizing equipment—Otto, whatever his faults, insisted on thoroughness: Sandy, considerably recovered now that he was on dry land, checked his props, Hendriks his sound equipment, the Count his camera equipment, Eddie his electrical gear, and I myself what little medical kit I had along. By three o'clock, when it was already dusk, we had everything stowed away, cubicles allocated and camp-beds and sleeping-bags placed in those: the jetty was now quite empty of all the gear that had been unloaded there.

We lit the oil stoves, left a morose and muttering Eddie— with the doleful assistance of the Three Apostles—to get the diesel generator working and made our way back to the *Morning Rose*, myself because it was essential that I speak to Smithy, the others because the hut was still miserably bleak and freezing whereas even the much-maligned *Morning Rose* still offered a comparative haven of warmth and comfort. Very shortly after our return a variety of incidents occurred in short and eventually disconcerting succession.

At ten past three, totally unexpectedly and against all indications, the conning-tower fitted snugly over the flange of the midship section. Six bolts were immediately fitted to hold it in position—there were twenty-four altogether—and the work-boat at once set about the task of towing the unwieldy structure into the almost total shelter offered by the right angle formed by the main body of the jetty and its north-facing arm.

At three-fifteen the unloading of the foredeck cargo began and, with Smithy in charge, this was undertaken with efficiency and dispatch. Partly because I didn't want to disturb him in his work, partly because it was at that moment impossible to speak to Smithy privately, I went below to my cabin, removed a small rectangular cloth-bound package from the base of my medical bag, put it in a small purse-string duffel bag and went back on top.

This was at three-twenty. The unloading was still less than twenty per cent completed but Smithy wasn't there. It was almost as though he had awaited my momentary absence to betake himself elsewhere. And that he had betaken himself elsewhere there was no doubt. I asked the winchman where he had gone, but the winchman, exclusively preoccupied with a job that had to be executed with all dispatch, was understandably vague about Smithy's whereabouts. He had either gone below or ashore, he said, which I found a very helpful remark. I looked in his cabin, on the bridge, in the chart-house, the saloon and all the other likely places. No Smithy. I questioned passengers and crew with the same result. No one had seen him, no one had any idea whether he was aboard or had gone ashore, which was very understandable because the darkness was now pretty well complete and the harsh light of the arc lamp now rigged up to aid unloading threw the gangway into very heavy shadow so that anyone could be virtually certain of boarding or leaving the *Morning Rose* unnoticed.

Nor was there any sign of Captain Imrie. True, I wasn't looking for him, but I would have expected him to be making his presence very much known. The wind was almost round to the south-south-east now and still freshening, the *Morning Rose* was beginning to pound regularly against the jetty wall with a succession of jarring impacts and a sound of screeching metal that would normally have had Imrie very much in evidence indeed in his anxiety to get rid of all his damned passengers and their equipment in order to get his ship out to the safety of the open sea with all speed. But he wasn't around, not any place I could see him.

At three-thirty I went ashore and hurried up the jetty to the huts. They were deserted except for the equipment hut where Eddie was blasphemously trying to start up the diesel. He looked up as he saw me.

'Nobody could ever call me one for complaining, Dr Marlowe, but this bloody—'

'Have you seen Mr Smith? The mate?'

'Not ten minutes ago. Looked in to see how we were getting on. Why? Is there something—'

'Did he say anything?'

'What kind of thing?'

'About where he was going? What he was doing?'

'No.' Eddie looked at the shivering Three Apostles, whose blank expressions were of no help to anyone. 'Just stood there for a couple of minutes with his hands in his pockets, looking at what we were doing and asking a few questions, then he strolls off.'

'See where he went?'

'No.' He looked at the Three Apostles, who shook their heads as one. 'Anything up, then?'

'Nothing urgent. Ship's about to sail and the skipper's looking for him.' If that wasn't quite an accurate assessment of how matters stood at that moment, I'd no doubt it would be in a very few minutes. I didn't waste time looking for Smithy. If he had been hanging around with apparent aimlessness at the camp instead of closely supervising the urgent clearing of the foredeck, which one would have expected of him and would normally have been completely in character, then Smithy had a very good reason for doing so: he just wanted, however temporarily, to become lost.

At three-thirty-five I returned to the *Morning Rose*. This time Captain Imrie was very much in evidence. I had thought him incapable of becoming frantic about anything, but as I looked at him as he stood in the wash of light at the door of the saloon I could see that I could have been wrong about that. Perhaps 'frantic' was the wrong term, but there was no doubt that he was in a highly excitable condition and was mad clear through. His fists were balled, what could be seen of his face was mottled red and white, and his bright blue eyes were snapping. With commendable if lurid brevity he repeated to me what he'd clearly told a number of people in the past few minutes. Worried about the deteriorating weather—that wasn't quite the way he'd put it—he'd had Allison try to contact Tunheim for a forecast. This Allison had been unable to do. Then he and Allison had made the discovery that the transceiver was smashed beyond repair. And just over an hour or so previously the receiver had been in order—or Smith had said it was, for he had then written down the latest weather forecast. Or what he *said* was the latest weather forecast. And now there was no sign of Smith. Where the hell was Smith?

'He's gone ashore,' I said.

'Ashore? Ashore? How the hell do you know he's gone ashore?' Captain Imrie didn't sound very friendly, but then, he was hardly in a friendly mood.

'Because I've just been up in the camp talking to Mr Harbottle, the electrician. Mr Smith had just been up there.'

'Up there? He should have been unloading cargo. What the hell was he doing up there?'

'I didn't see Mr Smith,' I explained patiently. 'So I couldn't ask him.'

'What the hell were *you* doing up there?'

'You're forgetting yourself, Captain Imrie. I am not responsible to you. I merely wished to have a word with him before he left. We've become quite friendly, you know.'

'Yes you have, haven't you?' Imrie said significantly. It didn't mean anything, he was just in a mood for talking significantly. 'Allison!'

'Sir?'

'The bo'sun. Search-party ashore. Quickly now, I'll lead you myself.' If there had ever been any doubt as to the depth of Captain Imrie's concern there was none now. He turned back to me but as Otto Gerran and Goin were now standing beside me I wasn't sure whether he was addressing me or not. 'And we're leaving within the half-hour, with Smith or without him.'

'Is that fair, Captain?' Otto asked. 'He may just have gone for a walk or got a little lost—you see how dark it is—'

'Don't you think it bloody funny that Mr Smith should vanish just as I discover that a radio over which he's been claiming to receive messages is smashed beyond repair?'

Otto fell silent but Goin, ever the diplomat, stepped in smoothly.

'I think Mr Gerran is right, Captain. You could be acting a little bit unfairly. I agree that the destruction of your radio is a serious and worrisome affair and one that is more than possibly, in light of all the mysterious things that have happened recently, a very sinister affair. But I think you are wrong immediately to assume that Mr Smith has any connection with it. For one thing, he strikes me as much too intelligent a man to incriminate himself in so extremely obvious a fashion. In the second place, as your senior officer who knows how vitally important a piece of equipment your radio is, why should he do such a wanton thing? In the third place, if he were trying to escape the consequences of his actions, where on earth could he escape to on Bear Island? I do not suggest anything as simple as an accident or amnesia: I'm merely suggesting that he may have got lost. You could at least wait until the morning.'

I could see Captain Imrie's fists unballing, not much, just a slight relaxation, and I knew that if he weren't wavering he was at least on the point of considering, a state of approaching uncertainty that lasted just as long as it took Otto to undo whatever Goin might have been on the point of achieving.

'That's it, of course,' he said. 'He just went to have a look around.'

'What? In the pitch bloody dark?' It was an exaggeration but a pardonable one. 'Allison! Oakley! All of you. Come on!' He lowered his voice a few decibels and said to us: 'I'm leaving within the half-hour, Smith or no Smith. Hammerfest, gentlemen, Hammerfest and the law.'

He hurried down the gangway, half a dozen men close behind. Goin sighed. 'I suppose we'd better lend a hand.' He left and Otto, after hesitating for a moment, followed.

I didn't, I'd no intention of lending a hand, if Smithy didn't want to be found then he wouldn't be. Instead I went down to my cabin, wrote a brief note, took the small duffel bag with me and went in search of Haggerty. I had to trust somebody, Smithy's most damned inconvenient disappearing trick had left me with no option, and I thought Haggerty was my best bet. He was stiff-necked and suspicious and, since Imrie's questioning of him that morning, he must have become even more suspicious of me: but he was no fool, he struck me as being incorruptible, he was, I thought, amenable to an authoritative display of discipline and, above all, he'd spent twenty-seven years of his life in taking orders.

It was fifteen minutes' touch and go, but at last he grudgingly agreed to do what I asked him to.

'You wouldn't be making a fool out of me, Dr Marlowe?' he asked.

'You'd be a fool if you even thought that. What would I have to gain?'

'There's that, there's that.' He took the small duffel bag reluctantly. 'As soon as we're safely clear of the island—'

'Yes. That, and the letter. To the captain. Not before.'

'Those are deep waters, Dr Marlowe.' He didn't know how deep, I was close to drowning in them. 'Can't you tell me what it is all about?'

'If I knew that, Haggerty, do you think I'd be remaining behind on this godforsaken island?'

For the first time he smiled. 'No, sir, I don't really think you would.'

Captain Imrie and his search-party returned only a minute or two after I'd gone back up to the upper deck. They returned without Smithy. I was surprised neither by their failure to find him nor the brevity of their search—an elapsed time of only twenty minutes. Bear Island, on the map, may be only the veriest speck in the high Arctic, but it does cover an area of 73 square miles and it must have occurred to Captain Imrie very early on indeed that to attempt to search even a fraction of one per cent of that icily mountainous terrain in darkness was to embark upon a monumental folly. His fervour for the search had diminished to vanishing point: but his failure to find Smithy had, if anything, increased his determination to depart immediately. Having ensured that the last of the foredeck cargo had been unloaded and that all of the film company's equipment and personal effects were ashore, he and Mr Stokes courteously but swiftly shook hands with us all as we were ushered ashore. The derricks were already stayed in position and the mooring ropes singled up: Captain Imrie was not about to stand upon the order of his going.

Otto, properly enough, was the last to leave. At the head of the gangway, he said: 'Twenty-two days it is, then, Captain Imrie? You'll be back in twenty-two days?'

'I won't leave you here the winter, Mr Gerran, never fear.' With both the mystery and his much-unloved Bear Island about to be left behind, Captain Imrie apparently felt that he could permit himself a slight relaxation of attitude. 'Twenty-two days? At the very outset. Why, man, I can be in Hammerfest and back in seventy-two hours. I wish you all well.'

With this Captain Imrie ordered the gangway to be raised and went up to the bridge without explaining his cryptic remark about the seventy-two hours. It was more likely than not that what he had in mind at that very moment was, indeed, to be back inside seventy-two hours with, his manner seemed to convey, a small regiment of heavily-armed Norwegian police. I wasn't concerned: I was as certain as I could be that, if that were indeed what he had in mind, he would change his mind before the night was out.

The navigation lights came on and the *Morning Rose* moved off slowly northwards from the jetty, slewed round in a half-circle and headed down the Sor-hamna, her engine note deepening as she picked up speed. Opposite the jetty again Captain Imrie sounded his hooter—only the captain could have called it a siren—twice, a high and lonely sound almost immediately swallowed up in the muffling blanket of snow: within seconds, it seemed, both the throb of the engine and the pale glow of the navigation lights were lost in the snow and the darkness.

For what seemed quite some time we all stood there, huddled against the bitter cold and peering into the driving snow, as if by willing it we could bring the lights back into view again, the engine throb back into earshot. The atmosphere was not one of voyagers happily arrived at their hoped-for destination but of castaways marooned on an Arctic desert island.

The atmosphere inside the big living cabin was not much of an improvement. The oil heaters were functioning well enough and Eddie had the diesel generator running so that the black heaters on the walls were just beginning to warm up, but the effects of a decade of deep-freeze were not to be overcome in the space of an hour: the inside temperature was still below freezing. Nobody went to their allocated cubicles for the excellent reason that they were considerably colder than the central living space. Nobody appeared to want to talk to anybody else. Heissman embarked upon a pedantic and what promised to be lengthy lecture about Arctic survival, a subject concerning which his long and intimate acquaintance with Siberia presumably made him uniquely qualified to speak, but there were no takers, it was questionable whether he was even listening to himself. Then he, Otto and Neal Divine began a rather desultory discussion of their plans for—weather permitting—the following day's shooting, but obviously they hadn't their hearts even in that. It was, eventually, Conrad who put his finger on the cause of the general malaise, or, more accurately, expressed the thought that was in the mind of everybody with the possible exception of myself.

He said to Heissman: 'In the Arctic, in winter, you require torches. Right?'

'Right?'

'We have them?'

'Plenty, of course. Why?'

'Because I want one. I want to go out. We've been in here now, all of us, how long, I don't know, twenty minutes at least, and for all we know there may be a man out there sick or hurt or frostbitten or maybe fallen and broken a leg.'

'Oh, come now, come now, that's pitching it a bit strongly, Charles,' Otto said. 'Mr Smith has always struck me as a man eminently able to take care of himself.' Otto would probably have said the same thing if he'd been watching Smithy being mangled by a polar bear: because of both nature and build Otto was not a man to become unnecessarily involved in anything even remotely physical.

'If you don't really care, why don't you come out and say so?' This was a new side of Conrad to me and he continued to develop his theme at my expense. 'I'd have thought you'd have been the first to suggest this, Dr Marlowe.' I might have been, too, had I not known considerably more about Smithy than he did.

'I don't mind being the second,' I said agreeably.

In the event, we all went, with the exception of Otto, who complained of feeling unwell, and Judith Haynes who roundly maintained that it was all nonsense and that Mr Smith would come back when he felt like it, an opinion which I held myself but for reasons entirely different from hers. We were all provided with torches and agreed to keep as closely together as possible or, if separated, to be back inside thirty minutes at the latest.

The party set off in a wide sweep up the escarpment fronting the Sor-hamna to the north. At least, the others did. I headed straight for the equipment hut where the diesel generator was thudding away reassuringly, for it was unlikely that any one of us would be missed—no one would probably be aware of the presence of any other than his immediate neighbours—and the best place to sit out a wild goose chase was the warmest and most sheltered spot I could find. With my torch switched off so as not to betray my presence I opened the door of the hut, passed inside, closed the door, took a step forward and swore out loud as I stumbled over something comparatively yielding and almost measured my length on the planked floor. I recovered, turned and switched on my torch.

A man was lying stretched out on the floor and to my total lack of surprise it proved to be Smithy. He stirred and groaned, half-turned, raised a feeble arm to protect his eyes from the bright glare of the torch, then slumped back again, his arm falling limply by his side, his eyes closed. There was blood smeared over his left cheek. He stirred uneasily, moving from side to side and moaning in that soft fashion a man does when he is close to the borderline of consciousness.

'Does it hurt much, Smithy?' I asked.

He moaned some more.

'Where you scratched your cheek with a handful of frozen snow,' I said.

He stopped moving and he stopped moaning.

'The comedy act we'll keep for later in the programme,' I said coldly. 'In the meantime, will you kindly get up and explain to me why you've behaved like an irresponsible idiot?'

I placed the torch on the generator casing so that the beam shone upwards. It didn't give much light, just enough to show Smithy's carefully expressionless face as he got to his feet.

'What do you mean?' he said.

'PQS 182131, James R. Huntingdon, Golden Green and Beirut, currently and wrongly known as Joseph Rank Smith, is who I mean.'

'I guess I'm the irresponsible idiot you mean,' Smithy said. 'It would be nice to have introductions all round.'

'Dr Marlowe,' I said. He kept the same carefully expressionless face. 'Four years and four months ago when we took you from your nice cosy job as Chief Officer in that brokendown Lebanese tanker we thought you had a future with us. A bright one. Even four months ago we thought the same thing. But here, now, I'm very far from sure.'

Smithy smiled but his heart wasn't in it. 'You can't very well fire me on Bear Island.'

'I can fire you in Timbuctoo if I want to,' I said matter-of-factly. 'Well, come on.'

'You might have made yourself known to me.' Smithy sounded aggrieved and I supposed I would have been also in his position. 'I was beginning to guess. I didn't know there was anyone else aboard apart from me.'

'You weren't supposed to know. You weren't supposed to guess. You were supposed to do exactly what you were told. Just that and no more. You remember the last line in your written instructions? They were underlined. A quotation from Milton. *I* underlined it.'

' "They also serve who only stand and wait",' Smithy said. 'Corny, I thought it at the time.'

'I've had a limited education,' I said. 'Point is, did you stand and wait? Did you hell! Your orders were as simple and explicit as orders could ever be. Remain constantly aboard the *Morning Rose* until contacted. Do not, under any circumstances, leave the vessel even to step ashore. Do not, repeat not, attempt to conduct any investigations upon your own, do not seek to discover anything, at all times behave like a stereotype merchant navy officer. This you failed to do. I wanted you aboard that ship, Smithy. I *needed* you aboard —now. And where are you—stuck in a godforsaken hut on Bear Island. Why in God's name couldn't you follow out simple instructions?'

'OK. My fault. But I thought I was alone. Circumstances alter cases, don't they? With four men mysteriously dead and four others pretty close to death—well, damn it all, am I supposed to stand by and do *nothing*? Am I supposed to have *no* initiative, nor to think for myself even once?'

'Not till you're told to. And now look where you've left me—one hand behind my back. The *Morning Rose* was my other hand and now you've deprived me of it. I wanted it on call and close to hand every hour of the day and night. I might need it at any time—and now I haven't got it. Is there anybody aboard that blasted trawler who could maintain position just off-shore in the darkest night or bring her up the Sor-hamna in a full blizzard? You know damn well there's not. Captain Imrie couldn't bring her up the Clyde on a midsummer's afternoon.'

'You have a radio with you then? To communicate with the trawler?'

'Of course. Built into my medical case—no more than a police job, but range enough.'

'Be rather difficult to communicate with the *Morning Rose*'s transceiver lying in bits and pieces.'

'How very true,' I said. 'And why is it in bits and pieces? Because on the bridge you started talking freely and at length about shouting for help over that self-same radio and whistling up the NATO Atlantic forces if need be, while all the time some clever-cuts was taking his ease out on the bridge wing drinking in every word you said. I know, there were fresh tracks in the snow—well, my tracks, but re-used, if you follow me. So, of course, our clever-cuts hies himself off and gets himself a heavy hammer.'

'I could have been more circumspect at that, I suppose. You can have my apologies if you want them but I don't see them being all that useful at this stage.'

'I'm hardly in line myself for a citation for distinguished services, so we'll leave the apologies be. Now that you're here—well, I won't have to watch my back so closely.'

'So they're on to you—whoever *they* are?'

'Whoever *they* are are unquestionably on to me.' I told him briefly all I knew, not all I thought I knew or suspected I knew, for I saw no point in making Smithy as confused as myself. I went on: 'Just so we don't act at cross-purposes, let me initiate any action that I—or we—may think may have to be taken. I need hardly say that that doesn't deprive you of initiative if and when you find yourself or think you find yourself physically threatened. In that event, you have my advance permission to flatten anybody.'

'That's nice to know.' Smithy smiled briefly for the first time. 'It would be even nicer to know who it is that I'm likely to have to flatten. It would be even nicer still to know what you who are, I gather, a fairly senior Treasury official, and I, whom I know to be a junior one, are doing on this god-damned island anyway.'

'The Treasury's basic concern is money, always money, in one shape or other, and that's why we're here. Not our money, not British money, but what we call international dirty money, and all the members of the Central Banks co-operate very closely on this issue.'

'When you're as poor as I am,' Smithy said, 'there's no such thing as dirty money.'

'Even an underpaid civil servant like yourself wouldn't touch this lot. This is all ill-gotten gains, illegal loot from the days of World War II. This money has all been earned in blood and what has been recovered of it—and that's only a fraction of the total—has almost invariably been recovered in blood. Even as late as the spring of 1945 Germany was still a land of priceless treasures: by the summer of that year the cupboard was almost entirely bare. Both the victors and the vanquished laid their sticky fingers on every imaginable object of value they could clap eyes on—gold, precious stones, old masters, securities—German bank securities issued forty years ago are still perfectly valid—and took off in every conceivable direction. I need hardly say that none of those involved saw fit to declare their latest acquisitions to the proper authorities.' I looked at my watch. 'Your worried friends are scouring Bear Island for you—or a very small part of it, anyway. A half-hour search. I'll have to bring in your unconscious form in about fifteen minutes.'

'It all sounds pretty dull to me,' Smith said. 'All this loot, I mean. Was there much of it?'

'It all depends what you call much. It's estimated that the Allies—and when I say "Allies" I mean Britain and America as well as the much-maligned Russians—managed to get hold of about two-thirds of the total. That left the Nazis and their sympathizers with about a paltry one-third, and the conservative estimate of that one-third—conservative, Smithy—is that it amounts to approximately £350 million. Pounds sterling, you understand.'

'A thousand million all told?'

'Give or take a hundred million.'

'That childish remark about this being a dull subject. Strike it off the record.'

'Granted. Now this loot has found its way into some very odd places indeed. Some of it, inevitably, lies in secret numbered bank-accounts. Some of it—there is no question about this—lies in the form of specie in some of the very deepest Austrian Alpine lakes and has so far proved irrecoverable. I know of two Raphaels in the cellar gallery of a Buenos Aires millionaire, a Michaelangelo in Rio, several Halses and Rubenses in the same illegal collection in New York, and a Rembrandt in London. Their owners are either people who have been in, were in, or are closely connected to the governments or armed forces of the countries concerned: there's nothing the governments concerned can do about it and there are no signs that they're particularly keen to do anything about it anyway, they themselves might be the ultimate beneficiaries. As lately as the end of 1970 an international cartel went on to the market with £30 millions' worth of perfectly valid German securities issued in the 'thirties, approaching in turn the London, New York and Zürich markets, but the Federal Bank of Germany refused to cash those until proper owner identification was established: the point is that it's an open secret that those securities were taken from the vaults of the Reichsbank in 1945 by a special Red Army unit who were constituted as the only legalized military burglars in history.

'But that's only the tip of the iceberg, so to speak; the vast bulk of this immense fortune is hidden because the war is still too recent and people—the illegal owners—still too scared to convert their treasures into currency. There's a special Italian Government Recovery Office that deals exclusively with this matter, and its boss, one Professor Siviero, estimates that there are at least seven hundred old masters, many of them virtually priceless, still untraced, while another expert, a Simon Wiesenthal of the Austrian Jewish Documentation Service, says virtually the same thing—he, incidentally, maintains that there are countless highly-wanted characters, such as top-ranking officers in the SS, who are living in great comfort from hundreds of numbered bank accounts scattered throughout Europe.

'Siviero and Wiesenthal are the acknowledged legal experts in this form of recovery Unfortunately, there are known to be a handful of people—they amount to certainly not more than three or four—who are possessed of an equal or even

169

greater expertise in this matter, but who unfortunately are lacking in the high principles of their colleagues, if that is the word, who operate on the right side of the law. Their names are known but they are untouchable because they have never committed any known crimes, not even fraudulent conversion of stocks, because the stocks are always good, the claimants always proven. They are, nevertheless, criminals operating on an international level. We have the most skilful and successful of the lot with us here on Bear Island. His name is Johann Heissman.'

'Heissman!'

'None other. He's a very gifted lad is our Johann.'

'But Heissman! How can that be? Heissman? What kind of sense can that make? Why it's only two years—'

'I know. It's only two years since Heissman made his spectacular escape from Siberia and arrived in London to the accompaniment of lots of noise and TV cameras and yards of newspaper space and enough red carpet to go from Tilbury to Tomsk, since which time he has occupied himself exclusively with his old love of film-making, so how can it possibly be Heissman?

'Well, it can be Heissman and it is Heissman for our Johann is a very downy bird indeed. We have checked, in fact, that he was a movie studio partner of Otto in Vienna just before the war and that they did, in fact, attend the same gymnasium in St Polten, which is not all that far away. We do know that Heissman ran the wrong way while Otto ran the right way at the time of the Anschluss, and we do know that Heissman, because of his then Communist sympathies, was a very welcome guest of the Third Reich. What followed was one of those incredibly involved double and treble dealing spy switches that occurred so frequently in central Europe during the war. Heissman was apparently allowed to escape to Russia, where his sympathies were well known, and then sent back to Germany where he was ordered to transmit all possible misleading but still acceptable military information back to the Russians.'

'Why? Why did he do it?'

'Because his wife and two children were captured at the same time as he was. A good enough reason?' Smithy nodded. 'Then when the war was over and the Russians overran Berlin and turned up their espionage records, they found out what

Heissman had really been doing and shipped him to Siberia.'

'I would have thought they would have shot him out of hand.'

'They would have, too, but for one small point. I told you that Heissman was a very downy bird and that this was a treble deal. Heissman was, in effect and actually, working throughout the war for the Russians. For four years he faithfully sent back his misleading reports to his masters and even though he had the help of the German Intelligence in the preparation of his coded messages, they never once latched on to the fact that Heissman was using his own overlaid code throughout. The Russians simply spirited him away at the end of the war for his own safety and allegedly sent him to Siberia. Our information is that he's never been to Siberia: we believe that his wife and two married daughters are still living very comfortably in Moscow.'

'And he has been working for the Russians ever since?' Smithy was looking just faintly baffled and I had some fellow-feeling for him, Heissman's masterful duplicity was not for ready comprehension.

'In his present capacity. During his last eight years in his Siberian prison, Heissman, in a variety of disguises, has been traced in North and South America, South Africa, Israel and, believe it or not, in the Savoy Hotel in London. We know but we cannot prove that all those trips were in some way concerned with the recovery of Nazi treasure for his Russian masters—you have to remember that Heissman had built up the highest connections in the Party, the SS and the Intelligence: he was almost uniquely qualified for the task. Since his "escape" from Siberia he has made two pictures in Europe, one in Piedmont, where an old widow complained that some tattered old paintings had been stolen from the loft of her barn, the other in Provence, where an old country lawyer called in the police about some deed boxes that had been removed from his office. Whether either pictures or deed boxes were of any value we do not know: still less can we connect either disappearance with Heissman.'

'This is an awful lot to take in all at once,' Smithy complained.

'It is, isn't it?'

'OK if I smoke?'

'Five minutes. Then I've got to drag you back by the heels.'

'By the shoulders, if it's all the same to you.' Smithy lit his cigarette and thought a bit. 'So what you've got to find out is what Heissman is doing on Bear Island.'

'That's why we're here.'

'You've no idea?'

'None. Money, it's got to be money. This would be the last place on earth I'd associate with money and maybe that association would be wrong anyway. Maybe it's only a means to the money. Johann, as I trust you've gathered by this time, is a very devious character indeed.'

'Would there be a tie-up with the film company? With his old friend Gerran? Or would he just be making use of them?'

'I've simply no idea.'

'And Mary Stuart? The secret rendezvous girl? What could the possible connection be there?'

'Same answer. We know very little of her. We know her real name—she's never made any attempt to conceal that—age, birthplace and that she's a Latvian—or comes from what used to be Latvia before the Russians took it over. We also know—and this information she hasn't volunteered—that it was only her mother who was Latvian. Her father was German.'

'Ah! In the Army perhaps? Intelligence? SS?'

'That's the obvious connection to seek. But we don't know. Her immigration forms say that her parents are dead.'

'So the department has been checking on her too?'

'We've had a rundown on everyone here connected with Olympus Productions. We may as well have saved ourselves the trouble.'

'So no facts. Any hunches, feelings?'

'Hunches aren't my stock in trade.'

'I somehow didn't feel they would be.' Smithy ground out his cigarette. 'Before we go, I'd like to mention two very uncomfortable thoughts that have just occurred to me. Number one. Johann Heissman is a very big-time very successful international operative? True?'

'He's an international criminal.'

'A rose by any other name. The point is that those boys avoid violence wherever possible, isn't that true?'

'Perfectly true. Apart from anything else, it's beneath them.'

'And have you ever heard Heissman's name being associated with violence?'

'There's no record of it.'

'But there's been a considerable amount of violence, one way or the other, in the past day or two. So if it isn't Heissman, who's behind the strong-arm behaviour?'

'I don't say it isn't Heissman. The leopard can change his spots. He may be finding himself, for God knows what reason, in so highly unusual a situation that he has no option other than to have recourse to violence. He may, for all we know, have violent associates who don't necessarily represent his attitude. Or it may be someone entirely unconnected with him.'

'That's what I like,' Smithy said. 'Simple straightforward answers. And there's the second point that may have escaped your attention. If our friends are on to you the chances are that they're on to me too. That eavesdropper on the bridge.'

'The point had not escaped my attention. And not because of the bridge, although that may have given pause for thought, but because you deliberately skipped ship. It doesn't matter what most of them think, one person or possibly more is going to be convinced that you did it on purpose. You're a marked man, Smithy.'

'So that when you drag me back there not everyone is going to feel genuine pangs of sorrow for poor old Smithy? Some may question the *bona fides* of my injuries?'

'They won't question. They'll damn well know. But we have to act as if.'

'Maybe you'll watch my back too? Now and again?'

'I have a lot on my mind, but I'll try.'

I had Smithy by the armpits, head lolling, heels and hands trailing in the snow, where two flashlights picked us up less than five yards from the door of the main cabin.

'You've found him then?' It was Goin, Harbottle by his side. 'Good man!' Even to my by now hypersensitive ear Goin's reaction sounded genuine.

'Yes. About quarter of a mile away.' I breathed very quickly and deeply to give them some idea as to what it must have been like to drag a two-hundred-pound dead-weight over uneven snow-covered terrain for such a distance. 'Found him in the bottom of a gully. Give me a hand, will you?'

They gave me a hand. We hauled him inside, fetched a camp-cot and stretched him out on this.

'Good God, good God, good God!' Otto wrung his hands, the anguished expression on his face testimony to the fresh burden now added to the crippling weight of the cross he was already carrying. 'What's happened to the poor fellow?' The only other occupant of the cabin, Judith Haynes, had made no move to leave the oil stove she was monopolizing, unconscious men being borne into her presence might have been so routine an affair as not even to merit the raising of an eyebrow.

'I'm not sure,' I said between gasps. 'Heavy fall, I think, banged his head on a boulder. Looked like.'

'Concussion?'

'Maybe.' I probed through his hair with my fingertips, found a spot on the scalp that felt no different from anywhere else, and said: 'Ah!'

They looked at me in anxious expectancy.

'Brandy,' I said to Otto. I fetched my stethoscope, went through the necessary charade, and managed to revive the coughing, moaning Smithy with a mouthful or two of brandy. For one not trained to the boards, he put up a remarkable performance, high-lighted, at its end, with a muted series of oaths and an expression of mingled shock and chagrin when I gently informed him that the *Morning Rose* had sailed without him.

During the course of the histrionics most of the other searchers wandered in in twos or threes. I watched them all carefully without seeming to, looking for an expression that was other than surprise or relief, but I might have spared myself the trouble: if there was one or more who was neither surprised nor relieved he had his emotions and facial muscles too well schooled to show anything. I would have expected nothing else.

After about ten minutes our concern shifted from a now obviously recovering Smithy to the fact that two members of the searching party, Allen and Stryker, were still missing. After the events of that morning I felt the absence of those two, of all of us, to be rather coincidental; after fifteen minutes I felt it odd, and after twenty minutes I felt it downright ominous, a feeling that was clearly shared by nearly everyone there. Judith Haynes had abandoned her squatter's rights by her oil stove and was walking up and down in short, nervous steps, squeezing her hands together. She stopped in front of me.

'I don't like it, I don't like it!' Her voice was strained and anxious, it could have been acting but I didn't think so. 'What's keeping him? Why is he so long? He's out there with that Allen fellow. Something's wrong. I know it is, I *know* it.' When I didn't answer she said: 'Well, aren't you going out to look for him?'

'Just as you went out to look for Mr Smith here,' I said. It wasn't very nice, but then I didn't always feel so very kind to other people as Lonnie did. 'Maybe your husband will come back when *he* feels like it.'

She looked at me without speaking, her lips moving but not speaking, no real hostility in her face, and I realized for the second time that day that her rumoured hatred for her husband was, in fact, only a rumour and that, buried no matter how deep, there did exist some form of concern for him. She turned away and I reached for my torch.

'Once more into the breach,' I said. 'Any takers?'

Conrad, Jungbeck, Heyter and Hendriks accompanied me. Volunteers there were in plenty but I reasoned that not only would increased numbers get in one another's way, but the chances of someone else becoming lost would be all the greater. Immediately after leaving the hut the five of us fanned out at intervals of not more than fifteen feet and moved off to the north.

We found Allen inside the first thirty seconds: more accurately, he found us, for he saw our torches—he'd lost his own—and came stumbling towards us out of the snow and the darkness. 'Stumbled' was the operative word, he was weaving and swaying like one far gone in alcohol or exhaustion, and when he tried to speak his voice was thick and slurred. He was shivering like a man with the ague. It seemed not only pointless but cruel to question him in that condition so we hurried him inside.

I had a look at him as we sat him on a stool by an oil stove and I didn't have to look twice or very closely to see that this hadn't exactly been Allen's day. Allen had been in the wars again and the damage that had been inflicted on him this time at least matched up to the injuries he'd received that morning. He had two nasty cuts above what had been up till then his undamaged eye, a bruised and scratched right

175

cheek, and blood came from both his mouth and nose, blood already congealed in the cold but his worst injury was a very deep gash on the back of the head, the scalp laid open clear to the bone. Someone had given young Allen a very thorough going over indeed.

'And what happened to you this time?' I asked. He winced as I started to clean up his face. 'Or should I say, do you know what happened to you?'

'I don't know,' he said thickly. He shook his head and drew his breath in sharply as some pain struck through either head or neck. 'I don't remember. I don't remember.'

'You've been in a fight, laddie,' I said. 'Again. Someone's cut you up, and quite badly.'

'I know. I can feel it. I don't remember. Honest to God, I don't remember. I—I just don't know what happened.'

'But you must have seen him,' Goin said reasonably. 'Whoever it was, you must have been face to face with him. God's sake, boy, your shirt's torn and there's at least a couple of buttons missing from your coat. And he *had* to be standing in front of you when he did this to you. Surely you must have caught a glimpse of him at least.'

'It was dark,' Allen mumbled. 'I didn't see anything. I didn't feel anything, all I knew was that I woke up kind of groggy like in the snow with the back of my head hurting. I knew I was bleeding and—*please,* I don't know *what* happened.'

'Yes you do, yes you do!' Judith Haynes had pushed her way to the front. The transformation that had taken place in her face was as astonishing as it was ugly, and although her morning performance had partially prepared me for something of this kind, and though this expression was different from the one that had disfigured her face that time, it was still an almost frightening thing to watch. The red gash of the mouth had vanished, the lips drawn in and back over bared teeth, the green eyes were no more than slits and, as had happened that morning, the skin was stretched back over her cheekbones until it appeared far too tight for her face. She screamed at him: 'You damned liar! Wanted your own back, didn't you? You dirty little bastard, what have you done with my husband? Do you hear me? Do you hear me? What have you done with him, damn you? Where is he? Where did you leave him?'

Allen looked up at her in a half-scared astonishment, then

shook his head wearily. 'I'm sorry, Miss Haynes, I don't know what—'

She hooked her long-nailed fingers into talons and lunged for him, but I'd been waiting for it. So had both Goin and Conrad. She struggled like a trapped wild-cat, screaming invective at Allen, then suddenly relaxed, her breath coming in harsh, rasping sobs.

'Now then, now then, Judith,' Otto said. 'That's no—'

'Don't you "now then" me, you silly old bastard!' she screamed. Filial respect was clearly not Judith Haynes's strong point, but Otto, though clearly nervous, accepted his daughter's abuse as if it were a matter of course. 'Why don't you find out instead what this young swine's done to my husband? Why don't you? Why don't you!' She struggled to free her arms and as she was trying to move away we let her go. She picked up a torch and ran for the door.

'Stop her,' I said.

Heyter and Jungbeck, big men both, blocked her flight.

'Let me go, let me out!' she shouted. Neither Heyter nor Jungbeck moved and she whirled round on me. 'Who the hell are you to—I want to go out and find Michael!'

'I'm sorry, Miss Haynes,' I said. 'You're in no condition to go to look for anyone. You'd just run wild, no trace of where you'd been, and in five minutes' time you'd be lost too and perhaps lost for good. We're leaving in just a moment.'

She took three quick steps towards Otto, her fists clenched, her teeth showing again.

'You let him push me around like this?' This with an incinerating glare in my direction. 'Spineless, that's you, absolutely spineless! Anybody can walk over you!' Otto blinked nervously at this latest tirade but said nothing. 'Aren't I supposed to be your bloody daughter? Aren't you supposed to be the bloody boss? God's sake, who gives the orders about here? You or Marlowe?'

'Your father does,' Goin said. 'Naturally. But, without any disrespect to Dr Marlowe, we don't hire a dog just to bark ourselves. He's a medical man and we'd be fools not to defer to him in medical matters.'

'Are you suggesting I'm a medical case?' All the colour had drained from her cheeks and she looked uglier than ever. 'Are you? Are you, then? A mental case, perhaps?'

Heaven knows I wouldn't have blamed Goin if he'd said

'yes' straight out and left it at that, but Goin was far too balanced and diplomatic to say any such thing, and besides, he'd clearly been through this sort of crisis before. He said, quietly but not condescendingly: 'I'm suggesting no such thing. Of course you're distressed, of course you're over-wrought, after all it is your husband that's missing. But I agree with Dr Marlowe that you're not the person to go looking for him. We'll have him back here all the quicker if you co-operate with us, Judith.'

She hesitated, still halfway between hysteria and rage, then swung away. I taped the gash on Allen's head and said: 'That'll do till I come back. Afraid I'll have to shave off a few locks and stitch it.' On the way to the door I stopped and said quietly to Goin: 'Keep her away from Allen, will you?'

Goin nodded.

'And for heaven's sake keep her away from Mary darling.'

He looked at me in what was as close to astonishment as he was capable of achieving. 'That kid?'

'That kid. She's next on the list for Miss Haynes's attentions. When Miss Haynes gets around to thinking about it, that is.'

I left with the same four as previously. Conrad, the last out, closed the door behind him and said: 'Jesus! My charming leading lady. What a virago she is!'

'She's a little upset,' I said mildly.

'A little upset! Heaven send I'm in the next county if she ever gets really mad. What the hell do you think can have happened to Stryker?'

'I have no idea,' I said, and because it was dark I didn't have to assume an honest expression to go with the words. I moved closer to him so that the others, already fanned out in line of search, couldn't hear me. 'Seeing we're such a bunch of odd-balls anyway, I hope an odd request from another odd-ball won't come amiss.'

'You disappoint me, Doctor. I thought you and I were two of the very few halfway normal people around here.'

'By the prevailing standards, any moderate odd-ball is normal. You know anything of Lonnie's past?'

He was silent for a moment, then said: 'He has a past?'

'We all have a past. If you think I mean a criminal past, no. Lonnie hasn't got one. I just want to find out if he was married or had any family. That's all.'

'Why don't you ask him yourself?'

'If I felt free to ask him myself, would I be asking you?' Another silence. 'Your name really Marlowe, Doc?'

'Marlowe, as ever was. Christopher Marlowe. Passport, birth certificate, driving licence—they're all agreed on it.'

'Christopher Marlowe? Just like the playwright, eh?'

'My parents had literary inclinations.'

'Uh-huh.' He paused again. 'Remember what happened to your namesake—stabbed in the back by a friend before his thirtieth birthday?'

'Rest easy. My thirtieth birthday is lost in the mists of time.'

'And you're really a doctor?'

'Yes.'

'And you're really something else too?'

'Yes.'

'Lonnie. Marital status. Children or no. You may rely on Conrad's discretion.'

'Thanks,' I said. We moved apart. We were walking to the north for two reasons—the wind, and hence the snow, were to our backs and so progress was easier in that direction, and Allen had come stumbling from that direction. In spite of Allen's professed total lack of recall of what had happened, it seemed likely to me that we might find Stryker also somewhere in that direction. And so it proved.

'Over here! Over here!' In spite of the muffling effects of the snow Hendriks's shout sounded curiously high-pitched and cracked. 'I've found him, I've found him!'

He'd found him all right. Michael Stryker was lying face down in the snow, arms and legs outspread in an almost perfectly symmetrical fashion. Both fists were clenched tight. On the snow, beside his left shoulder, lay a smooth elliptical stone which from its size—it must have weighed between sixty and seventy pounds—better qualified for the name of boulder. I stooped low over this boulder, bringing the torch close, and at once saw the few dark hairs embedded in the dark and encrusted stain. Proof if proof were required, but I hadn't doubted anyway that this was what had been used to smash in the back of Stryker's skull. Death would have been instantaneous.

'He's dead!' Jungbeck said incredulously.

'He's all that,' I said.

'And murdered!'

'That too.' I tried to turn him over on his back but Conrad
and Jungbeck had to lend their not inconsiderable weights
before this was done. His upper lip was viciously split all the
way down from the nostril, a tooth was missing and he had a
peculiar red and raw-looking mark on his right temple.

'By God, there must have been a fight,' Jungbeck said
huskily. 'I wouldn't have thought that kid Allen had had
it in him.'

'I wouldn't have thought so either,' I said.

'Allen?' Conrad said. 'I'd have sworn he was telling the
truth. Could he—well, do you think it could have happened
when he was suffering from amnesia?'

'All sorts of funny thing can happen when you've had a
bump on the head,' I said. I looked at the ground around the
dead man, there were footprints there, not many, already faint
and blurred from the driving snow: there was no help to be
gained from that quarter. I said: 'Let's get him back.'

So we carried the dead man back to the camp and it wasn't,
in spite of the uneven terrain and the snow in our faces, as
difficult a task as it might have been for the same reason
that I'd found it so difficult to turn him over—the limbs had
already begun to stiffen, not from the onset of rigor mortis,
for it was too soon for that yet, but from the effects of the
intense cold. We laid him in the snow outside the main cabin.
I said to Hendriks: 'Go inside and ask Goin for a bottle of
brandy—say that I sent you back for it, that we need it to
keep us going.' It was the last thing I would ever have recom-
mended to keep anyone warm in bitter outdoor cold, but it
was all I could think of on the spur of the moment. 'Tell
Goin—quietly—to come here.'

Goin, clearly aware that there was something far amiss,
walked out casually and casually shut the door behind him,
but there was nothing casual about his reaction when he saw
Stryker lying there, his gashed and marble-white face a death's
head in the harsh light of several torches. Goin's own face
was clear enough in the backwash of light reflected from the
snow. The shocked expression on his face he could have
arranged for: the draining of blood that left it almost as white
as Stryker's he couldn't.

'Jesus Christ!' he whispered. 'Dead?'

I said nothing, just turned the dead man over with Conrad's

and Jungbeck's help again. This time it was more difficult. Goin made a strange noise in his throat but otherwise didn't react at all, I suppose he'd nothing left to react with, he just stood there and stared as the driving snow whitened the dead man's anorak and, mercifully, the fearful wound in the occiput. For what seemed quite a long time we stood there in silence, gazing down at the dead man: I was aware, almost subconsciously, that the wind, now veering beyond south, was strengthening, for the thickening snow was driving along now almost parallel to the ground: I do not know what the temperature was, but it must have been close on thirty degrees below freezing. I was dimly aware that I was shaking with the cold: looking around, I could see that the others were also. Our breaths froze as they struck the icy air, but the wind whipped them away before the vapour had time to form.

'Accident?' Goin said hoarsely. 'It could have been an accident?'

'No,' I said. 'I saw the boulder that was used to crush his skull in.' Goin made the same curious noise in his throat again, and I went on: 'We can't leave him here and we can't take him inside. I suggest we leave him in the tractor shed.'

'Yes, yes, the tractor shed,' Goin said. He really didn't know what he was saying.

'And who's going to break the news to Miss Haynes?' I went on. God alone knew that I didn't fancy doing it.

'What?' He was still shocked. 'What was that?'

'His wife. She'll have to be told.' As a doctor, I supposed I was the one to do it, but the decision was taken from my hands. The cabin door was jerked abruptly open and Judith Haynes, her two dogs by her ankles, stood there framed against the light from the interior, with Otto and the Count just vaguely discernible behind her. She stood there for some little time, a hand on either door jamb, quite immobile and without any expression that I could see, then walked forward in a curiously dreamlike fashion and stooped over her husband. After a few moments she straightened, looked around as if puzzled, then turned questioning eyes on me, but only for a moment, for the questioning eyes turned up in her head and she crumpled and fell heavily across Stryker's body before I or anyone could get to her.

Conrad and I, with Goin following, brought her inside

and laid her on the camp-cot so lately occupied by Smithy. The cocker spaniels had to be forcibly restrained from joining her. Her face was alabaster white and her breathing very shallow. I lifted up her right eyelid and there was no resistance to my thumb: it was only an automatic reaction on my part, it hadn't even occurred to me that the faint wasn't genuine. I became aware that Otto was standing close by, his eyes wide, his mouth slightly open, his hands clenched together until the ivory knuckles showed.

'Is she all right?' he asked hoarsely. 'Will she—'

'She'll come to,' I said.

'Smelling salts,' he said. 'Perhaps—'

'No.' Smelling salts, to hasten her recovery to the bitter reality she would have to face.

'And Michael? My son-in-law? He's—I mean—'

'You saw him,' I said almost irritably. 'He's dead, of course he's dead.'

'But how—but how—'

'He was murdered.' There were one or two involuntary exclamations, the shocked indrawing of breath, then a silence that became intensified with the passing of seconds by the hissing of the Coleman lamps. I didn't even bother to look up to see what the individual reactions might be for I knew by now that I'd learn nothing that way. I just looked at the unconscious woman and didn't know what to think. Stryker, the tough, urbane, cynical Stryker had, in his own way, been terrified of this woman. Had it been because of the power she had wielded as Otto's daughter, his knowledge that his livelihood was entirely dependent on her most wayward whim—and I could imagine few more gifted exponents of the wayward whim than Judith Haynes? Had it been because of her pathological jealousy which I knew beyond all question to exist, because of the instant bitchiness which could allegedly range from the irrational to the insane, or had she held over his head the threat of some nameless blackmail which could bring him at once to his knees? Had he, in his own way, even loved his wife and hoped against hopeless hope that she might reciprocate some of this and been prepared to suffer any humiliation, any insult, in the hope that he might achieve this or part of it? I'd never know, but the questions were academic anyway, Stryker no longer concerned me, I was only turning them over in my mind wondering in what way they could throw any light on Judith Haynes's totally unexpected reaction to Stryker's death. She had despised him, she must have despised him for his dependence upon her, his weakness, his meek acceptance of insult, the fear he had displayed before me, for the emptiness and nothingness that had lain concealed behind so impressively masculine a façade. But had she loved him at the same time, loved him for what he had been or might have been, or was she just desolated at the loss of her most cherished whipping-boy, the one sure person in the world upon whom she knew she could with impunity vent her wayward spleen whenever the fancy took her? Even without her awareness of it, he might have become an integral, an indispensable part of her existence, an insidiously woven warp in the weft of her being, always dependable, always there, always ready to hand when she most needed him even when that need was no more than to absorb the grey corrosive poison eating away steadily at the edges of her mind. Even the most tarnished cornerstone can support the most crumbling edifice: take that away and the house comes tumbling down. The traumatic reaction to Stryker's death could, paradoxically, be the clinching manifestation of a complete and irredeemable selfishness: the as yet unrealized realization that she was the most pitiful of all creatures, a person totally alone.

Judith Haynes stirred and her eyes fluttered open. Memory came back and she shuddered. I eased her to a sitting position and she looked dully around her.

'Where is he?' I had to strain to hear the words.

'It's all right, Miss Haynes,' I said, and, just to compound that fatuous statement, added: 'We'll look after him.'

'Where is he?' she moaned. 'He's my husband, my husband. I want to see him.'

'Better not, Miss Haynes.' Goin could be surprisingly gentle. 'As Dr Marlowe says, we'll take care of things. You've seen him already and no good can come—'

'Bring him in. Bring him in.' A voice devoid of life but the will absolute. 'I must see him again.'

I rose and went to the door. The Count barred my way. His aquiline, aristocratic features held a mixture of revulsion and horror. 'You can't do that. It's too ghastly—it's—it's macabre.'

'What do you think that I think it is?' I felt savage but

I know I didn't sound that way, I think I only sounded tired. 'If I don't bring him in, she'll just go outside again. It's not much of a night for being outside.'

So we brought him in, the same three of us, Jungbeck and Conrad and myself, and we laid him on his back so that the fearful wound in the occiput didn't show. Judith Haynes rose from her camp-cot, moved slowly towards him like a person in a dream and sank to her knees. Without moving, she looked at him for some moments then reached out and gently touched the gashed face. No one spoke, no one moved. Not without effort, she pulled his right arm close in to his side, made to do the same with his left, noticed that the fist was still clenched and carefully prised it open.

A brown circular object lay in the palm of his hand. She took it, placed it in the palm of her own hand, straightened —still on her knees—and swung in a slow semi-circle showing us what she held. Then, her hand outstretched towards him, she looked at Allen. We all looked at Allen.

The brown leather button in her hand matched the still remaining buttons on Allen's torn coat.

CHAPTER NINE

I'm not sure how long the silence went on, a silence that the almost intolerable hiss of the lamps and the ululating moan of the south wind served only to deepen. It must have lasted at least ten seconds, although it seemed many times as long, a seemingly interminable period of time during which nobody moved and nothing moved, not even eyes, for Allen's eyes were fixed on the button in Judith Haynes's hand in fascinated uncomprehension, while every other eye in the room was on Allen. That one small leather-covered button held us all in thrall.

Judith Haynes was the first to move. She rose, very slowly, as if it called for a tremendous effort of both mind and muscle, and stood there for a moment, as if irresolute. She seemed quiet now and very resigned and because this was the wrong reaction altogether I looked past her towards Conrad and Smithy and caught the eyes of both. Conrad lowered his eyes briefly as if in acknowledgment of a signal, Smithy shifted his gaze towards Judith Haynes and when she began to move away from the body of her husband both of them moved casually towards each other to block off her clearly intended approach to Allen. Judith Haynes stopped, looked at them and smiled.

'That won't be necessary at all,' she said. She tossed the button to Allen who caught it in involuntary reaction. He held it in his hand, staring at it, then looked up in perplexity at Judith Haynes, who smiled again. 'You'll be needing that, won't you?' she said, and walked in the direction of her allocated room.

I relaxed and was aware that others were doing so also, for I could hear the slow exhalation of breaths of those standing closest to me. I looked away from Judith Haynes to Allen, and that was a mistake because I had relaxed too soon, I'd been instinctively aware that the seemingly quiet and sad resignation had been wholly out of character but had put it down to the effects of the shattering shock she had just received.

'You killed him, you killed him!' Her voice was an insane scream, but no more insane than the demented fury with which she was attacking Mary Darling who had already stumbled over backwards, the other woman falling on top of her, clawing viciously with hooked fingers. 'You bitch, you whore, you filthy slut, you—you murderess! You're the person who killed him! You killed my husband! You! You!' Sobbing and shrieking maniacal invective at the terrified and momentarily paralysed Mary Darling who had already lost her big hornrimmed spectacles, Judith Haynes wound one hand round the unfortunate Mary's hair and was reaching for her eyes with the other when Smithy and Conrad got to her. Both were big strong men but she fought with such crazed and tigerish ferocity—and they had at the same time to cope with two equally hysterical dogs—that it took them quite some seconds to pull her clear, and even then she clung with the strength of madness to Mary's hair, a grip that Smithy ruthlessly and without hesitation broke by squeezing her wrist until she shrieked with pain. They dragged her upright and she continued to scream hysterically with all the strength of her lungs, no longer attempting even to mouth words, just that horrible nerve-drilling shrieking like some animal in its dying agony, then the sound abruptly ceased, her legs buckled and Smithy and Conrad eased her to the floor.

Conrad looked at me. 'Act two?' He was breathing heavily and looked pale.

'No. This is real. Will you please take her to her cubicle?' I looked at the shocked and sobbing Mary but she didn't need any immediate assistance from me, for Allen, his own injuries forgotten, had dropped to his knees beside her, raised her to a sitting position and was using a none too clean handkerchief to dab at the three deep and ugly scratches that had been torn down the length of her left cheek. I left them, went into my cubicle, prepared a hypodermic and entered the cubicle where Judith Haynes had been taken. Smithy and Conrad were standing watchfully by and had been joined by Otto, the Count and Goin. Otto looked at the syringe and caught my arm.

'Is that—is that for my daughter? What are you going to do to her? It's all over now, man—good God, you can see she's unconscious.'

'And I'm going to see that she bloody well stays that way,' I said. 'For hours and hours and hours. That way it's best for her and best for all of us. All right, I'm sorry for your daughter, she's had a tremendous shock, but medically I'm not concerned with that, I'm just concerned with how best to treat her for the condition she's in now, which is frankly unbalanced, unstable and highly dangerous. Or do you want to have a look at Mary Darling again?'

Otto hesitated but Goin, calmly reasonable as always, came to my help. 'Dr Marlowe is perfectly right, Otto—and it's for Judith's own good, after such a shock a long rest can only help. This is the best thing for her.'

I wasn't so sure about that, I'd have preferred a strait-jacket, but I nodded my thanks to Goin, administered the injection, helped bundle her into a zipped sleeping-bag, saw that she was covered over and above that with a sufficiency of blankets and left her. I took the dogs with me and put them in my own cubicle—I don't much like having animals, especially highly-strung ones, in the company of a person under sedation.

Allen had Mary Darling seated on a bench now but was still dabbing her cheek. She'd stopped sobbing now, was just breathing with long quivering in-drawn gasps and, scratches apart, didn't seem much the worse for an experience that must have been as harrowing as it was brief. Lonnie was standing a few feet away, looking sorrowfully at the girl and shaking his head.

'Poor, poor lassie,' he said quietly. 'Poor little girl.'

'She'll be all right,' I said. 'If I do a halfway job the scratches won't even scar.' I looked at Stryker's body and decided that its removal to the tractor shed was clearly the first priority: apart from Lonnie and Allen, no one had eyes for anything else, and even although out of sight would not necessarily be out of mind, the absence of that mutilated body could hardly fail to improve morale.

'I wasn't talking about young Mary.' Lonnie had my attention again. 'I was thinking about Judith Haynes. Poor, lonely lassie.' I looked at him closely but I should have known him well enough by then to realize that he was incapable of either dissimulation or duplicity: he looked as sad as he sounded.

'Lonnie,' I said, 'you never cease to astonish me.' I lit the oil stove, put some water on to heat, then turned to Stryker. Both Smithy and Conrad were waiting and words were unnecessary. Lonnie insisted on coming with us, to open doors and hold a flash-light: we left Stryker in the tractor shed and went back to the main cabin. Smithy and Conrad went inside but Lonnie showed no intentions of following them. He stood there as if deep in thought, seemingly oblivious of a wind now strong enough to have to lean against, of a thickening driving snow now approaching the proportions of a blizzard, of the intense and steadily deepening cold.

'I think I'll stay out here a bit,' he said. 'Nothing like a little fresh air to clear the head.'

'No, indeed,' I said. I took the torch from him and directed its beam at the nearest hut. 'In there. On the left.' Wherever else Olympus Productions may have fallen short in the commissariat department, it hadn't been in the line of alcoholic stimulants.

'My dear fellow.' He retrieved his torch with a firm grasp. 'I personally supervised its storage.'

'And not even a lock to contend with,' I said.

'And what if there was? Otto would give me the key.'

'Otto would give you a key?' I said carefully.

'Of course. Do you think I'm a professional safe-cracker who goes around festooned with strings of skeleton keys? Who do you think gave me the keys to the lounge locker on the *Morning Rose*?'

'Otto did?' I said brightly.

'Of course.'

'What kind of blackmail are you using, Lonnie?'

'Otto is a very, very kind man,' Lonnie said seriously. 'I thought I'd told you that?'

'I'd just forgotten.' I watched him thoughtfully as he plodded purposefully through the deep snow towards the provisions hut, then went inside the main cabin. Most of the people inside, now that Stryker had gone, had transferred their attention to Allen, who was clearly self-consciously aware of this, for he no longer had his arm around Mary, although he still dabbed at her cheek with a handkerchief. Conrad, who had clearly become more than a little smitten by Mary Stuart for he'd sought out her company whenever possible in the past two days, was sitting beside her chafing one of her hands—I assumed she'd been complaining of the temperature which was still barely above freezing—and although she seemed half-reluctant and was smiling in some embarrassment, she wasn't objecting to the extent of making a song and dance about it. Otto, Goin, the Count and Divine were talking in low voice near one of the oil stoves: Divine, not surprisingly, was there not in the capacity of a contributor to the conversation, but as a bar-tender for he was laying out glasses and bottles under Otto's fussy direction. Otto beckoned me across.

'After what we've just been through,' he said, 'I think we're all badly in need of a restorative.' That Otto should be lashing out so recklessly with his private supplies was sufficient indication of the extent to which he had been shaken. 'It will also give us time to decide what to do with him.'

'Who?'

'Allen, of course.'

'Ah. Well, I'm sorry, I'm afraid you gentlemen will have to count me out for both drink and deliberations.' I nodded to Allen and Mary Darling, both of whom were watching us with some degree of apprehension. 'A little patching up to do there. Excuse me.'

I took the now hot water from the oil stove, brought it into my cubicle, put a white cloth on the rickety table that was there, laid out a basin, instruments and what medicaments I thought I'd require, then returned to where Conrad and Mary Stuart were sitting in the main body of the cabin. Like all the other little groups in the cabin they were talking in voices so low as to be virtually whispering, whether from a desire for privacy or because they still felt themselves to be in the presence of death I didn't know. Conrad, to my complete lack of surprise, was now industriously massaging her other hand, and as that was her left or faraway one I assumed that he hadn't had to fight for it.

I said: 'I'm sorry to interrupt the first-aid but I want to patch up young Allen a bit. I wonder if Mary dear will look after Mary darling for a bit?'

'Mary dear?' Conrad raised an inquiring eyebrow.

'To distinguish her from Mary darling,' I explained. 'It's what I call her when we're alone in the long watches of the night.' She smiled slightly but that was her only reaction.

'Mary dear,' Conrad said appreciatively. 'I like it. May I call you that?'

'I don't know,' she said mock-seriously. 'Perhaps it's copyright.'

'He can have the patent under licence,' I said. 'I can always rescind it. What were you two being so conspiratorial about?'

'Ah, yes,' Conrad said. 'Your opinion, Doc. That stone out there, I mean the lump of rock Stryker was clobbered with. I'd guess the weight about seventy pounds. Would you?'

'The same.'

'I asked Mary here if she could lift a rock like that above her head and she said don't be ridiculous.'

'Unless she's an Olympic weight-lifter in disguise, well, yes, you are ridiculous. She couldn't. Why?'

'Well, just look at her.' He nodded across at the other Mary. 'Skin and bone, just skin and bone. Now how—'

'I wouldn't let Allen hear you.'

'You know what I mean. A rock that size. "Murderess", Judith Haynes called her. Well, so OK, she was out there looking with the others, but how on earth—'

'I think Miss Haynes had something else in mind,' I said. I left them, beckoned to Allen, then turned to Smithy who was sitting close by. 'I require a surgery assistant. Feeling up to it now?'

'Sure.' He rose. 'Anything to take my mind off Captain Imrie and the report he must be writing out about me right now.'

There was nothing I could do to Allen's face that nature couldn't do better so I concentrated on the gash on the back of his head. I froze it, shaved the area around it, and jerked my head to Smithy to have a look. He did this and his eyes widened a little but he said nothing. I put eight stitches in the wound and covered it with plaster. During all of this we hadn't exchanged a word and Allen was obviously very conscious of this.

He said: 'You haven't got much to say to me, have you, Dr Marlowe?'

'A good tradesman doesn't talk on the job.'

'You're just thinking what all the others are thinking, aren't you?'

'I don't know. I don't know what all the others are thinking. Well, that's it. Just comb your hair straight back and no one will know you're prematurely bald.'

'Yes. Thank you.' He turned and faced me, hesitated and said: 'It does look pretty black against me, doesn't it?'

'Not to a doctor.'

'You—you mean you *don't* think I did it?'

'It's not a matter of thinking. It's a matter of knowing. Look, all in all you've had a pretty rough day, you're more shaken up than you realize, and when that anaesthetic wears off you're going to hurt a bit. Your cubicle's next to mine, isn't it?'

'Yes, but—'

'Go and lie down for a couple of hours.'

'Yes, but—'

'And I'll send Mary through when I've finished with her.'

He made to speak, then nodded wearily and left. Smithy said: 'That was nasty. The back of his head, I mean. It must have been one helluva clout.'

'He's been lucky that his skull isn't fractured. Doubly lucky in that he's not even concussed.'

'Uh-huh.' Smithy thought for a moment. 'Look, I'm not a doctor and I'm not very good at coining phrases, but doesn't this put a rather different complexion upon matters?'

'I am a doctor and it does.'

He thought some more. 'Especially when you have a close look at Stryker?'

'Especially that.'

I brought Mary Darling in. She was very pale, still apprehensive and had a little-girl-lost look about her, but she had herself under control. She looked at Smithy, made as if to speak, hesitated, changed her mind and let me get on with doing what I could. I cleaned and disinfected the scratches, taped them up carefully and said: 'It'll itch like fury for a bit, but if you can resist the temptation to haul the plasters off then you'll have no scars.'

'Thank you, Doctor. I'll try.' She looked very wan. 'Can I speak to you, please?'

'Of course.' She looked at Smithy and I said: 'You can speak freely. I promise you it will go no farther.'

'Yes, yes, I know, but—'

'Mr Gerran is dispensing free scotch out there,' Smithy said, and made for the door. 'I'd never forgive myself if I passed up an experience that can happen only once in a lifetime.'

She had me by the lapels even before Smithy had the door fully closed behind him. There was a frantic worry in her face, a sick misery in the eyes that made me realize just how much it had cost her to maintain her composure while Smithy had been there.

'Allen didn't do it, Dr Marlowe! He didn't, I know he didn't, I swear he didn't. I know things look awful for him, the fight they had this morning, and now this other fight and that button in—in Mr Stryker's hand and everything. But I know he didn't, he told me he didn't, Allen couldn't tell a lie, he wouldn't tell me a lie! And he couldn't hurt anything, I mean just not kill anybody, I mean hurt anybody, he just couldn't do it! And *I* didn't do it.' Her fists clenched until the knuckles showed she was even, for some odd reason, trying to shake me now, and tears were rolling down her face; whatever she'd known in her short life hadn't prepared her for times and situations like those. She shook her head in despair. 'I didn't, I didn't! A murderess, that's what she called me! In front of everybody, she called me a murderess! I couldn't kill anybody, Dr Marlowe, I—'

'Mary.' I stopped the hysterical flow by the simple process of putting my fingers across her lips. 'I seriously doubt whether you could dispose of a fly without worrying yourself sick afterwards. You and Allen together—well, if it were a particularly obnoxious fly you just might manage it. I wouldn't bet on it, though.'

She took my hand away and stared at me: 'Dr Marlowe, do you mean—'

'I mean you're a silly young goose. Together, you make a fine pair of silly young geese. It's not that I just don't believe that Allen or you had anything to do with Stryker's death. I *know* you hadn't.'

She sniffed a bit and then she said: 'You're an awfully kind person, Dr Marlowe. I know you're trying to help us—'

'Oh, do shut up,' I said. 'I can prove it.'

'Prove it? Prove it?' There was some hope in the sick eyes, she didn't know whether to believe me or not, and then it seemed that she decided not to, for she shook her head again and said numbly: 'She said I killed him.'

'Miss Haynes was speaking figuratively,' I said, 'which is not the same thing at all, and even then she was wrong. What she meant was that you were the precipitating factor in her husband's death, which of course you weren't.'

'Precipitating factor?'

'Yes.' I took her hands from my now badly crushed lapels, held them in mine and looked at her in my best avuncular fashion. 'Tell me, Mary darling, have you ever dallied in the moonlight with Michael Stryker?'

'Me? Have I—'

'Mary?'

'Yes,' she said miserably. 'I mean no, no, I didn't.'

'That's very clear,' I said. 'Let's put it this way. Did you ever give Miss Haynes reason to suspect that you had been? Dallying, I mean.'

'Yes.' She sniffed again. 'No. I mean he did.' I kept my baffled expression in cold storage and looked at her encouragingly. 'He called me into his cabin, just the day we left Wick, that was. He was alone there. He said that he wanted to discuss some things about the film with me.'

'A change from etchings,' I said.

She looked at me uncomprehendingly and went on: 'But it wasn't about the film he wanted to talk. You must believe me, Dr Marlowe. You must!'

'I believe you.'

'He closed the door and grabbed me and then—'

'Spare my unsullied mind the grisly details. When the villain was forcing his unwelcome attentions upon you there came the pit-a-pat of feminine footsteps in the corridor outside, whereupon the villain rapidly assumed a position where you appeared to be forcing your unwelcome attentions upon him and when the door opened—to reveal, of course, none other than his better half—there he was, fending off the licentious young continuity girl and crying, "No, no, Nanette, control yourself, this can never be," or words to that effect.'

'More or less.' She looked more miserable than ever, then her eyes widened. 'How did you know?'

'The Strykers of this world are pretty thick upon the ground. The ensuing scene must have been pretty painful.'

'There were two scenes,' she said dully. 'Something like it happened on the upper deck the following night. She said she was going to report me to her father—Mr Gerran. He said—not when she was there, of course—that if I tried to make trouble he'd have me fired. He was a director, you know. Later, when I got, well, friendly with Allen, he said he'd get us both fired if need be and make sure that neither of us would ever again get a job in films. Allen said that this was all wrong, why should we accept this when neither of us had done anything, so—'

'So he tried to make him see the error of his ways this morning and got clobbered for his pains. Don't worry, you've neither of you anything to worry about. You'll find your wounded knight-errant next door, Mary.' I smiled and gently touched the swollen cheek. 'This should be something to see. Love's young dream in sticking-plaster. You do love him, don't you, Mary?'

'Of course.' She looked at me solemnly. 'Dr Marlowe.'

'I'm wonderful?'

She smiled, almost happily, and left. Smithy, who must have been watching for her departure, came in almost at once and I told him what had been said.

'Had to be that, of course,' he said. 'The truth's always obvious when it's hung up in front of you and you're beaten over the head with a two-by-four to make you take notice. And now?'

'And now, I think, three things. The first, to clear the names of the two love-birds next door: that's not important at this stage, but they're sensitive souls and I think they'd like to be on speaking terms with the rest of the company again. Second thing is, I've no intention of being stranded here for the next twenty-two days—two days is a lot more like it: who knows, I might be able to pressure unknown or unknowns into precipitate action.'

'I should have thought there had been enough of that already,' Smithy said.

'You may have a point. Third thing is, I could make life a great deal easier and safer for both of us if we had every person so busy watching every other person that it would make it a great deal more difficult for the disaffected to creep up upon our backs unawares.'

'You touch upon a very sympathetic nerve,' Smithy said. 'Your plan into action and at once, I say. A small chat with the assembled company?'

'A small chat with the assembled company. I suggested a couple of hours' lie-down to Allen but I think he and Mary should be there. Would you?'

Smithy left and I went into the living area. Goin, Otto and the Count, all armed with glasses as was almost every other person there, were still in solemn and low-voiced conclave. Otto beckoned me across.

'One moment,' I said. I went outside, coughed and caught my breath as the bitter air cut into my lungs, then trudged against that snow-filled gale across to the provisions hut. Lonnie was seated on a packing case, lovingly examining the amber contents of a glass against the light from his torch.

'Ha!' he said. 'Our peripatetic healer. You know, when one consumes a noble wine like this—'

'Wine?'

'A figure of speech. When one consumes a noble scotch like this, half the pleasure lies in the visual satisfaction. Ever tried it in the darkness? Flat, stale, strangely lacking in bouquet. There's a worthwhile monograph here, I'm sure.' He waved his glass in the direction of the crates of bottles by one wall. 'Harking back to my earlier allusions to the hereafter, if they can have bars in Bear Island then surely—'

'Lonnie,' I said, 'you're missing out on the largesse stakes. Otto is dispensing noble wine at this very moment. He's using very large glasses.'

'I was on the very point of leaving.' He tilted his head and swallowed rapidly. 'I have a dread of being thought a misanthrope.'

I took this friend of the human race back to the main cabin and counted those there. Twenty-one, myself included, as it should have been: the twenty-second and last, Judith Haynes, was deeply unconscious and would be so for hours. Otto beckoned me a second time and I went across.

'We've been having what you might call a council of war,' Otto said importantly. 'We've arrived at a conclusion and would like to have your opinion.'

'Why mine? I'm just an employee, like everyone else here, apart, of course, from the three of you—and Miss Haynes.'

'Consider yourself a co-opted director,' the Count said generously. 'Temporary and unpaid, of course.'

'Your opinion would be valued,' Goin said precisely.

'Opinion about what?'

'Our proposed measures for dealing with Allen,' Otto said. 'I know that in law every man is presumed innocent until proved otherwise. Nor do we have any wish to be inhumane. But simply in order to protect ourselves—'

'I wanted to talk to you about that,' I said. 'About protecting ourselves. I wanted to talk to everybody about that. In fact, that's what I propose to do this very moment.'

'You propose to do what?' Otto could arrange his eyebrows in a very forbidding fashion when he put his mind to it.

'A brief address only,' I said. 'I'll take up hardly any of your time.'

'I can't permit that,' Otto said loftily. 'At least, not until you give us some idea what you have in mind and then we may or may not give our consent.'

'Your permission or lack of it is irrelevant,' I said indifferently. 'I don't require permission when I'm talking about something that may affect lives—you know, the difference between living and dying.'

'I forbid it. I would remind you of what you have just reminded me.' Otto had forgotten about the need for conducting delicate matters in conspiratorial murmurs and we had the undivided attention of everyone in the cabin. 'You are an employee of mine, sir!'

'And I'll now perform my last act as a dutiful employee.' I poured myself a measure of Otto's scotch which, as he and several others were drinking it, I presumed to be safe to drink. 'Health to one and all,' I said, 'and I don't mean that lightly or in the conventional sense. We're going to need it all before we leave this island, and let each one of us hope that he or she is not the one who is going to be abandoned by fortune. As for being your employee, Gerran, you can consider my resignation as being effective as from this moment. I do not care to work for fools. More importantly, I do not care to work for those who may be both fools and knaves.'

This, at least, had the effect of reducing Otto to silence for, to judge by the indigo hue his complexion was assuming, he appeared to be having some little difficulty in his breathing. The Count, I observed, had a mildly speculative expression on his face, while Goin's face held the impassivity of one withholding judgement. I looked round the cabin.

I said: 'It is, I know, belabouring the obvious to say that this trip of ours, so far, has been singularly luckless and ill-starred. We have been plagued by a series of tragic and extraordinarily strange events. We had Antonio die. This might have been the merest mischance: it might equally well

196

be that he was the victim of a premeditated murder or the hapless victim of a misplaced murder attempt that was aimed at someone else. Exactly the same can be said of the two stewards, Moxen and Scott. Similar attempts may or may not have been aimed at Mr Gerran, Mr Smith, Oakley and young Cecil here: all I can say with certainty is that if I hadn't been so lucky as to be in the vicinity when they were struck down at least three of those might have died. You may wonder why I make such a fuss about what could have been a simple, if deadly, outbreak of food poisoning: it is because I have reason to believe, without being able to prove it, that a deadly poison called *aconitine,* which is indistinguishable in appearance from horseradish, was introduced at specific points into the evening meal we had on the occasion when those people were struck down.'

I checked to see if I had the attention of those present and I've never made a more superfluous check. They were so stunned that they hadn't even got to the lengths of looking at each other: Otto's liquid largesse wholly forgotten, they had eyes only for me, ears only for what I was saying, the average university lecturer would have found it a dream of paradise: but then the average university lecturer rarely had the doubtful fortune to chance upon such wholly absorbing subject-matter as I had to hand.

'And then we have the mysterious disappearance of Halliday. I have no doubt that the cause of his death could be established beyond doubt if an autopsy could be carried out, but as I've equally no doubt that the unfortunate Halliday lies on the floor of the Barents Sea this can never be possible. But it is my belief—and this, again, is but conjecture—that he died not from any form of food poisoning but because he had a nightcap from a poisoned whisky bottle that was intended for me.' I looked at Mary Stuart: huge eyes and parted lips in a white shocked face, but I was the only one who saw it.

I pulled down the collar of my duffel-coat and showed them the impressively large and impressively multi-coloured bruise on the left-hand side of my neck

'This, of course, could have been self-inflicted. Or maybe I just slipped somewhere and banged myself. Or take this odd business of the smashed radio. Somebody with an aversion to radios, perhaps, and suchlike outward manifestations of what we choose to call progress, or someone who found the Arctic just too much for him and had to take it out on something —you know, the equivalent of going cafard in the desert.

'So far, nothing but conjecture. An extraordinary and even more extraordinarily unconnected series of violent and tragic mishaps, one might claim, coincidence is an accepted part of life. But not, surely, coincidence multiplied up to the nth degree like this; that would have to lie at the very farthest bounds of possibility. I think you would admit that if we could prove the existence, beyond any doubt, of a carefully premeditated and carefully executed crime, then the other violent happenings must cease to be regarded as conjectural coincidences and considered as being what they then would be, deliberately executed murders in pursuit of some goal that can't yet even be guessed at but must be of overwhelming importance.'

They weren't admitting anything, or, at least, if they were admitting anything to themselves they weren't saying it out loud, but I think it was really a case of their minds having stopped working, not all their minds, there had to be one exception, probably more.

'And we have this one proven crime,' I went on. 'The rather clumsily executed murder of Michael Stryker which was at the same time an attempt, and not a very clever attempt, to frame young Allen here for something he never did. I don't think the murderer had any special ill-will towards Allen, well, no more than he seems to have for the general run of mankind: he just wanted to divert any possible suspicion from himself. I think if you'd all had time enough to think about it you'd have come to the eventual conclusion that Allen couldn't possibly have had anything to do with it: with a doctor in the house, if you'll excuse the phrase, he hadn't a hope in hell.

'Allen says he has no recollection at all about what happened. I believe him absolutely. He's sustained a severe blow on the back of the head—the scalp is open to the bone. How he escaped a fractured skull, far less concussion, I can't imagine. It certainly must have rendered him unconscious for a considerable period. Which leads one to assume that this assailant was still in excellent shape after what was clearly his *coup de grâce*. Are we to assume then that Allen, after having been knocked senseless, immediately leapt up and smote his assailant hip and thigh? That doesn't make any kind of sense at all. What does make sense, what is the only answer, is that the unknown crept up behind Allen and laid him out, not with his hands but with some heavy and solid object—probably a stone, there's more than enough lying around. Having done this, he proceeded to cut the unconscious Allen up about the face, ripped his coat and tore off a couple of buttons—all to give the very convincing impression that he'd been in a fight.

'The same thing, but this time on a lethal scale, happened to Stryker. I'm convinced that it was no accident that Allen was merely knocked unconscious while Stryker was killed—our friend, who must be a bit of an expert in such matters, knew just how much weight to bring to bear in each case, by no means as easy a matter as you might think. Then this ghoul, in a stupid attempt to create the impression that Stryker had been the other party to the fight, proceeded to rough up Stryker's face as he had done Allen's: I leave it to you to form your own estimate of just how evil must be the mind of a man who will deliberately set about mutilating the face of a dead man.'

I left them for a little to form their own estimates. For the most part they looked neither sick nor revolted: their reactions were mainly of shock and minds still consciously fighting against comprehension. No glances were exchanged, no eyes moved: their eyes were only for me.

'Stryker had a split upper lip, a tooth missing and a reddish rough mark on his temple which I think must have been caused by another stone—very probably all the injuries were inflicted in this fashion to avoid any tell-tale marking of the hands or knuckles. Had those injuries been sustained in the course of a fight there would have been extensive bleeding and fairly massive bruising: there were no signs of either because Stryker was dead and circulation had ceased before those wounds were caused. To complete what he thought would be a most convincing effect, the murderer then closed the dead man's hand round one of the buttons torn from Allen's coat. Incidentally, there were no signs whatever of the churned-up snow one would have expected to find at the scene of a fight: there were two sets of tracks leading to the place where Stryker lay, one set leading away. No fuss, no commotion, just a quick if not particularly clean dispatch.'

I sipped some more of Otto's scotch—it must have come from his own private supply for it was excellent stuff—then asked in my best lecturer's fashion: 'Are there any questions?'

Predictably, there were none. They were all clearly far too busy asking themselves questions to have any time to put any to me.

I went on: 'I think you'd agree, then, that it now seems extremely improbable that any of the four previous deaths were the results of innocent coincidence. I think that only the most gullible and the most naïve would now be prepared to believe that those deaths were unconnected and not the work of the same agent. So what we have is, in effect, a mass murderer. A man who is either mad, a pathological killer, or a vicious and evil monster who finds it essential to murder with what can be only an apparent indiscrimination in order to achieve God knows what murky ends. He may, it is possible, be all three of those at once. Whatever he is or whoever he is, he's in this cabin now. I wonder which one of you it is?'

For the first time their eyes left me as they looked quickly and furtively at one another as if in the ludicrous hope that they might by this means discover the identity of the killer. None of them examined one another as closely as I observed them all over the rim of my glass; if one pair of eyes remained fixed on mine it could only be because its owner knew who the murderer was and didn't have to bother to look around: but I knew, even as I watched them, that I had no real foundation for any such hope, the murderer may have been no great shakes at physiology, but he was far too clever to walk into what, for an intelligent man with five deaths on his conscience, must have been a very obvious trap indeed. I was certain that there wasn't a pair of eyes before me that didn't flicker surreptitiously around the cabin. I waited patiently until I had their combined attention again.

'I have no idea who this murderous fiend may be,' I said, 'but I think I can with certainty say who it isn't. Counting the absent Miss Haynes, there are twenty-two of us in this cabin: to nine of those I cannot see that any suspicion can possibly attach.'

'Merciful God!' Goin muttered. 'Merciful God! This is monstrous, Dr Marlowe, unbelievable. One of us here, one of the people we know, one of our friends has the blood of five people on his hands? It can't be! It just can't be!'

'Except that you know that it must be,' I said. Goin made no reply. 'To begin with, I myself am in the clear, not because I know I am—we could all claim that—but because two hostile acts have been committed against my person, one of which was intended to be lethal. Further, I was bringing in Mr Smith here when Stryker was killed and Allen injured.' This last was the truth but not the whole truth, but only the killer himself would know that and as he was already on to me his opinion was unimportant because he couldn't possibly voice it. 'Mr Smith is in the clear because not only was he unconscious at the time, he was a nearly fatal victim of the poisoner's activities and it's hardly likely that he would go around poisoning himself.'

'Then that let's me out, Dr Marlowe!' The Duke's voice was a cracked falsetto, hoarse with strain. 'It wasn't me, it couldn't—'

'Agreed, Cecil, it wasn't you. Apart from the fact that you were another poisoning victim, I don't think—well, I'm not being physically disparaging but I'd think it very unlikely that you could have hoisted that rock that was used to kill Stryker. Mr Gerran, too, is above suspicion: not only was he poisoned but he was in the cabin here at the time of Stryker's death. Allen, obviously, could have had nothing to do with it and neither did Mr Goin here, although you'll have to take my word for that.'

'What does that mean, Dr Marlowe?' Goin's voice was steady.

'Because when you first saw Stryker's body you turned as white as the proverbial sheet. People can do lots of things with their bodies, but they can't switch on and off the epidermal blood supply at will. Had you been prepared for the sight you saw you wouldn't have changed colour. You did. So you weren't prepared. Our two Marys here we'll have to leave out of the reckoning for it would have been a physical impossibility for either of them to have attacked Stryker with that rock. And Miss Haynes, of course, doesn't come into the reckoning at all. Which, by my count, leaves thirteen potential suspects in all.' I looked round the cabin and counted. 'That's right. Thirteen. Let's hope it's going to be a very unlucky number for one of you.'

'Dr Marlowe,' Goin said. 'I think you should consider

withdrawing your resignation.'

'Consider it withdrawn. I was beginning to wonder what I'd do for food anyway.' I looked at my now empty glass, then at Otto. 'Seeing that I'm now back on the strength, as it were, would it be in order—'

'Of course, of course.' Otto, looking stricken, sunk heavily on to a providentially sturdy stool and insofar as it was possible for over two hundredweights of lard to look like a punctured balloon, he looked like a punctured balloon. 'Dear God, this is ghastly. One of us here is a murderer. One of us here has killed five people!' He shivered violently although the temperature had by this time risen well above freezing point. 'Five people. Dead. And the man who did it is here!'

I lit a cigarette, sipped a little more of Otto's scotch and waited for some further contributions to the conversation. Outside, the wind had strengthened until it was now a high and lonesome moaning sound that set the teeth on edge, a moan that regularly climbed up the register into a weird and eldritch whistling as the wind gusted and fell away, everyone appeared to be listening to it and listening intently, a weirdly appropriate litany for the fear and the horror that was closing in on their minds, a fit requiem for the dead Stryker. A whole minute dragged by and no one spoke so I took up the conversational burden again.

'The implications will not have escaped you,' I said. 'At least, when you have had as much time to think about them as I've had, they won't. Stryker is dead—and so are four others. Who should want them dead? Why should they have died? Is there a reason, a purpose behind those slayings? Have we a psychopathic murderer amongst us? If there is a purpose, has it been achieved? If it hasn't—or if the killer is a psychopath —which one of us is going to be next? Who is going to die tonight? Who is going to go to his cubicle tonight knowing that anyone, a crazed killer, it may be, is going to enter at any time—or even, possibly, one's own room-mate may be waiting his turn with a knife or a suffocating pillow? In fact, I should think that the room-mate possibility might be by far the more likely—for who would do anything so crazily obvious as that? Except, of course, a crazy man. So, before us, we have what you might call a sleepless vigil. Perhaps we can all keep it up for one night. But for twenty-two nights— can we keep it up for twenty-two nights? Is there any of us here who can be sure of still being alive when the *Morning Rose* returns?'

From their expressions and the profound silence that greeted this last question it was apparent that no one was prepared to express any such certainty. When I came to consider it myself, instead of just asking them to do so, I realized that the question of continued existence applied more particularly and more strongly to myself than to any of the others, for if the killer were no wayward psycho who struck out as the fancy took him but was an ice-cold and calculating murderer with a definite objective in view, then I was convinced that I was first on his calling list. I didn't for a moment think that any attempt to dispose of me would be because that was any part of the killer's preconceived plans but solely because I represented a threat to those plans.

'And how are we going to comport ourselves from now on?' I said. 'Do we now polarize into two groups, the nine acknowledged innocent giving a very wide berth and a leery eye to the thirteen potentially guilty even although this is going to be a mite hard on, say, twelve of the latter? Shall we be like oil and water and resolutely refuse to mix? Or about your shooting plans for tomorrow. Mr Gerran and the Count, I believe, are heading for the fells tomorrow, a goodie and a potential baddie—Mr Gerran is going to make sure that he has at least another goodie along with him to watch his back? Heissman is taking the work-boat to reconnoitre possible locations along the Sor-hamna and perhaps a bit farther south. I believe Jungbeck and Heyter here have volunteered to go along with him. Three of those, you note, whose innocence is not proved. Any white sheep going to go along with black wolf or wolves who may come back and sorrowfully explain that the poor sheep fell over the side and that in spite of their heroic efforts the poor fellow perished miserably? And those splendid precipices at the south of the island—one little well-timed nudge, a deft clicking together of the ankles—well, sixteen hundred feet is a considerable drop, especially when you bear in mind that it's straight down all the way. A perplexing and difficult problem, isn't it, gentlemen?'

'This is preposterous,' Otto said loudly. 'Absolutely preposterous.'

'Isn't it?' I said. 'A pity we can't ask Stryker his opinion about that. Or the opinions of Antonio and Halliday and

Moxen and Scott. When your pale ghost looks down from Limbo, Mr Gerran, and watches you being lowered into a hole in the frozen snow—do you think it will still look preposterous?'

Otto shuddered and reached for the bottle. 'What in God's name are we going to do?'

'I've no idea,' I said. 'You heard what I just said to Mr Goin. I have reverted to the position of employee. I haven't got my shirt on this film as I heard Mr Goin say to Captain Imrie that you had, I'm afraid this is a decision to arrive at at directorial level—well, the three directors that are still capable of making decisions.'

'Would our employee mind telling us what he means?' Goin tried to smile but it didn't come off, his heart wasn't in it.

'Do you want to go ahead with shooting all your scenes up here or don't you? It's up to you. If we all stay here in the cabin permanently, at least half a dozen awake at any given time, looking with all their eyes and listening with all their ears, then the chances are high that we'll all still be in relatively mint condition by the time the twenty-two days are up. On the other hand, of course, that means that you won't get any of your film shot and you'll lose all your investment. It's a problem I wouldn't like to have to face. That's excellent scotch you have there, Mr Gerran.'

'I can see that you appreciate it.' Otto would have liked a touch of asperity in his voice, but all he managed to do was to sound worried.

'Don't be so mean.' I helped myself. 'These are times that try men's souls.' I wasn't really listening to Otto, I was barely listening to myself. Once before, since leaving Wick, on the occasion when the Count had said something about a surfeit of horseradish, certain words had had the effect of a touch-paper being applied to a trail of gun-powder, triggering off a succession of thoughts that came tumbling in one after the other almost faster than my mind could register them, and now the same thing had happened again, only this time the words had been triggered off by something I'd said myself. I became aware that the Count was speaking, presumably to me. I said: 'Sorry, mind on other things, you know.'

'I can see that.' The Count was looking at me in a thoughtful fashion. 'All very well to opt out of responsibility, but what would *you* do?' He smiled. 'If I were to co-opt you again as a temporary unpaid director?'

'Easy,' I said, and the answer did come easily—as the result of the past thirty seconds' thinking. 'I'd watch my back and get on with the ruddy film.'

'So.' Otto nodded, and he, the Count and Goin looked at one another in apparent satisfaction. 'But now, this moment, what would you do?'

'When do we have supper?'

'Supper?' Otto blinked. 'Oh, about eight, say.'

'And it's now five. About to have three hours' kip, that's what I'm going to do. And I wouldn't advise anyone to come near me, either for an aspirin or with a knife in their hand, for I'm feeling very nervous indeed.'

Smithy cleared his throat. 'Would I get clobbered if I asked for an aspirin now? Or something a bit more powerful to make a man sleep? I feel as if my head has been on a butcher's block.'

'I can have you asleep in ten minutes. Mind you, you'll probably feel a damn sight worse when you wake up.'

'Impossible. Lead me to the knock-out drops.'

Inside my cubicle I gripped the handle of the small square double-plate-glazed window and opened it with some difficulty. 'Can you do that with yours?'

'You do have things on your mind. No mangers allocated for uninvited guests.'

'All the better. Bring a cot in here. You can borrow one from Judith Haynes's room.'

'Of course,' he said. 'There's a spare one there.'

CHAPTER TEN

Five minutes later, wrapped to the eyes against the bitter cold, the driving snow and that wind that was now howling, not moaning, across the frozen face of the island, Smithy and I stood in the lee of the cabin, by my window which I'd wedged shut against a wad of paper: there was no handle on the outside to pull it open again, but I had with me a multi-tooled Swiss army knife that could pry open just about anything. We looked at the vaguely seen bulk of the cabin, at the bright light—Coleman lamps have an intensely white flame—streaming from one of the windows in the central section and the pale glimmer of smaller lights from a few of the cubicles.

'No night for an honest citizen to be taking a constitutional,' Smithy said in my ear. 'But how about bumping into one of the less honest ones?'

'Too soon for him or them to be stirring abroad,' I said. 'For the moment the flame of suspicion burns too high for anyone even to clear his throat at the wrong moment. Later, perhaps. But not now.'

We went directly to the provisions store, closed the door behind us and, since the hut was windowless, switched on both our torches. We searched through all the bags, crates, cartons and packages of food and found nothing untoward.

'What are we supposed to be looking for?' Smithy asked.

'I've no idea. Anything, shall we say, that shouldn't be here.'

'A gun? A big black ribbed bottle marked "Deadly Poison"?'

'Something like that.' I lifted a bottle of Haig from a crate and stuck it in my parka pocket. 'Medicinal use only,' I explained.

'Of course.' Smithy made a farewell sweep of his torch beam round the walls of the hut: the beam steadied on three small highly varnished boxes on an upper shelf.

'Must be very high grade food in those,' Smithy said. 'Caviar for Otto, maybe?'

'Spares medical equipment for me. Mainly instruments. No

poisons. Guaranteed.' I made for the door. 'Come on.'

'Not checking?'

'No point. Be a bit difficult to hide a sub-machine-gun in one of those.' The boxes were about ten inches by eight.

'OK to have a look, all the same?'

'All right.' I was a bit impatient. 'Hurry it up, though.' Smithy opened the lids of the first two boxes, glanced cursorily at the contents and closed them again. He opened the third box and said: 'Broken into your reserves already, I see.'

'I have not.'

'Then somebody has.' He handed over the box and I saw the two vacant moulds in the blue felt.

'Somebody has indeed,' I said. 'A hypodermic and a tube of needles.'

Smithy looked at me in silence, took the box, closed the lid and replaced it. He said: 'I don't think I like this very much.'

'Twenty-two days could be a very long time,' I said. 'Now, if we could only find the stuff that's going to go inside this syringe.'

'If. You don't think somebody may have borrowed it for his own private use? Somebody on the hard stuff who's bent his own plunger? One of the Three Apostles, for instance? Right background, after all—pop world, film world, just kids?'

'No, I don't think that.'

'I don't think so either. I wish I did.'

We went from there to the fuel hut. Two minutes was sufficient to discover that the fuel hut had nothing to offer us. Neither had the equipment hut although it afforded me two items I wanted, a screwdriver from the tool-box Eddie had used when he was connecting up the generator, and a packet of screws. Smithy said: 'What do you want those for?'

'For the screwing up of windows,' I said. 'A door is not the only way you can enter the cubicle of a sleeping man.'

'You don't trust an awful lot of people, do you?'

'I weep for my lost innocence.'

There was no temptation to linger in the tractor shed, not with Stryker lying there, his face ghastly in the reflected wash from the torches, his glazed eyes staring unseeingly at the ceiling. We rummaged through tool-boxes, examined metal panniers, even went to the length of probing fuel tanks, oil tanks and radiators: we found nothing.

We made our way down to the jetty. From the main cabin it was a distance of just over twenty yards and it took us five minutes to find it. We did not dare use our torches, and with that heavy and driving snow reducing visibility to virtually arm's length, we were blind people moving in a blind world. We edged our way very gingerly out to the end of the jetty—the snow had covered up the gaps in the crumbling limestone and, heavily clad as we were, the chances of surviving a tumble into the freezing waters of the Sor-hamna were not high—located the work-boat in the sheltered north-west angle of the jetty and climbed down into it by means of a vertical iron ladder that was so ancient and rusty that the outboard ends of some of the rungs were scarcely more than a quarter of an inch in diameter.

On a dark night the glow from a torch can be seen from a considerable distance even through the most heavily falling snow but now that we were below the level of the jetty wall we switched our torches on again, though still careful to keep them hooded. A quick search of the work-boat revealed nothing. We clambered into the fourteen-footer lying alongside and had the same lack of success. From here we transferred ourselves to the mock-up submarine—an iron ladder had been welded both to its side and the conning-tower.

The conning-tower had a platform welded across its circumference at a distance of about four feet from the top. A hatch in this led to a semi-circular platform about eighteen inches below the flange to which the conning-tower was secured: from here a short ladder led to the deck of the submarine. We went down and shone our torches around.

'Give me subs any time,' Smithy said. 'At least they keep the snow out. That apart, I don't think I'd care to settle down here.'

The narrow and cramped interior was indeed a bleak and cheerless place. The deck consisted of transverse spaced wooden planks held in position at either side by large butterfly nuts. Beneath the planks we could see, firmly held in position, rows of long narrow grey-painted bars—the four tons of cast-iron that served as ballast. Four square ballast tanks were arranged along either side of the shell—those could be filled to give negative buoyancy—and at one end of the shell stood a small diesel, its exhaust passing through the deck-head as far as the top of the conning-tower, to which it was bolted: this engine was coupled to a compressor unit for emptying the ballast tanks. And that, structurally, was all that there was to it: I had been told that the entire mock-up had cost fifteen thousand pounds and could only conclude that Otto had been engaged in the producers' favourite pastime of cooking the books.

There were several other disparate items of equipment. In a locker in what I took to be the after end of this central mock-up were four small mushroom anchors with chains, together with a small portable windlass: immediately above these was a hatch in the deck-head which gave access to the upper deck: the anchors could only be for mooring the model securely in any desired position. Opposite this locker, securely lashed against a bulkhead, was a lightweight plastic reconstruction of a periscope that appeared to be capable of operating in a sufficiently realistic fashion. Close by were three other plastic models, a dummy three-inch gun, presumably for mounting on the deck, and two model machine-guns which would be fitted, I imagined, somewhere in the conning-tower. In the for'ard end of the craft were two more lockers: one held a number of cork life-jackets, the other six cans of paint and some paint-brushes. The cans were marked 'Instant Grey'.

'And what does that mean?' Smithy asked.

'Some sort of quick-drying paint, I should imagine.'

'Everything shipshape and Bristol fashion,' Smithy said. 'I wouldn't have given Otto the credit.' He shivered. 'Maybe it isn't snowing in here, but I'd have you know that I'm very cold indeed. This place reminds me of an iron tomb.'

'It isn't very cosy. Up and away.'

'A fruitless search, you might say?'

'You might. I didn't have many hopes anyway.'

'Is that why you changed your mind about their getting on with the making of the film? One minute indifference, the next advising them to press on? So that you could, perhaps, examine their quarters and their possessions when they're out?'

'Whatever put such a thought in your mind, Smithy?'

'There are a thousand snowdrifts where a person could hide anything.'

'That's a thought that's also in my mind.'

We made the trip from the jetty to the main cabin with much greater ease than we had the other way for this time we had the faint and diffuse glow of light from the Colemans to guide us. We scrambled back inside our cubicle without too much difficulty, brushed the snow from our boots and upper clothing and hung the latter up: compared to the interior of the submarine shell the warmth inside the cubicle was positively genial. I took screwdriver and screws and started to secure the window, while Smithy, after some references to the low state of his health, retrieved the bottle I'd taken from the provisions shed and took two small beakers from my medical box. He watched me until I had finished.

'Well,' he said, 'that's us safe for the night. How about the others?'

'I don't think most of the others are in any danger because they don't offer any danger to the plans of our friend or friends.'

'Most of the others?'

'I think I'll screw up Judith Haynes's window too.'

'Judith Haynes?'

'I have a feeling that she is in danger. Whether it's grave danger or imminent danger I have no idea. Maybe I'm just fey.'

'I shouldn't wonder,' Smithy said ambiguously. He drank some scotch absently. 'I've just been thinking myself, but along rather different lines. When, do you think, is it going to occur to our directorial board to call some law in or some outside help or, at least, to let the world know that the employees of Olympus Productions are dying off like flies and not from natural causes either?'

'That's the decision you would arrive at?'

'If I wasn't a criminal, or, in this case, the criminal and had very powerful reasons for not wanting the law around, yes, I would.'

'I'm not a criminal but I've very powerful reasons for not wanting the law around either. The moment the law officially steps into the picture every criminal thought, intent and potential action will go into deep freeze and we'll be left with five unresolved deaths on our hands and that'll be the end of it, for there's nothing surer than that we haven't got a thing to hang on anyone yet. There's only one way and that's by giving out enough rope for a hanging job.'

'What if you give out too much rope and our friend, instead of hanging himself, hangs one of us instead? What if there's murder?'

'In that case we'd have to call in the law. I'm here to do a job in the best way I can but that doesn't mean by any means I can: I can't use the innocent as sacrificial pawns.'

'Well, that's some relief. But if the thought does occur to them?'

'Then obviously we'll have to try to contact Tunheim—there's a Meteorological Office radio there that should just about reach the moon. Or we'll have to offer to try to contact Tunheim. It's less than ten miles away but in weather conditions like these it might as well be on the far side of Siberia. If the weather eases, it might be possible. The wind's veering round to the west now and if it stayed in that quarter a trip by boat up the coast might be possible—pretty unpleasant, but just possible. If it goes much north of west, it wouldn't—those are only open work-boats and would be swamped in any kind of sea. By land—if the snow stopped—well, I just don't know. In the first place, the terrain is so broken and mountainous that you couldn't possibly use the little Sno-Cat—you'd have to make it on foot. You'd have to go well inland, to the west, to avoid the Misery Fell complex for that ends in cliffs on the east coast. There are hundreds of little lakes lying in that region and I've no idea how heavily they may be frozen over, maybe some of them not very much, maybe just enough to support a covering of snow and not a man—and I believe some of those lakes are over a hundred feet deep. You might be ankle-deep, knee-deep, thigh-deep, waist-deep in snow. And apart from being bogged-down or drowned, we're not equipped for winter travel, we haven't even got a tent for an overnight stop—there isn't a hope of you making it in one day—and if the snow started falling again and kept on falling I bet Olympus Productions haven't even as much as a hand compass to prevent you from walking in circles until you drop dead from cold or hunger or just plain old exhaustion.'

' "You, you, you",' Smithy said. 'You're always talking about me. How about you going instead?' He grinned. 'Of course, I could always set off for there, search around till

I found some convenient cave or shelter, hole up there for the night, and return the next day announcing mission impossible.'

'We'll see how the cards fall.' I finished my drink and picked up screwdriver and screws. 'Let's go and see how Miss Haynes is.'

Miss Haynes seemed to be in reasonable health. No fever, normal pulse, breathing deeply and evenly: how she would feel when she woke was another matter altogether. I screwed up her window until nobody could have entered her room from the outside without smashing their way in—and breaking through two sheets of plate glass would cause enough racket to wake up half the occupants of the cabin. Then we went into the living area of the cabin.

It was surprisingly empty. At least ten people I would have expected to be there were absent, but a quick mental count of the missing heads convinced me that there was no likely cause for alarm in this. Otto, the Count, Heissman and Goin, conspicuously absent, were probably in secret conclave in one of their cubicles discussing weighty matters which they didn't wish their underlings to hear. Lonnie had almost certainly betaken himself again in his quest for fresh air and I hoped that he hadn't managed to lose himself between the cabin and the provisions hut. Allen, almost certainly, had gone to lie down again, and I presumed that Mary darling who appeared to have overcome a great number of her earlier inhibitions, had returned to her dutiful hand-holding. I couldn't imagine where the Three Apostles had got to nor was I particularly worried: I was sure that there was nothing to fear from them other than permanent damage to the ear drums.

I crossed to where Conrad was presiding over a three-burner oil cooker mounted on top of a stove. He had two large pans and a large pot all bubbling away at once, stew, beans and coffee, and he seemed to be enjoying his role of chef not least, I guessed, because he had Mary Stuart as his assistant. In another man I would have looked for a less than altruistic motive in this cheerful willingness, the hail-fellow-well-met leading man playing the democrat to an admiring gallery, but I knew enough of Conrad now to realize that this formed no part of his nature at all: he was just a naturally helpful character who never thought to place him self above his fellow-actors. Conrad, I thought, must be a very *rara avis* indeed in the cinema world.

'What's all this, then?' I said. 'You qualified for this sort of thing? I thought Otto had appointed the Three Apostles as alternate chefs?'

'The Three Apostles had it in mind to start improving their musical technique in this very spot,' Conrad said. 'I did a self-defence trade with them. They're practising across in the equipment hut—you know, where the generator is.'

I tried to imagine the total degree of cacophony produced by their atonal voices, their amplified instruments and the diesel engine in a confined space of eight by eight, but my imagination wasn't up to it. I said: 'You deserve a medal. You too, Mary dear.'

'Me?' She smiled. 'Why?'

'Remember what I said about the goodies pairing off with the baddies? Delighted to see you keeping a close eye on our suspect here. Haven't seen his hand hovering suspiciously long over one of the pots, have you?'

She stopped smiling. 'I don't think that's funny, Dr Marlowe.'

'I don't think it is either. A clumsy attempt to lighten the atmosphere.' I looked at Conrad. 'Can I have a word with the chef?'

Conrad looked at me briefly, speculatively, nodded and turned away. Mary Stuart said: 'That's nice. For me, I mean. Why can't you have a word with him here?'

'I'm going to tell him some funny stories. You don't seem to care much for my humour.' I walked away a few paces with Conrad and said: 'Had a chance of a word with Lonnie yet?'

'No. I mean, I haven't had an opportunity yet. Is it that urgent?'

'I'm beginning to think it may be. Look, I haven't seen him there but I'm certain as can be that Lonnie is across in the provisions hut.'

'Where Otto keeps all those elixirs of life?'

'You wouldn't expect to find Lonnie in the fuel shed? Diesel and petrol aren't his tipples. I wonder if you could go across there, seeking liquid solace from this harsh and weary world, from Bear Island, from Olympus Productions, from whatever you like, and engage him in crafty conversation. Touch upon the theme of how you're missing your family. Anything. Just get him to tell you about his.'

He hesitated. 'I like Lonnie. I don't like this job.'

'I'm past caring now about people's feelings. I'm just concerned with people's lives—that they should keep on living, I mean.'

'Right.' He nodded and looked at me soberly. 'Taking a bit of a chance, aren't you? Enlisting the aid of one of your suspects, I mean.'

'You're not on my list of suspects,' I said. 'You never were.'

He looked at me for some moments then said: 'Tell that to Mary dear, will you?' He turned and made for the outer door. I returned to the oil cooker. Mary Stuart looked at me with her usual grave and remote lack of expression.

I said: 'Conrad tells me to tell you that I've just told him —you're following me?—that he's not on my list of suspects and never was.'

'That's nice.' She gave me a little smile but there was a touch of winter in it.

'Mary,' I said, 'you are displeased with me.'

'Well.'

'Well what?'

'Are you a friend of mine?'

'Of course.'

'Of course, of course.' She mimicked my tone very creditably. 'Dr Marlowe is a friend of all mankind.'

'Dr Marlowe doesn't hold all mankind in his arms all night long.'

Another smile. This time there was a touch of spring in it. She said: 'And Charles Conrad?'

'I like him. I don't know what he thinks about me.'

'And I like him and I know he likes me and so we're all friends together.' I thought better of saying 'of course' again and just nodded. 'So why don't we all share secrets together?'

'Women are the most curious creatures,' I said. 'In every sense of the word "curious".'

'Please don't be clever with me.'

'Do you always share secrets?' She frowned a little, as if perplexed, and I went on: 'Let's play kiddies' games, shall we? You tell me a secret and I'll tell you one.'

'What on earth do you mean?'

'This secret assignation you had yesterday morning. In the snow and on the upper deck. When you were being so very affectionate with Heissman.'

I'd expected some very positive reaction from this and was correspondingly disappointed when there was none. She looked at me, silently thoughtful, then said: 'So you were spying on us.'

'I just happened to chance by.'

'I didn't see you chancing by.' She bit her lip, but not in any particularly discernible anguish. 'I wish you hadn't seen that.'

'Why?' It had been briefly in my mind to be heavily ironic but I could hear a little warning bell tinkling in the distance.

'Because I don't want people to know.'

'That's obvious,' I said patiently. 'Why?'

'Because I'm not very proud of it. I have to make a living, Dr Marlowe. I came to this country only two years ago and I haven't got any qualifications for anything. I haven't even got any qualifications for what I'm doing now. I'm a hopeless actress. I know I am. I've just got no talent at all. The last two films I was in—well, they were just awful. Are you surprised that people give me the cold shoulder, why they're wondering out loud why I'm making my third film with Olympus Productions? Well, you can guess now: Johann Heissman is the why.' She smiled, just a very small smile. 'You are surprised, Dr Marlowe? Shocked, perhaps?'

'No.'

The little smile went away. Some of the life went from her face and when she spoke her voice was dull. 'It is so easy, then, to believe this of me?'

'Well, no. The point is that I just don't believe you at all.'

She looked at me, her face a little sad and quite uncomprehending. 'You don't believe—you don't believe this of me?'

'Not of Mary Stuart. Not of Mary dear.'

Some of the life came back and she said almost wonderingly: 'That's the nicest thing anybody's ever said to me.' She looked down at her hands, as if hesitating, then said, without looking up: 'Johann Heissman is my uncle. My mother's brother.'

'Your uncle?' I'd been mentally shuffling all sorts of possibilities through my mind, but this one hadn't even begun to occur to me.

'Uncle Johann.' Again the little, almost secret smile, this time with what could have been an imagined trace of mischief: I wondered what her smile would be like if she ever smiled in pure delight or happiness. 'You don't have to believe me. Just go and ask him yourself. But privately, if you please.'

Dinner that night wasn't much of a social success. The atmosphere of cheerful good fellowship which is required to make such communal get-togethers go with a swing was noticeably lacking. This may have been due, partially, to the fact that most people either ate by their solitary selves or, both sitting and standing, in scattered small groups around the cabin, their attention almost exclusively devoted to the unappetizing goulash in the bowls held in their hands: but it was mainly due to the fact that everybody was clearly and painfully aware that we were experiencing the secular equivalent of our own last supper. For the interest in the food was not all-absorbing: frequently, but very very briefly, a pair of eyes would break off their rapt communion with the stew and beans, glance swiftly around the cabin, then return in an oddly guilty defensiveness to the food as if the person had hoped in that one lightning ocular sortie to discover some unmistakable tell-tale signs that would infallibly identify the traitor in our midst. There were, needless to say, no such overt indications of self-betrayal on display, and the problem of identification was deepened and confused by the fact that most of those present exhibited a measure of abnormality in their behaviour that would ordinarily have given rise to more than a modicum of suspicion anyway: for it is an odd characteristic of human nature that even the most innocent person who knows himself or herself to be under suspicion tends to over-react with an unnatural degree of casual indifference and insouciant concern that serves only to heighten the original suspicion.

Otto, clearly, was not one of those thus afflicted. Whether it was because he knew himself to be one of those who was regarded as being completely in the clear or because, as chairman of the company and producer of the film, he regarded himself as being above and apart from the problems that afflicted the common run of mankind, Otto was remarkably

216

composed and, astonishingly, even forceful and assertive. Unlikely though it had appeared up to that moment, Otto, normally so dithering and indecisive, might well be one of those who only showed of their best in the moments of crisis. There was certainly nothing dithering or indecisive about him when he rose to speak at the end of the meal.

'We are all aware,' said Otto briskly, 'of the dreadful happenings of the past day or two, and I think that we have no alternative to accepting Dr Marlowe's interpretation of the events. Further, I fear we have to accept as very real the doctor's warnings as to what may happen in the near future.

'Those are inescapable facts and entirely conceivable possibilities so please don't for a moment imagine that I'm trying to minimize the seriousness of the situation. On the contrary, it would be impossible to exaggerate it, impossible to exaggerate an impossible situation. Here we are, marooned in the high Arctic and beyond any reach of help, with the knowledge that there are those of us who have come to a violent end and that this violence may not yet be over.' He looked unhurriedly around the company and I did the same: I could see that there were quite a number who were as impressed by Otto's calm assessment of the situation as I was. He went on: 'It is precisely because the state of affairs in which we find ourselves is so unbelievable and so abnormal that I suggest we comport ourselves in the most rational and normal fashion possible. A descent into hysteria will achieve no reversal of the awful things that have just occurred and can only harm all of us.

'Accordingly, my colleagues and I have decided that, subject, of course, to taking every possible precaution, we should proceed with the business in hand—the reason why we came to this island at all—in as normal a fashion as possible. I am sure you will all agree with me that it is much better to have our time and attention taken up—I will not say gainfully employed—by working steadily at something purposive and constructive rather than sit idly by and have those awful things prey upon our minds. I do not suggest that we can pretend that those things never happened: I do suggest that it will benefit all of us if we act as if they hadn't.

'Weather permitting, we will have three crews in the field tomorrow.' Otto wasn't consulting, he was telling: I'd have done the same in his place. 'The main group, under Mr

217

Divine here, will go north up Lerner's Way—a road built through to the next bay about the turn of the century, although I don't suppose there are many traces left of it now. The Count, Allen and Cecil here will, of course, accompany him. I intend to go along myself and I'll want you there too, Charles.' This to Conrad.

'You'll require me along, Mr Gerran?' This from Mary Darling, her hand upraised like a little girl in class.

'Well, it'll be nearly all background—' He broke off, glanced at Allen's battered face, then looked again at Mary with what I took to be a roguish smile. 'If you wish to, certainly. Mr Hendriks, with Luke, Mark and John here, will try to capture for us all the sounds of the island—the winds on the fells, the birds on the cliffs, the waves breaking against the shore. Mr Heissman here is taking a hand-camera out in the boat to seek out some suitable seaward locations—Mr Jungbeck and Mr Heyter, who have nothing on tomorrow, have kindly volunteered to accompany him.

'These, then, are our decisions for tomorrow's programme. But the most important decision of all, which I have left to the last, is in no way connected with our work. We have decided that it is essential that we seek help with all possible speed. By help I mean the law, police or some such recognized authority. It is not only our duty, it may well be essential for our own self-preservation, to have a thorough and expert investigation made as quickly as is humanly possible. To call for help we need a radio and the nearest is at the Norwegian Meteorological Station in Tunheim.' I carefully refrained from looking at Smithy and was confident that he would reciprocate. 'Mr Smith, your presence here may prove to be a blessing—you are the only professional seaman amongst us. What would be the chances of reaching Tunheim by boat?'

Smithy was silent for a few seconds to lend weight to his observations, then said: 'In the present conditions so poor that I wouldn't even consider trying it, not even in these desperate circumstances. We've had very heavy weather recently, Mr Gerran, and the seas won't subside for quite some time. The drawback with those work-boats is that if one does encounter rough seas ahead you can't do what you would normally do, that is, turn and run before the sea: those boats are completely open at the back and would almost certainly be pooped—that is, they'd fill up with water and sink. So you'd have to be pretty certain of your weather before you set out.'

'I see. Too dangerous for the moment. When the sea moderates, Mr Smith?'

'Depends upon the wind. It's backing to the west right now and if it were to stay in that quarter—well, it's feasible. If it moves round to the north-west or beyond, no. Not on.' Smithy smiled. 'I wouldn't say that an overland trip would be all that easier, but at least you wouldn't be swamped in heavy seas.'

'Ah! So you think that it is at least possible to reach Tunheim on foot?'

'Well, I don't know. I'm no expert on Arctic travel, I'm sure Mr Heissman here—I'm told he's been giving a lecture about this already—is much more qualified to speak about it than I am.'

'No, no.' Heissman waved a deprecating hand. 'Let's hear what you think, Mr Smith.'

So Smithy let them hear what he thought, which was more or less a verbatim repetition of what I'd said to him in our cubicle earlier. When he'd finished, Heissman, who probably knew as much about winter travel in Arctic regions as I did about the back side of the moon, nodded sagely and said: 'Succinctly and admirably put. I agree entirely with Mr Smith.'

There was a thoughtful silence eventually broken by Smithy who said diffidently: 'I'm the supernumerary here. If the weather eases, I don't mind trying.'

'And now I have to disagree with you,' Heissman said promptly. 'Suicidal, just suicidal, my boy.'

'Not to be thought of for an instant,' Otto said firmly. 'For safety—for mutual safety—nothing short of an expedition would do.'

'I wouldn't want an expedition,' Smithy said mildly. 'I don't see that the blind leading the blind would help much.'

'Mr Gerran.' It was Jon Heyter speaking. 'Perhaps I could be of help here.'

'You?' Otto looked at him in momentary perplexity, then his face cleared. 'Of course. I'd forgotten about that.' He said in explanation: 'Jon here was my stuntman in *The High Sierra*. A climbing picture. He doubled for the actors who

219

were terrified or too valuable for the climbing sequences. A really first-class alpinist, I assure you. How about that then, eh, Mr Smith?'

I was about to wonder how Smithy would field that one when he answered immediately. 'That's about the size of the expedition I'd have in mind. I'd be very glad to have Mr Heyter along—he'd probably have to carry me most of the way there.'

'Well, that's settled then,' Otto said. 'Very grateful to you both. But only, of course, if the weather improves. Well, I think that covers everything.' He smiled at me. 'As co-opted board member, wouldn't you agree?'

'Well, yes,' I said. 'Except with your assumption that everyone will be here in the morning to play the parts you have assigned to them.'

'Ah!' Otto said.

'Precisely,' I said. 'You weren't seriously contemplating that we should *all* retire for the night, were you? For certain people with certain purposes in mind there is no time like the still small hours. When I say "people", I'm not going out-with the bounds of this cabin: when I say "purposes", I refer to homicidal ones.'

'My colleagues and I have, in fact, discussed this,' Otto said. 'You propose we set watches?'

'It might help some of us to live a little longer,' I said. I moved two or three steps until I was in the centre of the cabin. 'From here I can see into all five corridors. It would be impossible for any person to leave or enter any of the cubicles without being observed by a person standing here.'

'Going to call for a rather special type of person, isn't it?' Conrad said. 'Someone with his neck mounted on swivels.'

'Not if we have two on watch at the same time,' I said. 'And as the time's long gone when anybody's hurt feelings are a matter of any importance, two people on watch who are not only watching the corridors but watching each other. A suspect, shall we say, and a non-suspect. Among the non-suspects, I think we might gallantly exclude the two Marys. And I think that Allen too could do with a full night's sleep. That would leave Mr Gerran, Mr Goin, Mr Smith, Cecil and myself. Five of us, which would work out rather well for two-hour watches between, say, 10 p.m. and 8 a.m.'

'An excellent suggestion,' Otto said. 'Well, then, five volunteers.'

There were thirteen potential volunteers and all thirteen immediately offered their services. Eventually it was agreed that Goin and Hendriks should share the ten to midnight watch, Smith and Conrad the midnight to two, myself and Luke the two to four, Otto and Jungbeck the four to six, and Cecil and Eddie the six to eight. Some of the others, notably the Count and Heissman, protested, not too strongly, that they were being discriminated against: the reminder that there would be still another twenty-one nights after this one was sufficient to ensure that the protest was no more than a token one.

The decision not to linger around in small talk and socializing was reached with a far from surprising unanimity. There was, really, only one thing to talk about and nobody wished to talk about it in case he had picked the wrong person to talk to. In ones and twos, and within a very few minutes, almost everybody had moved off to their cubicles. Apart from Smithy and myself, only Conrad remained and I knew that he wished to talk to me. Smithy glanced briefly at me, then left for our cubicle.

'How did you know?' Conrad said. 'About Lonnie and his family?'

'I didn't. I guessed. He's talked to you?'

'A little. Not much. He had a family.'

'Had?'

'Had. Wife and two daughters. Two grown-up girls. A car crash. I don't know if they hit another car, I don't know who was driving. Lonnie just clammed up as if he had already said too much. He wouldn't even say whether he had been in the car himself, whether anyone else had been present, not even when it had taken place.'

And that was all that Conrad had learnt. We talked in a desultory fashion for some little time, and when Goin and Hendriks appeared to begin the first watch I left for my cubicle. Smithy was not in his camp-bed. Fully clothed, he was just removing the last of the screws I'd used to secure the window frame: he'd the flame of the little oil lamp turned so low that the cubicle was in semi-darkness.

'Leaving?' I said,

'Somebody out there.' Smithy reached for his anorak and I did the same. 'I thought maybe we shouldn't use the front door.'

'Who is it?'

'No idea. He looked in here but his face was just a white blur. He doesn't know I saw him, I'm sure of that, for he went from here and shone a torch through Judith Haynes's window, and he wouldn't have done that if he thought anyone was watching.' Smithy was already clambering through the window. 'He put his torch out but not before I saw where he was heading. Down to the jetty, I'm sure.'

I followed Smithy and jammed the window shut as I had done before. The weather was very much as it had been earlier, still that driving snow, the deepening cold, the darkness and that bitter wind which was still boxing the compass and had moved around to the south-west. We moved across to Judith Haynes's window, hooded our torches to give thin pencil beams of light, picked up tracks in the snow that led off in the direction of the jetty, and were about to follow them when it occurred to me that it might be instructive to see where they came from. But we couldn't find where they came from: whoever the unknown was he'd walked, keeping very close to the walls, at least twice round the cabin, obviously dragging his feet as he had gone, so that it was quite impossible to discover which cubicle window he'd used as an exit route from the cabin. That he should have so effectively covered his tracks was annoying: that he should have thought to do it at all was disconcerting for it plainly demonstrated at least the awareness that such late-night sorties might be expected.

We made our way quickly but cautiously down to the jetty, giving the unknown's tracks a prudently wide berth. At the head of the jetty I risked a quick flash with the narrowed beam of my torch: a single line of tracks led outwards.

'Well, now,' Smithy said softly. 'Our lad's down at the boats or the sub. If we go to investigate we might bump into him. If we go down to the end of the jetty for a quick look-see and don't bump into him he's still bound to see our tracks on his return trip. We want to make our presence known?'

'No. No law against a man taking a stroll when he feels like it, even though it is in a blizzard. And if we declare ourselves you can be damn sure he'll never put another foot wrong as long as we remain on Bear Island.'

We withdrew to the shelter of some rocks only a few yards distant along the beach, an almost wholly superfluous precaution in that close to zero visibility.

'What do you think he's up to?' Smithy said.

'Specifically, no idea. Generally, anything between the felonious and the villainous. We'll check down there when he's gone.'

Whatever purpose he'd had in mind, it hadn't taken him long to achieve it for he was gone within two minutes. The snow was so thick, the darkness so nearly absolute, that he might well have passed by both unseen and unheard had it not been for the erratic movement of the small torch he held in his hand. We waited for some seconds then straightened.

'Was he carrying anything?' I said.

'Same thought here,' Smithy said. 'He could have been. But I couldn't swear to it.'

We followed the double tracks in the snow down to the end of the jetty, where they ended at the head of the iron ladder leading down to the submarine mock-up. No question but this was where he'd gone, for apart from the fact that there was nowhere else where he could have been his footprints were all over the hull and, when we'd climbed into it, the platform in the conning-tower. We dropped down into the hull of the submarine.

Nothing was changed, nothing appeared to be missing from our earlier visit. Smithy said: 'I've taken a sudden dislike to this place. Last time we were here I called it an iron tomb. I wouldn't want it to be our tomb.'

'You feel it might?'

'Our friend seemingly didn't take anything away. But he must have had some purpose in coming here so I assume he brought something. On the track record to date that purpose wouldn't be anything I'd like and neither would be that something he brought. How would it be if he'd planted something to blow the damn thing up?'

'Why would he want to do a crazy thing like that?' I didn't feel as disbelieving as I sounded.

'Why has he done any of the crazy things he's done? Right now, I don't want a reason. I just want to know whether, as of now, and here and now, he's just done another crazy thing. What I mean is, I'm nervous.'

He wasn't the only one. I said: 'Assuming you're right, he couldn't blow this thing up with a little itsy-bitsy piece of plastic explosive. It would have to be something big enough to make a big bang. So, a delayed-action fuse.'

'To give him time to be asleep in his innocent bed when the explosion goes off? I'm more nervous than ever. I wonder how long he figured it would take him to get back to his bed.'

'He could do it in a minute.'

'God's sake, why are we standing here talking?' Smithy flashed his torch around. 'Where the hell would a man put a device like that?'

'Against a bulkhead, I'd say. Or on the bottom.'

We examined the deck first but all the bars of iron ballast and their securing wooden battens appeared to be undisturbed and firmly in place. There was just no room there for even the smallest explosive device. We turned to the rest of the hull, looked behind the mushroom anchors, among the chains, under the compressor unit and the windlass and behind the plastic models of periscope and guns. We found nothing. We even peered at the cleaning plates on the ballast tanks to see if any of those could have been unscrewed but there were no marks on them. And there was certainly no place where such a device could have been attached to the bulkheads themselves without being instantly detectable.

Smithy looked at me. It was difficult to say whether he was perplexed or, like me, increasingly and uncomfortably conscious of the fact that if such a time device did exist time might be swiftly running out. He looked towards the fore end of the hull and said: 'Or he might just have dropped it in one of those lockers. Easiest and quickest place to hide anything, after all.'

'Most unlikely,' I said, but I reached there before he did. I ran the beam of the torch over the paint locker and then the light steadied on a wooden batten close by the floor of the locker. I kept the light where it was and said to Smithy: 'You see it too?'

'A giveaway piece of fresh and unmelted snow. From a boot.' He reached for the lid of the locker. 'Well, time's a-wasting. Better open the damn thing.'

'Better not.' I'd caught his arm. 'How do you know it's not booby-trapped?'

'There's that.' He'd snatched back his hand like a man seeing a tiger's jaws closing on it. 'It would save the cost of a time-fuse. How do we open it then?'

'Gradually. It's unlikely that he had the time to rig up anything so elaborate as an electrical trigger, but if he did there'll be contacts in the lid. More likely, if anything, a simple pull cord. In either event nothing can operate in the first two inches of lift for he must have left at least that space to withdraw his hand.'

So we gingerly opened the lid those two inches, examined the rim and what we could see of the interior of the locker and found nothing. I pushed the locker lid right back. There was no sign of any explosive. Nothing had been put inside. But something had been removed—two cans of the quick-dry paint and two brushes.

Smithy looked at me and shook his head. Neither of us said anything. The reasons for removing a couple of paint cans were so wholly inconceivable that, clearly, there was nothing that could be gainfully said. We closed the locker, climbed up the conning-tower and regained the pier. I said: 'It's very un-likely that he would have taken them back to the cabin with him. After all, they're large cans and not easy things to hide in a tiny cubicle, especially if any of your friends should chance to come calling.'

'He doesn't have to hide them there. As I said earlier, there are a thousand snowdrifts where you can hide practically anything.'

But if he'd hidden anything he hadn't hidden them in any of the snowdrifts between the jetty and the cabin, for his tracks led straight back to the latter without any deviation to either side. We followed the footprints right back close up to the cabin walls and there they were lost in the smudged line of tracks that led right round the cabin's perimeter. Smithy hooded his torch and examined the tracks for some seconds.

He said: 'I think that track's wider and deeper than it was before. I think that someone—and it doesn't have to be the same person—has been making another grand tour of the cabin.'

'I think you're right,' I said, I led the way back to the

window of our own cubicle and was about to pull it open when some instinct—or perhaps it was because I was now subconsciously looking for the suspicious or untoward in every possible situation—made me shine my torch on the window-frame. I turned to Smithy. 'Notice something?'

'I notice something. The wad of paper we left jammed between the window and frame—well, it's no longer jammed between window and frame.' He shone his torch on the ground, stopped and picked something up. 'Because it was lying down there. A caller or callers.'

'So it would seem.' We clambered inside, and while Smithy started screwing the window back in place I turned up the oil lamp and started to look around partly for some other evidence to show that an intruder had been there, but mainly to try to discover the reason for his being there. Inevitably, my first check was on the medical equipment, and my first check was my last, and very brief it was too.

'Well, well,' I said. 'Two birds with one stone. We're a brilliant pair.'

'We are?'

'The lad you saw with his face pressed against that window. Probably had it stuck against it for all of five minutes until he'd made sure he'd been seen. Then, to make certain you were really interested, he went and shone his torch into Judith Haynes's window. No two actions, he must have calculated, could have been designed to lure us out into the open more quickly.'

'He was right at that, wasn't he?' He looked at my opened medical kit and said carefully: 'I'm to take it, then, that there's something missing there?'

'You may so take it.' I showed him the velvet-lined gap in the tray where the something missing had been. 'A lethal dose of morphine.'

CHAPTER ELEVEN

'Four bells and all's well,' Smithy said, shaking my shoulder. Neither the call nor the shake was necessary. I was by this time, even in my sleep, in so keyed-up a state that his turning of the door-handle had been enough to have me instantly awake. 'Time to report to the bridge. We've made some fresh coffee.'

I followed him into the main cabin, said a greeting to Conrad who was bent over pots and cups at the oil stove, and went to the front door. To my surprise the wind, now fully round to the west, had dropped away to something of not more than the order of a Force 3, the snow had thinned to the extent that it promised to cease altogether pretty soon, and I even imagined I could see a few faint stars in a clear patch of sky to the south, beyond the entrance of the Sorhamna. But the cold, if anything, was even more intense than it had been earlier in the night. I closed the door quickly, turned to Smithy and spoke softly.

'You're very encouraging,' Smithy said. 'What makes you so sure that those five—' He broke off as Luke, yawning and stretching vastly, entered the main cabin. Luke was a thin, awkward, gangling creature, a tow-headed youth urgently in need of the restraining influences of either a barber or a ribbon.

I said: 'Do you see him as a gun for hire?'

'I could have him up for committing musical atrocities with a guitar, I should think. Otherwise—yes, I guess. Very little threat to life and limb. And, yes again, that would go for the other four too.' He watched as Conrad went into one of the passages, carrying a cup of coffee. 'I'd put my money on our leading man any day.'

'Where on earth is *he* off to?'

'Bearing sustenance for his lady-love, I should imagine. Miss Stuart spent much of our watch with us.'

I was on the point of observing that the alleged lady-love had a remarkable predilection for moving around in the darker watches of the night but thought better of it. That

Mary Stuart was involved in matters dark and devious—Heissman's being her uncle didn't even begin to account for the earlier oddity of her behaviour—I didn't for a moment doubt: that she was engaged in any murderous activities couldn't for a moment believe.

Smithy went on: 'It's important that I reach Tunheim?'

'It hardly matters whether you do or not. With Heyter along, only the weather and the terrain can decide that. If you have to turn back, that's fine with me, I'd rather have you here: if you get to Tunheim, just stay there.'

'Stay there? How can I stay there? I'm going there for help, am I not? And Heyter will be shouting to come back.'

'I'm sure they'll understand if you explain that you're tired and need a rest. If Heyter makes a noise, have him locked up—I'll give you a letter to the Met. officer in charge.'

'You'll do that, will you? And what if the Met. officer point-blank refuses?'

'I think you'll find some people up there who'll be only too happy to oblige you.'

He looked at me without a great deal of enthusiasm. 'Friends of yours, of course?'

'There's a visiting meteorological team from Britain staying there briefly. Five of them. Only, they're not meteorologists.'

'Naturally not.' The lack of enthusiasm deteriorated into a coldness that was just short of outright hostility. 'You play your cards mighty close to the chest, don't you, Dr Marlowe?'

'Don't get angry with me. I'm not asking you that, I'm telling you. Policy—I obey orders, even if you don't. A secret shared is never a secret halved—even a peek at my card and who knows who's kibitzing? I'll give you that letter early this morning.'

'OK.' Smithy was obviously restraining himself with no small difficulty. He went on morosely: 'I suppose I shouldn't be too surprised to find even the *Morning Rose* up there?'

'Let me put it this way,' I said. 'I wouldn't put it beyond the bounds of possibility.'

Smithy nodded, turned and walked to the oil stove where Conrad, now returned, was pouring coffee. We sat for ten minutes, drinking and talking about nothing much, then Smithy and Conrad left. The next hour or so passed without event except that after five minutes Luke fell sound asleep and stayed that way. I didn't bother to wake him up, it wasn't necessary, I was in an almost hypernatural state of alertness: unlike Luke, I had things on my mind.

A door in a passage opened and Lonnie appeared. As Lonnie, by his own account, wasn't given to sleeping much and as he wasn't on my list of suspects anyway, this was hardly call for alarm. He came into the cabin and sat heavily in a chair by my side. He looked old and tired and grey and the usual note of badinage was lacking in his tone.

'Once again the kindly healer,' he said, 'and once again looking after his little flock. I have come, my boy, to share your midnight vigil.'

'It's twenty-five to four,' I said.

'A figure of speech.' He sighed. 'I have not slept well. In fact, I have not slept at all. You see before you, Doctor, a troubled old man.'

'I'm sorry to hear that, Lonnie.'

'No tears for Lonnie. For me, as for most of pitiful mankind, my troubles are of my own making. To be an old man is bad enough. To be a lonely old man, and I have been lonely for many years, makes a man sad for much of the time. But to be a lonely old man who can no longer live with his conscience—ah, that is not to be borne.' He sighed again. 'I am feeling uncommonly sorry for myself tonight.'

'What's your conscience doing now?'

'It's keeping me awake, that's what it's doing. Ah, my boy, my boy, to cease upon the midnight with no pain. What more could a man want when it's evening and time to be gone?'

'This wine-shop on the far shore?'

'Not even that.' He shook his head mournfully. 'No welcoming arms in paradise for the lost Lonnies of this world. Haven't the right entry qualifications, my boy.' He smiled and his eyes were sad. 'I'll pin my hopes on a small four-ale bar in purgatory.'

He lapsed into silence, his eyes closed and I thought he was drifting off into sleep. But he presently stirred, cleared his his throat and said apparently apropos of nothing. 'It's always too late. Always.'

'What's always too late, Lonnie?'

'Compassion is, or understanding or forgiveness. I fear that Lonnie Gilbert has been less than he should have been. But it's always too late. Too late to say I like you or I love you

229

or how nice you are or I forgive you. If only, if only, if only. It is difficult to make your peace with someone if you're looking at that person and he's lying there dead. My, my, my.' As if with an immense effort, he pushed himself to his feet. 'But there's still a little shred of something that can be saved. Lonnie Gilbert is now about to go and do something that he should have done many, many years ago. But first I must arm myself, some life in the ancient bones, some clarity in the faded mind, in short, prepare myself for what I'm ashamed to say I still regard as the ordeal that lies ahead. In brief, my dear fellow, where's the scotch?'

'I'm afraid Otto has taken it with him.'

'A kind fellow, Otto, none kinder, but he has his parsimonious side to him. But no matter, the main source of supply is less than a Sunday's march away.' He made for the outer door but I stopped him.

'One of those times, Lonnie, you're going to go out there, sit down there, go to sleep and not come back again because you'll be frozen to death. Besides, there's no need. There's some in my cubicle. Same source of supply, I assure you. I'll fetch it. Just keep your eye open in my absence, will you?'

It didn't matter very much whether he kept his eyes open or not for I was back inside twenty seconds. Smithy, clearly, was a heavier sleeper than I was for he didn't stir during my brief visit.

Lonnie helped himself copiously, drained his glass in a few gulps, gazed at the bottle longingly then set it firmly aside. 'Duty completed, I shall return and enjoy this at my leisure. Meantime, I am sufficiently fortified.'

'Where are you going?' It was difficult to imagine what pressing task he had on hand at that time of the night.

'I am in great debt to Miss Haynes. It is my wish—'

'To Judith Haynes?' I know I stared at him. 'It was my understanding that you could with but difficulty look at her.'

'In great debt,' he said firmly. 'It is my wish to discharge it, to clear the books, you might say. You understand?'

'No. What I do understand is that it's only three-forty-five. If this business has been outstanding, as you said, for so many years, surely it can wait just another few hours. Besides, Miss Haynes has been sick and shocked and she's under sedatives. As her doctor, and whether she likes it or not, I am her doctor, I can't permit it.'

'And as a doctor, my dear fellow, you should understand the necessity for immediacy. I have worked myself up to this, screwed myself, as it were, to the sticking-point. Another few hours, as you say, and it may be too late. The Lonnie Gilbert you see before you will almost certainly have reverted to the bad old, cowardly old, selfish old, clay-souled Lonnie of yore, the Lonnie we all know so well. And then it will always be too late.' He paused and switched his argument. 'Sedatives, you say. How long do the effects of those last?'

'Varies from person to person. Four hours, six hours, maybe as much as eight.'

'Well, there you are then. Poor girl's probably been lying awake for hours, just longing for some company, although not, in all likelihood, that of Lonnie Gilbert. Or has it escaped your attention that close on twelve hours have elapsed since you administered that sedative?'

It had. But what had not escaped my attention was that Lonnie's relationship vis-à-vis Judith Haynes had been intriguing me considerably for some time. It might, I thought, be very helpful and, with regard to a deeper penetration of the fog of mystery surrounding us, more than a little constructive if I could learn something of the burden of what Lonnie had in mind to say to Judith Haynes. I said: 'Let me go and see her. If she's awake and I think she's fit to talk, then OK.'

He nodded. I went to Judith Haynes's room and entered without knocking. The oil lamp was turned up and she was awake, stretched out under the covers with only her face showing. She looked ghastly, which was the way I had expected her to look, with the titian hair emphasizing the drawn pallor of her face. The usually striking green eyes were glazed and lack-lustre and her cheeks were smudged and streaked with tears. She looked at me indifferently as I pulled up a stool, then looked as indifferently away.

'I hope you slept well, Miss Haynes,' I said. 'How are you feeling?'

'Do you usually come calling on patients in the middle of the night?' Her voice was as dull as her eyes.

'I don't make a practice of it. But we're taking turns keeping watch tonight, and this happens to be my turn. Is there anything that you want?'

'No. Have you found out who killed my husband?' She was so preternaturally calm, under such seemingly iron control, that I suspected it to be the prelude to another uncontrollable hysterical outburst.

'No. Am I to take it from that, Miss Haynes, that you no longer think that young Allen did?'

'I don't think so. I've been lying here for hours, just thinking, and I don't think so.' From the lifeless voice and the lifeless face I was pretty sure she was still under the influence of the sedative. 'You will get him, won't you? The man who killed Michael. Michael wasn't as bad as people thought, Dr Marlowe, no, he really wasn't.' For the first time a trace of expression, just the weary suggestion of a smile. 'I don't say he was a kind man or a good one or a gentle one, for he wasn't: but he was the man for me.'

'I know,' I said, as if I understood, which I only partially did. 'I hope we get the man responsible. I think we will. Do you have any ideas that could help?'

'My ideas are not worth much, Doctor. My mind doesn't seem to be very clear.'

'Do you think you could talk for a bit, Miss Haynes? It wouldn't be too tiring?'

'I am talking.'

'Not to me. To Lonnie Gilbert. He seems terribly anxious to speak to you.'

'Speak to me?' Tired surprise but not outright rejection of the idea. 'Why should Lonnie Gilbert wish to speak to me?'

'I don't know. Lonnie doesn't believe in confiding in doctors. All I gather is that he feels that he's done you some great wrong and he wants to say "sorry". I think.'

'Lonnie say "sorry" to me!' Astonishment had driven the flat hopelessness from her voice. 'Apologize to *me*? No, not to me.' She was silent for a bit, then she said: 'Yes, I'd very much like to see him now.'

I concealed my own astonishment as best I could, went back to the main cabin, told an equally astonished Lonnie that Judith Haynes was more than prepared to meet him, and watched him as he went along the passage, entered her room and closed the door behind him. I glanced at Luke. He appeared, if anything, to be more soundly asleep than ever absurdly young to be in this situation, a pleased smile on his face: he was probably dreaming of golden discs. I walked quietly along the passage to Judith Haynes's room: there was nothing in the Hippocratic oath against doctors listening at closed doors.

It was clear that I was going to have to listen very closely indeed for although the door was only made of bonded ply, the voices in the room were being kept low and I could hear little more than a confused murmur. I dropped to my knees and applied my ear to the keyhole. The audibility factor improved quite remarkably.

'You!' Judith Haynes said. There was a catch in her voice, I wouldn't have believed her capable of any of the more kindly emotions. 'You! To apologize to me! Of all people, you!'

'Me, my dear, me. All those years, all those years.' His voice fell away and I couldn't catch his next few words. Then he said: 'Despicable, despicable. For any man to go through life, nurturing the animosity, nay, my dear, the hatred—' He broke off and there was silence for some moments. He went on: 'No forgiveness, no forgiveness. I know he can't—I know he couldn't have been so bad, or even really bad at all, you loved him and no one can love a person who is bad all through, but even if his sins had been black as the midnight shades—'

'Lonnie!' The interruption was sharp, even forceful. 'I know I wasn't married to an angel, but I wasn't married to any devil either.'

'I know that, my dear, I know that. I was merely saying—'

'Will you listen! Lonnie, Michael wasn't in that car that night. Michael was never near that car.'

I strained for the answer but none came. Judith Haynes went on: 'Neither was I, Lonnie.'

There was a prolonged silence, then Lonnie said in a voice so low that it was a barely heard whisper: 'That's not what I was told.'

'I'm sure it wasn't, Lonnie. My car, yes. But I wasn't driving it. Michael wasn't driving it.'

'But—you won't deny that my daughters were—well, incapable, that night. And that you were too. And that you made them that way?'

'I'm not denying anything. We all had too much to drink

that night—that's why I've never drunk since, Lonnie. I don't know who was responsible. All I know is that Michael and I never left the house. Good God, do you think I *have* to tell you this—now that Michael is dead?'

'No. No, you don't. Then—then who was driving your car?'

'Two other people. Two men.'

'Two men. And you've been protecting them all those years?'

'Protecting? No, I wouldn't use the word "protecting". Except inadvertently. No, I didn't put that well, I mean—well, any protection given was just incidental to something else we really wanted. Our own selfish ends, I suppose you could call it. Everybody knows well enough that Michael and I—well, we were criminals but we always had an eye on the main chance.'

'Two men.' It was almost as if Lonnie hadn't been listening to a word she'd said. 'Two men. You must know them.'

Another silence, then she said quietly: 'Of course.'

Once more an infuriating silence, I even stopped breathing in case I were to miss the next few words. But I wasn't given the chance either to miss them or to hear them for a harsh and hostile voice behind me said: 'What in the devil do you think you are doing here, sir?'

I refrained from doing what I felt like doing, which was to let loose with a few choice and uninhibited phrases, turned and looked up to find Otto's massively pear-shaped bulk looming massively above me. His fists were clenched, his puce complexion had darkened dangerously, his eyes were glaring and his lips were clamped in a thin line that threatened to disappear at any moment.

'You look upset, Mr Gerran,' I said. 'In point of fact, I was eavesdropping.' I pushed myself to my feet, dusted off the knees of my trousers, straightened and dusted off my hands. 'I can explain everything.'

'I'm waiting for your explanation.' He was fractionally more livid than ever. 'It should be interesting, Dr Marlowe.'

'I only said I can explain everything. *Can*, Mr Gerran. That doesn't mean I've got any intention of explaining anything. Come to that, what are you doing here?'

'What am I—what am I—?' He spluttered into outraged speechlessness, the year's top candidate for an instant coronary.

'God damn your impudence, sir! I'm about to go on watch! What are you doing at my daughter's door? I'm surprised you're not looking through that keyhole, Marlowe, instead of listening at it!'

'I don't have to look through keyholes,' I said reasonably. 'Miss Haynes is my patient and I'm a doctor. If I want to see her I just open the door and walk in. Well, then, now that you're on watch, I'll be on my way. Bed. I'm tired.'

'Bed! Bed! By God, I swear this, Marlowe, you'll regret —who's in there with her?'

'Lonnie Gilbert.'

'Lonnie Gilbert! What in the name of hell—stand aside, sir! Let me pass!'

I barred his way—physically. It was like stopping a small tank upholstered in Dunlopillo, but I had the advantage of having my back to the wall and he brought up a foot short of the door. 'I wouldn't, if I were you. They're having a rather painful moment in there. Lost, one might say, in the far from sweet remembrance of things past.'

'What the devil do you mean? What are you trying to tell me, you—you eavesdropper?'

'I'm not trying to tell you anything. Maybe, though, you'd tell me something? Maybe you would like to tell me something about that car crash—I assume that it must have been in California—in which Lonnie Gilbert's wife and two children were killed a long long time ago?'

He stopped being livid. He even stopped being his normal puce. Colour drained from his face to leave it ugly and mottled and stained with grey. 'Car crash?' He'd a much better control over his voice than he had over his complexion. 'What do you mean, "car crash", sir?'

'I don't know what I mean. That's why I'm asking you. I heard Lonnie, just snippets, talking about his family's fatal car crash, and as your daughter seemed to know something about it I assumed you would too.'

'I don't know what he's talking about. Nor you.' Otto, who seemed suddenly to have lost all his inquisitorial predilections, wheeled and walked up the passage to the centre of the cabin. I followed and walked to the outer door. Smithy was in for a hike, I thought, no doubt about it now. Although the cold was as intense as ever, the snow had stopped, the west wind dropped away to no more than an icily gentle breeze—

the fact that we were now in the lee of the Antarcticfjell might have accounted for that—and there were quite large patches of star-studded sky all around. There was a curious lightness, a luminescence in the atmosphere, too much to be accounted for by the presence of stars alone. I walked out a few paces until I was clear of the main cabin, and low to the south I could see a three-quarter moon riding in an empty sky.

I went back inside and as I closed the door I saw Lonnie crossing the main living area, heading, I assumed, for his cubicle. He walked uncertainly, like a man not seeing too well, and as he went by close to me I could see that his eyes were masked in tears: I would have given a lot to know just what it was that had been responsible for those tears. It was a mark of Lonnie's emotional upset that he did not so much as glance at the still three-quarter-full bottle of scotch on the small table by which Otto was sitting. He didn't even so much as look at Otto: more extraordinarily still, Otto didn't even look up at Lonnie's passing. In the mood he'd been in when he'd accosted me outside his daughter's door I'd have expected him to question Lonnie pretty closely, probably with both hands around the old man's neck: but Otto's mood, clearly, had undergone a considerable sea-change.

I was walking towards Luke, bent on rousing the faithful watchdog from his slumbers, when Otto suddenly heaved his bulk upright and made his way down the passage towards his daughter's cubicle. I didn't even hesitate, in for a penny, in for a pound. I followed him and took up my by now accustomed station outside Judith Haynes's door, although this time I didn't have to have resource to the keyhole again as Otto, in what was presumably his agitation, had left the door considerably ajar. Otto was addressing his daughter in a low harsh voice that was noticeably lacking in filial affection.

'What have you been saying, you young she-devil? What have you been saying? Car crash? Car crash? What lies have you been telling Gilbert, you blackmailing little bitch?'

'Get out of here!' Judith Haynes had abandoned the use of her dull and expressionless voice, although probably involuntarily. 'Leave me, you horrible, evil, old man. Get out, get out, get out!'

I leaned more closely to the crack between door and jamb. It wasn't every day one had the opportunity to listen to those family tête-à-têtes.

'By God, and I'll not have my own daughter cross me.' Otto had forgotten the need to talk in a low voice. 'I've put up with more than enough from you and that other idle worthless bastard of a blackmailer. What you did—'

'You dare to talk of Michael like that?' Her voice had gone very quiet and I shivered involuntarily at the sound of it. 'You talk of him like that and he's lying dead. Murdered. My husband. Well, Father dear, can I tell you about something you *don't* know that *I* know he was blackmailing you with? Shall I, Father dear? And shall I tell it to Johann Heissman too?'

There was a silence, then Otto said: 'You venomous little bitch!' He sounded as if he was trying to choke himself.

'Venomous! Venomous!' She laughed, a cracked and chilling sound. 'Coming from you, that's rich. Come now, Daddy dear, surely you remember 1938—why, even *I* can remember it. Poor old Johann, he ran, and ran, and ran, and all the time he ran the wrong way. Poor Uncle Johann. That's what you taught me to call him then, wasn't it, Daddy dear? Uncle Johann.'

I left, not because I had heard all that I wanted to hear but because I thought that this was a conversation that was not going to last very long and I could foresee a degree of awkwardness arising if Otto caught me outside his daughter's door a second time. Besides—I checked the time—Jungbeck, Otto's watch-mate, was due to make his appearance just at that moment and I didn't want him to find me where I was and, very likely, lose no time in telling his boss about it. So I returned to Luke, decided that there was no point in awakening him only to tell him to go to sleep again, poured myself a sort of morning nightcap and was about to savour it when I heard a feminine voice scream 'Get out, get out, get out', and saw Otto emerging hurriedly from his daughter's cubicle and as hurriedly close the door behind him. He waddled swiftly into the middle of the cabin, seized the whisky bottle without as much as by-your-leave—true, it was his own, but he didn't know that—poured himself a brimming measure and downed half of it at a gulp, his shaking hand spilling a fair proportion of it on the way up to his mouth.

'That was very thoughtless of you, Mr Gerran,' I said reproachfully. 'Upsetting your daughter like that. She's really a very sick girl and what she needs is tender affection, a measure of loving care.'

'Tender affection!' He was on the second half of his glass now and he spluttered much of it over his shirt front. 'Loving care! Jesus!' He splashed some more scotch into his glass and gradually subsided a little. By and by he became calm, almost thoughtful: when he spoke no one would have thought that only a few minutes previously his greatest yearning in life would have seemed to be to disembowel me. 'Maybe I wasn't as thoughtful as I ought to have been. But a hysterical girl, very hysterical. This actress temperament, you know. I'm afraid your sedatives aren't very effective, Dr Marlowe.'

'People's reactions to sedatives vary greatly, Mr Gerran. And unpredictably.'

'I'm not blaming you, not blaming you,' he said irritatedly. 'Care and attention. Yes, yes. But some rest, a damned good sleep is more important, if you ask me. How about another sedative—a more effective one this time? No danger in that, is there?'

'No. No harm in it. She did sound a bit—what shall we say?—worked up. But she's rather a self-willed person. If she refuses—'

'Ha! Self-willed! Try, anyway.' He seemed to lose interest in the subject and gazed moodily at the floor. He looked up without any enthusiasm as Jungbeck made a sleepy entrance, turned and shook Luke roughly by the shoulder. 'Wake up, man.' Luke stirred and opened bleary eyes. 'Bloody fine guard you are. Your watch is over. Go to bed.' Luke mumbled some sort of apology, rose stiffly and moved off.

'You might have let him be,' I said. 'He'll have to get up for the day inside a few hours anyway.'

'Too late now. Besides,' Otto added inconsequentially, 'I'm going to have the lot of them up inside two hours. Weather's cleared, there's a moon to travel by, we can all be where we want to be and ready to shoot as soon as there's enough light in the sky.' He glanced along the corridor where his daughter's cubicle was. 'Well, aren't you going to try?'

I nodded and left. Ten minutes' time—in the right circumstances which in this case were the wrong ones—can bring about a change in a person's features which just lies within the bounds of credibility. The face that had looked merely drawn so very recently, now looked haggard: she looked her real age and then ten hard and bitter years after that. She wept in a sore and aching silence and the tears flowed steadily down her temples and past the earlobes, the damp marks spreading on the grey rough linen of her pillow. I would not have thought it possible that I could ever feel such deep pity for this person and wish to comfort her: but that was how it was. I said: 'I think you should sleep now.'

'Why?' Her hands were clenched so tightly that the ivory of the knuckles showed. 'What does it matter? I'll have to wake up, won't I?'

'Yes, I know.' It was the sort of situation where, no matter what I said, the words would sound banal. 'But the sleep would do you good, Miss Haynes.'

'Well, yes,' she said. It was hard for her to speak through the quiet tears. 'All right. Make it a long sleep.'

So, like a fool, I made it a long sleep. Like an even greater fool I went to my cubicle and lay down. And, like the greatest fool of all, I went to sleep myself.

I slept for over four hours and awoke to an almost deserted cabin. Otto had indeed been as good as his word and had had everyone up and around at what they must have regarded as the most unreasonable crack of dawn. Understandably enough, neither he nor anyone else had seen fit to wake me: I was one of the few who had no functions to perform that day.

Otto and Conrad were the only two people in the main quarter of the cabin. Both were drinking coffee, but as both were heavily muffled they were clearly on the point of departure. Conrad said a civil good morning. Otto didn't bother. He informed me that the Count, Neal Divine, Allen, Cecil and Mary Darling had taken off with the Sno-Cat and cameras along Lerner's Way and that he and Conrad were following immediately. Hendriks and the Three Apostles were abroad with their sound-recording equipment. Smithy and Heyter had left over an hour previously for Tunheim. Initially, I found this vaguely disturbing, I would have thought that Smithy would have at least woken and spoken to me before leaving. On reflection, however, I found this omission less than disturbing: it was a measure of Smithy's confidence in

239

himself and, by implication, my unspoken confidence in himself, that he had not thought it necessary to seek either advice or reassurance before his departure. Finally, Otto told me, Heissman and his hand-held camera, along with Jungbeck, had taken off on his location reconnaissance in the sixteen-foot work-boat: they had been accompanied by Goin, who had volunteered to stand in for the now absent Heyter.

Otto stood up, drained his cup and said: 'About my daughter, Dr Marlowe.'

'She'll be all right.' She would never again be all right.

'I'd like to talk to her before I go.' I couldn't begin to imagine a reason why he should wish to talk to her or she to him, but I refrained from comment. He went on: 'You have no objections? Medical ones, I mean?'

'No. Just straightforward commonsense ones. She's under heavy sedation. You couldn't even shake her awake.'

'But surely—'

'Two or three hours at the very least. If you don't want my advice, Mr Gerran, why ask for it?'

'Fair enough, fair enough. Leave her be.' He headed towards the outer door. 'Your plans for the day, Dr Marlowe?'

'Who's left here?' I said. 'Apart from your daughter and myself?'

He looked at me, his brows levelled in a frown, then said: 'Mary Stuart. Then there's Lonnie, Eddie and Sandy. Why?'

'They're asleep?'

'As far as I know. Why?'

'Someone has to bury Stryker.'

'Ah, yes, of course. Stryker. I hadn't forgotten, you know, but—yes, of course. Yes, yes. You—?'

'Yes.'

'I am in your debt. A ghastly business, ghastly, ghastly, ghastly. Thank you again, Dr Marlowe.' He waddled purposefully towards the door. 'Come, Charles, we are overdue.'

They left. I poured myself some coffee but had nothing to eat for it wasn't a morning for eating, went outside into the equipment shed and found myself a spade. The frozen snow was not too deep, not much more than a foot, but the permafrost had set into the ground and it cost me over an hour and a half and, what is always dangerous in those high latitudes, the loss of much sweat before I'd done what had to be done. I returned the spade and went inside quickly to change:

it was a fine clear morning of bitter cold with the sun not yet in the sky, but no morning for an overheated man to linger.

Five minutes later, a pair of binoculars slung round my neck, I closed the front door softly behind me. Despite the fact that it was now close on ten o'clock, Eddie, Sandy, Lonnie and Mary Stuart had not as yet put in an appearance. The presence of the first three would have given me no cause for concern for all were notorious for their aversion to any form of physical activity and it was extremely unlikely that any would have suggested that they accompany me on my outing: Mary Stuart might well have done so, for any number of reasons: curiosity, the wish to explore, because she'd been told to keep an eye on me, even, maybe, because she would have felt safer with me than being left behind at the cabin. But whatever her reasons might have been I most definitely didn't want Mary Stuart keeping an eye on me when I was setting out to keep an eye on Heissman.

But to keep an eye on Heissman I had first of all to find him, and Heissman, inconveniently and most annoyingly, was nowhere to be seen. The intention, as I had understood it, was that he, with Jungbeck and Goin, should cruise the Sorhamna in the sixteen-footer, in search of likely background material. But there was no trace of their boat anywhere in the Sor-hamna, and from where I stood in the vicinity of the cabin I could take in the whole sweep of the bay at one glance. Against the remote possibility that the boat might have temporarily moved in behind one of the tiny islands on the east side of the bay I kept the glasses on those for a few minutes. Nothing stirred. Heissman, I was sure, had left the Sor-hamna.

He could have moved out to the open sea to the east by way of the northern tip of the island of Makehl, but this seemed unlikely. The northerly seas were white-capped and confused, and apart from the fact that Heissman was as far removed from the popular concept of an intrepid seaman as it was possible to imagine it seemed unlikely that he would have forgotten Smithy's warning the previous day about the dangers inherent in taking an open-pooped boat out in such weather. Much more likely, I thought, he'd moved south out of the Sor-hamna into the sheltered waters of the next bay to the south, the Evjebukta.

I, too, made my way south. Initially, I moved in a south-westerly direction to give the low cliffs of the bay as wide a berth as possible, not from any vertiginous fear of heights but because Hendriks and the Three Apostles were down there somewhere recording, or hoping to record, the cries of the kittiwake gulls, the fulmars, the black guillemots which were reputed to haunt those parts: I had no reason to fear anything at their hands, I just didn't want to go around arousing too much curiosity.

The going, diagonally upwards across a deceptively easy-looking slope, proved very laborious indeed. Mountaineering ability was not called for, which in view of my lack of expertise or anything resembling specialized equipment, was just as well: what was required was some form of in-built radar to enable me to detect the presence of hidden fissures and sudden dips in the smooth expanse of white, and in this, unfortunately, I was equally lacking, with the result that I fell abruptly and at fairly regular intervals into drifts of newly-formed snow that at times reached as high as my shoulders. There was no physical danger in this, the cushioning effect of newly-driven snow is almost absolute, but the effort of almost continuously extricating myself from those miniature ravines and struggling back up to something resembling terra firma—which even then had seldom less than twelve or fifteen inches of soft snow—was very wearing indeed. If it were so difficult for me to make progress along such relatively simple ground I wondered how Smithy and Heyter must be faring in the so much more wildly rugged mountainous terrain to the north.

It took me just on an hour and a half to cover less than a mile and arrive at a vantage point of a height of about five hundred feet that enabled me to see into the next bay—the Evjebukta. This wide U-shaped bay, stretching from Kapp Malmgren in the north-east to Kap Kolthoff in the south-west, was just over a mile in length and perhaps half of that in width: the entire coastline of the bay consisted of vertical cliffs, a bleak, forbidding and repellent stretch of grey water and precipitous limestone that offered no haven to those in peril on the sea.

I stretched out gratefully on the snow and, when the thumping of my heart and the rasping of my breathing had quietened sufficiently for me to hold a pair of binoculars steady, I

used them to quarter the Evjebukta. It was completely bereft
of life. The sun was up now, low over the south-eastern
horizon, but even although it was in my eyes, visibility was
good enough and the resolution of the binoculars such that
I could have picked up a sea-gull floating on the waters. There
were some little islands to the north of the bay and, of
course, there were the cliffs immediately below me that blocked
off all view of what might be happening at their feet: but if
the boat was concealed either behind an island or under
the cliffs, it was most unlikely that Heissman would remain
in such positions long for there would be nothing to detain
him.

I looked south beyond the tip of Kapp Kolthoff and there,
beyond the protection of the headland, the sun glinted off the
broken tops of white water. I was as certain as one could be
without absolute proof that they would not have ventured
beyond the protection of the point: Heissman's unseamanlike
qualities apart, Goin was far too prudent a man to step
unheedingly into anything that would even smack of danger.

How long I lay there waiting for the boat to appear either
from behind an island or out from under the concealment of
the nearest cliffs I didn't know: what I did know was that
I suddenly became aware of the fact that I was shaking with
the cold and that both hands and feet were almost completely
benumbed. And I became aware of something else. For
several minutes now I'd had the binoculars trained not on
the north end of the bay but at the foot of the cliffs to the
south on a spot where, about three hundred yards north-
west of the tip of Kapp Kolthoff, there was a peculiar indentation in the cliff walls. Partly because of the fact that it
appeared to bear to the right and out of sight behind one of the
cliff-faces guarding the entrance, and partly because, due to
the height of the cliffs and the fact that the sun was almost
directly behind, the shadows cast were very deep, I was unable
to make out any details beyond this narrow entrance. But
that it was an entrance to some cove beyond I didn't doubt.
Of any place within the reach of my binoculars it was the
only one where the boat could have lain concealed: why
anyone should wish to lie there at all was another matter
altogether, a reason for which I couldn't even guess at. One
thing was for certain, a landward investigation from where
I lay was out of the question: even if I didn't break my neck

in the minimum of the two-hour journey it would take me to get there, nothing would be achieved by making such a trip anyway, for not only did the descent of those beetling black cliffs seem quite suicidal but, even if it were impossibly accomplished, what lay at the end of it removed any uncertainty about the permanency of the awaiting reception: for there was no foreshore whatever, just the precipitous plunge of those limestone walls into the dark and icy seas.

Stiffly, clumsily, I rose and headed back towards the cabin. The trip back was easier than the outwards one for it was downhill, and by following my own tracks I was able to avoid most of the involuntary descents into the sunken snow-drifts that had punctuated my climb. Even so, it was nearer one o'clock than noon when I approached the cabin.

I was only a few paces distant when the main door opened and Mary Stuart appeared. One look at her and my heart turned over and something cold and leaden seemed to settle in the pit of my stomach. Dishevelled hair, a white and shocked face, eyes wild and full of fear, I'd have had to be blind not to know that somewhere, close, death had walked by again

'Thank God!' Her voice was husky and full of tears. 'Thank God you're here! Please come quickly. Something terrible has happened.'

I didn't waste time asking her what, clearly I'd find out soon enough, just followed her running footsteps into the cabin and along the passage to Judith Haynes's opened door. Something terrible had indeed happened, but there had been no need for haste. Judith Haynes had fallen from her cot and was lying sideways on the floor, half-covered by her blanket which she'd apparently dragged down along with her. On the bed lay an opened and three parts empty bottle of barbiturate tablets, a few scattered over the bed: on the floor, its neck still clutched in her hand, lay a bottle of gin, also three-part empty. I stooped and touched the marble forehead: even allowing for the icy atmosphere in the cubicle, she must have been dead for hours. Make it a long sleep, she'd said to me: make it a long sleep.

'Is she—is she—?' The dead make people speak in whispers.

'Can't you tell a dead person when you see one?' It was brutal of me but I felt flooding into me that cold anger that was to remain with me until we'd left the island.

'I—I didn't touch her. I—'

'When did you find her?'

'A minute ago. Two. I'd just made some food and coffee and I came to see—'

'Where are the others? Lonnie, Sandy, Eddie?'

'Where are—I don't know. They left a little while ago—said they were going for a walk.'

A likely tale. There was only one reason that would make at least two of the three walk as far as the front door. I said: 'Get them. You'll find them in the provision shed.'

'Provision shed? Why would they be there?'

'Because that's where Otto keeps his scotch.'

She left. I put the gin bottle and barbiturate bottle to one side, then I lifted Judith Haynes on to the bed for no better reason than that it seemed cruel to leave her lying on the wooden floor. I looked quickly around the cubicle, but I could see nothing that could be regarded as untoward or amiss. The window was still screwed in its closed position, the few clothes that she had unpacked neatly folded on a small chair. My eye kept returning to the gin bottle. Stryker had told me and I'd overheard her telling Lonnie that she never drank, had not drunk alcohol for many years: an abstainer does not habitually carry around a bottle of gin just on the off-chance that he or she may just suddenly feel thirsty.

Lonnie, Eddie and Sandy came in, trailing with them the redolence of a Highland distillery, but that was the only evidence of their sojourn in the provision shed; whatever they'd been like when Mary had found them, they were shocked cold sober now. They just stood there, staring at the dead woman and saying nothing: understandably, I suppose, they thought there was nothing they could usefully say.

I said: 'Mr Gerran must be informed that his daughter is dead. He's gone north to the next bay. He'll be easy to find—you've only got to follow the Sno-Cat's tracks. I think you should go together.'

'God love us all.' Lonnie spoke in a hushed and anguished reverence. 'The poor girl. The poor, poor lassie. First her man—and now this. Where's it all going to end, Doctor?'

'I don't know, Lonnie. Life's not always so kind, is it? No need to kill yourselves looking for Mr Gerran. A heart attack on top of this we can do without.'

'Poor little Judith,' Lonnie said, 'And what do we tell

Otto she died of? Alcohol and sleeping tablets—it's a pretty lethal combination, isn't it?'

'Frequently.'

They looked at each other uncertainly, then turned and left. Mary Stuart said: 'What can I do?'

'Stay there.' The harshness in my voice surprised me almost as much as it clearly surprised her. 'I want to talk to you'.

I found a towel and a handkerchief, wrapped the gin bottle in the former and the barbiturate bottle in the latter. I had a glimpse of Mary watching me, wide-eyed, in what could have been wonder or fear or both, then crossed to examine the dead woman, to see whether there were any visible marks on her. There wasn't much to examine—although she'd been in bed with blankets over her, she'd been fully clothed in parka and some kind of fur trousers. I didn't have to look long. I beckoned Mary across and pointed to a tiny puncture exposed by pushing back the hair on Judith Haynes's neck. Mary ran the tip of her tongue across dry lips and looked at me with sick eyes.

'Yes,' I said. 'Murdered. How do you feel about that, Mary dear?' The term was affectionate, the tone not.

'Murdered!' she whispered. 'Murdered!' She looked at the wrapped bottles, licked her lips again, made as if to speak and seemingly couldn't.

'There may be some gin inside her,' I conceded. 'Possibly even some barbiturate. I'd doubt it though—it's very hard to make people swallow anything when they're unconscious. Maybe there are no other fingerprints on the bottles—they could have been wiped off. But if we find only her forefinger and thumb round the neck—well, you don't drink three-quarters of a bottle of gin holding it by the finger and thumb.' She stared in fascinated horror at the pin-prick in the neck and then I let the hair fall back. 'I don't know, but I think an injection of an overdose of morphine killed her. How do you feel about it, Mary dear?'

She looked at me pitifully but I wasn't wasting my pity on the living. She said: 'That's the second time you said that. Why did you say that?'

'Because it's partly your fault—and it may be a very large part—that she's dead. Oh, and very cleverly dead, I assure you. I'm very good at finding those things out—when it's too damn late. Rigged for suicide—only, I knew she never drank. Well?'

'I didn't kill her! Oh, God, I didn't kill her! I didn't, I didn't, I didn't!'

'And I hope to God you're not responsible for killing Smithy too,' I said savagely. 'If he doesn't come back, you're first in line as accessory. After murder.'

'Mr Smith!' Her bewilderment was total and totally pathetic. And I was totally unmoved. She said: 'Before God, I don't know what you're talking about.'

'Of course not. And you won't know what I'm talking about when I ask you what's going on between Gerran and Heissman. How could you—a sweet and innocent child like you? Or you wouldn't know what's going on between you and your dear loveable Uncle Johann?'

She stared at me in a dumb animal-like misery and shook her head. I struck her. Even although I was aware that the anger that was in me was directed more against myself than at her, still it could not be contained and I struck her, and when she looked at me the way a favourite pet would look at a person who has shot it but not quite killed it, I lifted my hand again but this time when she closed her eyes and flinched away, turning her head to one side, I let my hand drop helplessly to my side, then did what I should have done in the first place, I put my arms around her and held her tight. She didn't try to fight or struggle, just stood quite still. She had nothing left to fight with any more.

'Poor Mary dear,' I said. 'You've got no place left to run to, have you?' She made no answer, her eyes were still closed. 'Uncle Johann is no more your uncle than I am. Your immigration papers state that your father and mother are dead. It is my belief that they are still alive and that Heissman is no more your mother's brother than he is your uncle. It is my belief that he is holding them as hostage for your good conduct and that he is holding you as hostage for theirs. I don't just think that Heissman is up to no good, I know he is, for I don't just think he's a criminal operating on an international scale, I know that too. I know that you're not Latvian but strictly of German ancestry. I know too that your father ranked very highly in the Berlin councils of war.' I didn't know that at all, but it had become an increasingly safe guess. 'And I know too that there's a great deal of money involved, not in hard cash but in negotiable securities. All this is true, is it not?'

There was a silence then she said dully. 'If you know so much, what's the good in pretending any more.' She pushed back a little and looked at me through defeated eyes. 'You're not a real doctor?'

'I'm real enough, but not in the ordinary way of things, for which any patients I might have had would probably feel very thankful as I haven't practised these past good few years. I'm just a civil servant working for the British Government, nothing glamorous or romantic like Intelligence or counter-Intelligence, just the Treasury, which is why I'm here because we've been interested in Heissman's shenanigans for quite some time. I didn't expect to run into this other bus-load of trouble though.'

'What do you mean?'

'Too long to explain, even if I could. I can't, yet. And I've things to do.'

'Mr Smith?' She hesitated. 'From the Treasury too?' I nodded and she went on: 'I've been thinking that.' She hesitated again. 'My father commanded submarine groups during the war. He was also a high Party official, very high, I think. Then he disappeared—'

'Where was his command?'

'For the last year, the north—Tromso, Trondheim, Narvik, places like that, I'm not sure.' I was, all of a sudden I was, I knew it had to be true.

I said: 'Then disappearance. A war criminal?' She nodded. 'And now an old man?' Another nod. 'And amnestied because of age?'

'Yes, just over two years ago. Then he came back to us—Mr Heissman brought us all together, I don't know how.'

I could have explained Heissman's special background qualifications for this very job, but it was hardly the moment. I said: 'Your father's not only a war criminal, he's also a civil criminal—probably an embezzler on a grand scale. Yet you do all this for him?'

'For my mother.'

'I'm sorry.'

'I'm sorry too. I'm sorry for all the trouble I've given you Do you think my mother will be all right?'

'I think so,' I said, which, considering my recent disastrous record in keeping people alive, was a pretty rash statement on my part.

'But what can we *do*? What on earth can we do with all those terrible things happening?'

'It's not what *we* can do. I know what to do. It's what you are going to do.'

'I'll do anything. Anything you say. I promise.'

'Then do nothing. Behave exactly as you've been behaving. Especially towards Uncle Johann. But never a word of our talk to him, never a word to anyone.'

'Not even to Charles?'

'Conrad? Least of all to him.'

'But I thought you liked—'

'Sure I do. But not half as much as our Charles likes you. He'd just up and clobber Heissman on the spot. I haven't,' I said bitterly, 'been displaying very much cleverness or finesse to date. Give me this one last chance.' I thought a bit about being clever, then said: 'One thing you can do. Let me know if you see anyone returning here. I'm going to look around a bit.'

Otto had almost as many locks as I had keys. As befitted the chairman of Olympus Productions, the producer of the film and the *de facto* leader of the expedition he carried a great number of bits and pieces of equipment with him. Most of the belongings were personal and most of these clothes, for although Otto, because of his spherical shape, was automatically excluded from the list of the top ten best-dressed men, his sartorial aspirations were of the most soaring, and he carried at least a dozen suits with him although what he intended to do with them on Bear Island was a matter for conjecture. More interestingly, he had two small squat brown suitcases that served merely as cover for two metal deed-boxes.

Those were hasp-bound with imposing brass padlocks that a blind and palsied pick-lock could have opened in under a minute, and it didn't take me much longer. The first contained nothing of importance, that was, to anyone except Otto: they consisted of hundreds of press clippings, no doubt carefully selected for the laudatory nature of their contents, and going back for twenty-odd years, all of them unanimous in extolling Otto's cinematic genius: precisely the sort of ego-feeding nourishment that Otto would carry around with him. The second deed-box contained papers of a purely financial nature, recorded Otto's transactions, incomes and outgoes over a number of years, and would have proved, I felt certain, fascinating reading for any Inland Revenue Inspector or law-abiding accountant, if there were any such around, but my interest in them was minimal: what did interest me though, and powerfully, was a collection of cancelled cheque-books, and as I couldn't see that those were going to be of any use to Otto in the Arctic I pocketed them, checked that everything was as I had found it, and left.

Goin, as befitted the firm's accountant, was also much given to keeping things under lock and key, but because the total of his impediments didn't come to much more than a quarter of Otto's, the search took correspondingly less time. Again as befitted an accountant, Goin's main concern was clearly with matters financial, and as this coincided with my own current interest I took with me three items that I judged likely to be handsomely rewarding of more leisured study. Those were the Olympus Productions salary lists, Goin's splendidly-padded private bank-book and a morocco diary that was full of items in some sort of private code but was nonetheless clearly concerned with money, for Goin hadn't bothered to construct a code for the columns of pounds and pence. There was nothing necessarily sinister about this: concern for privacy, especially other people's privacy, could be an admirable trait in an accountant.

In the next half-hour I went through four cubicles. In Heissman's I found what I had expected to find, nothing. A man with his background and experience would have discovered many years ago that the only safe place to file his records was inside his head. But he did have some innocuous items—I supposed he had used them in the production of the Olympus manifesto for the film—which were of interest to me, several large-scale charts of Bear Island. One of those I took.

Neal Divine's private papers revealed little of interest except a large number of unpaid bills, IOUs and a number of letters, all of them menacing in varying degrees, from an assortment of different bankers—a form of correspondence that went well with Divine's nervous, apprehensive and gener ally down-trodden mien. At the bottom of an old-fashioned Gladstone in the Count's room I found a small black automatic, loaded, but as an envelope beside it contained a current London licence for a gun this discovery might or might not have significance: the number of law-abiding people in law-abiding Britain who for divers law-abiding reasons consider it prudent to own a gun are, in their total, quite remarkable. In the cubicle shared by Jungbeck and Heyter I found nothing incriminating. But I was intrigued by a small brown paper packet, sealed, that I found in Jungbeck's case. I took this into the main cabin where Mary Stuart was moving from window to window—there were four of them—keeping watch.

'Nothing?' I said. She shook her head. 'Put on a kettle, will you.'

'There's coffee there. And some food.'

'I don't want coffee. A kettle—water—half an inch will do.' I handed her the packet. 'Steam this open for me, will you?'

'Steam—what's in it?'

'If I knew that I wouldn't ask you to open it.'

I went into Lonnie's cubicle but it held nothing but Lonnie's dreams—an album full of faded photographs. With few exceptions, they were of his family—clearly Lonnie had taken them himself. The first few showed a dark attractive girl with a wavy shoulder-length thirties hair-do holding two babies who were obviously twins. Later photographs showed that the two babies were girls. As the years had passed Lonnie's wife, changing hairstyles apart, had changed remarkably little while the girls had grown up from page to page, until eventually they had become two rather beautiful youngsters very closely resembling their mother. In the last photograph, about two-thirds of the way through the album, all three were shown in white summer dresses of an unconscionable length leaning against a dark open roadster: the two girls would then have been about eighteen. I closed the album with that guilty and uncomfortable feeling you have when you stumble, however inadvertently, across another man's private dreams.

I was crossing the passage to Eddie's room when Mary called me. She had the package open and was holding the contents in a white handkerchief. I said: 'That's clever.'

'Two thousand pounds,' she said wonderingly. 'All in new five-pound notes.'

'That's a lot of money.' They were not only new, they were in consecutive serial number order. I noted down the first and last numbers, tracing would be automatic and immediate: somebody was being very stupid indeed or very confident indeed. This was one item of what might be useful evidence that I did not appropriate but locked up again, re-sealed, in Jungbeck's case. When a man has that much money around he's apt to check on its continued presence pretty frequently.

Neither Eddie's nor Hendriks's cubicles revealed any item of interest, while the only thing I learned from a brief glance at Sandy's room was that he was just that modicum less scrupulous in obtaining his illicit supplies than Lonnie: Sandy stocked up on Otto's scotch by the bottleful. The Three Apostles' quarters I passed up: a search in there would, I was convinced, yield nothing. It never occurred to me to check on Conrad.

It was just after three o'clock, with the light beginning to fade from the sky, when I returned to the main cabin. Lonnie and the other two should have contacted Otto and the others a long time ago, their return, I should have thought, was considerably overdue. Mary, who had eaten—or said she had—gave me steak and chips, both of the frozen and pre-cooked variety, and I could see that she was worried. Heaven knew she had enough reason to be worried about a great number of things, but I guessed that her present worry was due to one particular cause.

'Where on earth can they all be?' she said. 'I'm *sure* something must have happened to them.'

'He'll be all right. They probably just went farther than they intended, that's all.'

'I hope so. It's getting dark and the snow's starting—' She broke off and looked at me in embarrassed accusation. 'You're very clever, aren't you?'

'I wish to God I were,' I said, and meant it. I pushed my almost uneaten meal away and rose. 'Thank you. Sorry, and it's nothing to do with your cooking, but I'm not hungry. I'll be in my room.'

'It's getting dark,' she repeated inconsequentially.

'I won't be long.'

I lay on my cot and looked at my haul from the variou

cabins. I didn't have to look long and I didn't have to be possessed of any outstanding deductive powers to realize the significance of what I had before me. The salary lists were very instructive but not half so enlightening as the correspondence between Otto's cheque-books and Goin's bank-book. But the map—more precisely the detailed inset of the Evjebukta—was perhaps the most interesting of all. I was gazing at the map and having long, long thoughts about Mary Stuart's father when Mary Stuart herself came into my room.

'There's someone coming.'

'Who?'

'I don't know. It's too dark and there's snow falling.'

'What direction?'

'That way.' She pointed south.

'That'll be Hendriks and the Three Apostles.' I wrapped the papers up into a small towel and handed them to her. 'Hide those in your room.' I turned my medical bag upside down, brought a small coach-screwdriver from my pocket and began to unscrew the four metal studs that served as floor-rests.

'Yes, yes, of course.' She hesitated. 'Do you mind telling me—'

'There are shameless people around who wouldn't think twice of searching through a man's private possessions. Especially mine. If I'm not here, that's to say.' I'd removed the base and now started working free the flat black metal box that had fitted so snugly into the bottom.

'You're going out.' She said it mechanically, like one who is beyond surprise. 'Where?'

'Well, I'm not dropping in at the local, and that's for sure.' I took out the black box and handed it to her. 'Careful. Heavy. Hide that too—and hide it well.'

'But what—'

'Hurry up. I hear them at the door.'

She hurried up. I screwed the base of the bag back in position and went into the main cabin. Hendriks and the Three Apostles were there and from the way they clapped their arms together to restore circulation and in between sipped the hot coffee that Mary had left on the stove, they seemed to be more than happy to be back. Their happiness vanished abruptly when I told them briefly of Judith Haynes's death, and although, like the rest of the company, none of them had any cause to cherish any tender feelings towards the dead woman, the simple fact of the death of a person they knew and that this fresh death, suicide though it had been, had come so cruelly swiftly after the preceding murders, had the immediate effect of reducing them to a state of speechless shock, a state from which they weren't even beginning to recover when the door opened and Otto lurched in. He was gasping for air and seemed close to exhaustion, although such symptoms of physical distress, where Otto was concerned, were not in themselves necessarily indicative of recent and violent exertion: even the minor labour of tying his shoelaces made Otto huff and puff in an alarming fashion. I looked at him with what I hoped was a proper concern.

'Now, now, Mr Gerran, you must take it easy,' I said solicitously. 'I know this has been a terrible shock to you—'

'Where is she?' he said hoarsely. 'Where's my daughter? How in God's name—'

'In her cubicle.' He made to brush by me but I barred his way. 'In a moment, Mr Gerran. But I must see first that—well, you understand?'

He stared at me under lowered brows, then nodded impatiently to show that he understood, which was more than I did, and said: 'Be quick, please.'

'Seconds only.' I looked at Mary Stuart. 'Some brandy for Mr Gerran.'

What I had to do in Judith Haynes's cubicle took only ten seconds. I didn't want Otto asking awkward questions about why I'd so lovingly wrapped up the gin and barbiturate bottles, so, holding them gingerly by the tops of the necks, I unwrapped them, placed them in reasonably conspicuous positions and summoned Otto. He hung around for a bit, looking suitably stricken and making desolate sounds, but offered no resistance when I took his arm, suggested that he was achieving nothing by remaining there and led him outside.

In the passage he said: 'Suicide, of course?'

'No doubt about that.'

He sighed. 'God, how I reproach myself for—'

'You've nothing to reproach yourself with, Mr Gerran. You saw how completely broken she was at the news of her husband's death. Just plain, old-fashioned grief.'

'It's good to have a man like you around in times like these,' Otto murmured. I met this in modest silence, led him back to his brandy and said: 'Where are the others?'

'Just a few minutes behind. I ran on ahead.'

'How come Lonnie and the other two took so long to find you?'

'It was a marvellous day for shooting. All background. We just kept moving on, every shot better than the last one. And then, of course, we had this damned rescue job. My God, if ever a location unit has been plagued with such ill luck—'

'Rescue job?' I hoped I sounded puzzled, that my tone didn't reflect my sudden chill.

'Heyter. Hurt himself.' Otto lowered some brandy and shook his head to show the burden of woes he was carrying. 'He and Smith were climbing when he fell. Ankle sprained or broken, I don't know. They could see us coming along Lerner's Way, heading more or less the way they'd gone, though they were much higher, of course. Seems Heyter persuaded Smith to carry on, said he'd be all right, he'd attract our attention.' Otto shook his head and drained his brandy. 'Fool!'

'I don't understand,' I said. I could hear the engine of the approaching Sno-Cat.

'Instead of just lying there till we came within shouting distance he tried to hobble down the hill towards us. Of course his blasted ankle gave way—he fell into a gully and knocked himself about pretty badly. God knows how long he was lying there unconscious, it was early afternoon before we heard his shouts for help. A most damnable job getting him down that hill, just damnable. Is that the Sno-Cat out there?'

I nodded. Otto heaved himself to his feet and we went towards the front door together. I said: 'Smithy? Did you see him?'

'Smith?' Otto looked at me in faint surprise. 'No, of course not. I told you, he'd gone on ahead.'

'Of course,' I said. 'I'd forgotten.'

The door opened from the outside just as we reached it. Conrad and the Count entered, half-carrying a Heyter who could only hop on one leg. His head hung exhaustedly, his chin on his chest, and his pale face was heavily bruised on both the right cheek and temple.

We got him on to a couch and I eased off his right boot.

The ankle was swollen and badly discoloured and bleeding slightly where the skin had been broken in several places. While Mary Stuart was heating some water, I propped him up, gave him some brandy, smiled at him in my most encouraging physician's fashion, commiserated with him on his ill luck and marked him down for death,

CHAPTER TWELVE

Otto's stocks of liquid cheer were taking a severe beating. It is a medical commonplace that there are those who, under severe stress, resort to the consumption of large quantities of food. Olympus Productions Ltd harboured none of those. The demand for food was non-existent, but, in a correspondingly inverse proportion, alcoholic solace was being eagerly sought, and the atmosphere in the cabin was powerfully redolent of that of a Glasgow public house when a Scottish soccer team has resoundingly defeated its ancient enemies from across the border. The sixteen people scattered around the cabin—the injured Heyter apart—showed no desire to repair to their cubicles, there was an unacknowledged and wholly illogical tacit assumption that if Judith Haynes could die in her cubicle anyone could. Instead, they sat scattered around in twos and threes, drinking silently or conversing in murmurs, furtive eyes forever moving around the others present, all deepening a cheerless and doom-laden air which stemmed not from Judith Haynes's death but from what might or might not be yet another impending disaster: although it was close on seven now, with the darkness total and the snow falling steadily out of the north, Heissman, Goin and Jungbeck had not yet returned.

Otto, unusually, sat by himself, chewing on a cigar but not drinking: he gave the impression of a man who is wondering what fearsome blow fate now has in store for him. I had talked to him briefly some little time previously and he had given it as his morose and unshakable opinion that all three of them had been drowned: none of them, as he had pointed out, knew the first thing about handling a boat. Even if they managed to survive more than a few minutes in those icy waters, what hope lay for them if they did swim to shore? If they reached a cliff-face, their fingers would only scrabble uselessly against the smoothly vertical rock until their strength gave out and they slid under: if they managed to scramble ashore at some more accessible point, the icy air would reach through their soaked clothes to their soaked bodies and freeze them to death almost instantly. If they didn't turn up, he said, and now he was sure they wouldn't, he was going to abandon the entire venture and wait for Smithy to bring help, and if that didn't come soon he would propose that the entire company strike out for the safety of Tunheim.

The entire company had momentarily fallen silent and Otto, looking across the cabin to where I was standing, gave a painful smile and said, as if in a desperate attempt to lighten the atmosphere: 'Come, come, Dr Marlowe, I see you haven't got a glass.'

'No,' I said. 'I don't think it's wise.

Otto looked around the cabin. If he was being harrowed by the contemplation of his rapidly dwindling stocks he was concealing his grief well. 'The others seem to think it's wise.'

'The others don't have to take into account the danger of exposing opened pores to zero temperatures.'

'What?' He peered at me. 'What's that supposed to mean?'

'It means that if Heissman, Jungbeck and Goin aren't back here in a very few minutes I intend to take the fourteen-footer and go to look for them.'

'What!' This in a very different tone of voice. Otto hauled himself painfully to his feet as he always did when he was preparing to appear impressive. 'Go to look for them? Are you mad, sir? Look for them, indeed. On a night like this, pitch dark, can't see a hand in front of your nose. No, by God, I've already lost too many people, far too many. I absolutely forbid it.'

'Have you taken into account that their engine may have just failed? That they're just drifting helplessly around, freezing to death by the minute while we sit here doing nothing?'

'I have and I don't believe it possible. The boat engines were overhauled completely before our departure and I know that Jungbeck is a very competent mechanic. The matter is not to be contemplated.'

'I'm going anyway.'

'I would remind you that that boat is company property.'

'Who's going to stop me taking it?'

Otto spluttered ineffectually, then said: 'You realize—'

'I realize.' I was tired of Otto. 'I'm fired.'

'You'd better fire me too then,' Conrad said. We all turned to look at him. 'I'm going along with him.'

I'd have expected no less from Conrad, he, after all, had been the one to initiate the search for Smithy soon after our landing. I didn't try to argue with him. I could see Mary Stuart with her hand on his arm, looking at him in dismay: if she couldn't dissuade him, I wasn't going to bother to try.

'Charles!' Otto was bringing the full weight of his authority to bear. 'I would remind you that you have a contract—'

'——— the contract,' Conrad said.

Otto stared at him in disbelief, clamped his lips quite shut, wheeled and headed for his cubicle. With his departure everybody, it seemed, started to speak at the same time. I crossed to where the Count was moodily drinking the inevitable brandy. He looked up and gave me a cheerless smile.

'If you want a third suicidal volunteer, my dear boy—'

'How long have you known Otto Gerran?'

'What's that?' He seemed momentarily at a loss, then quaffed some more brandy. 'Thirty-odd years. It's no secret. I knew him well in pre-war Vienna. Why do you—'

'You were in the film business then?'

'Yes and no.' He smiled in an oddly quizzical fashion. 'Again it's on the record. In the halcyon days, my dear fellow, when Count Tadeusz Leszczynsky—that's me—was, if not exactly a name to be conjured with, at least a man of considerable means. I was Otto's angel, his first backer.' Again a smile, this time amused. 'Why do you think I'm a member of the board?'

'What do you know of the circumstances of Heissman's sudden disappearance from Vienna in 1938?'

The Count stopped being amused. I said: 'So that's not on the record.' I paused to see if he would say anything and when he didn't I went on: 'Watch your back, Count.'

'My—my back?'

'That part of the anatomy that's so subject to being pierced by sharp objects or rapidly moving blunt ones. Or has it not occurred to you that the board of Olympus are falling off their lofty perches like so many stricken birds? One lying dead outside, another lying dead inside, and two more at peril or perhaps even perished on the high seas. What makes you think you should be so lucky? Beware the slings and arrows, Tadeusz. And you might tell Neal Divine and Lonnie to beware of the same things, at least while I'm gone. Especially Lonnie—I'd be glad if you made sure he doesn't step outside this cabin in my absence. Very vulnerable things, backs.'

The Count sat in silence for some moments, his face not giving anything away, then he said: 'I'm sure I don't know what you're talking about.'

'I never for a moment thought you would.' I tapped the bulky pocket of his anorack. 'That's where it should be, not lying about uselessly in your cabin.'

'What, for heaven's sake?'

'Your 9 mm Beretta automatic.'

I left the Count on this suitably enigmatic note and moved across to where Lonnie was making hay while the sun shone. The hand that held his glass shook with an almost constant tremor and his eyes were glassy but his speech was as intelligible and lucid as ever.

'And once again our medical Lochinvar or was it Launcelot gallops forth to the rescue,' Lonnie intoned. 'I can't tell you, my dear boy, how my heart fills with pride—'

'Stay inside when I'm gone, Lonnie. Don't go beyond that door. Not once. Please. For me.'

'Merciful heavens!' Lonnie hiccoughed on a grand scale. 'One would think I am in danger.'

'You are. Believe me, you are.'

'Me? Me?' He was genuinely baffled. 'And who would wish ill to poor old harmless Lonnie?'

'You'd be astonished at the people who would wish ill to poor old harmless Lonnie. Dispensing for the moment with your homilies about the innate kindness of human nature will you promise me, really promise me, that you won't go out tonight?'

'This is so important to you, then, my boy?'

'It is.'

'Very well. With this gnarled hand on a vat of the choicest malt—'

I left him to get on with what promised to be a very lengthy promise indeed and approached Conrad and Mary Stuart who seemed to be engaged in an argument that was as low-pitched as it was intense. They broke off and Mary Stuart put a beseeching hand on my arm. She said: 'Please Dr Marlowe. Please tell Charles not to go. He'll listen to you, I know he will.' She shivered. 'I just *know* that something awful is going to happen tonight.'

'You may well be right at that,' I said. 'Mr Conrad, you are not expendable.'

I could, I immediately realized, have lighted upon a more fortunate turn of phrase. Instead of looking at Conrad she kept looking at me and the implications of what I'd said dawned on me quite some time after they had clearly dawned on her. She put both hands on my arm, looked at me with dull and hopeless eyes, then turned and walked towards her cubicle.

'Go after her,' I said to Conrad. 'Tell her——'

'No point. I'm going. She knows it.'

'Go after her and tell her to open her window and put that black box I gave her on the snow outside. Then close her window.'

Conrad looked at me closely, made as if to speak, then left. He was nobody's fool, he hadn't even given a nod that could have been interpreted as acknowledgment.

He was back within a minute. We pulled on all the outer clothes we could and furnished ourselves with four of the largest torches. On the way to the door, Mary Darling rose from where she was sitting beside a still badly battered Allen. 'Dr Marlowe.'

I put my head to where I figured her ear lay behind the tangled platinum hair and whispered: 'I'm wonderful?'

She nodded solemnly, eyes sad behind the huge horn-rimmed glasses, and kissed me. I didn't know what the audience thought of this little vignette and didn't much care: probably a last tender farewell to the good doctor before he moved out forever into the outer darkness. As the door closed behind us, Conrad said complainingly: 'She might have kissed me too.'

'I think you've done pretty well already,' I said. He had the grace to keep silent. With our torches off we moved across to what shelter was offered from the now quite heavily falling snow by the provisions hut and remained there for two or three minutes until we were quite certain that no one had it in mind to follow us. Then we moved round the side of the main cabin and picked up the black box outside Mary Stuart's window. She was standing there and I'm quite sure she saw us but she made no gesture or any attempt to wave goodbye: it seemed as if the two Marys had but one thought in common.

We made our way through the snow and the darkness down to the jetty, stowed the black box securely under the stern-sheets, started up the outboard—5½ horsepower only, but enough for a fourteen-footer—and cast off. As we came round the northern arm of the jetty Conrad said: 'Christ, it's as black as the Earl of Hell's waistcoat. How do you propose to set about it?'

'Set about what?'

'Finding Heissman and company, of course.'

'I couldn't care if I never saw that lot again,' I said candidly. 'I've no intention of trying to find them. On the contrary, all our best efforts are going to be brought to bear to avoid them.' While Conrad was silently mulling over this volte-face, I took the boat, the motor throttle right back for prudence's sake, just over a hundred yards out until we were close into the northern shore of the Sor-hamna and cut the engine. As the boat drifted to a stop I went for'ard and eased anchor and rope over the side.

'According to the chart,' I said, 'there are three fathoms here. According to the experts, that should mean about fifty feet of rope to prevent us from drifting. So, fifty feet. And as we're against the land and so can't be silhouetted, that should make us practically invisible to anyone approaching from the south. No smoking, of course.'

'Very funny,' Conrad said. Then, after a pause, he went on carefully: 'Who are you expecting to approach from the south?'

'Snow White and the Seven Dwarfs.'

'All right, all right. So you don't think there's anything wrong with them?'

'I think there's a great deal wrong with them, but not in the sense you mean.'

'Ah!' There was a silence which I took to be a very thoughtful one on his part. 'Speaking of Snow White.'

'Yes?'

'How about whiling away the time by telling me a fairy story?'

So I told everything I knew or thought I knew and he listened in complete silence throughout. When I finished I waited for comment but none came, so I said: 'I have your promise that you won't clobber Heissman on sight?'

'Reluctantly given, reluctantly given.' He shivered. 'Jesus, it's cold.'

'It will be. Listen.'

At first faintly, intermittently, through the falling snow and against the northerly wind, came the sound of an engine, closing: within two minutes the exhaust beat was sharp and distinct. Conrad said: 'Well, would you believe it. They got their motor fixed.'

We remained quietly where we were, bobbing gently at anchor and shivering in the deepening cold, as Heissman's boat rounded the northern arm of the jetty and cut its engine. Heissman, Goin and Jungbeck didn't just tie up and go ashore immediately, they remained by the jetty for over ten minutes. It was impossible to see what they were doing, the darkness and the snow made it impossible to see even the most shadowy outlines of their forms, but several times we could see the flickering of torch beams behind the jetty arm, several times I heard distinctly metallic thuds and twice I imagined I heard the splash of something heavy entering the water. Finally, we saw three pin-points of light move along the main arm of the jetty and disappear in the direction of the cabin.

Conrad said: 'I suppose, at this stage, I should have some intelligent questions to ask.'

'And I should have some intelligent answers. I think we'll have them soon. Get that anchor in, will you?'

I started up the outboard again and, keeping it at its lowest revolutions, moved eastwards for another two hundred yards, then turned south until, calculating that the combination of distance and the northerly wind had taken us safely out of earshot of the cabin, I judged the moment had come to open the throttle to its maximum.

Navigating, if that was the word for it, was easier than I had thought it would be. We'd been out more than long enough now to achieve the maximum in night-sight and I had little difficulty in making out the coastline to my right: even on a darker night than this it would have been difficult not to distinguish the sharp demarcation line between the blackness of the cliffs and the snow-covered hills stretching away beyond them. Neither was the sea as rough as I had feared it might be: choppy, but no more than that, the wind could hardly have lain in a more favourable quarter than it did that night.

Kapp Malmgren came up close on the starboard hand and I turned the boat more to the south-west to move into the Evjebukta, but not too much, for although the cliffs were easily enough discernible, objects low in the water and lying against their black background were virtually undetectable and I had no wish to run the boat on to the islands that I had observed that morning in the northern part of the bay.

For the first time since we'd weighed anchor Conrad spoke. He was possessed of an exemplary patience. Clearing his throat, he said: 'Is one permitted to ask a question?'

'You're even permitted to receive an answer. Remember those extraordinary stacks and pinnacles close by the cliffs when we were rounding the south of the island in the *Morning Rose*?'

'Oh blessed memory,' Conrad said yearningly.

'No need for heartbreak,' I said encouragingly. 'You'll be seeing her again tonight.'

'What!'

'Yes, indeed.'

'The *Morning Rose*?'

'None other. That is to say, I hope. But later. Those stacks were caused by erosion, which in turn was caused by tidal streams, storm waves and frost—island used to be much bigger than it is now, bits of it are falling into the sea all the time. This same erosion also caused caves to form in the cliffs. But it formed something else—I knew nothing about it until this afternoon—which I think must be unique in the world. Two or three hundred yards in from the southern tip of this bay, a promontory called Kapp Kolthoff, is a tiny horseshoe-shaped harbour—I saw it through the binoculars this morning.'

'You did?'

'I was out for a walk. At the inner end of this harbour there is an opening, not just any opening, but a tunnel that goes clear through to the other side of Kapp Kolthoff. It must be at least two hundred yards in length. It's called Perleporten. You have to have a large-scale map of Bear Island to find it. I got my hands on a large-scale map this afternoon.'

'That length? Straight through? It must be man-made.'

'Who the hell would spend a fortune tunnelling through two hundred yards of rock from A to B, when you can sail from A to B in five minutes? I mean, in Bear Island?'

'It's not very likely,' Conrad said. 'And you think Heissman and his friends may have been here?'

'I don't know where else they could have been. I looked every place I could look this morning in the Sor-hamna and in this bay. Nothing.'

Conrad said nothing, which was one of the things I liked about a man whom I was beginning to like very much. He could have asked a dozen questions to which there were as yet no answers, but because he knew there were none he refrained from asking them. The *Evinrude* kept purring along with reassuring steadiness and in about ten minutes I could see the outline of the cliffs on the south of the Evjebukta looming up. To the left, the tip of Kapp Kolthoff was clearly to be seen. I imagined I could see white breakers beyond.

'There can't possibly be anyone to see us,' I said, 'and we don't need our night-sight any more. I know there are no islands in the vicinity. Headlamps would be handy.'

Conrad moved up into the bows and switched on two of our powerful torches. Within two minutes I could see the sheer of dripping black cliffs less than a hundred yards ahead. I turned to starboard and paralleled the cliffs to the north-west. One minute later we had it—the eastward facing entrance to a tiny circular inlet. I throttled the motor right back and moved gingerly inside and almost at once we had it—a small semi-circular opening at the base of the south cliff. It seemed impossibly small. We drifted towards it at less than one knot. Conrad looked back over his shoulder.

'I'm claustrophobic.'

'Me too.'

'If we get stuck?'

'The sixteen-footer is bigger than this one.'

'*If* it was here. Ah, well, in for a penny, in for a pound.'

I crossed my mental fingers that Conrad would have cause to remember those words and eased the boat into the tunnel. It was bigger than it looked but not all that bigger. The waves and waters of countless æons had worn the rock walls as smooth as alabaster. Although it held a remarkably true direction almost due south it was clear, because of the varying widths and the varying heights of the tunnel roof, that the hand of man had never been near the Perleporten; then, suddenly, when Conrad called out and pointed ahead and to the right, that wasn't so clear any more.

The opening in the wall, no more, really, than an indentation hardly distinguishable from one or two already passed, was, at its deepest, no more than six feet, but it was bounded by an odd flat shelf that varied from two to five feet in width. It looked as if it had been man-made, but then, there were so many curiously shaped rock formations in those parts that it might just possibly have resulted from natural causes. But there was one thing about that place that absolutely was in no way due to natural causes: a pile of grey-painted metal bars, neatly stacked in criss-cross symmetry.

Neither of us spoke. Conrad switched on the other two torches, pivoted their heads until they were facing upwards, and placed them all on the shelf, flooding the tiny area with light. Not without some difficulty we scrambled on to the shelf and looped the painter round one of the bars. Still without speaking I took the boat-hook and probed the bottom: it was less than five feet below the surface, and a very odd kind of rock it felt too. I guddled around some more, let the hook strike something at once hard and yielding and hauled it up. It was a half-inch chain, corroded in places, but still sound. I hauled some more and the end of another rectangular bar, identical in size to those on the shelf and secured to the chain by an eye-bolt, came into sight. It was badly discoloured. I lowered chain and bar back to the bottom.

Still in this uncanny silence I took a knife from my pocket and tested the surface of one of the bars. The metal, almost certainly lead, was soft and yielding, but it was no more than a covering skin, there was something harder beneath. I dug the knifeblade in hard and scraped away an inch of the lead. Something yellow glittered in the lamp-light.

'Well, now,' Conrad said. 'Jackpot, I believe, is the technical term.'

'Something like that.'

'And look at this.' Conrad reached behind the pile of bars and brought up a can of paint. It was labelled 'Instant Grey'.

'It seems to be very good stuff,' I said. I touched one of the bars. 'Quite dry. And, you must admit, quite clever. You saw off the eye-bolt, paint the whole lot over, and what do you have?'

'A ballast bar identical in size and colour to the ballast bars in the mock-up sub.'

'Ten out of ten,' I said. I hefted one of the bars. 'Just right for easy handling. A forty-pound ingot.'

'How do you know?'

'It's my Treasury training. Current value—say thirty thousnd dollars. How many bars in that pile, would you say?'

'A hundred. More.'

'And that's just for starters. Bulk is almost certainly still under water. Paint-brushes there?'

'Yes.' Conrad reached behind the pile but I checked him. 'Please not,' I said. 'Think of all those lovely fingerprints.'

Conrad said slowly: 'My mind's just engaged gear again.' He looked at the pile and said incredulously: 'Three million dollars?'

'Give or take a few per cent.'

'I think we'd better leave,' Conrad said. 'I'm coming all over avaricious.'

We left. As we emerged into the little circular bay we both looked back at the dark and menacing little tunnel. Conrad said: 'Who discovered this?'

'I have no idea.'

'Perleporten. What does that mean?'

'The gates of Pearl.'

'They came pretty close at that.'

'It wasn't a bad try.' The journey back was a great deal more unpleasant than the outward one had been, the seas were against us, the icy wind and the equally icy snow were in our faces, and because of the same snow the visibility was drastically reduced. But we made it inside an hour. Almost literally frozen stiff but at the same time contradictorily shaking with the cold, we tied the boat up. Conrad clambered up on to the jetty. I passed him the black box, cut about thirty feet off the boat's anchor rope and followed. I built a rope cradle round the box, fumbled with a pair of catches and opened a hinged cover section which comprised a third of the top plate and two-thirds of a side plate. In the near total darkness switches and dials were less than half-seen blurs, but I didn't need light to operate this instrument, which was a basically very simple affair anyway. I pulled out a manually operated telescopic aerial to its fullest extent and turned two switches. A dim green light glowed and a faint hum, that couldn't have been heard a yard away, came from the box.

'I always think it's so satisfactory when those little toys work,' Conrad said. 'But won't the snow gum up the works?'

'This little toy costs just over a thousand pounds. You can immerse it in acid, you can boil it in water, you can drop it from a four-story building. It still works. It's got a little sister that can be fired from a naval gun. I don't think a little snow will harm, do you?'

'I wouldn't think so.' He watched in silence as I lowered the box, pilot light facing the stonework, over the south arm of the pier, secured the rope to a bollard, made it fast round its base and concealed it with a scattering of snow. 'What's the range?'

'Forty miles. It won't require a quarter of that tonight.'

'And it's transmitting now?'

'It's transmitting now.'

We moved back to the main arm of the pier, brushing footmarks away with our gloves. I said: 'I wouldn't think they would have heard us coming back, but no chances. A weather eye, if you please.'

I was down inside the hull of the mock-up sub and had rejoined Conrad inside two minutes. He said: 'No trouble?'

'None. The two paints don't quite match. But you'd never notice it unless you were looking for it.'

We were not greeted like returning heroes. It would not be true to say that our return, or our early return, was greeted with anything like disappointment, but there was definitely an anti-climactic air to it; maybe they had already expended all their sympathies on Heissman, Jungbeck and Goin, who had claimed, predictably enough, that their engine had broken down in the late afternoon. Heissman thanked us properly enough but there was a faint trace of amused condescension to his thanks that would normally have aroused a degree of antagonism in me were it not for the fact that my antagonism towards Heissman was already so total that any deepening of it would have been quite impossible. So Conrad and I contented ourselves with making a show of expressing our relief to find the three voyagers alive while not troubling very much to conceal our chagrin. Conrad especially, was splendid at this: clearly, he had a considerable future as an actor.

The atmosphere in the cabin was almost unbearably funereal. I would have thought that the safe return of five of their company might have been cause for some subdued degree of rejoicing, but it may well have been that the very fact of our being alive only heightened the collective awareness of the dead woman lying in her cubicle. Heissman tried to tell us about the marvellous backgrounds he had found that day and I couldn't help reflecting that he was going to have a most hellishly difficult job in setting up camera and sound crews within the extraordinarily restrictive confines of the Perleporten tunnel: Heissman desisted when it became clear that no one was listening to him. Otto made a half-hearted attempt to establish some kind of working relationship with me and even went to the length of pressing some scotch upon me, which I accepted without thanks but drank nevertheless. He tried to make some feebly jocular remark about open pores and it being obvious that I didn't intend venturing forth again that night, and I didn't tell him, not just yet, that I did indeed intend to venture forth again that night but that as my proposed walk would take me no farther than the jetty it was unlikely that all the open pores in the world would incapacitate me.

I looked at my watch. Another ten minutes, no more. Then we would all go for that little walk, the four directors of Olympus Productions, Lonnie and myself. Just the six of us, no more. The four directors were already there and, given the time Lonnie normally took to regain contact with reality after a prolonged session with the only company left in the world that gave him any solace, it was time that he was here also. I went down the passage and into his cabin.

It was bitterly cold in there because the window was wide open, and it was wide open because that was the way that Lonnie had elected to leave his cubicle, which was quite empty. I picked up a torch that was lying by the rumpled cot and peered out of the window. The snow was still falling and steadily but not so heavily as to obscure the tracks that led away from the window. There were two sets of tracks. Lonnie had been persuaded to leave: not that he would have required much persuasion.

I ignored the curious looks that came my way as I went quickly through the main cabin and headed for the provisions hut. Its door was open but Lonnie was not there either. The only sure sign that he had been there was a half-full bottle of scotch with its screw-top off. So much for Lonnie and his mighty oath taken with his hand on a vat of the choicest malt.

The tracks outside the hut were numerous and confused: it was clear that my chances of isolating and following any particular set of those was minimal. I returned to the cabin and there was no lack of immediate volunteers for the search: Lonnie had never made an unwitting enemy in his life.

It was the Count who found him, inside a minute, face down in a deep drift behind the generator shed. He was already shrouded in white, so he must have been lying there for some time. He was clad in only shirt, pullover, trousers and what appeared to be a pair of ancient carpet slippers. The snow beside his head was stained yellow where the contents—or part of the contents—of yet another bottle, still clutched in his right hand, had been spilt.

We turned him over. If ever a man looked like a dead man it was Lonnie. His skin was ice-cold to the touch, his face the colour of old ivory, his glazed unmoving eyes were open to the falling snow, and there was no rise and fall to his chest, but on the off-chance that there might just be some substance in the old saw that a special providence looks after little children and drunks, I put my ear to his chest and thought I detected a faint and far-off murmur.

We carried him inside and laid him out on his cot. While oil heaters, hot-water bags and heated blankets were being brought in or prepared—apart from the general esteem in which Lonnie was held, everyone seemed almost pathetically eager to contribute to something constructive—I used my stethoscope and established that he did indeed have a heart-beat if such a term could be applied to something as weak and as fluttering as the wings of a wounded captive bird. I thought briefly of a heart stimulant and brandy and dismissed both ideas, both, in his touch-and-go condition, were as likely to kill him off as to have any good effect. So we just concentrated on heating up the frozen and lifeless-seeming body as quickly as possible, while four people continuously massaged ominously white feet and hands t try to restore some measure of circulation.

Fifteen minutes after we'd first found him he was perceptibly breathing again, a shallow and gasping fight for air, but breathing nevertheless. He was now as warm as artificial aids could make him, so I thanked the others and told them they could go: I asked the two Marys to stay behind as nurses, because I couldn't stay myself: by my watch, I was already ten minutes late.

Lonnie's eyes moved. No other part of him did, but his eyes moved. After a few moments they focused blearily on me: he was as conscious as he was likely to be for a long time.

'You bloody old fool!' I said. It was no way to talk to a man with one foot still halfway through death's door, but it was the way I felt. 'Why did you do it?'

'Aha!' His voice was a far-off whisper.

'Who took you out of here? Who gave you the drink?' I was aware that the two Marys had at first stared at me, then at each other, but the time was gone when it mattered what anyone thought.

Lonnie's lips moved soundlessly a few times. Then his eyes flickered shiftily and he gave a drunken cackle, no more than a faint rasping sound deep in his throat. 'A kind man,' he whispered weakly. 'Very kind man.'

I would have shaken him except for the fact that I would certainly have shaken the life out of him. I restrained myself with a considerable effort and said: 'What kind man, Lonnie?'

'Kind man,' he muttered. 'Kind man.' He lifted one thin wrist and beckoned. I bent towards him. 'Know something?' His voice was a fading murmur.

'Tell me, Lonnie.'

'In the end—' His voice trailed away.

'Yes, Lonnie?'

He made a great effort. 'In the end—' there was a long pause, I had to put my ear to his mouth—'in the end, there's only kindness.' He lowered his waxen eyelids.

I swore and I kept on swearing until I realized that both girls were staring at me with shocked eyes, they must have thought that I was swearing at Lonnie. I said to Mary Stuart: 'Go to Conrad—Charles. Tell him to tell the Count to come to my cubicle. Now. Conrad will know how to do it.'

She left without a question. Mary Darling said to me:

'Will Lonnie live, Dr Marlowe?'

'I don't know, Mary.'

'But—but he's quite warm now—'

'It won't be exposure that will kill him, if that's what you mean.'

She looked at me, the eyes behind the hornrims at once earnest and scared. 'You mean—you mean he might go from alcoholic poisoning?'

'He might. I don't know.'

She said, with a flash of that almost touching asperity that could be so characteristic of her: 'You don't really care, do you, Dr Marlowe?'

'No, I don't.' She looked at me, the pinched face shocked, and I put my arm round the thin shoulders. 'I don't care, Mary, because he doesn't care. Lonnie's been dead a long time now.'

I went back to my cubicle, found the Count there and wasted no words. I said: 'Are you aware that that was a deliberate attempt on Lonnie's life?'

'No. But I wondered.' The Count's customary cloak of badinage had fallen away completely.

'Do you know that Judith Haynes was murdered?'

'Murdered!' The Count was badly shaken and there was no pretence about it either.

'Somebody injected her with a lethal dose of morphine. Just for good measure, it was my hypodermic, my morphine.' He said nothing. 'So your rather illegal bullion hunt has turned out to be something more than fun and games.'

'Indeed it has.'

'You know you have been consorting with murderers?'

'I know now.'

'You know now. You know what interpretation the law will put on that?'

'I know that too.'

'You have your gun?' He nodded. 'You can use it?'

'I am a Polish count, sir.' A touch of the old Tadeusz.

'And very impressive a Polish count should look in a witness-box too,' I said. 'You are aware, of course, that your only hope is to turn Queen's Evidence?'

'Yes,' he said. 'I know that too.'

CHAPTER THIRTEEN

'Mr Gerran,' I said, 'I'd be grateful if you, Mr Heissman, Mr Goin and Tadeusz here would step outside with me for a moment.'

'Step outside?' Otto looked at his watch, his three fellow directors, his watch again and me in that order. 'On a night like this and at an hour like this? Whatever for?'

'Please.' I looked at the others in the cabin. 'I'd also be grateful if the rest of you remained here, in this room, till I return. I hope I won't be too long. You don't have to do as I ask and I'm certainly in no position to enforce my request, but I suggest it would be in your own best interests to do so. I know now, I've known since this morning, who the killer amongst us is. But before I put a name to this man I think it is only fair and right that I should first discuss the matter with Mr Gerran and his fellow directors.'

This brief address was received, not unsurprisingly, in total silence. Otto, predictably, was the one to break the silence: he cleared his throat and said carefully: 'You claim to know this man's identity?'

'I do.'

'You can substantiate this claim?'

'Prove it, you mean?'

'Yes.'

'No, I can't.'

'Ah!' Otto said significantly. He looked around the company and said: 'You're taking rather much upon yourself, are you not?'

'In what way?'

'This rather dictatorial attitude you've been increasingly adopting. Good God, man, if you've found, or think you've found our man, for God's sake tell us and don't make this big production out of it. It ill becomes any man to play God, Dr Marlowe, I would remind you that you're but one of a group, an employee, if you like, of Olympus Productions, just like—'

'I am not an employee of Olympus Productions. I am an

273

employee of the British Treasury who has been sent to investigate certain aspects of Olympus Productions Ltd. Those investigations are now completed.'

Otto over-reacted to the extent that he let his jaw drop. Goin didn't react much but his smooth and habitually bland face took on a wary expression that was quite foreign to it. Heissman said incredulously: 'A Government agent! A secret service—'

'You've got your countries mixed up. Government agents work for the US Treasury, not the British one. I'm just a civil servant and I've never fired a pistol in my life, far less carried one. I have as much official power as a postman or a Whitehall clerk. No more. That's why I'm asking for co-operation.' I looked at Otto. 'That's why I'm offering you what I regard as the courtesy of a prior consultation.'

'Investigations?' Clearly, I'd lost Otto at least half a minute previously. 'What kind of investigations? And how does it come that a man hired as doctor—' Otto broke off, shaking his head in the classic manner of one baffled beyond all hope of illumination.

'How do you think it came that none of the seven other applicants for the post of medical officer turned up for an interview? They don't teach us much about manners in medical school but we're not as rude as that. Shall we go?'

Goin said calmly: 'I think, Otto, that we should hear what he has to say.'

'I think I'd like to hear what you have to say too,' Conrad said. He was one of the very few in the cabin who wasn't looking at me as if I were some creature from outer space.

'I'm sure you would. However, I'm afraid you'll have to remain. But I would like a private word with you, if I may.' I turned without waiting for an answer and made for my cubicle. Otto barred my way.

'There's nothing you can have to say to Charles that you can't say to all of us.'

'How do you know?' I brushed roughly by him and closed the door when Conrad entered the cubicle. I said: 'I don't want you to come for two reasons. If our friends arrive, they may miss me down at the jetty and come straight here—I'd like you in that case to tell them where I am. More importantly, I'd like you to keep an eye on

Jungbeck. If he tries to leave, try to reason with him. If he won't listen to reason, let him go—about three feet. If you can just kind of naturally happen to have a full bottle of scotch or suchlike in your hand at the time, then clobber him with all you have. Not on the head—that would kill him. On the shoulder, close in to the neck. You'll probably break the odd bone: in any event it will surely incapacitate him.'

Conrad didn't as much as raise an eyebrow. He said: 'I can see why you don't bother with guns.'

'Socially and otherwise,' I said, 'a bottle of scotch is a great leveller.'

I'd taken a Coleman storm lantern along with me and now hung it on a rung of the vertical iron ladder leading down from the conning-tower to the interior of the submarine mock-up: its harsh glare threw that icily dank metallic tomb into a weirdly heterogeneous mélange of dazzling white and inkily black geometrical patterns. While the others watched me in a far from friendly silence, I unscrewed one of the wooden floor battens, lifted and placed a ballast bar on top of the compressor and scraped at the surface with the blade of my knife.

'You will observe,' I said to Otto, 'that I am not making a production of this. Prologues dispensed with, we arrive at the point without waste of time.' I closed my knife and inspected the handiwork it had wrought. 'All that glitters is not gold. But does this look like toffee to you?'

I looked at them each in turn. Clearly, it didn't look like toffee to any of them.

'A total lack of reaction, a total lack of surprise.' I put my knife back in my pocket and smiled at the stiffening attitudes of three out of the four of them. 'Scout's honour, we civil servants never carry guns. And why should there be surprise even at the fact of my knowledge—all four of you have been perfectly well aware for some time that I am not what I was engaged to be. And why should any of you express surprise at the sight of this gold—after all, that was the only reason for your coming to Bear Island in the first place.'

They said nothing. Curiously enough, they weren't even looking at me, they were all looking at the gold ingot as if it were vastly more important than I was, which, from their point of view, was probably a perfectly understandable priority preference.

'Dear me, dear me,' I said. 'Where are all the instant denials, the holier-than-thou clutching of the hearts, the outraged cries of "What in God's name are you talking about?" I would think, wouldn't you, that the unbiased observer would find this negative reaction every bit as incriminating as a written confession?' I looked at them with what might have been interpreted as an encouraging expression, but again—apart from Heissman's apparently finding it necessary to lubricate his lower lip with the tip of his tongue—I elicited no response, so I went on: 'It was, as even your defending counsel will have to admit in court, a clever and well thought-out scheme. Would any of you care to tell me what the scheme was?'

'It is my opinion, Dr Marlowe,' Otto said magisterially, 'that the strain of the past few days has made you mentally unbalanced.'

'Not a bad reaction at all,' I said approvingly. 'Unfortunately, you're about two minutes too late in coming up with it. No volunteers to set the scene, then? Do we suffer from an excess of modesty or just a lack of co-operation? Wouldn't you, for instance, Mr Goin, care to say a few words? After all, you are in my debt. Without me, without our dramatic little confrontation, you'd have been dead before the week was out.'

'I think Mr Gerran is right,' Goin said in that measured voice he knew so well how to use. 'Me? About to die?' He shook his head. 'The strain for you must have been intolerable. Under such circumstances, as a medical man, you should know that a person's imagination can easily—'

'Imagination? Am I imagining this forty-pound gold ingot?' I pointed to the ballast bars below the battens. 'Am I imagining those other fifteen ingots there? Am I imagining the hundred-odd ingots piled on a rock shelf inside the Perleporten? Am I imagining the fact that your total lack of reaction to the word Perleporten demonstrates beyond question that you all know what Perleporten is, where it is and what its significance is? Am I imagining the score of other lead-sheathed ingots still under water in the Perleporten? Let's stop playing silly little games for your own game is up. As I say, quite a clever little game while i lasted. What better cover for a bullion-recovery trip to the Arctic than a film unit—after all, film people are widely regarded as being eccentric to the extent of being lunatic so that even their most ludicrous behaviour is accepted as being normal within its own abnormal context? What better time to set out to achieve the recovery of this bullion than when there are only a few hours' daylight so that the recovery operation can be carried out through the long hours of darkness? What better way of bringing the bullion back to Britain than by switching it with this vessel's ballast so that it can be slipped into the country under the eyes of the Customs authorities?' I surveyed the ballast. 'Four tons, according to this splendid brochure that Mr Heissman wrote. I'd put it nearer five. Say ten million dollars. Justifies a trip to even an out-of-the-way resort like Bear Island, I'd say. Wouldn't you?'

They wouldn't say anything.

'By and by,' I went on, 'you'd probably have manufactured some excuse for towing this vessel down to Perleporten so as to make the trans-shipment of the gold all that easier. And then heigh-ho for Merry England and the just enjoyment of the fruits of your labours. Could I be wrong?'

'No.' Otto was very calm. 'You're right. But I think you'd find it very hard to make a criminal case out of this. What could we possibly be charged with? Theft? Ridiculous. Finders, keepers.'

'Finders, keepers? A few miserable tons of gold? Your ambitions are only paltry, you're only skimming the surface of the available loot. Isn't that so, Heissman?'

They all looked at Heissman. Heissman, in turn, didn't appear particularly anxious to look at anyone.

'Why do you silly people think I'm here?' I said. 'Why do you think that, in spite of the elaborate smoke-screen you set up, the British Government not only knew that you were going to Bear Island but also knew that your purpose in going there was not as advertised? Don't you know that, in certain matters, European governments co-operate very closely? Don't you know that most of them share a keen interest in the activities of Johann Heissman? For what you don't know is that most of them know a great deal more about Johann Heissman than you do. Perhaps, Heissman, you'd like to tell them yourself—starting, shall we say, with the thirty-odd years you've been working for the Soviet government?'

Otto stared at Heissman, his huge jowls seeming to fall apart. Goin's facial muscles tightened until the habitual smooth blandness had vanished from his face. The Count's expression didn't change, he just nodded slowly as if understanding at last the solution of a long-standing problem. Heissman looked acutely unhappy.

'Well,' I said, 'as Heissman doesn't appear to have any intention of telling anyone anything, I suppose that leaves it up to me. Heissman, here, is a remarkably gifted specialist in an extremely specialized field. He is, purely and simply, a treasure-hunter, and there's no one in the business who can hold a candle to him. But he doesn't just hunt for the type of treasure that you people think he does: I fear he may have been deceiving you on this point, as, indeed, he has been deceiving you on another. I refer to the fact that a pre-condition of his cutting you into a share of the loot was that his niece, Mary Stuart, be employed by Olympus Productions. Having the nasty and suspicious minds that you do, you probably and rapidly arrived at the conclusion that she wasn't his niece at all—which she isn't—and was along for some other purposes—which she is. But not for the purposes which your nasty and suspicious minds attributed to her. For Heissman, Miss Stuart was essential for the achievement of an entirely different purpose which he kind of forgot to tell you about.

'Miss Stuart's father, you have to understand, was just as unscrupulous and unprincipled a rogue as any of you. He held very senior positions in both the German Navy and the Nazi Party and, like others similarly placed, used his power to feather his own nest—just as Hermann Goering did—when the war was seen to be lost, although he was smarter than Goering and managed to get out from under before the war-criminal round-up. The gold, although this will probably never be proved, almost certainly came from the vaults of Norwegian banks, and a man with all the resources of the German Navy behind him would have had no trouble in choosing such a splendidly isolated spot as Perleporten in Bear Island and having the stuff transferred there. Probably by submarine. Not that it matters.

'But it wasn't just the gold that was transported to Perleporten, which is why Mary Stuart is here. Feathers weren't enough for Dad's nest, nothing less than swansdown would do. The swansdown almost certainly took the form of either bank bonds or securities, probably obtained—I wouldn't say purchased—in the late thirties. Such securities are perfectly redeemable even today. An attempt was recently made to sell £30 millions' worth of such securities through foreign exchange, but the West German Federal Bank wouldn't play ball because proper owner-identification was lacking. But there wouldn't be any problem about owner-identification this time, would there, Heissman?'

Heissman didn't say whether there would or there wouldn't.

'And where are they?' I said. 'Nicely welded up in a dummy steel ingot?' As he still wasn't being very forthcoming, I went on: 'No matter, we'll have them. And then you're never going to have the pleasure of seeing Mary Stuart's father put his signature and fingerprints on those documents and of checking that they match up.'

'You're sure of that?' Heissman said. He had recovered his normal degree of composure, which meant that he was very composed indeed.

'In a changing world like ours who can be sure of anything? But with that proviso, yes.'

'I think you've overlooked something.'

'I have?'

'Yes. We have Admiral Hanneman.'

'That's Miss Stuart's father's true name?'

'You didn't even know that?'

'No. It's of no relevance. And no, I haven't overlooked that fact. I shall attend to that matter shortly. After I have attended to your friends. Maybe that's the wrong word, maybe they're not your friends any more. I mean, they don't *look* particularly friendly, do they?'

'Monstrous!' Otto shouted. 'Absolutely monstrous. Unforgivable! Diabolical! Our own partner!' He spluttered into an outraged silence.

'Despicable,' Goin said coldly. 'Absolutely contemptible.'

'Isn't it?' I said. 'Tell me, does this moral indignation stem from this revelation of the depths of Heissman's perfidy or merely because he omitted to cut you in on the proceeds of the cashing of the securities? Don't bother answering that question, it's purely rhetorical, as villains you're dyed in the same inky black as Heissman. What I mean is, most of you spend a great deal of time and careful thought in concealing from the other members of the board of Olympus Productions just what the true natures of your activities are. Heissman is hardly alone in this respect.

'Take the Count here. Compared to the rest of you he was a vestal angel, but even he dabbled in some murky waters. For over thirty years now he's been a member of the board and has had a free meal ticket for life because he happened to be in Vienna when the *Anschluss* came, when Otto headed for the States and Heissman was spirited away. Heissman was spirited away because Otto had arranged for him to be so that he could take all the film company's capital out of the country: Otto was never a man to hesitate when it came to selling a friend down the river.

'What Otto didn't know but what the Count did but carefully refrained from telling him was that Heissman's disappearance had been entirely voluntary. Heissman had been a German secret agent for some time and his adopted country needed him. What his adopted country didn't know was that Russia had adopted him even before they had, but this isn't germane to the main point: that Otto believed he had betrayed a friend for gold and that the Count knew it. Unfortunately, it's going to be very hard to prove anything against the Count, and not being a grasping man by nature, never having asked for anything more than his salary, there's nothing to demonstrate blackmail which is why I've chosen him—and he's accepted—as the person to turn Queen's Evidence against his fellow directors on the board.'

Heissman now joined Otto and Goin in giving the Count the kind of look they had so lately given him.

'Or take Otto,' I went on. 'For years he'd been embezzling very large sums of money from the company, virtually bleeding it white.' It was now the turn of Heissman and the Count to stare at Otto. 'Or take Goin. He discovered about the embezzling and for two or three years he's been blackmailing Otto and bleeding *him* white. In sum, you constitute the most unpleasant, unprincipled and depraved bunch it's ever been my misfortune to encounter. But I haven't even scratched the surface of your infamy, have I? Or the infamy of one of you. We haven't even discussed the person responsible for the violent deaths that have taken place. He is, of course, one of you. He is, of course, quite, quite mad and will end his days in Broadmoor: although I have to admit that there's been a certain far from crazy logic in his thinking and actions. But a prison for the insane—one regrets the abolition of the death penalty—is a certainty: it may well be, Otto, as well as being the best you can hope for, that you won't live long after you get there.' Otto said nothing, the expression on his face remained unchanged. I went on: 'For your hired killers, of course, Jungbeck and Heyter, there will be life sentences in maximum security jails.'

The temperature in that icily cold metallic tomb had fallen to many degrees below freezing point, but everyone appeared to be completely unaware of the fact: the classic example of mind over matter, and heaven knew that minds could rarely have been more exclusively and almost obsessively possessed than those of the men in those weird and alien surroundings.

'Otto Gerran is an evil man,' I said, 'and the enormity of his crimes scarcely comes within the bounds of comprehension. However, one has to admit that he has had the most singularly wretched luck in his choice of business associates, and those associates must be held partly to blame for the terrible events that happened, for their extraordinary cupidity and selfishness drove Otto into a corner from which he could escape only by resorting to the most desperate measures.

'We have already established that three of you here have been blackmailing Otto steadily over the years. His other two fellow directors, his daughter and Stryker, joined wholeheartedly in what had become by this time a very popular pastime. They, however, used a very different basis for their blackmail. This basis I cannot as yet prove but the facts, I believe, will be established in time. The facts are concerned with a car crash that took place in California over twenty years ago. There were two cars involved. One of those belonged to Lonnie Gilbert and had three women inside—

his wife and two daughters, all of whom appeared to be considerably the worse for drink at the time. The other car belonged to the Strykers—but the Strykers were not in their car. The two people who were had, like Lonnie's family, been at the same party in the Strykers' house and, like Lonnie's family, were in an advanced state of intoxication. They were Otto and Neal Divine. Isn't that so, Otto?'

'There's nothing of this rubbish that can be proved.'

'Not yet. Now, Otto was driving the car, but when Divine recovered from the effects of the crash he was convinced— no doubt by Otto—that he had been at the wheel. So for years now Divine has been under the impression that he owes his immunity from manslaughter charges purely to Otto's silence. The salary lists show—'

'Where did you get the salary lists from?' Goin asked.

'From your cubicle—where I also found this splendid bank book of yours. The lists show that Divine has been receiving only a pittance in salary for years. How admirable is our Otto. He not only makes a man take the responsibility for deaths which he himself has caused but in the process reduces that man to the level of a serf and a pauper. The blackmailed doing some blackmailing on his own account. Makes for a pretty picture all round, does it not?

'But the Strykers knew who had really caused the crash, for Otto had been driving when they left the house. So they sold their silence in return for jobs on the board of Olympus Productions and vastly inflated salaries. You are a lovable, lovable lot, aren't you? Do you know that this fat monster here actually tried to have Lonnie murdered tonight? Why? Because Judith Haynes, very shortly before she died, had told Lonnie the truth of what had happened in the car crash: so, of course, Lonnie would have been a danger to Otto as long as he had lived.

'I don't know who suggested this film expedition as a cover for getting the bullion. Heissman, I suppose. Not that it matters. What matters is that Otto saw in this proposed trip a unique and probably never to be repeated opportunity to solve all his troubles at one stroke. The solution was simple—eliminate all his five partners, including his daughter whom he hated as much as she hated him. So he gets himself two guns for hire, Heyter and Jungbeck—no question about the hire aspect, I found two thousand pounds in five-pound notes in Jungbeck's case this afternoon: two alleged actors of whom no one but Otto had ever heard.

'In effect, Otto would clear his board in one fell sweep. He'd get rid of the people he hated and who hated him. He'd buy enough time by their deaths to conceal his embezzlement. He'd collect very considerable insurance money and get back in the black with the help of accommodating accountants who can be as venal as the next lot. He would get all that lovely gold for himself. And, above all, he'd be for ever free of the continuous blackmail that had dominated his life and warped his mind until it drove him over the edge of insanity.' I looked at Goin. 'Do you understand now what I mean by saying that without me you'd have been dead by the end of the week?'

'Yes. Yes, I think so. I have no option other than to believe you are right.' He looked at Otto in a kind of wonder. 'But if he was only after the board of directors—'

'Why should others die? Ill luck, ill management, or some-one just got in his way. The first intended victim was the Count, and this was where the ill luck came in. Not the Count's—Antonio's. Otto, as I think digging into his past will show, is a man of many parts. Among some of the more esoteric skills acquired were some relating to either chemistry or medicine: Otto is at home with poisons. He is also, as so many very fat men are, extremely gifted at palming articles. At the table on the night when Antonio died the food, as usual, was served from the side table at the top of the main table where Otto sat. Otto introduced some aconite—only a pinch was necessary—into the horseradish on the plate intended for the Count. Unfortunately for poor Antonio, the Count has a profound dislike of horseradish and passed his on to the vegetarian Antonio. And so Antonio died.

'He tried to poison Heissman at the same time. But Heissman wasn't feeling in the best of form that evening, were you, Heissman—you will recall that you left the table in a great hurry, your plate untouched. The economical Haggerty, instead of consigning this clearly untouched plate to the gash bucket, put it back in the casserole from which the two stewards, Scott and Moxen, were served later that night—and from which the Duke stole a few surreptitious mouthfuls. Three became very ill, two died—all through ill luck.'

'Aren't you overlooking the fact that Otto himself was poisoned?' the Count said.

'Sure he was. By his own hand. To obviate any suspicion that might fall on him. He didn't use aconite though—all that was required was some relatively harmless emetic and some acting. This, incidentally, was why Otto sent me off on a tour of the *Morning Rose*—not to check on sea-sickness but to see who else he might have poisoned by accident. His reaction when he heard of Antonio's death was unnaturally violent—though I didn't get the significance at the time.

'Matters took another tragic turn later that evening. Two people came to check my cabin in my absence—one was either Jungbeck or Heyter and the other was Halliday,' I looked at Heissman. 'He was your man, wasn't he?'

Heissman nodded silently.

'Heissman was suspicious of me. He wanted to check on my *bona fides* and examined my cases—had them examined, rather, by Halliday. Otto was suspicious and one of his hired men discovered that I'd been reading an article about aconite. One death more or less wasn't going to mean much to Otto now, so he planned to eliminate me, using his favourite eliminator—poison. In a bottle of scotch. Unfortunately for Halliday, who had come to see if he could lay hands on the medical case that I'd taken up to the saloon, he drank the night-cap intended for me.

'The other deaths are easy to explain. When the party was searching for Smithy, Jungbeck and Heyter clobbered Allen and killed Stryker in this clumsy attempt to frame Allen. And, during the night, Otto arranged for the execution of his own daughter. He was on watch with Jungbeck and the murder could only have occurred during that time.' I looked at Otto. 'You should have checked on your daughter's window—I'd screwed it shut so that it was impossible for anyone to have entered from the outside. I'd also found that a hypodermic and a phial of morphine had been stolen. You don't have to admit any of this—both Jungbeck and Heyter will sing like canaries.'

'I admit everything.' Otto spoke with a massive calm. 'You are correct in every detail. Not that I see that any of it is going to do you any good.' I'd said that he was an artist in palming things and he proceeded to prove it. The very unpleasant-looking little black automatic that he held in his hand just seemed to have materialized there.

'I don't see that that's going to do you any good either,' I said. 'After all, you've just admitted that you're guilty of everything I claimed you were.' I was standing directly under the conning-tower hatchway, where I'd deliberately and advisedly positioned myself as soon as we'd arrived, and I could see things that Otto couldn't. 'Where do you think the *Morning Rose* is now?'

'What was that?' I didn't much like the way his pudgy little hand tightened round the butt of his gun.

'She never went farther than Tunheim where there have been people up there waiting to hear from me. True, they couldn't hear by direct radio contact, because you'd had one of your hard men smash the trawler's receiver, hadn't you? But before the *Morning Rose* left here I'd left aboard a radio device that tunes into a radio homer. They had clear instructions as to what to do the moment that device was actuated by the homer transmitter. It's been transmitting for almost ninety minutes now. There are armed soldiers and police officers of both Norway and Britain aboard that trawler. Rather, they were. They're aboard this vessel now. Please take my word for it. Otherwise we have useless bloodshed.'

Otto didn't take my word for it. He stepped forward quickly, raising his gun as he peered up towards the conning-tower. Unfortunately for Otto, he was standing in a brightly-lit spot while peering up into the darkness. The sound of a shot, hurtful to the ears in that enclosed space, came at the same instant as his scream of pain, followed by a metallic clunk as the gun falling from his bloodied hand struck a bar of bullion.

'I'm sorry,' I said. 'You didn't give me time to tell you that they were specially picked soldiers.'

Four men descended into the body of the vessel. Two were in civilian clothes, two in Norwegian Army uniforms. One of the civilians said to me: 'Dr Marlowe?' I nodded, and he went on: 'Inspector Matthewson. This is Inspector Nielson. It looks as if we were on time?'

'Yes, thank you.' They weren't in time to save Antonio

and Halliday, the two stewards, Judith Haynes and her husband. But that was entirely my fault. 'You were very prompt indeed.'

'We've been here for some time. We actually saw you go below. We came ashore by rubber dinghy from the outside, north of Makehl. Captain Imrie didn't much fancy coming up the Sor-hamna at night. I don't think he sees too well.'

'But I do.' The harsh voice came from above. 'Drop that gun! Drop it or I'll kill you.' Heyter's voice carried utter conviction. There was only one person carrying a gun, the soldier who had shot Otto, and he dropped it without hesitation at a sharp word from the Norwegian inspector. Heyter climbed down into the hull, his eyes watchful, his gun moving in a slight arc.

'Well done, Heyter, well done.' Otto moaned from the pain of his shattered hand.

'Well done?' I said. 'You want to be responsible for another death? You want this to be the last thing Heyter ever does, well or not?'

'Too late for words.' Otto's puce face had turned grey, the blood was dripping steadily on to the gold. 'Too late.'

'Too late? You fool, I knew that Heyter was mobile. You'd forgotten I was a doctor, even if not much of one. He'd a badly cut ankle inside a thick leather boot. That could only have been caused by a compound fracture. There was no such fracture. A sprained ankle doesn't cut the skin open. A self-inflicted injury. As in killing Stryker, so in killing Smith—a crude and total lack of imagination. You did kill him, didn't you, Heyter?'

'Yes.' He turned his gun on me. 'I like killing people.'

'Put that gun down or you're a dead man.'

He swore at me, viciously and in contempt, and was still swearing when the red rose bloomed in the centre of his forehead. The Count lowered his Beretta, dark smoke still wisping from its muzzle, and said apologetically, 'Well, I *was* a Polish count. But we do get out of practice, you know.'

'I can see that,' I said. 'A rotten shot but I guess it's worth a royal pardon at that.'

On the jetty, the police inspectors insisted on handcuffing Goin, Heissman and even the wounded Otto. I persuaded them that the Count was not a danger and further persuaded them to let me have a word with Heissman while they made their way up to the cabin. When we were alone I said: 'The water in the harbour there is below the normally accepted freezing point. With those heavy clothes and your wrists handcuffed behind your back you'll be dead in thirty seconds. That's the advantage of being a doctor, one can be fairly definite about those things.' I took him by the arm and pushed him towards the edge of the jetty.

He said in a high-strained voice: 'You had Heyter deliberately killed, didn't you?'

'Of course. Didn't you know—there's no death penalty in England now. Up here, there's no problem. Goodbye, Heissman.'

'I swear it! I swear it!' His voice was now close to a scream. 'I'll have Mary Stuart's parents released and safely reunited. I swear it! I swear it!'

'It's your life, Heissman.'

'Yes.' He shivered violently and it wasn't because of the bitter wind. 'Yes, I know that.'

The atmosphere in the cabin was extraordinarily quiet and subdued. It stemmed, I suppose, from that reaction which is the inevitable concomitant of profound and still as yet unbelieving relief. Matthewson, clearly, had been explaining things.

Jungbeck was lying on the floor, his right hand clutching his left shoulder and moaning as if in great pain. I looked at Conrad, who looked at the fallen man and then pointed to the broken shards of glass on the floor.

'I did as you asked,' he said. 'I'm afraid the bottle broke.'

'I'm sorry about that,' I said. 'The scotch, I mean.' I looked at Mary Darling, who was sobbing bitterly, and at Mary Stuart who was trying to comfort her and looked only fractionally less unhappy. I said reprovingly: 'Tears, idle tears, my two Marys. It's all over now.'

'Lonnie's dead.' Big blurred eyes staring miserably from behind huge glasses. 'Five minutes ago. He just died.'

'I'm sorry,' I said. 'But no tears for Lonnie. His words, not mine. "He hates him who would on the rack of this rough world stretch him out longer."'

She looked at me uncomprehendingly. 'Did he say that?'

'No. Chap called Kent.'

'He said something else,' Mary Stuart said. 'He said we were to tell the kindly healer—I suppose he meant you—to bring his penny to toss for the first round of drinks in some bar. I didn't understand. A four-ale bar.'

'It wouldn't have been in purgatory?'

'Purgatory? Oh, I don't know. It didn't make any sense to me.'

'It makes sense to me,' I said. 'I won't forget my penny.'